PRAISE FOR *BLACK*

An NBC *Today Show* Book Club Pick

t YA Book of 2018

Book of the Year

2018 Must-Read

st Selection

rafted high fantasy about
a society in which survival depends on falconry; even bird
haters will be spellbound . . . *Black Wings Beating*
is its own wondrous thing."
—*The New York Times Book Review*

"*Black Wings Beating* gives us **irresistible, complex
characters** in a **propulsive, adventure-filled story**,
pulling off the rare trick of leaving its readers satisfied but
undeniably excited for a second volume."
—NBC's *Today Show*

★ "A well-crafted fantasy featuring diverse characters,
this book is a strong selection for all libraries serving teens."
—*School Library Journal*, **starred review**

★ "Readers will be swept away in this book's talons."
—*Kirkus Reviews*, **starred review**

"Stock up—this one will make the rounds."
—*Booklist*

"Fantasy fans should find a worthwhile combination
of familiar tropes and novel world building to make
this a series to keep an eye on."
—*The Bulletin*

RED
SKIES
FALLING

RED
SKIES
FALLING

ALEX LONDON

THE SKYBOUND SAGA **BOOK II**

**SQUARE
FISH**

FARRAR STRAUS GIROUX NEW YORK

SQUARE
FISH

An imprint of Macmillan Publishing Group, LLC
120 Broadway, New York, NY 10271
fiercereads.com

Square Fish and the Square Fish logo are trademarks of Macmillan and
are used by Farrar Straus Giroux under license from Macmillan.

Our books may be purchased in bulk for promotional, educational, or business use. Please
contact your local bookseller or the Macmillan Corporate and Premium Sales Department
at (800) 221-7945 ext. 5442 or by email at MacmillanSpecialMarkets@macmillan.com.

Library of Congress Cataloging-in-Publication Data

Names: London, Alex, author.
Title: Red skies falling / Alex London.
Description: New York : Farrar Straus Giroux, 2019. |
Series: Skybound saga ; book 2 | Summary: Orphaned twins Kylee and Brysen
    continue to fight for survival and power in the remote valley of the Six Villages.
Identifiers: LCCN 2018046457 | ISBN 978-1-250-61988-4 (paperback) |
    ISBN 978-0-374-30686-1 (ebook)
Subjects: | CYAC: Falconry—Fiction. | Brothers and sisters—Fiction. |
    Twins—Fiction. | Fantasy.
Classification: LCC PZ7.L84188 Re 2018 | DDC [Fic]—dc23
LC record available at https://lccn.loc.gov/2018046457

Originally published in the United States by Farrar Straus Giroux
First Square Fish edition, 2020
Book designed by Elizabeth H. Clark
Square Fish logo designed by Filomena Tuosto

1 3 5 7 9 10 8 6 4 2

LEXILE: 910L

This one's for Maddie, though I don't think I'll let her read it for a decade or two.

—A. L.

THE FROZEN LANDS
DEMON'S BEAK
NAMELESS GAP
NECKLACE RIVER
UPPER JAW
BLUE SHEEP PASS
GRASSLAND PLAINS
CARDINAL'S CREST RIDGE
KYLEE & BRYSEN'S HOUSE
BLOOD BIRCH FOREST
SIX VILLAGES
UZTAR

LOWER JAW

SKY CASTLE

RISHL BRONZE PITS

PARSH DESERT

TALON FORTRESS

THE ASSASSIN

THERE ARE MORE DIFFERENCES BETWEEN AN ASSASSIN AND A murderer than there are shapes in the clouds, but that makes no difference to the victims.

Yirol could forgive the lack of distinction made by those she was about to kill, but she found the lack of distinction by those she served deeply insulting, even though she would never say as much. Rising to the position she now held—signed and sealed as the apex assassin for the Council of Forty—took political cunning as well as mental ruthlessness. She was no common murderer and would never let her passions or desires dictate her dispatches. She did her job, and she did it by the most effective means necessary to its particular requirements. She had no love of poisons but would deploy them if called for. She truly enjoyed bladeplay but would never employ it on a job meant to look like a hunting accident. An assassin was herself the blade, whatever tools she wielded. And yet, to the kyrgs of the Council of Forty, she was defined by the corpses she created, not the efficiency with which she created them.

And now the young man kneeling in front of her kept calling her a murderer, which she found irksome.

"Please," he begged. "You don't have to do this. You don't have to be a murderer."

Yirol shook her head and squatted so her eyes were level with her target's. "A murderer kills for reasons of the heart— for want or hate or lust or a little of each," she explained. "I want nothing from you, and I feel no hate for you. As to lust . . ." She hooked a finger under his chin. He had kind eyes and a boyish face in spite of the stubble. Light-brown skin that shone like desert glass, his youth a sun lighting him from within. How many ice-wind seasons did he have behind him? Twenty? Not many more than that, certainly. His full lips had yet to know all the kisses they were meant for, and now, thanks to Yirol, they never would.

She leaned in and let her own lips touch his cheek. She heard his breath catch as she whispered in his ear, "*That* would be a reason to let you live." She leaned back, and he looked at her hopefully. They always looked at her that way, imagining that her kindness might save them.

It would not.

The practiced blade came up in her other hand, silently spun from its sheath on her wrist, and made a clean slice across the pulsing artery in his neck. His shocked eyes went wide, and his hands grabbed at her wrists, tugging, as his life bled away. She held firm, stared down with the same expression as the statue of the ancient falconer watching over the courtyard from its high plinth. The artist had carved Valyry the Gloveless with as much emotion as the stone hawk that perched on her fist, and Yirol appreciated the sculptor's stoic skill. She didn't like the newer sculptures filled with lifelike emotions, as if the great heroes of Uztar's past were made great by their humanity, not by their triumph over it. Greatness, she knew, only came to those who could stand as stone against the buffeting winds that blew through every living heart.

The great and the dead share one trait, she thought. *Imperviousness.*

She waited for the young man to collapse and join the unfeeling dead, then she turned him over with her foot so that his lifeless eyes could stare up at the stars. Someone would want to give him a sky burial. There would be wailing and lamentation, as there always was for her younger targets, but the life of the city would move on, as it must, as she had helped it to do. The kyrgs of the Council of Forty had decided that this young noble was a danger to Uztar, but that danger had now been eliminated.

Yirol did not wonder what danger this young man might've been. That was not her purview. She'd followed him for days through the city's winding streets. He'd only left the gates for close hunts with his cast of falcons, always with different young men and women of the Uztari nobility for company and a team of valets to serve their wants and needs, and then in the evening he either threw or attended rich dinners and decadent dances. In her youth, Yirol had attended such dances, too, before she'd found her calling in the assassins' guild.

Looking down at the dead boy, she wondered how many boys just like him she had killed in her time, whether for debts owed or politics played poorly. She preferred the kills that went like this, quick and smooth and peaceful. The violent endings were the ones that haunted. They suggested a lack of discipline or planning on her part, and she hated to think someone's end could've been made easier had she only worked a little harder. Pretty though he was, she'd likely forget this boy's death before the next moon rose.

Except . . . this is odd. The boy's skin had taken on a kind of texture it hadn't had before. His eyes seemed misshapen. A trick of the light?

Yirol bent down and wiped the blood from her blade on his shirt. She found the material strange, like a pelt. And had the shirt been this color before, the same light brown as his skin? As she stared at the body, it was like looking into a reflection in a mountain lake. She saw the young man, but through him, rippling, she saw something else, a double vision of horns bursting from his head, an elongated face and the hooves of a beast. While nothing moved, everything shifted. Her head spun.

She leapt up and away and poised herself to fight, but what she meant to fight was unclear. She now stood over the dead body of a mountain elk where the young man's corpse had been.

You can never plan for everything, she told herself. *You've missed something vital, and now you'll pay dearly for your failure.*

"You should see the look on your face," a young man spoke from behind her. She whirled and flung her knife, but he dodged and the blade sparked against the stone and clattered away. He was the mirror image of the noble she'd just killed . . . or thought she'd killed. He was dressed finely in a black tunic and black pants. His bare arms were brushed with the light golden powder that some hunters wore to mask their scent from prey. It'd become a fashion statement in the last few seasons, finding its way from practical use in the brush to cosmetic use in the parlors of the elite. And this young man was certainly one of the elite. If he survived this night, he would be named to the kyrg, one of the Council of Forty, and the Council had wanted to avoid that outcome.

Yirol had never before failed an assignment. She drew another blade from the sheath on her arm as she kicked back gently at the prone elk, making sure it was still dead and still where she'd left it. She had the courtyard layout memorized and was plotting her next move.

You're a failure, she thought. *End yourself now before the Council does it for you.*

"What trick is this?" she demanded, knowing these thoughts were not her own. "How are you doing that?"

"I'm not doing a thing," the young lord said, then looked up. "It is." A wide-winged shadow drifted in a spiral over the box of sky framed by the courtyard. As it whirled, it lowered, visible only by what it blotted out. It was the largest bird of prey Yirol had ever seen, but it was more than its size that rooted her feet to the stones. This bird was darkness itself, oblivion on the wing. She knew its name, or at least, she knew what it was called: the ghost eagle.

The assassin stepped back over the elk's body as she searched for her route out of the courtyard. She'd been an assassin long enough to know when she was outmatched, when retreat was not cowardice but prudence. She never entered a space without at least two escape routes, and yet now, her mind was cloudy, her thoughts scattered. All she saw were high stone walls. Where had all the doorways gone?

"*REEEEE*," the terrible bird shrieked, making one great flapping turn high overhead, preparing to dive.

You're careless. You forgot your way out, Yirol thought.

"No, I didn't," she said out loud, arguing with herself, trying to clear her head. The ghost eagle's shriek was rumored to unleash horrors in the mind, but these things were lies. It was just a bird.

"It was a strange thing watching you slit an elk's throat, thinking it to be me," the young man said. "But they say the ghost eagle can torment your thoughts before tearing you to pieces. Philosophers claim the world is nothing but what we perceive it to be. Our minds can make an elk into a man, a door into a wall, a dream into a nightmare. If all the world is air and thought, then that which masters thought masters all."

Yirol spun and searched. They were in her head, the eagle or the man. She put her hand out to make sure the stone of the wall was real, was solid. Somehow she had been tricked into believing that which wasn't there. She'd whispered in an elk's ear and listened to an elk's plaintive cries, then answered them with words. She remembered it clearly now, as it actually happened, not as she had hallucinated it. And now, as realization dawned, she heard the young man laughing at her.

"I know . . . nasty stuff, this eagle's tricks. Hard to know what's real, isn't it?" The young man chuckled. "Some think the bird is magic. Personally, I think it has a mind so different from ours that it's not bound by the same rules of consciousness that we are. It can alter consciousness—its own or others'—to suit its needs. Of course, this isn't really a concern of yours at the moment, is it?"

"*REEEEEE*," the eagle screeched, and her vision of the young man wobbled. She saw herself standing where he had been, looked down at her hands and saw the light dust of powder he wore. She focused on her breath, regained herself. Her hands were her hands, his were his, and he stood across from her. The dead elk was still dead, still just an elk. She searched the sky for a sight of the eagle. How could you fight something that could muddle your thoughts so completely?

If she did not regain control of her mind's eye, that elk would be her last kill. She had to focus. She had to tame her perception. She looked at the statue of Valyry the Gloveless. A climb up the plinth, a leap off the stone falcon's head, and she'd be on the rooftop.

But running toward the sky would not save her. The sky belonged to the ghost eagle and to the dead.

She couldn't see any other ways out of the courtyard to the street, but there was a drain for snow melt, a drain that led down, under, into the depths of the city on the mountainside.

Even now, crystal-clear meltwaters flowed along its channels, guiding her path in the dark. Like a hunted rabbit, she would go to ground!

Like a frightened rabbit, she thought.

No, like a rabbit that survives.

She threw her blade straight up toward the black, winged shape in the night, more in the hopes of causing a distraction than to slow the attack.

"*Iryeem-na*," the young lord said, and Yirol had no time to wonder what that meant, because she was running for the drain as the ghost eagle dove, a scythe from the stars. Before she was even halfway to the sewer opening, the eagle swooped. Its massive talons tore her head from her body. She ran three more steps before she fell. The eagle rose away, clutching its grim trophy and painting the assassin's blood across the rooftops like a bee spreads pollen.

The eagle screeched, sending all who heard it into the dregs of their bottles or below the furs on their beds, and then eagle and young lord alike vanished into different shadows.

What was left of Yirol, the Council's assassin, would not be found till morning, after which a new kyrg would take his appointed place and a new apex assassin would be needed.

KYLEE

PARTNERS

1

"DO YOU WANT TO DIE LIKE THIS?" ÜKU SCREAMED.

The white-haired Owl Mother had the back of Kylee's tunic bunched in her hand, thrusting her forward, and that bunched fabric clutched between her shoulder blades by a wrinkled fist was the only thing holding Kylee over the precipice of the Sky Castle's walls. The clouds below roiled and broke against jagged cliffs.

"I could let go and spare us all the time you waste shambling to your death. If you plan to die so young, why not leap headlong for it?"

Kylee wanted to tell Üku that she did not want to die like this, had no intention of dying young, and that the featherbrained old woman better pull her back up. But she couldn't find her voice just then, so she swallowed and considered the strength in Üku's arm, how long she'd been holding Kylee, and how much longer she could. Finally, Kylee managed to scrape the word *no* from the gravel in her throat.

"Then show me the reason you're here," Üku snapped. "Show me how you plan to survive! Call the eagle to hunt. You know the word. Speak it!"

Kylee cleared her throat, focused her mind away from the sheer drop and onto the giant bird of prey that lurked somewhere in this dusky sky.

She searched the low clouds for any sign of the black-winged ghost eagle. She looked at the mountain elk idly picking their way up the cliff below the Sky Castle's walls, as comfortable on a nearly ice-smooth rock face with a foothold no bigger than a baby's skull as an eagle was on a breeze. They chewed cloudgrass without care or worry. None of the local hawks were big enough to take a mountain elk, and none of the nobles would risk injury to their finest hunting eagles just to catch some gamey meat.

But the ghost eagle was ten times the size of the next largest bird of prey, and there was no prey in the world it couldn't hunt, that it *wouldn't* hunt if Kylee could marshal the Hollow Tongue she'd been studying and *command* it.

"*Raakrah*," she said.

The elk stayed calm. How could they know a ghost eagle prowled the low clouds? When had that terror ever haunted the Sky Castle's air, and why should a bird of the night stalk them in the day? Their lives up to that point had offered no clues for the situation they were now in.

Just like me, Kylee thought.

The wind blew her cloak around her. The braid of her black hair whipped, and she felt Üku's arm shudder. How much longer could she hold Kylee there, tilted over the wall's edge?

Maybe the elk were right not to fear her.

The Hollow Tongue was the bird's lost language, known now only in fragments, and Kylee had little grasp of it, even after two full moon turnings spent studying. When you spoke the Hollow Tongue, you had to mean what you said, deeply and truly, or your words might as well be lies. No bird of prey ever listened to a lie. There was no word in the Hollow Tongue for lying. But there were infinite ways to say "kill."

"*Raakrah*," she said again.

Nothing happened.

The nobles and kyrgs and their valets, who had gathered on the outer walls to watch her, chattered nervously in huddled clumps. While there were others with some abilities in the Hollow Tongue, Kylee was the only one in the castle who had the interest of the ghost eagle, and so she had the interest

17

of everyone else, but she had yet to command the dreaded bird successfully.

"Think!" Üku scolded. "What have you learned?"

Earlier that afternoon, just as the air began to cool for the evening, Kylee and Grazim, Üku's only other student, had been learning to command colorful tulip hawks to fly between their fists, trading places.

The fact that she and Grazim hated each other made the exercise more interesting, and a few kyrgs and their valets had gathered to watch.

"*Toktott*," Üku had snapped just as the birds crossed in midair, and suddenly, the tulip hawks adjusted their flight paths, slammed their bodies into each other, and then bounced backward. After one or two more attempts to pass, they each gave up and returned to the girls' respective fists.

"*Toktott* means *to block* or *to stop*," Üku said. "If you are to overpower the command I have given them, you will have to mean your own command with greater force of will than I have with mine. The Hollow Tongue demands the perfect marriage of word, truth, and intent. To use it, you will have to truly *want* your bird to do as you wish. Find *your* truth and speak it."

"How can we speak our truth for someone's else's purpose?" Kylee asked.

"*That*," Üku replied, "is the fundamental question of your studies. The Hollow Tongue demands your full self: your history, your beliefs, your knowledge, your feelings, and your desires. Either you control those things, or they control you."

"Those are all the things that make you *you*," Kylee noted.

"Exactly," Üku agreed. "No one ever attained power over a bird of prey without first attaining power over themselves. Tame yourself and you can tame the world. So . . . what words might you use here, to tame this tulip hawk to the purpose? How might you make what you *must* do match what you *want* to do?"

"*Sif-sif*," Kylee suggested, the word for *trade* or *switch* that they had already been using.

"And yet that is not strong enough." Üku dismissed her guess. "What does *khostoon* mean?"

"Partner," Grazim said, puffed with pride at her vast vocabulary.

Üku nodded at the other girl, even smiled. "Very good. Your birds already know your relationships to them, but not to each other. You must *tell* them. A partner or an ally is a mighty thing, but the two of you must *believe* you are partners to overcome those who would get in your way."

Kylee blew a loose strand of hair from her eyes. There was no way she could truly see Grazim as her partner. Kylee had been born in the Six Villages, an Uztari town whose faith and fortunes were tied to falconry; while Grazim had been born to Altari priests who wandered the grasslands in exile, cursing falconry and all who practiced it. Grazim had run away to the Owl Mothers for shelter, for study, for purpose. Kylee had only come reluctantly, forced to study in order to protect her brother back home. Grazim resented Kylee's connection with the ghost eagle, and Kylee resented Grazim's eagerness to serve the Sky Castle. No amount of bird trading was going to change their mutual resentment. It'd be easier to kiss a vulture's tongue than to believe she could ever be Grazim's *partner*.

"*Khostoon*," they both said without conviction, and the frustrated bird on Kylee's fist did nothing in response.

"Girls, girls, girls," Üku clucked. "If you succumb to your adolescent squabbles, you will never master the power you have. Even the mightiest eagle can be bested by a unified flock. Try again!"

Grazim frowned. Kylee frowned back.

"*Khostoon*," they snarled in unison, again to no avail.

Üku looked at her feet. "I just don't know how to get through to either of you. Are you so weak-minded that you can find *nothing* to share with each other? You've more in common than you think."

Kylee gazed at the other girl, looking her up and down. Grazim had cut her blond hair short for training, and her skin was sun-darkened almost to the color of Kylee's own, but she had a feeling that sort of superficiality was not what Üku had meant. What could Kylee have in common with this officious, ambitious, and overall vicious lowland girl, who'd have happily knifed Kylee the day they'd met? Kylee, for her part, would've been happy never to have met her in the first place.

When the ghost eagle appeared on a parapet above, interrupting the training, it was a relief to both of them. Everyone watching their struggle with the tulip hawks scattered for cover, all but Üku, Kylee, and Grazim.

"Your *friend* came back," Grazim said, putting as much bite in her voice as she could, although the words tripped on her tongue and stumbled out of her mouth. It was impossible to look directly at the ghost eagle and not feel a pang of ancient fear. Some people were said to hallucinate in its presence, others to confess their darkest secrets, or the darkest secrets of other people. Alone among birds, the ghost eagle could shred the mind of its prey before its talons crushed the body.

Kylee swallowed. She would not let her own fear show in front of these people, even as the skin on her arms prickled beneath the great bird's black-eyed gaze.

The eagle stood as tall as a desert camel, and spread its wings wider than one. The ghost eagle was the only bird that could carry off a full-grown man or horse. It could weaken the most flint-hearted woman's resolve and had caused more than one little boy to wet himself. It was death and fear incarnate, and it had chosen Kylee for its attention. The kyrgs who ruled Uztar had taken notice.

It was when the ghost eagle shrieked over the courtyard and took flight again that Üku grabbed Kylee, dragged her up the stairs to the top of the wall, and thrust her over the ledge, where she now found herself.

"Maybe this will get through to you," Üku growled. "See there! In the distance along the river? That is your home. Even now the Six Villages are building barricades, preparing for war against our enemies. Your friends are there. Your mother is there. Your brother. If you do not master your power, they will *all* be slaughtered by the invasion of the Kartami hordes. *This* is your chance. Find the words! Command the ghost eagle to hunt for you! Show me why you are here! I'll ask you again: Do you want to die like this?"

"No!" She yelled it the second time. Then Kylee closed her eyes, thought of blood, death, and hunger, and searched for a word as if her life depended on it . . . because it did.

2

"*RAAKRAH*," KYLEE TRIED A THIRD TIME, AND FOR A THIRD TIME, nothing happened. The elk kept chewing the cloudgrass, scampering sideways up the cliff as calmly as hares graze in clover.

Üku pulled Kylee back from the wall's precipice, letting her stand upright on her own, balanced only a hairbreadth from the edge. She'd never had any intention of dropping Kylee off the wall, and now Kylee knew it. That did not, however, make her want to forgive the old woman for the threat.

Üku turned to Grazim, who had followed them up the stairs and now stood, arms crossed, in an exaggerated performance of impatience. "Why is Kylee's word not working?" Üku asked her.

"*Raakrah* is the word you would use to ask a bird of prey to hunt for you," Grazim said, standing beside the Owl Mother. "It can also mean *gather* or *find*."

The ghost eagle had never shown any interest in Grazim, the only other student of the Hollow Tongue the Sky Castle had found, but the Altari girl's skill gave her impressive influence over hawks and falcons and even a few of the lesser eagles. She loved showing off her superior knowledge and now offered Kylee a smug smile.

"Is that what you want, Kylee?" Üku asked. "For the ghost eagle to hunt for you? Are you hungry for wild elk? If you are, you have to mean it when you say it. Speak like you would a curse or confession or love song."

Grazim chuckled. Kylee was so not a singer of love songs. From the corner of her eye, Kylee saw the throng of kyrgs and their hangers-on huddled in the sheltered doorway of the tower opposite. Only one person was out on the wall in the open, exposed to the sky: a young noble, finely dressed with an embroidered falconer's glove on, though he had no bird in sight. His robe bore a bronze signet on the lapel, so he was a kyrg himself, one of the Forty. His dark eyes were set on her, not on the clouds below, and the line of his lips curved up on one side in a lopsided smirk shaped like a blade. Kylee had seen him watch her training before, but he'd never stood out from the crowd of onlookers until now.

Yval Birgund, the chief defense counselor and one of the more powerful kyrgs in the Sky Castle, stepped out beside the young noble and whispered in his ear. The young man nodded and continued to watch, his smirk settling into a needle-straight line.

The high wind howled around them where they stood. To their backs rose the huge city of the Sky Castle, hewn from the pink, gray, and black stone of the mountains. Its wall-ringed neighborhoods were stacked along the slopes, roofs and courtyards colliding with ramps and stairs at dizzying angles. Kylee turned back to the soothing open view in front of her, the cherry-red sunset sky draped over the Uztari plains. To her left, the rugged untamed mountains hooked around the plateau farther than eyes could see. To her right, the same, but the Necklace flowed along the range's base, shimmering with the last of the daylight as it fed the grasslands and foothills, and somewhere past the lower clouds in those foothills, the Six Villages waited, preparing for war.

Her brother was there, and his life was in Kylee's hands, or, to be accurate, in her voice. His life—all the Six Villagers' lives—depended on her voice speaking true. For an instant, she felt she could see him, not as in a memory, but like she was looking at him through a glazed window, watching him track a hawk through the foothills, his shock of gray hair ruffled by a breeze blowing down the mountains from where she now stood. He looked up toward the Sky Castle, like he was looking directly at her, though she was at least a full moon's march away. He was looking in the wrong direction, though. Behind him, danger lurked. Something loomed, something terrible, and she wanted to shout at him to turn around, to defend himself, or better yet, to run!

She nearly shouted, *Run!*, then caught herself, remembered where she was, and how very far from home. She couldn't see her brother. That was the ghost eagle's work, toying with her, as it would do until she could command it.

She tried to see the deadly arc the dread bird cut in the sky, tried to see through the crimson clouds into herself, to what she wanted most, what she could ask of this monstrous eagle that it might believe was true.

"REEEE!" it shrieked, and her thoughts bent with the blade of its cry.

Kill them all, she thought. *They brought you here; they're using you. Forget the elk. Find the words to make* them *prey. Return to your home, to your brother. To the life you want. They are in the way. Kill them all.*

She shuddered; knowing that the thoughts weren't hers didn't make them any less true. She wanted to go home; that was why the eagle had shown home to her, but if Uztar couldn't win the war against the Kartami, there would be no home to return to. She didn't have to like these people to share the same purpose with them. She didn't have to love the kingdom to serve it.

She thought to her lessons, lists of words with only partial definitions. Most of the Hollow Tongue was a mystery even to the Owl Mothers, who'd preserved it for generations. They had a few words they'd passed down, and tiny bits of text they'd managed to match to the words they knew. The written language was even more lost than the spoken one. Travelers and long-haulers talked of ruined shrines in the Parsh Desert that still carried whole sentences in the Hollow Tongue, but no one was even sure *who* had written them. It certainly wasn't the birds themselves.

Kylee knew the words for *feast* and *hunt* and *mercy* and *trade* and *falcon* and *owl* and, now, *block*. She'd learned other words, three or four dozen, but she couldn't recall them in this moment and cursed herself for not studying harder.

Nothing she *could* remember was useful here. And what good would a word do if she didn't know what to ask for? What good would all the words in any language be if you found yourself with nothing to say? What did Kylee *really* want?

She looked over her shoulder, back at Grazim's sour-fruit face, at Üku, who loathed her but had promised the kyrgs to train her. At the defense counselor, who had taken her from her home so that she might serve the kingdom and protect them from the Kartami, and at the strange young noble beside him, waiting, watching.

Images flashed in her mind, memories this time, real ones, not hallucinations—she and her brother and their friend Nyall tackling the ghost eagle and binding it; her brother and his beloved goshawk, Shara, winning a fight in the battle pits; laughing with her friend Vyvian while a gaggle of battle boys tried to flirt with her; she and Brysen learning to climb together, coaching each other up, anchoring each other's ropes, going higher together than they ever could alone.

She knew what to say.

"*Khostoon*," she said, and suddenly a black streak broke through the low clouds like a hurled spear, lanced straight up the cliff, and grazed the castle wall, making everyone duck, even those safely under the shelter of the stone parapet. The giant bird circled once, tucked its boulder-crushing talons and folded its wind-beating wings, and fell like lightning's shadow on an unsuspecting elk.

The elk brayed and grunted when the eagle crashed onto its back, vanishing beneath the giant bird's widespread wings. Together, both eagle and elk fell from the cliff. It looked like the weight was too much for the bird to carry. They tumbled into the cloud cover and vanished. Kylee felt her own breath falling with them, hope exhaled and not returning. Falconry was an art of loss, and even the tamest birds could leave you, even the most vicious birds could fail.

Stupid, Kylee cursed herself, and cursed all of Uztar for pinning their hopes in a war on one bird, no matter how powerful, and one girl, no matter how determined to save her family. *Stupid, stupid, stupid*, she thought, and then, before she knew why, she felt a smile blossom up in her and a sudden laugh escape her lips.

Flapping so powerfully that the clouds dissolved around its wings, the ghost eagle rose, bursting into the sky below the wall, clutching its massive quarry by the flesh of its back. The elk stirred and kicked, then hung limp as the eagle brought it higher and higher.

The laughter in Kylee's mind was not her own. The ghost eagle's fall had been . . . a joke? Had the eagle been *playing* with her?

Great, she thought, and knew the thought was hers. *My fate hangs on a giant killer bird with a sense of humor.*

All eyes followed the eagle's winding flight up into the reddening sky, then watched it swoop low and drop the massive beast. The elk let out a loud cry as it plummeted, then hit the top of the wall with a sickening thud in front of the cowering nobles.

Its body opened on impact like a split summer melon, splattering their finery with its insides. Even Defense Counselor

Birgund gasped. Only the young noble with the knife-blade smile stood resolute, his golden cheekbones and lightly pursed lips now splattered with elk's blood.

"*REEEE!*" the ghost eagle shrieked, diving away and disappearing. It abandoned its prey's remains, demonstrating that it had no interest in the hunt, nor even, really, in the kill. Only in Kylee's desires.

Khostoon *means partner*, she thought, and knew that the thought was a promise.

"Looks like I found a *partner* after all," she said to Üku, staring a warning at the Owl Mother never to threaten her again. She stretched her fingers, locked her thumbs across her chest in the winged salute of Uztari respect, and smiled a biting grin. "Thank you for teaching me the word I needed, Mem Üku." She looked at Grazim, then pointedly looked away. "I mean . . . that *we* needed."

As she marched down the steps back to the courtyard below, she walked with her hands behind her back. She hoped it appeared like defiant confidence.

In truth, she had to stop her hands from shaking.

Partner partner partner echoed in her mind in a voice that wasn't her own.

3

KYLEE STOOD TREMBLING IN THE SMALL CHAMBER JUST OFF THE
training courtyard. She could barely get her falconer's glove
off and onto one of the pegs on the wall. She simply dropped
her game bag and belt on the floor and let her face fall into her
hands. She wanted to scream. She wanted to go home. She
wanted to be anywhere but here, forced to meet everyone
else's expectations of her.

She had just done something no falconer in generations had
done, and rather than feeling liberated by her success, she felt
more trapped than ever. The moment she demonstrated mastery of the ghost eagle, she'd be deployed to war, and then

everyone would expect her to save them. What, she wondered, would her new "partner" expect?

She thought about her twin brother, Brysen. He'd had a goshawk named Shara, one he'd rescued from their father's wrath for losing at the battle pits, and he'd loved that bird and tended her every need, and she had hunted for him and battled for him. But still she had left him, and it had broken his heart. Had *they* been partners? Would the ghost eagle break Kylee's heart when it left, or just her mind? She could never love the ghost eagle, but she was bound to it regardless.

Traditional falconers trained their birds for several seasons with food and lures and hoods and leashes, taught them to recognize the falconer on sight, to return to their fists and eat from their hands. The falconers gave the birds names as part of the human urge to tame the wild with words, as if naming a river can control its flow or naming a hawk can harness its appetites. Speakers of the Hollow Tongue did not name their birds of prey. They knew that no name they gave the birds would be true, and the Hollow Tongue required truth. Kylee couldn't imagine calling the ghost eagle anything anyway, nor stroking its tail feathers or feeding it tiny cuts of meat from her hand while she whispered her secrets to it, the way Brysen had with Shara. Even so, she needed the ghost eagle to serve her. She had to keep it interested in their partnership, no matter how much the shine of its eyes and the echoes in her mind terrified her.

She had no doubt that what Üku said was true: If she failed to command the ghost eagle, her brother would die, either at the end of a Kartami blade or by one of the Council's assassins. To protect him, she had to keep the ghost eagle from fleeing her like Brysen's hawk had fled him.

A shadow filled the room, and Kylee whirled, reaching for the blade strapped to her upper arm.

"Whoa!" Nyall held his empty hands up where he stood in the waning light of the archway. "I heard you put on a show for the kyrgs. Word is already winging its way through the quarter."

Kylee relaxed and slumped back against the wall, glad it was he who'd come. Nyall's tall, broad-shouldered body filled the space like a door, which he took to be a part of his job, protecting Kylee's privacy when she needed it, keeping her company when she wanted it. He was the only person who'd come with her when she left the Six Villages, the only person at the Sky Castle who actually knew her.

"I did what they wanted," she told him.

"From the look on Üku's face when I passed her under the colonnade, it looked like you did something more than what they wanted," he replied as he came into the chamber to do his actual job as her valet, checking and maintaining her equipment.

It was strange to have a friend as an assistant. She didn't want to boss him around, and she didn't like to be served. Even in their military training, he was tasked as her second and instructed to follow her orders, though he had far more experience fighting than she did. He'd been a battle boy back in the Villages and knew the wounds a talon or a blade could make. He'd been on the giving and receiving ends of each more than a few times.

In spite of her discomfort with having a valet, he appeared to have no problem with their arrangement. He was enthusiastic about seeing Kylee as often as he could and deciding who had access to her and who did not. Because of her gift for the Hollow Tongue, she had a lot of callers in the castle. They did their best to curry favor with him in order to get to her. He enjoyed that part of the job as well, accepting their gifts and doling out tiny pieces of hope that she might eat a meal at their homes or come to their parties.

The long green coat he wore now had been a gift from a noble who'd wanted Kylee to command a very expensive fox-catcher falcon to hunt instead of sitting, fist-bound, flapping its wings but never flying when it saw prey. What good was having an impressive hawk if it wouldn't make a kill?

The kyrg was a junior counselor for district sewer-and-lighting maintenance, which was an unglamorous but very lucrative role, and the coat she'd given Nyall was made of fine green silk, lined with fox fur, and studded with glass buttons in a great array of colors. The stitching around all the pockets, collar, and cuffs was gold thread. The kyrg's husband had given Nyall the emerald studs he now wore in his ears. Kylee worried she'd end up having to pay the couple a visit as compensation for Nyall's outfit.

He'd tied his long coils of hair up like a regal nest on top of his head, and the dark skin of his long neck, she saw, was dusted with fine gold hunting powder. He'd even added a small tattoo on his neck: six black feathers for the Six Villages, a reminder of home or, more likely, a way to show he was proud of where he came from, even as he moved in the highest circles of power now.

She smiled at him while he rubbed oil into the leather of her glove to keep it supple, and he flashed his own bright smile back. That tattoo on his neck was just the kind of in-your-face joke Brysen would've enjoyed.

"Any news?" she asked him. When he wasn't working, Nyall spent a lot of time in the pubs that other valets frequented, and he usually knew the latest gossip. Hearing him share it reminded her of being home. She could almost imagine she and Brysen and their friend Vyvian were sitting around the Broken Jess, listening to news of birds caught and sold, hatchlings learning to fly, and battle boys learning to brawl.

Nyall smiled, and his mossy eyes shone. His dimples dented his dark cheeks like stones dropped into a deep mountain lake, and she understood why anyone with any romantic blood in their veins was more than happy to give Nyall gifts, even if it never got them any closer to a meeting with Kylee. He looked like a classic hero, one of the great falconers they sang of in stories: broad-shouldered, dark-skinned, and taller than her and her brother by two heads. He had the kind of arms people wanted to be wrapped in, the kind of shoulders the sky itself might want to cry on. No one understood why Kylee turned down his advances, and she never asked him if there were different favors he gave in exchange for the gifts he received. That was the sort of thing Brysen enjoyed discussing, not her.

Nyall pulled a letter from his jacket and passed it over. She unrolled it quickly, buoyed by the sloppy hand it was written in. Brysen's. The pigeon that brought the letter had hit a heavy mist, which had dampened the ink and made it runny. She had to guess at some of the words, but her brother wrote the way he spoke, and she could almost hear his voice through the creative spellings.

Hey Ky, hope all's good with the great and powerful kyrgs up there in the Sky Cassel. You running things yet? If not yet, I guess you'll replace Kyrg Bardu as the proctor by the next moon's end and start telling them all what to do. Got yer last letter. Sounds blazing there. Hot water piped from springs? Bet folks smell better than here. Don't worry, tho. I'm taking care, washing bedstuff sometimes even. Sorry I left that to you all those seasons. It's not the best fun.

Ma and I are getting on well enuff. She still prays most of the time and gives too much bronze to the Crawling Priests, but we're getting more and more Altari refugees from the grasslands every day and she's started doing wash for them, no cost. I tried to throw my own in the other day and she hissed at me, said she woodn't clean unholy bird scuzz off my shirts. I asked her was there such a thing as holy bird scuzz and wood she clean that? That's how I ended up doing my own lawndry.

Jowyn is still here. He took yer room. Don't worry! I'm not doing anything you woodn't approve of. Least not with him. JOKING! No time for that stuff. We help with the barrycades along the river on rainy days and

when the weather's fair, Jo goes out trapping with me.
Catching more than ever, selling them faster too, but
still . . . no Shara, tho I thought I saw her a couple
days ago. She's close, I can tell.

Brysen had started another line twice below that, something about his lost goshawk, but he'd scratched the lines out.
Kylee could sort of make out the phrase *give up* but wasn't sure
of the words surrounding them. Brysen wasn't usually the
giving-up type.

    Anyway, don't worry about us here. Stay safe and
  show them what a Six Villager can do. When you save all
  Uztar, I wanna see that Kyrg Birgund on his nees at yer
  feet, eating out of yer hand like a tame kestrel.
                    Yer handsum brother, if you remembr,
                                Brysen

Kylee laughed, glad to hear he and their mother hadn't
been fighting and even gladder that he hadn't fallen in love
with the strange owl boy who had come to live with them.
Jowyn had followed them home from the blood birch forest
when they'd caught the ghost eagle, exiled from the Owl
Mothers by Üku herself. Brysen had a heart that raced as fast

as a sparrow's and fell to predators just as often. She hoped he was being careful with it. It wasn't just her brother's heart she was worried about. She hoped he was being careful with all the parts of him that led him astray. Without her around, he could get into all sorts of trouble.

Thinking of Brysen peacocking around the Villages had her smiling, but Nyall had other news to deliver, and there were hints of it in Brysen's letter.

Altari refugees arriving in the Six Villages.

Barricades along the river.

Birds selling faster than ever and for higher prices.

"The Kartami are moving fast," Nyall said. "Huge flocks of birds in front of them, fleeing for the mountains, more than anyone can trap. Folks are afraid of scarcity as the kite warriors get closer because Kartami are killing every bird of prey they find and every falconer, too. Anyone who even does business with falconers. They took out two more long-hauler caravans full of grain for Zilynstar. Then they took Zilynstar, too. Slaughtered every Uztari and every bird and sent a few hundred Altari fleeing straight for the Six Villages."

"Brysen didn't mention that." She held up the letter.

"You think he wants you to worry about him? He'd lie lightning into a rainbow if it'd keep you from worrying."

"You think he'll go out and fight?"

Nyall actually laughed, which made Kylee laugh, too. Of course Brysen would fight. Brysen never let something like training, skill, or practice get in the way of a grand heroic gesture. If the Kartami kite warriors laid siege to the Six Villages, he'd be on the barricades before the first feathers flew.

"I have to stop the kite warriors before it comes to that," she said, any laughter leaving her voice instantly.

"You aren't the only one fighting them, you know?" He raised an eyebrow at her. Leave it to Nyall to remind her that the salvation of everything under the sky was not her responsibility alone. She wished she believed him.

"I'm the only one the ghost eagle listens to," she replied.

"You think you're ready?"

"Not even close." She bit her lip. "Much as I hate to admit it, I think I have to work harder with Üku and Grazim."

"I don't trust either of them."

"Me neither," she told him. "But if I'm going to keep the ghost eagle around and get it to do what I need, I'm going to have to know what I'm saying to it more than I do. I'm afraid that if I say the wrong thing, it'll kill the very people I'm trying to protect."

"Not killing the people you're trying to protect is pretty thoughtful of you," Nyall agreed. "I hope I'm one of them."

"What can I say?" She grinned at him. "Not getting my friends killed is the least I can do. I'm nothing if not thoughtful."

"You could never be nothing to me. You know, I think you're everyth—"

"Apologies for the intrusion," a man's voice cut into their conversation, and they both flinched, whirling to the open archway. Nyall already had his knife out, but the figure in the door held his hands up to show them empty, just as Nyall had when Kylee'd pulled her knife on him. Everyone in the Sky Castle had been jumpy ever since the headless body of the assassin Yirol had been found. "I must say, I was impressed by your demonstration today," the man added. "The finest minds in the city are singing your deeds all over town and embellishing the song with each telling. By sunset, rumors will have you riding the ghost eagle over the rooftops of the city while chanting the *Epic of the Forty Birds* in its original language."

Kylee looked the man up and down. He was that young kyrg with the bladed smile.

"Ryven," he introduced himself.

"*Kyrg* Ryven," Nyall added for emphasis. He had a comforting way of making sure Kylee always knew to whom she was speaking, so she didn't have to bother remembering everyone's names. She'd be lost in the city's social circles without

Nyall's help. In the Six Villages, she'd known basically the same people her whole life.

"Guilty of politics," Kyrg Ryven confessed. He rubbed the deliberate stubble on his cheeks while she looked him over. He seemed very aware of the impression he made: charming, insouciant, and a little dangerous. His teeth were slightly crooked, which meant he hadn't been born to wealth, but they were gleaming white, which meant he had wealth now.

He stepped into the room as Nyall sheathed his blade. "I've seen a speaker of the Hollow Tongue command a peregrine to bring a hare back to its tamer, but to see a ghost eagle drop a full-grown elk at a hunter's feet? Marvelous."

"You weren't afraid?" she asked him.

"I felt safe in your presence." Ryven offered his smile once more.

She didn't want to tell him his charm was wasted on her. He was more Brysen's type. Her lack of interest in a handsome grin hadn't been of much concern or of much value back in the Villages, but here in the seat of Uztari wealth and power, everything could be a weapon, and a kyrg didn't need to know she was immune to his seductions or anyone else's.

Let him try, she thought, *and in the trying, he'll reveal more of himself than I will of myself.*

Nyall stepped forward and made the winged salute, his

palms pressed over his heart, hooked thumbs and fingers spread like wings to either side. "To what do we owe the honor of this visit?"

"I'm having a party tonight," Ryven said. "And I'd like to invite Kylee to attend."

"She trains with the infantry early in the mornings," Nyall answered for her, which was both true and not a reason not to go to the party.

"Training tomorrow will be delayed until mid-sun," Ryven replied, not looking at Nyall. "I've already taken care of it. I'd be simply heartbroken if you failed to come. Unless, of course, you don't *want* to?"

She shook her head, knowing better than to offend a kyrg who could whisper in the ear of the defense counselor or even the proctor herself.

"I'll see you there, then." Kyrg Ryven saluted, then left them gaping after him with no opportunity to decline.

"Did he get an entire battalion's training delayed so that you could go to his party?" Nyall wondered.

Kylee nodded.

"Careful, Ky. Having the attention from a kyrg like that is like climbing in a lightning storm."

"Thrilling?" she offered, missing the freedom of her early-morning climbs.

"Tempting the sky," Nyall replied.

"We'll meet up after the party," she told him. "Maybe while I'm there, you can go have a drink or two at one of the pubs. Find out more about this kyrg. Put those dimples of yours to work."

"Hey!" Nyall protested. "I am more than just my pretty face!"

She laughed, but if she'd known that was the last time she'd see his smiling face, she'd have said something other than "Just don't drink too much sandthorn wine. I don't want to listen to your singing."

4

KYLEE LEFT THE MILITARY WING OF THE CASTLE AND CLIMBED THE
winding stairs to the sparse room that she and Grazim shared.
She needed to figure out what one wore to a fashionable young
kyrg's party. In her seventeen turns of the season, Kylee had
climbed treacherous cliffs, fought off killers and crooks, and
even bent death itself to her will, but it was choosing an outfit
that made her anxious.

She didn't want to look underdressed or overdressed or
like a foolish girl from the Villages who was trying too hard.
No one in the Six Villages dressed up for parties. They'd dress
for market days and for the Feast of the High Crossing, but
not even the Tamirs, the most powerful family in town, put

on fancy clothes for a party. Parties involved too much blood and bird scuzz.

She laid out a flock of finery across the bed. There were cream-colored leathers from a kyrg who controlled several tanneries; there was a kilt embroidered with modern interpretations of old Uztari patterns that a charming textile designer and his husband had given her; and there were more tailored vests and tunics and collars in more patterns and fabrics and styles than she could count. Everyone at the Sky Castle enjoyed fashion except for her.

She was tempted to summon Nyall to help her dress, but she'd never invited him to her private rooms before and didn't want to confuse him. She knew how he felt about her, and he knew that feeling was not something she would reciprocate. That balance had always worked fine for them, but she'd seen people do foolish things when a wild wind blew through their hearts, and she didn't want to tempt any breezes Nyall might feel blowing. It was an exhausting thing, being responsible not just for her own feelings but for his, too.

The sky made wind but also wings, she thought. She did what she was able to for the people she cared about, and if sparing Nyall's fragile feelings or her brother's ever-reckless heart were in her abilities, then that was what she would do. That was what she had *always* done.

"So you think the ghost eagle is your partner?" Grazim sneered from the doorway. Even if they hadn't shared the room, Kylee couldn't have kept her out. There were no doors, just an open archway, like in the equipment room, and she was told to count herself lucky for that. Regular military trainees were in long barracks, sleeping on pallets lined up side by side like falcon perches in the mews. Kylee and Grazim lived as well as officers twice their age. They even had their own water closet, although there was no door to that room, either.

"Are you angry because I used a new word before you could use it, or because the ghost eagle doesn't pay any attention to you?"

Grazim snorted. The culture she came from forbade falconry, which made her ability to use the Hollow Tongue intriguing to Kylee. The Altari saw the training and use of birds of prey as the highest blasphemy, of which Kylee's mother had always reminded her. She, too, was Altari, and, like Grazim, her ancestors had been exiled from the mountains by the first Uztari, the ones who built the Sky Castle and settled the foothills. Some Altari had their places in society as peddlers and herders, farmers and servants, but they were restricted in their movements and their trades and were eyed with skepticism as sympathizers to the Kartami fanatics. Kylee's own mother hadn't been able to work in the Six Villages, and though she could've simply denounced her culture, her zeal was too strong for compromise.

That choice had always enraged Kylee. If her mother had just been less fanatical, she could've worked, and if she'd worked, she could've left their father, and if she'd left their father, Brysen might've been spared the worst of his abuse. Instead, Brysen suffered countless seasons of berating and beatings and the one awful burning that had scarred half his body and turned his hair ash-gray. In a few more seasons, their father might've killed him. It took the man's death to set them free of him.

Kylee had the ghost eagle to thank for that. Maybe they'd been partners since long before she spoke that word today.

"The Hollow Tongue should not be *abused*," Grazim scolded.

"How did *I* abuse it?" Kylee uncrossed her arms and stared at her roommate.

The other girl untied her hair, shook it out, and sat on the edge of her bed. "You take shortcuts and disrespect the lessons Mem Üku takes pains to teach us. You've got talent but no skill."

"I don't see the difference," Kylee said, but she did see the difference. Talent came naturally; skill had to be earned. Talent and skill together were an unstoppable force. It was the former that had brought her here, but the latter she was meant to learn. Without skill, she risked being tamed by the ghost eagle, not the other way around.

"Your talent is an insult to the skill I've worked my whole life for," Grazim said, then added, "*Shyehnaah-tar.*"

Grazim's favorite raptor, a long-winged jackal hawk with brown-and-black-spotted feathers across its chest, fluttered into the room and landed on her fist. Grazim sighed and shook her head, looking pointedly away from Kylee even as the hawk kept its brilliant-orange eyes locked on her. "If I'd been born to falconry like you were, imagine what I could do."

"Yeah, it's too bad I was born so *lucky*, isn't it?" Kylee gave her a sarcastic smile. She was a long, long way from home, sharing a room with someone who hated her, watched over by an entire city, and held hostage by a threat against her brother's life from the most powerful kyrgs of Uztar. She'd have traded all her "luck" for a pigeon feather.

"I *will* be the first Altari-born ever to command soldiers for the Sky Castle," Grazim told her, "and I will do it with a mastery of the Hollow Tongue that I have earned. I will show every last one of these Uztari peacocks that my Altari lungs breathe out more excellence than they will know in their entire lives, and as I rise, so will all Altari with me. If you think I won't cut down some Six Villages girl of Uztar who's perched in my way, you've got another think coming."

"You think one accomplished Altari will make any of these kyrgs change their minds about your people or cede one bit of power to them? They'll use you, but they'll never respect you."

"Respect is taken," Grazim replied. "Not given."

"Well, you can't take from them what they don't have for you."

"Speak for yourself," Grazim grunted, then added with the lilt of a mockingbird, "Oh wait, speaking for yourself is what you have such a hard time doing, isn't it?"

"And I wonder why those hawks didn't believe we wanted to be partners?" Kylee scoffed. She wanted to loom over Grazim, but the hawk on the girl's fist kept its keen eyes fixed on her. One wrong move and the bird would fly from the fist, and Kylee didn't think she had the skill to call it off.

They stared at each other, each locked into their dislike for the other, resenting their talents and mistrusting their motivations. Kylee knew Grazim would be better as an ally than an enemy, but she couldn't even think how to make peace with the girl. She herself had never been ambitious like Grazim and didn't understand the drive. She'd worked hard to look after her melancholic mother and her broken-winged brother, but for herself, she'd never had bigger goals than getting by. Her little world of friends and family had always

been enough for her, and she had never asked for the burden
of the ghost eagle's attention. She hated being resented for
something she hadn't wanted in the first place.

"What is it that you want right now, Grazim?" she asked.
"Did you just come here to insult me?"

Grazim grunted and rolled her eyes to the ceiling. "I came
to tell you Mem Üku would like to have dinner with you pri-
vately tonight."

"Well, I have a kyrg's party, so please tell our illustrious
Owl Mother that I will have to speak to her in the morning."

"I am *not* your messenger," Grazim snarled.

"And yet here you are, bringing me a message."

"You want to party with that powdered kyrg, you tell Mem
Üku yourself."

"I'm sure she knows already," Kylee said. "She doesn't miss
much."

"You're just going to ignore her invitation?"

"I'm not ignoring her," Kylee said. "I just have plans."

"You know, not everyone worships you just because the
ghost eagle *sometimes* listens to you," Grazim said. "You should
be more careful."

"Is that a threat?"

"Not from me." Grazim looked at the hawk on her fist.
"Our gifts make us different, and there are people who fear
that difference. People who wish us harm."

"I can take care of myself," Kylee told her. "But thanks for your *genuine* concern."

"If I had half your natural gift for the Hollow Tongue, I'd—"

"You'd have the ghost eagle tear me to pieces," Kylee finished the girl's sentence. "I'm very glad you don't."

Grazim's nostril's flared and the freckles on her pale face seemed to darken. She looked like she was about to say something else but snapped her mouth shut instead. She stood with the unhooded hawk on her gloveless fist before marching back out through the arch and under the red-dusk sky. "Enjoy your party," she called back over her shoulder, and if Kylee hadn't known better, she'd have thought the other girl's feelings were hurt.

But Grazim didn't have feelings.

Kylee was alone again, her heart racing and her outfit options still strewn across her bed. Whichever one she chose, she'd be wearing her blade as an accessory. A party among the powerful was just like a hunting expedition, except everyone was a predator and everyone was prey.

THE EMPTY SKY

VAST FLOCKS FILLED THE SKY AHEAD OF ANON'S ARMY, A RIPPLING NET spreading from horizon to horizon, unfurling away in a honking, squawking, screeching cacophony of panic. Behind his army, the skies were empty and quiet save the vultures, which did not linger above for long. They rattled as they dropped on the corpses the army left in its wake.

The vultures fell, they fed, and then Anon's apprentice warriors slayed the carrion crunchers after they'd cleaned the bones. No sky burial for the Kartami's vanquished. Warriors burned the vultures' bodies and the leftover bones in huge pyres. Gray plumes of smoke rose behind the army, behind the flocks that fled them, and the plumes could be seen from one end of the plateau to the other. Pillars of smoke that held up an empty sky. These were the only monuments Anon built to his conquest, and all who saw the approaching pillars trembled.

Which was, of course, the point.

Anon was not a showman, like so many traveling pigeon flippers and songbird dancers he'd captured, but he understood the nature of a spectacle. Those performers who had repented their consort with the birds of prey, he allowed to serve the back of his columns, putting up and breaking down camp, piling bodies, and setting his army's deeds to song. A lucky few he sent ahead as refugees to spread these songs and, with them, fear.

A dirge for the lost settlements of Vala Dur; a lament for the slaughter of the great caravans of the Lower Parsh; an ode to a pair of fallen kite warriors who died in each other's arms during the battle for Vykiria Oasis but killed over a hundred Uztari hawkers before they caught that final breeze. Each song enlarged the myth, while each pillar of smoke showed the army's progress toward the Six Villages, toward the day when those who'd heard the songs could either surrender or become another verse.

Anon knew that his forces were outnumbered. Fearsome as they were, and so far undefeated, they did not have an army large enough to seize the Sky Castle, not even to hold the Six

Villages if he took them. But his forces could conquer the minds of their enemies before the first kite went aloft or the first spear was thrown.

His early advances had been ferocious. Each pair of kite warriors was told to spare no one. The warrior in the kite was to spear every person and every bird; the warrior in the barrow below to slice their heads from their bodies, to crush them beneath the barrow's wheels.

"We can show mercy later," Anon had explained to his commanders. "People remember little of what you do but *all* of how you make them feel. If, at first, we terrorize them, they will always think of us with terror. There are heroes whose lives are forever marred by one moment of weakness, and there are cowards who were brave once, in their youth, and who glide upon that reputation forever, no matter what ineffectual fools they later turn out to be. We will begin by blowing such a bloody wind across this plateau that even our gentlest breeze will make their fiercest warriors weep."

That was how they'd begun, but now, after conquering so much, he'd started to show mercy, to administer territory, to control trade and law and culture, which were all feathers of the same great bird: empire.

He had no interest in empire. He was destined to conquer, not to rule. Let those who came after him manage the new world he would make. That was not his destiny.

In his youth, standing before a ruined shrine of the First Falconers, its purpose and meaning long forgotten, Anon had had a vision. He had seen his fate. He was meant to free humanity from submission to the cult of birds and to bring down the sky that stalked them. Everything he had done since was bent to that great purpose. Even now, he had a plan, and it had little to do with seizing paltry patches of mud from the Uztari kyrgs who thought they ruled them.

He knew his great purpose as a river knows the course of its flow and a wind knows the season for freezing and for burning. Anon was the river, he was the wind, he was the ice and the flame of the world.

In the distance, racing toward him in the opposite direction of a fast and fleeing flock of sand gulls, starlings, and sparrows, was a lone glider, flying low on frayed silks.

With one arm, Anon slacked the line to the kite that drove his war barrow, slowing to a stop as the kite fell. At his cue, the barrows behind him slacked their lines as well. Almost instantly, his formation of rows and columns, over two thousand pairs of warriors, rolled to a dusty stop on the plains. The glider dipped, and the pilot landed at a run as her wings folded behind her. She slipped her harness and sprinted to Anon, knelt at his feet.

He gave her a skin of milk stout to clear her throat and strengthen her voice before she gave her report.

While he waited, he ran his hands along the smooth edge of his war barrow, tapped his fingers on the wooden strake around the rim. His first barrows had been built from scrounged wood and metal, collected over countless seasons of raids, but now the newer ones were built in his seized settlements, carved and forged for strength and speed. He'd added engineers to his ranks, and they had improved the system of ropes and pulleys that allowed the driver to launch a kite from the back of the barrow, harnessing the wind like the very birds they meant to destroy.

A fighter could then climb the rope, strap into the kite, and rain death down on all who rose up against them. Anon's barrow pairs ruled every patch of ground they crossed and every spot of sky above them.

But soon they'd face the real strength of Uztar, its professional soldiers, strong weapons, and skilled falconers. Add to that the speakers of the Hollow Tongue the Uztari had recruited and Anon's shards of the faithful would be ground to glass. If he did not find a way to hold the Uztari off until he could effect his true purpose, then all his sacrifice, all the blood he'd shed, would be for nothing. To endure against Uztar, he needed an advantage the kyrgs had not considered.

"They've built barricades along the river," the glider pilot reported. "But as you suspected, they left the mountains above the Villages largely undefended. A few falconers and hunting parties patrol the high passes—that's all."

"They know our war barrows can't operate up there," Anon said, "and they trust their falcons to guard against gliders we send aloft. They may even attempt retreat once the siege begins."

"Any retreat would send them through the blood birch forest," the scout noted. "The Owl Mothers would never let them pass through their territory."

"The Owl Mothers are in alliance with Uztar," Anon said. "We can't be sure what they will do. We can, however, be sure of what *we* will do. We set the pace of this war, not the Uztari heathens or their Altari collaborators. Us."

"Yes, Anon." The warrior bowed her head.

"So?" Anon stared at her, awaiting the report he wanted.

"As we were told, the boy goes into the crags and cliffs above the Villages every day to search for a hawk."

"He's a dealer in falcons," Anon said. "He will continue to go into the mountains searching for hawks. That is how all these filthy falconers earn their bronze."

"I'm sorry, I was not clear." She kept her eyes fixed on the dirt at her feet. "The boy is searching for one particular hawk: his boyhood falcon. Our spies say he loves this bird above all others. He lost it capturing the ghost eagle and believes she will fly back to him. He goes into the foothills to search for her every day."

Anon snorted. Of course the boy would love a bird. Love had driven him into the mountains to capture the ghost eagle in the first place—and had nearly put it squarely in Anon's control—but the sister's love for him had foiled those plans. As much as he'd have liked to kill the girl, he had no loyalists in the Sky Castle, no assassins to dispatch or spies to report back on her movements. The girl and her eagle were, for now, out of his reach.

But the boy. The boy was much closer at hand. The boy had locked eyes with the ghost eagle before, so fear of Anon's brutality was unlikely to sway him, but there was a force greater than fear, and this boy was still at its mercy.

Love.

Anon had seen it in battle a thousand times over. Lovers, siblings, parents, and children would all fight more ferociously for each other than any band of strangers assembled in training barracks. That was why his kite warriors fought in loving pairs—familial or romantic—and no pair had ever yet retreated. Even in death, they were not defeated. The frightened will fight, but lovers will conquer.

If the Sky Castle did not see the usefulness of such a boy, Anon certainly did. It was his very capacity for love that would make that boy as powerful a weapon as his sister was, even if he didn't know it yet. An ambitious heart would be harnessed.

"You've made arrangements?"

The glider pilot nodded. "For a few bronze, there are Uztari who will betray anyone, even fledgling boys."

Anon frowned. He did not like leaving a delicate operation to hired Uztari traitors.

"Remind me who your companion was?" he asked the glider pilot.

"My mother," the scout said. "She grew too ill to fight, so you blessed me with this task while she heals."

"Visit with her," Anon said. "And then select three squadrons of gliders to return with you. The main force will continue our roll toward the Villages, but your aerial assault will go ahead, test their defenses, and be in a position to grab the boy if your hirelings fail."

"Yes, Anon." She bowed again toward the dirt, the ground from which they came and to which they would return. He was glad to see her piety. No sky worshippers in his army.

"Thank you," he said, and the pilot ran off to visit with her mother while his army prepared for an evening's rest.

To keep them sharp while they gave his plan time to unfold, he'd have them hit another lowland town or two along the way to the Villages. Before his true siege of the Uztari nest began, he would raise a few more columns of smoke to the sky.

All Uztar will shudder at the huge flocks fleeing before them.

The thought made Anon glad. The boy would see them with heartache for his sister. The girl would see them farther away and be filled with anxiety for her brother.

And somewhere, Anon knew, the ghost eagle would see his burning pyres, too. He prayed the sky itself would tremble.

BRYSEN

THE HUNTED ONES

5

BRYSEN FOLLOWED THE SIGNS IN THE FADING DAYLIGHT. THE SNAG OF fluff on mountain hawthorn, the spot of blood speckling the jagged shale of a cliff face, the nervous cries of displaced crows as they burst from a copse of chir pine.

A hawk was near.

He looked out from the rocky slope where he'd crouched and saw a huge murmuration of starlings whirling against the pale pink sky. As the sun dropped behind the far mountain range, red coated its peaks, like teeth gnawing the horizon raw. The black cloud of birds oozed sideways, then spun straight up, a single mind in a thousand feathered bodies. They rose in a vortex, erupted apart, then merged into one mass again, undulating higher and higher, inventing new shapes as they flew. Augurs read fortunes in these shapes, saw the unfolding of fates, but Brysen had never had an interest in augury and tried not to think too much about fate. His had never been promising.

He knew that a solitary predator like a hawk wouldn't risk diving into the middle of a large flock of starlings, but any starling that strayed too far from the group's center might become a target. Surely the hawk he was chasing watched this aerial display from some hidden crevasse, waiting for a chance to strike. If Brysen could think like a hunter on the wing, he could find where his quarry hid.

He scanned the rocks, looking for the shape of a bird of prey, one that looked much like any other but that he would know from every other.

Shara.

His hawk.

Falconers lost their birds all the time. Raptors weren't like house pets, whose affections bound them to their masters; their hungry hearts didn't love the way a person's did. They stayed close when it suited them, flew to the fist for their own reasons, and could leave for even the smallest slight: an upraised voice, a paltry meal, an angry gesture, or a shock of fright.

Shara had flown off to escape the ghost eagle; he'd *sent* her away. It had been the only way to save her, but the wind and the sky didn't take intentions into account, and gone was gone no matter the reason. Any decent falconer would count Shara as a loss, and move on to trap and train a new bird. Brysen, however, was *not* a decent falconer. He was a dreamer; he counted on his dreams to lead him where past experience and the sum of expert opinion refused.

Shara knew the way home. Most hawks were territorial to some extent and preferred to hunt in familiar places. Brysen knew Shara would return, the way mountain laurel knows to flower when the wind begins to warm. He knew it because it simply had to happen. There was no him without her.

He also knew that was a load of birdbrained scuzz, but longing didn't care for logic, and he was allowed to believe things in the quiet of his mind even when he knew them to be lies. Without those quiet lies, how could anyone dream?

Nearly every day since losing his hawk, his boyfriend, his best friend, and his sister, he had gone up into the mountains to search for Shara—the only thing he might actually get back.

There! Hunched on a pile of boulders—looking like a boulder herself—he saw a mottled gray goshawk of Shara's coloring and Shara's size.

He whistled to his hunting partner, Jowyn, who crouched below him on the rocky slope under a grass-strewn blanket. Brysen could just see the boy's face, smeared with mud to obscure how pale it was—an unnatural white from seasons of drinking the sap of the blood birch forest. It camouflaged him perfectly in the snow of the high mountains but made him stand out brightly in the brown and gray foothills during the snowless melt-wind season.

Jowyn prepared to move, but before Brysen could signal him or take the first quiet step toward the hawk on the boulder, the huge flock of starlings turned and rushed straight for the mountain, screaming their skin-shaking shrieks.

Brysen had to duck as a thousand birds sluiced up the slope and flew over the ridge above him, making for the distant peaks and the frozen void beyond. For this season, that was the wrong direction for a flock to fly, but birds had been doing it for weeks. Every day now, huge flocks of every species imaginable surged across the smoking plains and up over the mountains. The skies were clotted with finches and chickadees, magpies and mallards, crows and ravens, geese, pigeons, and starlings.

Birds of prey hunted them all.

"The flocks are a bad sign," people in the Six said.

"Nothing goes that direction over the mountains," they said. "Not in our lifetime. Not in a hundred lifetimes."

"It's that gray-haired fledgling's fault," they said, meaning Brysen. "Never should've gone after the ghost eagle."

They didn't care that it was his sister who had the ghost eagle's attention, that it was she who'd spoken to it, who'd led it to the Sky Castle. The only thing Brysen had done was get betrayed by the boy he thought he loved and abandoned by the bird he thought would never leave him.

Not that these facts mattered. When people were scared, they looked for someone to blame, and Brysen, a half-Altari orphan with sky-blue eyes, prematurely gray hair, and a less-than-soaring reputation, was a fine target for blame.

"The flocks are fleeing the Kartami, nothing else," his friends tried to argue on his behalf, and that was probably the truth of it.

The warriors in their kite-driven barrows drew closer by the day. The flocks were fleeing them, and because of that, the falcons and hawks that hunted the birds were plentiful in the crags and crevasses of the mountains above the Six Villages. He'd trapped a few over the weeks of searching for Shara and sold them fast. He had a few others ready to sell in his mews at home right now, just as soon as he had the time to take them into town. First, though, he had to try for the one bird he actually cared about trapping, the one he had no intention of selling.

When he looked back for her, he saw she'd left her

boulder, startled by the huge flock of starlings, and was winging her way across a small gorge. It *was* her! He'd know her crooked-winged flying anywhere.

He ran after Shara, fully in the open, hoping her keen eyes would see him and she'd return. He slid down into a small meltwater stream, soaking his boots and pants halfway up his calves, then began to scramble on all fours up the loose stones toward the gnarly tree where Shara had settled, his eyes more fixed on the bird than on his handholds.

The loose rock gave way under him, and he slipped, scraped his face, and skittered on his belly back to the meltwater. The noise scared the hawk, and she launched herself from the branch, wings bursting open with power, legs thrust out, then tucked underneath as she flapped and turned, vanishing up and over the ridge in the same direction the starlings had flown.

"No," he whimpered after her in a tone that made him cringe at himself. Though his face stung, losing her when he'd been so close stung more. He knew he should probably give up. He should go home and sell the birds he'd already caught, but he had enough bronze these days thanks to the surging prices of raptors now that everyone feared there would soon be none left to catch. For the first time in his life, business was booming, and he couldn't have cared less. All he wanted was his old hawk back.

Bronze can buy fine birds and fare,
Homes well-furnished anywhere.
But what I need no bronze can earn,
My heart's repair, my love's return.

Brysen lay where he'd slid and felt sorry for himself, remembering bad poetry he'd heard Jowyn singing. He'd been *so close*, and yet, he'd failed. Another almost, another not-quite. Another failure in an oh-so-long line of failures.

Even in capturing the ghost eagle, it'd been his twin sister Kylee who'd triumphed; Kylee had caught the great bird's interest and gone off to the Sky Castle to master it. She might be the salvation of Uztari civilization, while Brysen, without the slightest gift to command a hawk in the Hollow Tongue, was still just some Six Villages kid, passing his days trapping raptors and plucking out a living from whatever bronze he could get for them, just like his dead scuzzard of a father before him.

He groaned and rolled onto his back to stare up at the pitiless half-blue sky that looked down on him, the sky that saw all his faults and all his pain and never intervened.

"Some help you are," he grumbled at the air.

For all he knew, Shara would fly over the plateau, summit the great mountains that ringed Uztar, and vanish into the frozen steppes beyond. This might've been the last glance he'd ever get at her, looking at her tail feathers as she flew away. He got that view of everyone he ever loved eventually. He'd watched them all leave.

"Story of my life," he told the empty sky.

"Hey. Are you all right?" Jowyn squatted beside him, assessing Brysen's bloody, scraped face and knuckles. Brysen pushed himself up slowly, glad for the blood and gravel on his face. It might hide the blush that was rising. He'd forgotten Jowyn was there while he'd been muttering at the sky. "Most people climb down a slope on their feet, not their face." Jowyn grinned at him. There was no dark mood that the unnaturally pale boy didn't try to lighten with a joke. He offered Brysen his kerchief to wipe the blood from his face.

Jowyn's exile from the Owl Mothers was changing his appearance, if not his personality. He was still snow-owl white, but his hair had grown back in, just as white. In the mountains, drinking the sap of the blood birch forest had not only paled him past any shade of human skin but also made his skin nearly impervious to the elements and extremely fast-healing. The longer he spent without the sap, the more those properties faded. Just two full moons into exile and he'd started to show the first signs that he was as human as anyone else. The day before, Jowyn had lamented a bug bite, which Brysen had to point out was actually a zit. This upset Jowyn even more.

The tattoos that ran up his left side from his toes to his

neck had darkened, showing black and ochre calligraphy in astonishing detail, beyond the skill of any Six Villages artist. To avoid questions about them in town, he'd taken to wearing tunics with long sleeves and high necks, as well as tall boots that he'd had to learn how to walk in. When he'd been in the Owl Mothers' covey, they'd always been barefoot. Only on the mountain, alone with Brysen, did he take off his shirt and shoes again, although even in the warmer air of the melt-wind season, he'd been getting cold. Goose bumps rose on his arms and across his chest. He shivered but would never actually admit to being cold. He never gave any indication that he missed the Owl Mothers, or the strength the blood birch sap had given him, or the forest he could never return to again on pain of death.

His eyes now were soft only with concern for Brysen, who looked away.

"I'm fine." Brysen sighed, letting Jowyn help him up. "Shara was here. She'll come back. And I'll come back until I catch her."

"Well, maybe she'll fly all the way back to—" Before Jowyn could finish, a scream echoed around them, followed by laughter. The scream was human, the laughter more like a blade dragged across a tongue. Both boys looked up toward the sounds. They were coming from the other side of the ridge Brysen had just slid down.

"Come on!" a voice shouted, thick with malice. "Acting like worms'll get you eaten like worms!"

The boys nodded at each other and, wordlessly, crawled up to the edge of the ridge, Brysen more careful with his footfalls this time. They looked into the gully below and saw the scene that had produced the screaming.

There was a blanket laid out on the ground. The contents of a traveler's pack had been spread out over the blanket—bladders of water and fermented milk, hard meats, and flat breads, but not much of anything else. It took Brysen a moment to see the people, because they'd backed all the way into the far shadow of the mountain with no way out.

There were two old men—one had a baby in his arms—and an old woman with a sturdy build. All three of the adults had surely seen better seasons. The baby cried while the man tried to shush it, and the old woman stood in front of him, thrusting her body between him and the huge griffon vulture, which had its beady eyes fixed on her.

The vulture was on a rough leash, and the man holding the other end had the top of his head shaved to the scalp in a twisted mirror of a vulture's pate. When he jerked the leash, the vulture snapped its beak, and the man laughed his knife-blade laugh.

He had three companions, who'd shaved the tops of their heads, too, and they echoed his laughter at the terror the big

carrion-eating bird inflicted. Though they all carried themselves like vultures, the other three had hawks on their fists
and curved bone-handled blades in their free hands. Brysen
noticed a copper band on the ankle of one of their hawks, and
even from a distance he could tell it was one from his shop,
Skybreaker Falconry. He'd clamped it onto that bird's ankle
with his own hands, but he hadn't sold a bird to these bandits.
This was a stolen hawk, and that put what passed for law in
the Six on Brysen's side no matter what he decided to do next.

"Huh? Huh?" the one with the stolen hawk teased, shoving
his fist forward, toward the captive group, and turning his
hand to make the bird rouse. It stood tall and opened its
wings. It had to do this for balance, but it looked terrifying to
those who didn't know how a bird behaved on the fist.

The trio flinched, even the woman in front, who tried not
to. They were Altari—had to be. Only Altari would be this
afraid of a trained bird, as terrified by the threat of violence
against their bodies as the threat of violence against their
souls. The Altari believed birds of prey were sacred and that
to harm one was as great a sin as training one to do harm.
They wouldn't defend themselves against these attackers even
if they could've, and the bandits knew it. These scum were
just the sort who preyed on Altari fleeing for their lives across
unfamiliar lands.

Someone should teach them a lesson.

"Don't like birds, do you, glass grinders?" the bandit sneered. "Maybe you shouldn't be up in these mountains then, huh? This is our land, not yours." He roused his hawk again. The man with the vulture kicked it forward so that it charged on its leash, a huge bird held back by a tiny strip of leather. The baby wailed, and the bandits laughed.

"What are you afraid of?" the vulture keeper cawed. "She only eats babies *after* they're dead! Don't Altari want sky burials, too?" He spit a thick green wad of hunter's leaf on the ground at their feet. The bandits were jacked up on the leaf, and likely on foothill gin, too, which would give Brysen an advantage if he cared to take them on. It could also make them more dangerous. That was the problem with facing off against drunks. Sometimes you could get away with a nimble step and their resolve collapsed. Sometimes any resistance to their whims incited more violence. The scars all over Brysen's back and sides read like a catalog of a drunkard's rages.

"Mud below," he muttered, thinking on his scuzzard of a father. He focused again on the drunks.

Could he take them? He was birdless. Could he face four men with hungry hawks and a massive griffon vulture?

Jowyn, sensing Brysen's intent, put a hand on his shoulder, shook his head no. Brysen nodded his head yes. Jowyn frowned. The pale boy hated violence. Before running away to the Owl

Mothers, he'd been the youngest son of the most brutal family in the Six Villages, and he'd decided never to give in to that part of himself. He was a gentle soul in an ungentle world. Jowyn could always make Brysen laugh, but at that moment, it would've been nice to have a friend by his side who was good in a fight—someone more like Nyall. Then again, Brysen didn't feel any need to protect Nyall, whereas the thought of keeping Jowyn safe made him glad. He liked having someone around who he could look after. Nyall didn't need him, but Brysen liked to think Jowyn did. A boy who wouldn't fight needed someone around him who would. That was just the way of the world. Predators and prey.

Brysen knew which one he wanted to be.

"Stay here," he urged his friend. "I'll handle this." He drew out his curved black blade—the only thing beside his sky-blue eyes that his father'd left him—and pulled away from Jowyn.

"Bry, don't," Jowyn whispered.

"Just watch my back," Brysen replied as he slid quietly over the lip of the ridge, plotting on his way down which of the vulture-faced thieves' throats he'd open first.

By the time his feet hit the ground, he'd decided to let his black-talon blade do the choosing.

6

THE VULTURE SAW BRYSEN FIRST. ITS HEAD SNAPPED AROUND AND
regarded him with wide black pupils ringed in red, like
eclipsed suns, and in that single heartbeat under its stare,
Brysen felt a chill as if a corpse had looked at him.

And then the hawks screeched, the bandits turned, and a
thrill warmed him, the rush that only comes when you know
all hell is about to break loose.

"Ah, here's some real prey." The bandit with the vulture
took a step toward Brysen, yanking the large bird by the leash.
Brysen's fist felt empty where his hawk should've been. He
wasn't even wearing a falconer's glove, just weather-beaten
pants the color of dried mud and a sleeveless tunic in the same

shade. His skin was barely a shade lighter than the clothes, and he blended in well on the melt-wind mountain, which was useful for trapping animals that relied on sight to survive.

"Well, if it isn't that famous Six Villages boy," one of the bandits said, grinning. "What do you think, Corrnyn? Will he be a gusher or a trickler when I cut him?"

Corrnyn, the one with the vulture, shrugged. "Doesn't matter much. We've a job to do. No cutting. Not fatally, anyway." The bandit loosed his hawk toward Brysen with a cry of "Utch!"

The hawk flew from the fist, its gray beak pointed for Brysen like an arrowhead and its talons rising. They had trained this bird to attack. They didn't know that the copper band on its ankle meant that *Brysen* had trained the same bird first, that he had tracked it over the low foothills two rising-wind seasons ago, had trapped it and brought it home, fed it by hand, tamed it to his fist, leashed it and lured it and taught it to return to him when he called. He and his mentor, Dymian, had trained this one together. The memory of Dymian stung but not so much as a talon to the face would.

He whistled three short bursts and held up his fist.

Birds have memory, especially when it comes to food, and it hadn't been that long since this one had eaten out of Brysen's hand. Thrasher, they'd named him, because he had thrashed so hard against his tether the first night that they wondered if they'd ever tame him. But they had, and now he came to Brysen. A hawk's heart was fickle, but its appetite endured.

Thrasher's wings opened, and the bird landed on Brysen's bare fist, fluffed his feathers, and looked at him, waiting for the food he had come to expect. Brysen took a small piece of raw rabbit from the game pouch on his side and the bird tucked in, tearing at the delicious prize. Thrasher's talons dug into Brysen's hand so hard, he had to curl his toes to keep from crying, but he didn't let the pain show. He had to stay calm to keep the bird calm. Corrnyn gawked.

"Nice try," Brysen told them. "But a hunter knows a hunter. And you all just look like bone-sucking scavengers to me."

"Grab him," Corrnyn urged, but the man whose hawk Brysen now held hesitated.

"Oh, fill your sack with stones," Corrnyn groaned. "It's the boy's sister who speaks the Hollow Tongue, and she's not here. This one's no more a killer than a canary is." He handed the vulture's leash to one of his companions and lunged toward Brysen. The move was sloppy and the man was unsteady on his feet. Brysen dodged to the left, parrying with the blade he held in his right hand. At the same time, he tossed the hawk on his fist skyward, whistling as he did.

The hawk flew up, over the lip of the gorge, and circled, waiting on as Brysen had trained him to do. That was back when Brysen thought he knew exactly the migration his life would take. But a wild wind had blown him to a new course: Dymian was dead, his sister was gone, and nothing felt familiar except the feel of a bird flying from the fist.

He wasn't like his sister; he couldn't speak to a bird of prey in the Hollow Tongue. That was a gift, and Brysen had never been one to receive gifts. He had, however, practiced and trained and hoped and fought, and he whistled Thrasher down to fight for him now.

"Utch!" another bandit yelled, launching his bird for Thrasher. The two hawks met midair in a tangle of talon and feather, screeching rage, while the third bandit's hawk flew over Brysen and attacked from behind. The bird harried him deeper into the gorge, where the sides were too steep for escape and the bandits had him pinned. The vulture and its keeper pecked and rattled at the Altari, keeping them against the back wall. One of the men had fallen into a coughing fit, and the woman tried to pat his back while still shielding him. None of them would be any help. Brysen looked up for Jowyn, thinking even unskilled help was better than no help at all, but he didn't see his friend on the ridge above.

Brysen really wished he'd made more of a plan before jumping down here. Heroic intentions alone weren't much good against well-practiced beak and blade, and if he was being honest with himself, he'd never been that great a fighter to begin with. If these bandits hadn't been drunk, he'd be dead already.

He blocked the first bandit's attack in time to duck a swipe from the second and sweep the legs out from under the one called Corrnyn. He turned the motion of his leg sweep into a thrusting uppercut with his blade, just missing a bandit's crotch, which made the man back off long enough for Brysen to stand.

He was readying for another attack when he felt the sharp twinge of talons on his back, a hawk's crushing grip on his shoulder blade. The pain staggered him. He tried to shake it loose, but its wings flapped around the sides of his head, smacking his cheeks, his ears, his eyes, blinding him. He managed to snatch the bird, yank its light body off, and throw it, hard, toward the rocks. When it hit and fell on its feet, it looked back at him with shock and fright, panting. Then it fluffed its feathers and flew away, straight out of the gorge, even as its tamer tried to whistle it back.

A lesson every falconer learns eventually: A mistreated hawk will always leave.

Above, the other hawk had gotten behind Thrasher and grabbed him by the neck. Thrasher, true to his name, thrashed wildly, but the more the bird struggled, the tighter the other hawk squeezed. As it flew higher and higher, it crushed the life out of Thrasher. The bird's body fell, dead, less than an arm's length from Brysen, and though he'd seen dead birds before, this one stung. It was his fault.

The victorious hawk dove at him. He braced himself for the impact, but it never came.

A streak of gray sliced the sky, knocking the attacking falcon off its course. The two birds tumbled together on the ground, rolling in the dust, until one stood with its foot on the other, squeezing the life from it as it had squeezed Thrasher.

Shara.

Praise the sky. Brysen smiled though his mouth was bleeding, and then a fist punched the smile straight off his face. A boot kicked Shara hard enough that Brysen felt it in his own ribs and the three old Altari refugees gasped. Then Corrnyn punched him to his knees as the Altari looked away.

This, Brysen thought through the pain, was why they were so easily dominated. Falconry was the spine of the kingdom— the source of wealth and power—and they weren't a part of it. Those willing to use birds of prey would always rule those who wouldn't. Now, Corrnyn loomed over Brysen and hauled him back to his feet by his hair.

On the ground, Shara fluttered but couldn't fly. The kick had hurt her wing, broken some feathers. Brysen wanted to run to her, to help her, but he was helpless in Corrnyn's grip.

"Curse of the sky on you," one of the old men muttered. "On all of you!"

"We got what we came for," Corrnyn told the others, turning Brysen around to tie his wrists behind him. "Kill the glass grinders. They made great bait for a sentimental soul." He leaned down to whisper, "Didn't they, Brysen?"

"I—" Brysen was baffled. They hadn't been robbing these people; they'd been luring Brysen to abduct *him*.

Just as the first bandit moved to cut the old Altari down, a rainbow kestrel painted a streak down the side of the gorge and strafed across Corrnyn's face, breaking his nose and startling him into dropping his knife. Brysen dove for it as the kestrel swooped up again with a proud screech.

"What the—?" Corrnyn staggered, gushing blood through the fingers cupped over his face.

Up on the ridge, Jowyn stood, but he hadn't cast the small, colorful hawk. Another figure stepped up to his side and held out a fist on which the rainbow kestrel settled and preened. Beside him, another figure held a second falcon on the fist, and then another stepped forward with a herder's buzzard, and then another and another. Brysen smiled when he recognized the friends that Jowyn had brought: the battle boys.

7

THE RAINBOW KESTREL TORE INTO A HUNK OF RAW MEAT CLUTCHED IN the smallest battle boy's colorful glove. Nyck.

Born the youngest of five sisters in a family of dedicated Uztari soldiers, Nyck had abandoned the family's military tradition, his childhood home, and the name they'd leashed to him at birth to take up working for the Tamir family. He'd risen from the battle pits of the Broken Jess to become the leader of his own motley scrum: the notorious battle boys, the most loyal, ferocious, and rowdy flock of miscreants Brysen had ever had the honor of calling his friends. They were half-hyped on hunter's leaf, ale-toasted, as brightly clad as parrots, and keen for a fight.

"Hey!" Nyck called down to Brysen as the kestrel ate from his fist. "I think these bone-eaters owe you an apology."

"You're not supposed to come up here!" Corrnyn shouted up at the boys. "You keep to the Villages, and we keep to the hills. That's the deal. If we start robbing each other's nests, there's no end to it."

Brysen couldn't believe how *offended* the bandit sounded. Like there were rules for robbing and kidnapping innocent people that the battle boys were breaking.

"We don't rob anybody," Nyck replied. "We protect our own, and if some folks want to pay us for our services, who are we to refuse?"

"You don't want to make our employer angry," Corrnyn warned. "He makes Mama Tamir look like a grub-eating—"

Nyck cut him off. "Listen, chickadee, I couldn't care less how you feather your nest, but Brysen's been my pal since we were kids, and you've put a knife on him. Sorry to say, that's all there is to it. Run off now. Anything else ends with your organs catching some sunlight."

The bandits looked to one another, then back up to the battle boys. They were outnumbered and on low ground. They'd never get out of the gorge alive if they fought, and they knew it.

"Mud take you!" Corrnyn spat at Brysen's feet. "When the Kartami come, we'll see whose guts catch sunlight."

"I can't wait," Nyck laughed. "But we *are* done talking to you." He moved his fist so his bird had to spread its wings to keep balance, showing its wingspan against the sun and casting a huge shadow below. The bandits ran, and Jowyn started climbing down, followed by Nyck and the rest.

Brysen rushed to Shara. She was panting and had pulled herself below the shade of a boulder. He scooped her up gently, tears chasing one another down his face. He hadn't meant their reunion to go like this. He'd never wanted her to come back to him just to be wounded again, in a stupid knife fight.

No, he thought. *I wanted her back any way she came.*

He cradled her in his arms so she couldn't flap and hurt herself further. She was smaller than he remembered, light as sun on a pond and just as delicate, like the slightest tremor would ripple her to oblivion. He could feel the rapid beat of her racing heart in her downy chest, and in her eyes, he saw her unmitigated terror.

"It's me," he whispered. "Bry." As if that word alone could calm her. "Don't worry," he promised. "I'll make this better. I'll fix you."

It was his fault she'd broken her feathers. Brysen didn't have much faith, but he did believe that a man was responsible for the wounds he made—at least, the kind of man he wanted to be. He'd made no shortage of wounds in his sixteen ice-winds in the world. But a bird's wounds, at least, he knew how to mend. He could fix a broken hawk.

He grabbed the Altari's thick blanket from where it lay discarded and swaddled Shara to keep her warm and still, then rummaged in his game sack for honey paste, sage balm, and a few loose feathers that were a close match to hers. He kept an assortment in his bag, just in case. Trapping and hunting could injure a raptor, so he always had the basic tools to help on hand. While he waited for Jowyn and the battle boys to get down the ridge, he held each feather up to the light to check the color, delicately smoothing them and arranging them on the ground. Hawking wasn't all talon and claw and bloody prey.

"What are you doing?" Jowyn asked, leaning over his shoulder while the battle boys went to talk to the old Altari about who they were and what had brought them up from the plains.

"I'll need to imp her new flight feathers," Brysen explained. "She won't be able to fly with the feathers she's broken, and if I leave them, they could get infected, but I can clean out the shafts, then slide new ones into place and graft them in with balm. They'll behave just like her own feathers until they molt and natural ones grow in."

"You've got an artist's eye," Jowyn observed, resting his hand on Brysen's back. Brysen tensed and looked over his shoulder at him. The pale boy had a half smile on his lips, fuller than a boy's had any business being, and the small flecks of gold that speckled Jowyn's gray eyes glistened in the fading light.

"Hurt hawks can't hunt." He shrugged the other boy's fingers off and studied his injured bird. Looking too long at Jowyn was like looking too long into a fire. You lost sight of anything that wasn't burning, and Brysen had been burned before.

He was going to be careful with his heart this time. Jowyn was his friend, nothing more. Anything else was just whistling heartbreak down from the sky.

"Help me hold her down," he said, and Jowyn came around in front of the blanket, squatted, and rested his hand across Shara's soft gray back as delicately as he'd rested it across Brysen's. Brysen unwrapped the bird. Their fingers brushed, and Brysen dared a glance up again.

Jowyn was watching the hawk, wide-eyed. In the mountains, the covey of boys that the Owl Mothers kept had no need for healing arts. They drank the sap of the blood birches and all was healed. Down here, bodies broke, bodies had to be mended.

Brysen wished he could stop himself from thinking about bodies. Those thoughts always turned to his own: the burn scars that covered him from waist to neck and how badly he wanted to be rid of them, those glossy-fleshed reminders of how pitiful and defenseless he'd been, how deserving of scorn. At least Shara's wounds he knew how to heal.

The battle boys and the Altari gathered around to watch, blocking his light. He waved them back and raised the curved black blade. He'd have liked to heat it over a flame, but there was no flame here in the mountain gorge, so he simply set to work on Shara's feathers, one at time, cutting the first broken one away, smearing the wound with sage balm and the replacement feather with honey paste and delicately sliding it into place.

"She's going to squirm," he warned Jowyn. "Hold her firmly."

Jowyn did, and Brysen held the feather still in its place. With his other hand, he stroked Shara, offering the proper prayer:

> *"Another's blood I'll mend with care,*
> *Another's pain I'll take to share,*
> *Another's wing will take to air."*

He felt stupid singing in front of everyone else, especially when his voice cracked, but he had to sing the song so the balm would work.

Jowyn smiled, which made Brysen's cheeks flush. He wanted to explain that it wasn't superstition that made him sing this prayer; it was just that the balm took exactly the amount of time to stick the feather in place as the prayer took to sing. But Jowyn's bright smile made him want to let the other boy think he was the type of person who'd sing to an injured bird just to make it feel better. Jowyn made him want to *be* that kind of person.

By the time the feathers were all imped and Shara was swaddled once again, the sun had already dipped past the horizon, and the mountains had blended into the purple sky, dark peaks scraping against dark sky. Brysen looked at his friends, looked at the chaos of footprints and blood in the dust at their feet.

"So how did Jowyn find you so conveniently?" he asked. "You all following me?"

Nyck laughed. "Don't flatter yourself. We were already here looking for *them*." He pointed at the three old Altari. "We saw their fire last night, and we get a full bronze a day to patrol this pass for glass grinders—I mean, Altari."

"And we *each* get a bronze for finding some," Glynnick interjected. He was one of the youngest, having lived through about as many ice-winds as he had hairs on his upper lip. But even baby birds can bite, and Brysen had seen poor fools underestimate Glynnick in a fight and pay the price.

"How come I never heard about this deal before?" Brysen was usually in on whatever schemes the battle boys had going.

"You haven't been around the Broken Jess much lately," Nyck said.

"I've been busy," Brysen told them. He didn't tell him how he'd lost his taste for gambling and hawk-battling after losing Shara, how he kind of liked spending time in the mountains alone with Jowyn now, and how he was pretty sure Jowyn didn't feel comfortable at the Broken Jess. Some friends you shared your feelings with, and some you didn't. The battle boys were tough and loyal and a blast to get blasted with, but they weren't *feelings* sort of friends.

"What are you supposed to do when you find the Altari?" he wondered. "Protect them from bandits? You the Home Guard now?"

The battle boys snickered, but Nyck silenced them with a gesture. "Kinda, but . . . well . . . not quite *protect* them . . . You know the Villages are already crowded as is, and with folks unsettled because of all the strange bird migrations and the Kartami pushing all these people off the plains . . . it's getting tense. To keep the peace, we're supposed to keep newcomers out."

"I see newcomers all the time."

"*Altari* newcomers," Nyck clarified. "They could be Kartami agents."

Brysen looked back at the old people. "You think these people are with the Kartami? They're running *from* the Kartami!"

Fentyr, the biggest battle boy, cut in, "How're we supposed to feed everyone who comes this way? They're being chased from the desert straight for us. You think that's an accident? The Kartami want us to have to feed all their refugees just to starve us out."

"You're describing a plague of locusts," Brysen said. "This is three haggards and a baby. People who need help. We can take them to the Six."

Fentyr snorted. "Since when did you join the Holy Order of the Feather Sweeps, huh? Taking in all the waywards of this world."

Fentyr wasn't just talking about the old refugees. He looked at Jowyn sideways. He was skeptical of this strange boy, who'd run away and come back but wouldn't even speak to his old family. It made people nervous, especially the battle boys, because it was Jowyn's old family for whom they worked.

The Tamir family were predators, and Mama Tamir—Jowyn's mother—was the apex predator. Doing work for them was as likely to end in death as in a payday.

"I don't want to take in everyone," Brysen argued. "But we can at least escort these four to safety."

"Glass grinders get the dirt's mercy, not the sky's. Always been that way," Fentyr said. Brysen stared him down for the slur. Brysen's ma had been called "glass grinder" countless times, usually by his father, but he refused to let his friends get away with the term. It was based on an old lie claiming that Altari crawled so much in the desert, they ground the sand to glass. The word was a way for the Uztari to grind them down the same.

Fentyr muttered an apology. You could always tell when someone had the capacity to be better than they were. They could feel shame. Only the shameless were truly irredeemable.

"We've always had Altari in the Villages," Brysen said, hoping the people behind him weren't offended by Fentyr.

"A few at a time, like your ma," Nyck said. "Never a crowd coming like this."

"Come on," Brysen pleaded. "They're only three and a baby. They can stay at my place."

Nyck bit his lower lip as he shook his head at Brysen, then turned it into a nod and an eye roll. "Why can't I ever say no to you?"

"My rugged good looks?" Brysen suggested.

"Your total ineptitude," Nyck replied. "You're helpless as a baby bird, and I guess I just have that mothering instinct. And you." He jutted his chin at Jowyn. "Some use you were."

"I found you, didn't I?" Jowyn replied, crossing his arms.

"And if you hadn't?" Nyck got in his face. "They were going to *take* Brysen, and you were going to let them."

"Hey, we were outnumbered!" Brysen stood in between the two boys, feeling the need to justify his newest friend's actions to his oldest ones. "Jowyn would've been taken, too."

"What*ever* would we have done without him?" Nyck sneered.

"So who were they? Why'd they come after you?" Fentyr asked.

"I don't know," Brysen said, wishing they'd questioned the bandits instead of letting them run off. "But there is someone in the Villages who might. She knows what every lowlife under a tern's flight is up to."

"But she hates you, Bry," Nyck noted. "Like . . . *deadly* hates you."

"Oh, scuzz," Jowyn cursed. He'd figured out who Brysen meant, and he was not happy about it.

"I know," Brysen said, looking straight into Jowyn's eyes. "But first thing tomorrow, we have to go see your mother, and I need you there in case she's tempted to kill me instead of answering my questions."

"What makes you think I can stop her from killing you?" he asked.

"You're her son who flew the coop," Brysen replied. "She'll be so glad you're back that she won't think of killing the one who brought you."

"My ma kills twice as many when she's happy as when she's

sad," Jowyn said. "Her birthday parties were always followed by weeks of funerals."

"I know," Brysen said. "But I need to know who's after me and why, and she might be able to tell me."

"You're perching a lot of hope on that word *might*," Jowyn said.

"No," Brysen told him. "I'm perching a lot of hope on *you*."

PATIENCE AND APPETITE

KYRG BARDU, AS PROCTOR OF THE COUNCIL OF FORTY, WAS THE MOST powerful person in Uztar, and she quite simply hated waiting. She stood in her dovecote in the middle of the round tower filled with niches for her prized pigeons and listened to them coo. She was trying to calm herself, to let the evening unfold as it would. She didn't like what had happened with the girl and the ghost eagle today. She didn't like anything that happened with the ghost eagle any day, though she'd soon be in a position to do something about it.

I used to be a patient person, she thought. She'd been appointed to her seat on the Council, rather than inheriting it like some, and she'd quietly worked her way up to the proctorship, one careful move at a time. Politics was a game of patience and appetite, like falcon training, and it was a game she played well.

And yet now, in the face of invasion and war, politics tired her. The kyrgs of the Council were quarrelsome—forty egos and forty sets of competing interests and forty hopes and forty fears and thirty-nine people who thought it was her job to care about what it was they wanted.

Some argued for sending emissaries to sue for peace with the Kartami so that trade routes could resume; others argued for total war, forced conscription of all fight-capable youths with even so much as peach fuzz under their arms. She had one kyrg who believed his beloved falcon was a Kartami hostage and that the Council should offer a huge ransom. Though the Kartami killed any trained birds of prey they captured, there was no talking sense to the distraught falconer. He'd paid a fortune for that peregrine, and he'd happily pay another for her return.

And then there was the business of Kyrg Ryven, the most troubling development. His ascension to the Council had cost Bardu her best assassin. How he'd managed to survive, she still didn't know. But he had, and he'd been seated and sealed by law, and now he was one of the Forty whom she was forced to concern herself with.

Except he *had* no concerns.

He brought her neither problems nor complaints, requests nor demands. He never offered her secrets or gossip and didn't invite her to his endless parties. He wanted, it seemed, nothing from her, and this worried Bardu more than anything.

A politician who didn't play politics was a dangerous predator indeed.

So she'd dispatched a spy, at no small expense, and she hoped this evening would provide her with some answers about the young kyrg *and* the young falconer on whom Uztar pinned its hopes. What she needed was control of both of them, and what she had right now was too little information on *either* of them. If Ryven was wooing the young woman, it could only be because of her relationship with the ghost eagle. Power perched on the strongest branch, and whoever controlled that bird was certainly strongest.

"Lywen!" she called for her hawk master, who was also her nephew, which gave him certain privileges other hawk masters did not enjoy. For one, being allowed anywhere near her pigeons, the birds she far preferred over hawks and eagles.

While an Uztari proctor who had no love for birds of prey was a scandal, the quality could also be useful. She was not in competition with the other kyrgs for the finest cast in her mews or the best hunt or the greatest fighting raptor. They needn't be jealous of her, and she needn't keep the finest birds she acquired and so could bestow them as gifts. Power wasn't always achieved by force, after all. A gift could be stronger than a threat, and she had offered plenty of gifts in her time.

To the Owl Mothers she'd given autonomy over their mountain lands and a regular supply of parentless boys to serve in their covey. To Kyrg Birgund she'd given rank and honor and the glory of commanding Uztar's forces. To the Altari girl, Grazim, she'd dangled status higher than any Altari before had achieved. The ambitious were as easy to master as a starving falcon. It didn't take much meat to call them to the fist.

What gift, she wondered, would let her master Kylee? What did that Six Villager girl want above all else?

Ryven was likely betting on romance, but Bardu knew from her spies that this was not likely to be of any interest to the young woman. Her brother was a raging blaze of desires, but Kylee's fire burned from a different fuel.

She claimed it was her brother's safety, but she'd left him behind with precious little resistance, which made Bardu doubt that was truly what she wanted, even if she still believed it was. What else would a girl like that want, a girl who'd spent her whole life caring for others, looking out for them and fixing their mistakes?

She had to figure it out before Ryven did. He was throwing

another party, and even with the ghost eagle flitting about the skies and war plaguing the plains, the people of this city above the clouds loved a party. Bardu did not have that luxury. While they enjoyed themselves, she needed to protect Uztar and to protect her position ruling it.

"Yes, mem." Lywen finally arrived, saluting with the wings across his heart. He smelled like hunter's leaf, and his green-tinted teeth suggested he'd been chewing and gambling with the apprentices in the battle pits again. She bit her tongue. Take away the boy's indulgences and she might erode his loyalty, which would be a shame. She'd never hear the end of it from her siblings if she had her own nephew assassinated.

She pretended not to smell him. "Our agent has arrived? She's prepared?"

"Yes, mem," Lywen confirmed, licking his lips and fidgeting with the tassel on a falcon's hood he was clutching for some reason. His falcon was not with him. Perhaps the battle pits hadn't gone well. "The girl's family was quite honored to send her for this task."

"A sackful of bronze certainly helped," Bardu scoffed. Six Villagers were nearly as famous for their spying families as they were for their falconers, and there was no greater honor to a spy than getting paid. Bardu wondered if the young woman they'd sent would ever see so much as a round of the bronze that had bought her service. Her family would likely keep it all. She also wondered if the spy could be trusted for candor. The spy had known Kylee for a long time, and young people tended to value friendship more than bronze.

"I don't like waiting," Bardu told her nephew. "I think I'd like to put some other insurance into place."

"Insurance?" It was a concept her nephew didn't grasp.

"In case our spy is not as useful as her family claims she will be."

"What do you have in mind?"

She looked up at her pigeons, at the last of the daylight that caught the mess of bluish feathers floating down from their niches. The walls were streaked with the white of dried bird scuzz, which Bardu never had cleaned away. She liked to re-member that even the gentlest birds produced impressive amounts of crap. It was an apt metaphor for Uztar.

"Who replaced Yirol after her untimely demise?"

"The assassin?" Lywen scratched his chin, as if he had any sort of stubble there. "I believe one of your former valets. Chitiycalania."

"Ah." Bardu smiled. "Chit. Good. Please send her a mes-sage from me: I have a job. Something to keep us all occupied until Kyrg Ryven's festivities are over."

She felt better now that she'd taken action. Kyrg Ryven's parties didn't start until long after sundown and didn't end until close to sunup, and she did not want to wait that long to exert a measure of power over the young woman who believed she might command the sky. She had to be tamed first, and Kyrg Bardu knew just how to do it.

The one difference between politics and falcon training was this: You couldn't tame a hawk with fear. Humans were a different story.

KYLEE

WHAT WINGS ASPIRE

8

THE SKY CASTLE HAD BEGUN AS A FORT, BUILT BY THE EARLY UZTARI who crossed the mountains from the frozen steppes on the other side. After they fought off the Altari, they established the stronghold on high ground to watch over the plateau and to maintain control over the sky above it. Kylee ran her fingers over the oldest stones. The chips and gashes made by war had been smoothed by time. The castle had grown out from the central fortress, the defensive walls transformed to inner courtyards. The halls that had once heard the screams of wounded warriors were now pens for livestock or mews for hawks. From this high castle, Uztari power grew and settlements expanded.

Over the generations, the castle had expanded from the central ring to accommodate more and more people. New circular walls traced the contours of the mountain, up and down and sideways, struggling to burst free from the limits of the landscape but bound by the relentless force of gravity. Any great plan laid by the founders of the first citadel had long been abandoned by the growth of the city, and its layout was like the pattern of drifting clouds.

High towers at the upper and lower central gates and on the two far sides gave a near-infinite view across the plateau and down into the castle, which was itself a series of structures built around pens and mews and courtyards. The older parts of the castle were more organized than the newer ones, but all were in a state of constant repair. An army of craftspeople and artisans worked tirelessly to keep the castle from crumbling down the mountain. The fact that it still stood was a triumph of stubbornness and wealth over wind and rain and war.

Hammering and clattering were the constant song of the city, with the shrieks and cries of birds punctuating the creative cursing of the artisans. The cacophony made Kylee tense as she walked the lamplit streets. She'd thought the Six Villages during the Hawkers' Market were loud, but the noise of the great city above the clouds made even the loudest festival she'd known as a girl seem soft as a chick's chirping.

The lamps that lit the street burned compressed bricks of

mountain grass and elk dung, and the fuel gave every street and walkway an odor of the wilderness, something feral and hunting. In finer homes, the fuel was perfumed, but the cost was too great for the public lamps, and so the direction of the mountain winds defined the odor of the city. Rich people were known to keep several homes within walking distance so they could decamp to sweeter smells depending on which way the evening breezes blew.

A warm, melting wind had blown off the miasma of dung in the air. The way from the garrison to Kyrg Ryven's residence was nearly the whole length of the city, and it was a pleasant night for a walk. Cloaked Uztari with hawks on their fists strolled around the curved lanes, wandering aimlessly. Their chattering was even more aimless; it was necessary in order to stay awake on the long vigils it took to accustom a new falcon to the fist. Wealthier people had valets to do this task for them, carrying new birds around for days without sleep until the hawk became completely used to being held and completely dependent on the one holding it for food and rest and companionship.

The whole process made Kylee think of breaking a prisoner. Behind all the gentleness in a falconer's care for her birds, there was a kind of brutality. Dominance through dependency. A falconer's kindness to a bird was the kindness of bait on a hook. It was power disguised as kindness.

She wondered if the invitation to Kyrg Ryven's party was the same sort of kindness.

All the kyrgs who made up the Council of Forty had chambers somewhere near the central citadel, where the business of administering Uztar took place, but few besides Kyrg Bardu actually lived there. The old buildings were cold and drafty and lacked modern comforts like hot-spring water and wide staircases. Every kyrg kept at least one secondary home in the newer districts to the east and west of the citadel. Kyrg Ryven had his palatial home in the southwest quarter of the city, high over the neighborhood the locals called the Peacock, because of the way colorful mountain flowers thrived in window boxes. Thanks to the abundant botanicals, perfumeries and herbalists had sprouted up, and the city's sprawling flower market thrived there, paying, of course, a tax to the kyrg who presided over the neighborhood, Ryven himself. His bronze was the product of beauty, bought and sold.

Kylee saw the house from a distance, long before she reached its gate. It perched above the neighborhood, a central oval of stone with two wings of smooth stone flanking it, terraces off each wing arrayed in a pattern like flight feathers, so the home suggested a falcon roused, about to fly. The home was grand, grander than Kylee could've imagined for someone so young, and she wondered if it belonged to his parents. Were they the reason he was on the Council of Forty? A kyrg's seat could be passed down to anyone the current holder chose. In most cases that was a child or spouse or lover, but some kyrgs offered up their seats for sale upon their death, to ensure their family's future wealth if not their power. Had Kyrg Ryven been given his seat, or had he bought his way to it?

A bitter taste of resentment tingled her teeth when she thought of someone who would never be buffeted by the winds of other people's expectations just because they had wealth. The things Kylee and her brother had to do just to survive were totally unknown to a man like Kyrg Ryven, who could invite a stranger to his home for a party and know that she would have to attend. In that moment, she could understand Grazim a little more. Whatever gifts or achievements you thought you had, there was someone soaring above them, casting a shadow down. Jealousy was a simple predator, but it hunted everyone—even Kylee.

Maybe that's why everyone fears the ghost eagle, she thought. *It doesn't look up with longing at anyone. Everything alive is below it.* Kylee'd have liked to know what that kind of freedom felt like, to be above it all, at the apex, longing for nothing and having your back scratched by the stars.

Ryven's house was as close as any Kylee had seen to starlight. It was higher even than the outer wall Üku had dangled her off earlier, higher than the city's watchtowers. Its roof rose almost to the height of the nearest mountain peak.

At the entrance, there were over a hundred steps whirling up in a wide turn from the end of the street to the front gate. The iron bars were draped with long vines of sparrow's ivy, which was just beginning to bud with orange flowers. Two spotted wood owls perched on either side of the gate. They were tethered in place but unhooded, watching Kylee's approach with black eyes in bright orange faces.

The owls match the flowers, she thought with astonishment.

When she stood in front of them, she checked the length of the leather leashes that bound the owls and saw that, indeed, she was within range if they chose to dive at her. Instead, one of them hooted, and the other swiveled its head to look off to the side, at a view over the silver clouds below. From the gate, she could look back over much of the city. She saw the curved streets like meltwater streams, the flickering lights of the dung-lamps shifting the scuttling shadows as people moved about their evening business. Around the tall towers that watched over every district, clouds of bats flew, feasting on the insects that were drawn to the lights from the windows. The bats told of warming weather, of the rushing of rivers and growing of crops on the grasslands. With the warmth came the fighting season and the certainty that Kartami attacks would grow more aggressive and faster and would soon reach the Six Villages.

She looked past the outer wall, across the ragged mountain

range, tracing the moonlit river as far as she could, hoping to see even a flicker of light from the distant Villages, but they were too far and the clouds hung too low, concealing the settlements from view. The Sky Castle might've been an island in a sea of stone and cloud, sitting so far above the rest of Uztar.

If Kylee was a sort of prisoner in the Sky Castle, it wasn't so bad a place to be. Kylee loved heights—another trait she shared with the ghost eagle. And the sooner she mastered that bird, the sooner she'd be free to leave.

But first she had to get into the party, and she had no idea how to get past the front gate. She looked at the impassive owls. Was this a test of her skill with the Hollow Tongue? Was she supposed to ask them for entry? She *did* want to go inside, wanted to see the view from the house and find out what the kyrg wanted from her, so maybe asking would work. She didn't know the Hollow Tongue for "open," so she tried asking in her own words.

"Uh . . . could you open?"

The owls blinked at her.

"If you please, dear madams?" she tried, thinking perhaps a kyrg's owls might stand on formality. She used a female honorific out of respect for the owls' nobility and the dominance of females of the species.

One of the owls shifted on its feet, but otherwise, nothing happened. She could feel the eyes of curious people on the street looking up at her. It wasn't like she was unknown in the Sky Castle: the girl the ghost eagle follows. She wished she'd worn a cloak. With a hood.

"Waiting for someone?" a girl called, making her way up the stairs behind Kylee.

"I . . ." Kylee wasn't sure how to explain that she couldn't figure out the way in. "Kyrg Ryven invited me," she said.

"I should hope so," the girl answered, climbing the last steps, paying no attention to the owls. "I'd hate to be at this kind of party without my best friend." When she lowered the hood of her cloak, Kylee felt like her heart had just caught a gliding breeze.

"Vy!" she cried. Vyvian was her closest friend in the Six Villages, aside from Nyall and her brother, and her presence on the steps of a kyrg's palace inside the Sky Castle was as surprising as it was welcome. "*What* are you doing here?"

"My mother dispatched me not long after you left," her friend told her. "Albyon was supposed to go, but he broke his leg dancing at the Broken Jess, so it was finally my turn to ply the family trade where it matters."

Kylee itched to hug her friend, but she stopped herself at the mention of "the family trade." Vyvian's family trade was spying, and it couldn't be a coincidence that her first visit to the Sky Castle happened to be at the same time as Kylee's. When they were kids, she used to talk about it like it was a nest of bone-sucking vultures, but she'd probably just been parroting her parents. Spying was big business in the Six Villages, and any spy who wanted to rise wanted to work at the Sky Castle.

If Vyvian had found her way to the very same party as Kylee, it was not by accident—broken leg or otherwise. Back when Kylee was just some Six Villages girl, Vyvian's work hadn't mattered much. But now that Kylee was in the center of Uztari power, Vyvian's friendship was a lot more complicated. A spy would want something from her, and it might not be clear what it was or what it would cost until after she'd gotten it.

All these hidden agendas made Kylee so tired. Why couldn't anything just be straightforward, like it was before the ghost eagle?

"I'm glad to see you," Kylee offered simply, which was true, if far from simple.

"And not just because I know how to get inside the gates?" Vyvian smiled and reached between a few strands of dangling ivy beside one of the owls. She revealed a thick cord of rope and pulled it. Somewhere above, a bell rang.

"I wonder how long it would have taken me to figure that out," Kylee laughed.

Vyvian laughed, too, sweet as song. "I'm sure someone would have come looking for you eventually. You *are* the guest of honor—you know that, right?"

Kylee shook her head. "I haven't done anything worth honoring."

"You've already done more than most of these finch-faced nobles could dream," Vyvian said. "You should hear the rumors about you back home. Everyone thinks you'll be the savior of Uztar. Some folks think you've already saved us."

"What about Brysen?" Kylee asked. The glide her heart had felt a moment ago turned to a nervous flapping, trying desperately to stay aloft. "How's he doing?"

Vyvian put her hand on Kylee's shoulder. "He's totally fine," she assured her. "He spends most days with the pale-skinned owl boy who followed you down the mountain. He claims they're just friends, but Albyon's been inconsolable about it. I think that's how he hurt himself, trying to get your brother's attention."

"And is Brysen . . . safe?" she asked.

"There are spies watching him," Vyvian whispered, "but I promise, it's no one from my family. We wouldn't do that."

Silent as a snow owl, the knowledge hovered in the air between them that her family would absolutely *do that*, that they might be the very ones *doing that*. Kylee supposed it was better her brother was being watched by people who knew him than by some strangers the Sky Castle had sent. Still, she wondered, if it came to it, if Kylee failed or if she displeased the

Council, would it fall to Vyvian's family to assassinate her brother? Would they *do that*, too?

"So how do you know about this party?" she asked, pivoting away from the fraught topic of her brother's fate. He was the reason Kylee was here, but she'd rather not spend all their time talking about him.

"It's what I do," Vyvian said, flipping her dark hair back behind her neck.

"Do you know anything about the host, Kyrg Ryven?"

Just as Vyvian was about to answer her question, the gate opened, and Vyvian charged forward, the two owls rotating their heads to watch the girls pass through and resume their winding way up to the front door. The stairs were lined with all manner of birds of prey carved from pink, black, gray, and white salt rock, which glowed from within, lighting the path. Two human guards stood beside the entrance, with large curved swords on their belts and tall, unhooded falcons on their left fists.

"He's the youngest kyrg ever seated," Vyvian whispered as they approached. "And there were kyrgs who didn't want him seated at all."

"Why not?"

"That's what I'm supposed to find out. He was an orphan taken in by a kyrg who died mysteriously while out hunting.

So far, all the information our clients have is mere mutterings and rumors. They want to know facts."

"Who *are* your clients?" Kyle asked.

Vyvian held up a finger and cocked her head. "Come on, Ky, you *know* I can't tell you that."

"So you aren't here because of me?" Kylee found herself both relieved and disappointed.

"You've heard the one about two birds and one stone, right?"

"Yeah," Kylee said. "I don't think I want to be one of those birds."

"Don't worry," Vyvian told her. "In this case, the stone thrower's on your side, and she has *excellent aim*. Just do me a favor."

"What's that?"

"Introduce me to our host."

"Oh." Kylee smiled. "The spy needs help with her spying. I see how it is!"

"It's not *that*." Vyvian laughed. "Well, not *just* that. You *have* seen him, right? I could definitely rest awhile on his perch."

At that Kylee rolled her eyes. Her friend was incorrigible. Vyvian had never seen a beautiful creature whose feathers she didn't want to ruffle, metaphorically speaking. And Kyrg Ryven had the sort of feathers that girls like Vyvian very much enjoyed ruffling.

"I'm sure he'll introduce himself to you." Kylee took

Vyvian's arm and leaned her head close to her friend's as they stepped up to the guards like a pair of swans. "You are with *me* after all, the *savior* of Uztar."

It felt good to laugh about it with a friend, even if that friend was a spy and a liar. When you got this close to power, Kylee realized, everyone was a spy and a liar, so it was important to keep close the liars you could trust and hope the knives they hid ended up in someone else's back.

9

THE TALL STONE DOORS OF KYRG RYVEN'S HOUSE OPENED AND THE
avalanche of sound and light nearly knocked Kylee back down
the stairs and halfway down the mountain. As she adjusted
her eyes and tried to figure out what could be producing all
the light, Kyrg Ryven himself stepped straight to the center of
the doorway, beaming, and beckoned them in, like he'd been
waiting there all along.

The moment she and Vyvian stepped inside, the room fell
silent. Counselors and merchants, valets and attendants, performers, servants, and sundry citizens of the Sky Castle
peered at her through the haze of pipe smoke and candles
under glass. They paused with small cakes halfway to their

lips or bubbling liquor and ale mid-swallow. Some had birds of prey hooded on their fists; others had songbirds in little cages worn like hats or breastplates. One woman had bright yellow goldfinches looped by the ankles side by side up her sleeves all the way to her shoulders, and another ring of them tied all the way around the brim of her hat. The birds were either used to being fashion or sedated with slump root, because none of them flapped or screamed like a bird bound to a dress should have.

Only Kyrg Ryven had dressed simply. He wore a long black utility kilt with silver buckles and straps on the pockets and a long black raven's feather at the end of his belt. His black tunic was sleeveless, to show off either his arms or his bicep armbands, each ringed with flat metal feathers. On a closer look, Kylee saw the black kilt and tunic were embroidered with detailed flocks of birds in black thread with just the tiniest hint of red that caught the light when he moved. It was far from simple; it was *subtle*, a distinction that Kylee also took as a warning. She'd have to be careful around him. His agenda might be as finely stitched as his outfit.

A servant came to take Kylee's cloak and presented her with a full bronze piece in its place, as no one would turn over their cloak for nothing, even in the warmer melt-wind season.

The moment her cloak was whisked away, the guests assessed the clothes she'd chosen, reading her outfit with the focus of augurs divining the meaning in the flight of birds, wondering who'd given these clothes to her, and what it meant that she'd chosen to wear them over others.

Except the guests would have to keep on guessing, because other than the cloak, the clothes she'd chosen were all her own. They were the clothes she'd been wearing when she left the Six Villages: simple leathers and wools colored with local dyes, a dagger strapped to her thigh, and a falconer's glove—one of her brother's—on her belt. She'd decided to dress like herself, like someone who was not beholden to these people, like someone who would not forget where she came from. She was here to win their war and protect her family. Everything else—even parties—was simply a means to that end. If she could've worn some fantastic outfit without it being forced to *mean something*, then maybe she would have, but this outfit sent the message she wanted to send: *I don't want to be here.*

Beside her, Vyvian cleared her throat. "I probably should've met you at your room."

Vyvian's outfit was the inverse of Ryven's, a slick white tunic of shimmering fabric that flowed as one piece into shining white pants. Her boots were calf height and covered in white owl feathers, and around each of her arms she wore a clear glass swan whose neck wrapped twice around her biceps. Their eyes were polished bronze. Each piece must have cost more than three seasons of spying in the Villages could pay. Sensing Kylee's surprise, she explained, "My family's clients do have some bronze to spare," and Kylee was more certain than ever that it was another kyrg who'd hired her friend and dispatched her to this party. Could it have been the defense counselor, Birgund? Or the proctor herself?

With every eye in the vast room looking at them, Kylee sensed how a grouse must feel with a hawk circling above. Or perhaps how it felt in those few terrible moments between the dive and the killing strike.

Once they'd been assessed, the party resumed its clamor.

"You look dashing," Ryven told them as he stepped forward to greet them properly. He gave the winged salute self-consciously, like someone skilled at etiquette but aware of its absurdity. Kylee returned the salute with matched irony, which seemed to please the young kyrg.

"This is my friend Vyvian, from home," Kylee introduced her.

"Ah yes, the other Six Villager who has joined us recently." Ryven smiled. "They say the great tradition of falconry was born in the Six Villages and practiced there with a grace even our finest hawk masters cannot match."

"*Grace* is not the word I'd use to describe a fight in the battle pits," Kylee offered.

"Well, we may be the head of the Uztari Empire, but you

spring from its heart, and we are honored to have falconers of such venerable pedigree here."

"The honor is mine." Vyvian smiled at him, not correcting that she was not, herself, a falconer, though his lingering gaze suggested he knew already.

"Venerable pedigree, huh?" Kylee cut in. "My da was a violent drunken rube, and my ma was an Altari runaway. I'm not sure it's my pedigree anyone here is interested in."

For a moment, Vyvian and Ryven both looked like she'd slapped them, then the young kyrg laughed and Vyvian laughed with him.

"Honesty is something we sorely lack here," Kyrg Ryven said. "And yet it is essential to those who would master the Hollow Tongue. An interesting contradiction, I think."

"Is it?" Kylee wondered. "All things are bound to their opposites, are they not?"

"So they say," Ryven answered her. "And yet to be unbound is to be free. Perhaps seeking freedom from our shadows is the calling of those who would walk in the sun."

"Unless we *are* the shadows," Kylee countered. In truth, she had no idea what they were talking about anymore, but it was fun to bat sentences back and forth like they were in a game whose rules the players invented as they played.

Vyvian looked between them, uninvited to their game and searching for a way in.

"Do you study the Hollow Tongue, Kyrg Ryven?" Vyvian tried with an almost invisible twitch of her lip that Kylee only noticed because of their long friendship. This was just the sort of news her clients would pay for, which Ryven seemed already to know, because he winked at her.

"Ah, if study alone could grant one the Hollow Tongue, our teachers would be the richest among us," Kyrg Ryven said. "And the kyrgs would compete for tutors the way they now compete for spies." Vyvian tensed, but Ryven pretended not to notice. "Of course, as Kylee knows, the Hollow Tongue can hardly be spoken by merely studying the words. I'm not sure even our mysterious and esteemed Owl Mothers understand its workings fully."

"If they did, they probably wouldn't need me," Kylee retorted, which drew a curious frown from the kyrg. He looked at Kylee the way a hawk watches a butterfly; there was no threat in his appraisal, but there was a clear sense that the power in this interaction was all his. Kylee'd have liked to shift the balance back somehow and thought her bluntness would show how little she cared about his flowery words, but he turned his back and led them through the crowded party, gesturing for a servant to bring them something to drink. A glass of spiced milk punch was pressed into Kylee's right hand, a delicate pastry into her left, and the servants flitted away before she could even see them.

Whispers passed between the guests, muttering details of her life.

". . . ghost eagle killed her father . . ."

". . . brother was in love with that Avestri boy . . . the dead one . . ."

"Ghost eagle killed him, too."

"The brother?"

"The Avestri boy . . ."

"I heard the brother did it . . ."

"I heard *she* did it . . ."

"So where's the brother?"

Kylee didn't like how much these people knew about her and also didn't like having her hands full in a strange environment, so she devoured the pastry quickly—it was filled with dried fruit and sweet cheese—then gulped back the drink. Servants took the empty glass from her as quickly as they'd first pressed it on her, and just as suddenly, another drink and another pastry appeared in her hands. The servants glanced sideways at the kyrg, as if for approval, but he didn't deign to look at his staff. Whatever his background, the young kyrg had certainly taken on some of the obnoxious manners of the spoiled rich. Kylee gave the servants her thanks before they busied themselves in the crowded party again.

Ryven must have kept a flock of glass crafters busy season in and season out. Everyone at the party was drinking from glass, not a stoneware cup in sight. Kylee found that focusing on the small details wealth accorded, rather than the big ones, kept her head from spinning. The glass was cool and the new pastry was sprinkled with bright green and red herbs.

"Mountain saffron!" One of the guests beamed at her. His skin was dark as Nyall's, but his hair was as amber as Grazim's freckles. He wore a quilted robe of colorful patches and clutched a drink in each hand. "Bet they don't have *that* in your Villages."

A glare from Ryven silenced the man and sent him melting away into the crowd like late ice on a rushing river.

Ryven led them toward a set of guarded doors on the opposite side of the entry hall, but held his hand up before they could pass through. "If you wouldn't mind, Vyvian, I'd like to speak to Kylee alone." She hesitated, but he beckoned a tall, thin woman over. "You would surely enjoy a chat with Kyrg Amye? She's the senior counselor for smiths here in the city, responsible for much of the weaponry our army will employ against the invaders. That's of interest to your family, no?" Vyvian balked, realizing that Ryven knew exactly who she was and what business she was in. "Kyrg Amye, please, meet my charming friend Vyvian. She has so many questions I'm sure you'd love to answer."

He then nudged Kylee forward to the doors. As she went, she realized she did not want to be alone with this kyrg with her hands full. He saw her indecision and motioned to a table by the door where she could set down her pastry—tragically untouched. It looked delicious. A bright-eyed sparrow hawk leashed beside the table looked from Kylee to the pastry, to Kylee again, then gleefully pecked away at the delicate, saffron-scented crust.

Ryven took the drink from her hand and passed it to Vyvian.

"A small consolation for borrowing your friend," he told her.

"A poor trade for me," Vyvian mused, "but how can I refuse the prettiest peacock here anything?"

"You flatter me," Ryven said.

"Who said I was talking about you?" Vyvian winked at Kylee and Ryven laughed.

He saluted her with more sincerity than he had when they'd entered. "To your highest health."

"And to yours," she replied, grinning, then gulped back the intoxicating brew, using the grand gesture as an excuse to lean into Kylee for a hug. "Be careful in there," she whispered in Kylee's ear, all whimsy drained from her voice. This was *not* meant for the kyrg to overhear. "Befriending the wrong person can be dangerous." Then she pulled away and laughed loudly. "Do leave some of his feathers unplucked for me!"

Kyrg Amye looked aghast as Kylee let Ryven show her through the doors and into a room as still as a windless winter sky.

10

WHEN THE DOORS CLOSED, THE PARTY'S NOISE VANISHED, AND THEY
were alone in a large room with three bare stone walls. Where
the fourth wall might've been, the night sky shone with starlight over the mountain peaks. No barrier or banister blocked
the view . . . or the fall.

"This is my study," Ryven said. "Ironically, the only place I
find myself able to maintain some privacy is a place completely
open to the elements."

"I shouldn't leave my friend alone too long," Kylee said.
"She'll scandalize your guests."

She kept one hand low, near the hilt of her dagger, and

assessed the space. The room was divided into thirds by great stone pillars that supported the ceiling above. They were intricately inscribed from top to bottom, but she didn't have time to look them over, because her eyes were struck by the only piece of furniture in the room: a stone table on which sat a large mechanical model of the migratory patterns of a dozen different kinds of birds.

There were flocks of bronze ravens, copper geese, silver pigeons, and brass waxwings. Starlings in jade and cardinals in ruby. Lone hawks and falcons carved from bone, golden eagles made of gold, and above them all, from a shining piece of stone blacker than an elk's eye: a massive ghost eagle. Each bird was held in place by a thin copper arm.

"My guests are used to scandal by now," Ryven told her as he crossed the room to the model and removed a small bone pin that locked the arms in place. With a breeze that the shape of the walls and pillars channeled from outside, the model began to move; each flock and bird responding to the wind and to one another in an intricate dance that mirrored their behavior in the sky. The jade starlings formed an undulating murmuration; the ruby cardinals flitted low, while the geese found their V shape and made straight lines across the diameter of the model. At different heights, hawks and eagles circled and dove, the tiny metal wings folding as they fell and clicking open as they swooped up again. Only the black-stone ghost eagle stayed still, quivering above it all.

This was artisanship like Kylee had never seen.

"Generations of thinkers have made a study of the patterns of birds from this very room," Ryven said. "This design follows the rules of their flight as best as we've observed them and as best as our finest craftspeople can manufacture."

"Is this like augury?"

Ryven shook his head. "I'm not trying to predict the future here. Rather, I'm trying to observe the present and understand the past. Only by understanding that can I craft the future. It's scholarship, not sorcery."

"You don't look like a scholar," she noted.

"And you don't look like someone who could command death itself from the sky, yet what you did today suggests it's foolish to assume a person is merely what they appear. 'We are great flocks contained in single skins.'"

She raised an eyebrow.

He cleared his throat. "That is from the great poet Symin," he said. "They were a nomadic poet some four hundred seasons ago, traveling from settlement to settlement and famed for profane verses."

"That verse didn't sound so profane."

"Most of their other poems are about sex and murder. They

were eventually killed in a battle pit by a kyrg whose honor, hunting ability, and physical prowess the poet had insulted. Or it was a lover's quarrel. The archives are unclear. Moths ate most of the records."

"So." Kylee looked around the open-walled chamber, listened to the wind howling off the mountains, and tried to hear the faint murmur of the party on the other side of the doors. "Did you bring me in here to tell me about poetry? I like poetry, but I don't think we need privacy to discuss it."

"Very true," Ryven said. "Poetry is best discussed in the open. Power, on the other hand, benefits from closed doors."

"Power?" Kylee's hand rested on her dagger's hilt as Kyrg Ryven stepped closer to her.

"Yes, Kylee," he said. "After what you did with the ghost eagle today, I believe you have greater power than even Üku imagines, and I'd like to teach you to use it."

"You?" Kylee narrowed her eyes at him, but her grip on her dagger loosened. "What could you teach me that Üku can't?"

"Not that she can't," Ryven said. "That she *won't*."

"Why wouldn't she—?" Kylee couldn't get the question out before the kyrg whispered one sharp word.

"*Talorum.*"

Like an inkpot spilled over the night horizon, a great black form blossomed in the air and spread its wings in a silent glide until it settled, high and keen, on the edge of the room that was open to the sky. Its black eyes blazed at Kylee and at the kyrg who'd called it by its name.

The ghost eagle.

11

THE GREAT EAGLE STOOD STILL AS STONE, WATCHING THEM WITH ITS malevolent eyes, and Kylee found she couldn't move, couldn't even open her lips to breathe, let alone speak. And still, the ghost eagle merely watched, the black crown of feathers on its head unwavering though the wind whipped around them. Its meat hook of a beak bent in an eagle's eternal frown, and then it took a step toward her, talons clicking on the stone.

"You know what that word means?" Ryven asked, barely above a whisper. "The name of the ghost eagle? *Talorum*. It means bound to death."

The eagle took another step, its sharp beak thrust forward as it walked, wings tucked against its back. Its head twitched, taking in the room. Step by step, it backed them toward the doors. Kylee hadn't been so close to it since the night she, Nyall, Jowyn, and Brysen had captured it. She could smell the acrid scent of blood and meat and high mountain air off its night-black feathers.

"Call it off," Kylee whispered.

"No," Ryven said flatly.

"Do it!" Kylee shouted, and startled the bird, who froze and swung its head toward her, eyes locked on hers. It opened its beak, let out the tiniest chirp, almost laughably small. In fact, it made her think of a laugh. Was the ghost eagle laughing at her again?

He's killed you, Kylee thought. *Before you could even get started, this foolish kyrg has killed you.*

"*You* can call it off," Ryven told her. "If you want to. You know you can."

She breathed heavily through her nose, searching for the word she needed. The eagle took another step toward her. She pulled the knife from her arm.

"Your brother isn't here now, Kylee," Ryven said. "No one to protect but yourself. Find the words. You're always saving others, dealing death for someone else's benefit. Save yourself now. Do this for you."

"*Khostoon, fliss*," she tried, telling the bird, her partner, to leave, but their connection didn't feel like a partnership right now. It didn't feel like anything but prey quivering in front of a predator. She looked over at Ryven; he looked at her.

He did this, she thought. *He's just like the others, trying to manipulate you. You should let him die.*

"*Kraas*," she said, and this the eagle obeyed. It turned and rushed for Kyrg Ryven, charging him on foot across the room until his back was pressed against the wall and the bird loomed over him. She saw its long black tongue as it opened its mouth, and suddenly, the kyrg pleaded.

"No, Kylee, tell it to *go*. Not to eat. To go!"

The great bird reared back its head to strike, ready to kill the smug kyrg who dared to manipulate her while his guests drank and gossiped outside the thick stone doors. She could let him die, right now. She could show them all its power. *Her* power. As the handsome kyrg cowered below the hooked black beak, Kylee knew there was no difference between the eagle's will and her own. What she wanted, it wanted.

And what she wanted was to be free of all these people thinking they could control her. She, like the bird, could not be controlled. Letting this man here be killed would make that very clear to every kyrg on the Council. She was her own person and would not be tethered to their whims.

But what then? Murdering a kyrg in his home was surely a crime. Would she pay for it alone, or would Nyall, too? Would Brysen? She saw it all play out in her mind, plain as pigeons.

The Council's rage, Brysen's arrest in the Six Villages, and her helplessness to stop it, ghost eagle or no.

"*Fliss*," she said, and the eagle's head swung around to her once more, met her eyes, and nearly knocked her back with its stare. For a moment, the terrible black bird looked disappointed; then it turned and ran for the open side of the room, head lowering along its body as its wings spread, and it flung itself out into the night, up and away. Flapping without a sound into the dark.

When Kylee turned back to point her knife at the stupid young kyrg, he was leaning against the wall and looking at her with a smirk. His arms were crossed, and he was unconcerned with the knife she had raised. His pleading had been a show.

"No one knows I speak the Hollow Tongue," he told her. "Or that the ghost eagle listens to me when I do, which is precisely why I am able to speak it. Everyone speaks it differently. The language itself comes from the heart of each speaker, their truest self."

As he pushed himself off the wall, Kylee pivoted, keeping the flight-path model between them. "Why keep it a secret? If you were open about it, you could lead the ghost eagle into war and Uztar wouldn't need me at all."

He rested his palm on the edge of the model across from her, leaned over the clicking and whirling metal birds. "You could say I speak from a place of deception. When I aim to deceive, the eagle obliges me. It *only* obeys me in deception."

"Like when you pleaded for your life just now?"

He nodded. "That Altari girl, Grazim, speaks the Hollow Tongue from her ambition and can only command raptors to serve that ambition, but the ghost eagle doesn't care for it. It chooses to ignore her words. Üku speaks from her desire to control others, and the ghost eagle does not want to give her that control. It has no love for the Owl Mothers and has never once obeyed one."

Kylee kept her jaw clenched, eyes narrowed. The model turned between them, metal birds shining flecks of moonlight back onto their faces. "How do you know all this?"

"Careful study," Ryven said as he slid the carved bone pin back into place and ceased the model's movements. "Which is how I know that you are a caretaker. All your life, you've cared for others—your mother, your brother. You speak from care, and when you do, the ghost eagle heeds you. It has always heeded you when you were playing the caretaker. Even now, the moment you chose to spare me was the moment it heard you."

"It heard me before that," she said. "When I told it to eat you."

"Yes." Ryven set his palms on the stone table and leaned toward her. "Exactly! Which is how I know there is more to you than being a caretaker. Üku wants you only speaking from that place that ties you to your brother, because then she can control you. But when you turned the bird on me, you spoke for yourself. For what *you* wanted. That is the power that Üku fears and will not teach you. But I will."

"Why? Why would you do that? Why should I even believe you if, like you say, your greatest truth is your power of deception?"

"You shouldn't trust me," he said. "But you don't have to trust me to be my partner."

"Your partner in what?"

"That will come out in time." He leaned back from the table and crossed over to her, looking once at the doors. Kylee followed his glance, wondered if anyone in that party had the slightest clue they'd been cavorting just a door's depth away from an enraged ghost eagle. The thought gave her chills, but the chills were not entirely unpleasant.

"They think I'm in here seducing you," Ryven said, "which is why I threw the party to begin with. It's what I'm known for, being surrounded by beauty . . ." Kylee tensed. "I would *never*," he continued. "I would never even suggest it. Right now, you have too little power and I've got too much. Your friend will tell tales to her masters, of course, the kind of tales she is wont to imagine. But you don't seem like someone who minds these sorts of rumors, especially when they're useful to you. My intentions toward you are not romantic. You've nothing to fear from me."

"I didn't say I was afraid," Kylee told him. "But I'm not naïve. Anyway, how would *that* rumor be useful to me?"

"It gives us an excuse to be alone together whenever we'd like," Ryven said. "And when we're alone, I can teach you how to be more than a caretaker, how to find the voice that will give you the power I know you want."

"All I want is to keep the people I love safe."

"No." Ryven looked closely at her. She felt his gaze like a wind blowing. "That is *not* all you want."

She met his eyes, unflinching. "What do you think I want?"

He considered her, and in his hesitation, she wondered what lie he was forming or what truth he was trying to make look like a lie. But before he could offer either, they were interrupted by a scream loud enough to carry through the stone doors, and the next moment, a bell rang in the wall. Ryven pulled a lever, which swung the doors open, letting the glare of the party spill through, but the chatter had fallen away.

Only one person was making any noise at all.

"Magra!" he yelled. "No! No! No!"

Ryven stepped out to the hall and when Kylee followed him, she saw the man in layers of silk scarves kneeling on the floor with a sparrow hawk in his hands, the one that had been leashed on the table by the doors. It was dead and limp in his palms. On the table, only a few crumbs of the pastry Kylee had left there remained.

She looked up questioningly at Vyvian, who stood on the other side of the weeping man, each of them wondering what they had missed while they'd been apart. Vyvian would want to know what had happened between Kylee and Kyrg Ryven—about which Kylee would have to lie—and Kylee wanted to know what was going on with this rich man and his dead bird.

Before she could begin to move toward her friend to ask, a shudder passed through Vyvian's fingers and she dropped the glass in her hand. It shattered at her feet and she looked at Kylee wide-eyed, stricken and white as a snow owl. She gagged once, then collapsed. The neck of the glass swan around her left arm snapped when she landed on it, the crystal-clear head clattering away on the stones. Kylee rushed across the crowd to hold her, to lift her off the shattered glass that speckled the stone floor where she'd fallen.

"Vy! Vy!" Kylee called. Her friend's eyes were glazed, her lips pale.

"I . . . I didn't . . . ," Vyvian said, and then her breath rattled. She seized and choked and died just like that in Kylee's arms.

Before Kylee could even articulate the word to herself, one of the guests shouted, "Poison!"

"Guards, seal the gates!" Ryven shouted. "Search every guest and every servant."

"Unholy scuzzard!" a valet yelled, drawing a knife from beneath his tray and rushing at Kylee.

"*Shyehnaah!*" she yelled, and in a flash, every hawk in the room leapt from its tamer's fist and set on the valet, on his face and hair, talons and beaks jabbing him.

"Ahh!" he screamed, swatting at them to no avail, while the guests cried for their birds, whose beaks came up bloody.

As the birds ripped the valet open on the floor of the lush hall, Ryven shouted at him. "Who sent you?"

The would-be assassin met his eyes through the flurry of wings over his face, and Kylee thought he might be about to answer, though he looked surprised to be asked the question. He was about to speak when a hawk at his cheek silenced him with a squeeze of her foot on his windpipe.

Kylee blanched while the hawks tore into the dead man's body. Richly dressed guests grew faint while others watched with morbid fascination, and Kylee sat with Vyvian's head cradled coldly in her lap. Her friend was dead, and she was sure the poison had been meant for her.

IN THE CUPS

NOT EVERY TALE TOLD BY A DRUNKARD IS A LIE, BUT IT TAKES SPECIAL skill to pluck the truth from the brightly plumed stories that flutter around a pub when the moon is high.

Nyall did not have this skill, but he did have a few quarter-bronzes to spend, and he was quick to buy anyone with a tale to tell a round or two.

"I hear Ryven got his seat on the Council by murder," said a man with a bright yellow songbird in a small cage in front of him. "Killed the kyrg who raised him."

"Nah," said another drinker. "They were lovers."

"She raised him; they weren't lovers."

"All kinds of people in this world," the songbird man

replied. "Coulda been lovers even though she raised him; he coulda murdered her, too."

"No, he's not the type to lie with a woman."

"I heard he's the type to lie with a dozen women."

"He lies with anyone who'll lie with him. And lie to anyone about it!"

The drunkards burst out laughing, and Nyall was left wondering if what anyone had said was true and if the young kyrg would try anything with Kylee. He clutched the stoneware cup in front of him so hard, it cracked. He hated the part of himself that got jealous, especially since Kylee was as likely to lie with the kyrg as she was to lie with an emu. She'd made it clear to Nyall since he'd first tried to kiss her a dozen seasons ago: She didn't want to kiss *anyone*. Not him, nor another boy, nor another girl. At first, he thought that just meant he had to try harder, but a talking-to from Vyvian had straightened him out there. She told him she'd slice his beloved hair off if he ever made Kylee uncomfortable again.

It'd been easy to be friends with Kylee ever since then. He'd let her know how he felt and let her know he didn't expect anything in return.

Yet he kept doing things for her anyway. Like following her into the mountains after the ghost eagle. Like following her to the Sky Castle. Like sitting in this ale house, trying to learn Kyrg Ryven's secrets.

"None of you know what you're talking about," a big woman said, sliding her powerful, square frame next to Nyall on the bench and tethering her hooded peregrine to the perch behind her. As soon as she settled in, the other drinkers turned away, found other tables, lost themselves in other conversations.

Nyall slowly drained his drink, letting the dregs dribble through the crack he'd made and using that time to assess the woman. She was tall—two heads taller than Nyall, and Nyall was not short. She was also wider and more muscular than two of him, and he was not slight. Her skin was as dark as his but with a redder hue, like molten rock, and she wore rich white pants and a red wool tunic with a white-gold brooch. The brooch showed a dove clutching a falcon in its talons: the signet of Kyrg Bardu. If Nyall was going to find something useful for Kylee here, this woman was surely the one who knew it.

Unfortunately, Nyall's cup had been quite full when he began drinking, and it was not the first he'd drained tonight in his quest for knowledge. By the time he set it down on the table, his head had started to spin and his tongue had lost a touch of dexterity.

"Sos you know Kyrgryven, eh?" he slurred. Not a great start to his investigation. He cleared his throat, sat up straighter. Thought about the spies in the Six Villages and how confidently they drank and talked, talked and drank, and never let the one interfere with the other. Vyvian had told him to take a gulp of pressed walnut oil before drinking so that he wouldn't get drunk, but he neither had pressed walnut oil in the Sky Castle nor knew where to get it. Also, taking a gulp of nut oil sounded gross.

"You've made acquaintance with the gentleman kyrg?" he tried again, overly formal to hide his drunkenness, which only amplified the effect. "*Scuzz,*" he muttered, which made the woman laugh.

"Chitiycalania," she introduced herself, offering the winged salute. "My friends call me Chit."

"Chit," Nyall repeated.

On his other side, an equally humongous man with eyes like cloudless sky and skin like canyon stone slid up against Nyall and pushed a cup of sandthorn wine in front of him. He, too, wore the emblem of the proctor.

"May your spirits soar," the man said, toasting him. Nyall, never one to defy two bruisers offering free drinks, knocked the libation back and gasped at the burning that slid down his throat. It had not been sandthorn wine at all but straight foothill gin. Either he or the room tilted sideways, and he gripped the table with both hands, hoping to right it or himself. He tried not to think about puking.

"Thought you'd appreciate a taste of home," Chit said.

"Tanks oo," he slurred.

"What would you like to know about the good kyrg?" Chit asked him, taking a delicate sip of the same watered-down wine she'd been nursing since she'd sat.

"Whashis story?" Nyall asked artlessly. Then, in a befuddled attempt to restore some subtlety to his spying, thought of Brysen, imagined how his best friend might play this game, and added, "He handsome."

"Oh?" The woman raised an eyebrow at Nyall. "Looking for romance with a kyrg?"

"No fer me," Nyall answered too quickly, undoing the groundwork he'd poorly laid. "I'm in love already?"

Why'd it come out like a question? *Get a grip, Nyall.* He cleared his throat again. Remembered Kylee's advice. Smiled to flash his dimples. He knew by Chit's reaction that it looked more like a grimace and neither she nor her partner were interested in the affections of a drunk young man like himself.

"You're in love with the bird talker," the man said, and Nyall nodded, though it hadn't been a question, then realized that these people should not have known he was in love with Kylee or even who he was to begin with. He was supposed to be a stranger here. "Your friend Vyvian is thorough in her reports. She'll go far here in the Sky Castle."

Vyvian. She was here?

Of course Kyrg Bardu had spies in the Six, and of course

Vyvian was one of them, and of course she'd followed Kylee here. She was close with Kylee and Brysen, and the moment they became important, so did she. Nyall had never kept any secrets from Vyvian, because he'd never thought of himself as someone who knew anything worth keeping secret. He'd always been suspicious of people who acted as if they might one day have power or need it.

Now he regretted his openness as much as he regretted that last drink. As soon as his head cleared, he'd have to warn Kylee about their friend's divided loyalties. In spite of that, he was looking forward to seeing her. Vyvian was the kind of friend you could always count on as long as you knew you could never *really* count on her. Kylee would be thrilled to know she was in the Sky Castle. It helped to have allies. A flock was stronger than a lone fledgling.

At the thought of Kylee, Nyall's stomach suddenly felt like a falcon in a dive. He searched for the words he needed. "We are jus frens," he managed to get out.

"Here's to vain hopes," Chit said, and downed her drink, and Nyall was surprised to find himself downing another one. When had they given him another one? Why had he drunk it? And did anyone in this pub know a decent cure for hiccups?

His plan was not going according to plan.

"So, Nyall?" the man asked, and Nyall swung his head around, his thick coils of hair smacking Chit in the shoulder. He had to bend his neck to look up at the man's face.

"How you knowin m'name like?" he asked, then cleared his throat again, fought back a hiccup that turned into a burp, and focused his eyes through the haze of drink. He rephrased himself as clearly as possible. "How, please, do you know my name, you, yes?"

At least he hadn't slurred.

The man laughed and signaled the barkeep for another drink. "You and Kylee are quite well-known," he said. "Especially after today. Some think she'll stop the Kartami. Some think she'll call down the wrath of the sky. Everyone thinks she's worth knowing."

"Mmmkay," Nyall said, trying to push the new cup of liquor away and spilling it in the process.

"We're told you were some kind of 'battle boy' back in the Six Villages," Chit said, making Nyall spin around to face her again as the liquor slowly spread across the table in a shimmering, herbaceous pool. His hair whacked the man in the chest this time. "What is that?"

"Means I got frens," Nyall said, squaring his shoulders. "Means I know how t'fight."

"Friends are a good thing," said Chit.

"A great thing," said the man.

"In fact, Kyrg Bardu would like to be *your* friend," said Chit.

"Why don't you come with us?" the man suggested.

"For a chat," added Chit, and it was not a suggestion.

"I—" Nyall said, but he was already being helped from his seat. Chit's falcon cocked its head beneath its hood as she nudged it onto her fist, gripping Nyall's upper arm with the other hand. It was almost like the bird was watching him with blinded eyes.

That was the last thing Nyall remembered of the night. The bird with blinded eyes.

When he woke, his head was pounding, but the headache was the least of his worries.

BRYSEN

THROUGH AWFUL GRACE

12

POWER IS A WIND; INVISIBLE BUT FOR THE BRANCHES IT SHAKES, THE walls it topples, and the wings it raises high. Power is a force some people fly on, and no one in the Six Villages flew higher on it than the Tamir family. They were as close to nobility as existed in this part of Uztar. Some distant kyrg held title over the region, but their claim to actually visit and assert authority had ended generations ago, when one of the Tamir clan fed that kyrg's toes to his own falcon one at a time until a concession was granted. All taxes would be paid, and the Villages would remain loyal to the Council of Forty so long as no interference was made with how the Tamirs ran things. While they were never granted a formal seat on the Council themselves, their rule over this little yet potent patch of civilization was never again questioned.

Until Brysen screwed it up.

Because of him, Mama Tamir's eldest son, Goryn, sat in some Sky Castle dungeon, and professional soldiers now had a garrison in the Six Villages. They said it was to oversee the construction of the barricades against the Kartami siege, but everyone knew they had their eyes on Mama Tamir, waiting for even the smallest excuse to execute Goryn, lock her and the rest of her family in chains, and seize the wealth they'd long hoarded. Wars were expensive, and though Mama Tamir helped fund this one with generous contributions of bronze, she never gave too much. She treated the Sky Castle like a tame falcon—always keeping it fed just enough so that it wouldn't turn on her, just hungry enough that it would keep coming back.

"We shouldn't be here," Jowyn warned Brysen as they walked up the narrow steps to the heavy stone doors that marked the entrance to Mama Tamir's favorite home. She had many around the Villages, not wanting her enemies to know in which she slept, but Nyck had told them where she'd be this morning—Skypool House, they called this one—and Brysen and Jowyn had set off to find her there.

"I've turned away every pigeon she's sent," Jowyn explained. "Haven't answered a single message. I even told her attendants that they'd have to drag me unconscious to see her and then explain to her why they'd injured her long-lost son. She's not going to be happy when I walk in with you, making demands."

"She's your mother," Brysen said, like that meant anything. Altari parents, like his own mother, felt a duty to raise their children, even if they weren't kind or nurturing or gentle about it. His mother's pious scolding showed, in her way, a kind of commitment to family that Uztari parents did not share. Uztari parents modeled their families on the birds— caring for the littlest children until they were old enough to fend for themselves, then pushing them from the nest. If they flew, they'd sometimes be welcomed back, sometimes fought off as competitors and forced to make their own way. If they fell, well . . . that was the will of the sky. Not everyone gets to soar.

Mama Tamir, at least, tried to keep her children around. She considered herself sentimental, which explained why she was so angry at the boy who'd had her first son arrested and was harboring her second, runaway son.

"You shouldn't be here," the first attendant at the door grunted at them, echoing Jowyn exactly. The Tamirs called their guards "attendants" because they'd never admit to need-ing guards at all. They did their own violence. It was a point of pride. If it came to killing him, Brysen was pretty sure Mama Tamir would do the deed herself.

"We need to talk to her," Brysen said, crossing his arms and staring up at the large woman, who had an unhooded sunset hawk on her fist. "Now."

"You need to go back home," the attendant said. "Look after those glass grinders you took in."

The sunset hawk cocked its head at him, shifted its feet on the fist while Brysen seethed. Not only was the attendant showing that she knew about the refugees, she was also demonstrating that she could use that slur right to his face and he couldn't do a thing about it.

"She will want to see *me*," Jowyn cut in before Brysen could find an insult to hurl and get a talon in his eye. "Of course, we could leave, and I could send my ma a message that I was turned away?"

The attendant narrowed her eyes at the pale boy but didn't have the nerve to insult a Tamir heir, no matter how estranged he was or how strange he looked. She stepped aside to let them pass but didn't bother pushing open the doors. Both boys had to lean on the stone with all their weight to get it to open. The sunset hawk screeched at them but didn't move.

Once through the doors, Brysen saw why this place was called Skypool House. It was carved directly into the mountain, but not by human hands. Ancient subterranean rivers had cut winding caverns into the mountain, and the smooth stone walls were striped in layers of minerals and sediment.

The result was more imaginative patterns and colors than any human art could've imagined. Morning light cut down through openings in the rock overhead, painting the halls and caverns pink. In the ice-wind season, these openings would fill the home with snow. The passages would be impassable, and the entire place would freeze. Brysen couldn't imagine the kind of wealth that allowed a person to have a home for just fair-weather days.

Somewhere, Brysen heard the flow of the ancient streams that had carved these caverns and now fed their baths and springs. No hauling water for the Tamir family; they had their own private rivers inside.

"Come on." Jowyn led the way along the halls.

He'd last been here as a little boy, but he still knew the winding way to his mother's sitting room. He trailed his fingertips along the smooth stone wall, and Brysen wondered what memories Jowyn's fingertips were tracing. He had suffered violence from his family, just like Brysen had, but he'd left them and meant never to return. Brysen still lived in the house that had been his torture chamber, even though his torturer was dead. Now Jowyn was walking in to see one of his own, and he was doing it for Brysen.

They both heard the screaming before they saw its source.

In a large chamber open to the sky, Mama Tamir stood on the edge of one of those flowing underground streams. In a niche in the wall above her, a river eagle watched the water hungrily, but was tethered in place. Jowyn's mother, her sturdy frame wrapped in a robe of raven's feathers and silk, had a handful of worm-meal, which she tossed in the water while making gentle clucking sounds. The screams were coming from the river.

"The worm-meal is so they don't eat too quickly and spoil their appetites," she said without looking back at Brysen and Jowyn. "Like some little boys used to do."

Jowyn stopped and tensed. Without warning, he grabbed Brysen's hands and held him back, too. He squeezed Brysen's fingers, more in warning than affection, but still Brysen's face heated . . . until he looked back and saw the terror on his friend's face.

"Don't get closer," Jowyn whispered.

Brysen didn't move, but he couldn't help looking. There was a man in the river, tied by the wrists and ankles to its banks, splayed out just below the surface. To breathe he had to strain his neck and lift his head. Upstream from him, downy-feathered eagle chicks pecked the worm-meal from the water and hopped about in play. Some of them still had blood on their tiny beaks from pecking at the chained-up man.

"Please," he coughed through a mouthful of water at Jowyn's mother. His face was a mess of bloody beak marks. "Please."

Jowyn's mother squatted over him. "You can drown any time you like," she said, running her fingers through his wet hair. "Or you can hang on until my little chicks are strong enough to fly and then I won't have to put your wife in here, too. Your choice. Think on it."

With that, she stood and turned to Brysen and her son. Jowyn let go of Brysen's hand, straightened his back. "Ma," he said with such a tremble that Brysen wanted to grab him and run, apologize for making him come here. Regret mobbed Brysen as fast as crows on carrion.

"Jo," she replied coldly. "You look . . ." She cleared her throat, looked him up and down. "Ridiculous."

Though they had similar features—a broad face; wide, heavy-lidded eyes; and ears that stuck out just a little farther than most people Brysen knew—mother and son did not look alike at all. Jowyn was shorter and lithe, where his mother was thick and bulky with muscle. His skin was nearly white as a snow owl, with hair just as white, while she had a light umber complexion and thick black hair. "Why the Owl Mothers do this to their boys, I'll never understand."

"The sap makes us strong," Jowyn said.

"*I* could've made you strong."

"Goryn would've killed me if I stayed."

"Goryn is gone now." Mama Tamir finally looked at Brysen. "Thanks to this one."

"I'm sorry for my role in your eldest son's fall, Mem Tamir." Brysen offered the winged salute with as much respect as his current terror would allow. His hands shook where he held them in front of his heart. Jowyn shifted his shoulders just slightly in front of Brysen, a tiny, protective gesture that would do nothing if the woman's wrath were unleashed, but it steadied Brysen's hands nonetheless. This was a feeling he thought he could get used to, if he had the chance. If he lived through this conversation.

Mama Tamir snorted. "Goryn's own ambitions failed him, and he deserved what he got. We don't coddle mistakes in my family. We do, however, demand amends. So . . . are you here to make amends?" She glanced at the gentle stream around the room's perimeter. There were more cleats where ropes could be tied, more spaces to hold prisoners.

"I've come to ask you a question," Jowyn said. "Someone tried to abduct Brysen, and we think you might know who it was."

"You assume it wasn't me?" She smiled. "Maybe this is how I planned to bring you home again. Taking your little lover there."

"We're not lovers!" Jowyn blurted too fast, and Brysen found it stung, even though it was true. He didn't have to say it *so* emphatically. "I mean . . . we're just friends. Anyway, we know it wasn't you."

She shook her head. "You run away from me, let me think you're dead for more changing seasons than I can count, then you come home white as a snow owl and ignore me until you *want* something, and then you come running back to the nest? That is very selfish of you, Jo. I'm not some Owl Mother who happily provides you everything you might want. A relationship is an exchange, and you ask for information but offer me nothing. Not even the gratitude a chick pays a hen, nor so much as an apology."

"I'm sorry, Ma," he said. "I never should have let you think I was dead."

She waved her hand dismissively. "You want to know who is after your 'friend' here, and why?"

Jowyn nodded.

"You want him to be protected?"

Jowyn nodded again.

"I would do anything my son asks of me," Mama Tamir told him. "However, you are still a stranger. You want to be my son again? Prove it." She drew a knife from her robe and set it on the banks of the stream, beside the man gagging in the water.

"You want me to kill that man?" If Jowyn could've looked paler, he would've then.

"He's an enemy of the family," his mother said. "We kill our enemies."

A small whimper escaped the water.

"It should not be hard," Mama Tamir said. "He is suffering, and you would end his suffering. Everyone wins."

"I . . ." Jowyn hesitated. His eyes met Brysen's; there was an apology in his glance. "I won't," he said at last. "I can't."

His mother sighed. "Then I can't help you. You're no son of mine. You're nothing to me. You may go and hope you do nothing else to disappoint me. There are things in this world worse than nothing."

"I'm sorry," Jowyn said to Brysen. "I can't kill this man."

Brysen shook his head. He was the one who was sorry. He never should've made them come here. He never should've dreamed that this woman would be anything other than the monster she'd always been. They'd simply have to prepare to defend themselves, even if they didn't know who they had to defend themselves against. "It's not your fault," Brysen said. "I'd never want you to kill for me."

"How moving," Jowyn's mother sneered as they turned to go. Mama Tamir called after them, but not to Jowyn. "Brysen could still be something to me."

They stopped. The air in the cave hung heavy with her words. The only sounds were the gentle trickle of the stream and the ugly gasps of the man in the water, trying not to drown.

"You've taken two sons of mine," she said when he turned

back to face her. "And still you live, which makes my reputation suffer. You are the one who should make amends."

Brysen waited. She would tell him what she wanted when she was ready. Asking would only demonstrate how much power she held over him. She seemed to appreciate his silence. She smiled and folded her thick hands in front of her.

"If I can't have a son," she told him, "I could use an assassin."

"Brysen is not an—" Jowyn started, but she cut him off with a look, as only a parent can.

"The debt is his, not yours," she snapped. "And so the choice is his, not yours."

Brysen braced himself. He'd never killed anyone, not even in a fight in the battle pits, but it wasn't like he was opposed to the idea of killing. He was a hunter, and hunters killed all the time without moralizing about it. He loved Shara, and she was as murderous a bird as could be. How many sparrows and rabbits had met their end by her tender talons? Why should he celebrate her killings but fear to do his own?

And yet, doing work for the Tamir clan was like hunting in a lightning storm: You might catch what you wanted, but you'd never know when the killing strike might fall from above.

Nevertheless, he found himself asking, "Who?"

"Bry . . . don't . . . ," Jowyn warned.

"The same person, in fact, who tried to abduct you," Jowyn's mother said. "The Kartami leader. He wants you for a hostage—to keep your sister and the ghost eagle out of the war. I want you to use that to get close to him, then cut his head from his body."

Brysen wasn't sure if the whimper he heard came from Jowyn or the man slowly dying in the stream or from his own throat, but Mama Tamir smiled and whistled for her attendant to usher them out.

"I see you're nervous," she said. "Take the night to think it over. Talk to your"—she gave her son a withering glance, then looked away from him like he was nothing more than a house finch—"*friend* about it. I think, by morning, you'll be eager to agree. In my experience, it is much better to be the hunter than the prey. And in the war to come, you will be one, or you will be the other."

13

"YOU ABSOLUTELY CANNOT DO THIS," JOWYN SAID AS THEY MADE their way back home through the Six Villages. "You're not an assassin."

Brysen kept his eyes forward as he walked. Usually at this time of the melt-wind season, you could hear the rush of the Necklace flowing high between its banks, but now the massive barricades rose beside the river, and the sounds of hammering, sawing, and shouting drowned out nature's song. Just over the top of the barricades, Brysen saw rising columns of gray smoke—the Kartami's vaporous flags—announcing the army's approach. The Villages had only a few days left before the Kartami arrived, and the crowds of Altari fleeing their advance choked the streets.

The only places the Altari avoided were the public mews, where birds of prey were kept, and the Broken Jess, where hawk battles were held. Although the crowd of Tamir attendants guarding the Jess with six-talon whips probably kept the Altari away as effectively as did their pious aversion to falconry sports.

Even though the Altari reviled falconry, they now relied on it for protection, crowding in from the Grassland Plains, desperate to get behind the barricades. Falconers stood sentinel at points along the wall, their birds on their fists, watching the approaching army with keen expectation. The Altari lived under the mantle of safety that the falconers on the barricades provided, but they were disgusted with the falconry that provided it. Brysen figured hypocrisy was a necessary part of survival in a world as unforgiving as this one.

Two soldiers were shaking down a haggard Altari man, demanding he account for himself, prove he wasn't a Kartami spy.

"I fled *from* the Kartami. Why would I help them?" the man pleaded as the soldiers bound his wrists and dropped a hood over his head. His muffled voice came through the fabric. "How can I prove something I'm not?"

Nearly everyone looked away as he was dragged off. To

defend him would invite suspicion, and even a suspicion of spying would get your tongue cut out. Wounded birds lash out with the most violence, and right now, the Six Villages were wounded and the Altari were unlucky enough to be in the grip of their talons.

Brysen stopped walking and waited for Jowyn to catch up. "What if I can end this war?" he asked the other boy. "What if your ma is right and the Kartami *are* trying to take me hostage so my sister won't fight? What if, instead, I can cut their great general down? How many thousands of lives would be saved? How many innocent people?"

"You think *my* ma cares about saving lives?" Jowyn shook his head. "What'd the mouse say to the kestrel when he was invited over for dinner?"

Jowyn always had a joke ready, but Brysen was not in the mood for jokes.

"The mouse didn't say anything." Jowyn offered the punch line unbidden. "Because it was the first course."

"I'm not a mouse," Brysen snapped.

"I didn't mean it like that," Jowyn said. "But you're not an assassin, either. You risked your life to help those refugees last night."

Brysen shrugged. "It was the least I could do."

"Your least tends to be a lot." Jowyn put a hand on Brysen's shoulder, which threatened to melt any counterargument he could muster. The warmth of that hand conspired with Jowyn's sharp jawline and long eyelashes to dismantle Brysen's reason and tangle his tongue. He could snare a kestrel in a crosswind, but he was hopeless against this gray-eyed boy's blinking. "Most people here aren't that generous."

"I'm not generous." Brysen's throat was dry. He swallowed too loudly, slid away from Jowyn's touch, and resumed walking. "I'm selfish."

"Yes, it's true." Jowyn laughed, catching up again. "Selfish people always risk their lives to save a group of ragged strangers, then invite them home and give them the food off their table. Totally selfish."

"It's not funny," Brysen said, not sure why he needed Jowyn, of all people, to understand that he didn't deserve praise. "If someone's only a little selfish, then he need only be a little selfless to balance it out, right?" he tried to explain. "But me? I *want* so much . . . I *have* to give even more. I'm not generous; I'm trying to keep a balance."

"You think it's a scale? Like weighing bronze for the market?"

Brysen nodded.

"Well, those Altari you helped aren't weighing what you did for them," Jowyn said. "And I'm not weighing why you took me in when the Owl Mothers exiled me, either . . . though I assume it was to take advantage of me." He smiled, and Brysen felt his face flush, but this time, he forced out a laugh, too. Banter was so much easier than sincerity, and he was lucky Jowyn couldn't stand a heavy mood too long.

He wondered how Jowyn would feel when one of Brysen's darker moods descended. He once went an entire season without bathing just because it didn't seem worth it. If that happened again, would that be the last he saw of this light-hearted owl boy?

But if Brysen were to end the war, to do the grand heroic thing, then even Jowyn would see his moods were worth putting up with. That was the scale he couldn't explain. Every brave or generous thing he did was part of a personal balancing act, one he'd always done. It was a way to prove to himself that he wasn't worthless, to do valuable things so that he'd have value. It never quite worked. Everyone still left him anyway.

But killing the leader of the Kartami horde was the sort of thing that made people want to sing songs about you, want to stay near you. No one ever celebrated some kid who'd fixed a hawk's wing and took in three old outcasts and a baby. There were thousands of dying birds and just as many desperate Altari. If he wanted to be heroic, he had to do something huge . . . just the thing Mama Tamir had proposed.

If he lived a safe and quiet life, letting his sister be the hero, he could look after the house and spend more time with

Jowyn. He could maybe even be happy for a while, but he knew it wouldn't last. The siege would begin. Jowyn would get to know him better. Everything would break apart, like it always did, unless he did something to change it. He didn't believe in augury; the future wasn't written in the sky. He was sure that he could—in spite of all evidence of his past failures—show the world that he mattered.

"Come on, Brysen." Jowyn kept arguing as they weaved through the crowded street, bumping shoulders with gruff Uztari soldiers and wary Altari wanderers alike. Brysen acted like he was taking in the sights—the half-empty barrels of the feed stores, the overpriced haggard hawks and disappointing hatchlings in the breeders' shops. He was doing his best not to look at Jowyn, because he so badly wanted to be convinced by him. "Think it through. My ma knows they'll probably kill you before you get a chance to kill their leader and then she'll have her revenge for what you did to Goryn, *or* you'll succeed and she'll get the glory for having sent you and you'll still probably get killed before you get away. Whatever happens, she wins and you lose. But I've seen you with Shara. You're a healer, Bry. Not a killer."

"There's a war starting, in case you hadn't noticed." Brysen gestured up at the falconers on the barricades. "Killers are what's needed now. Should I just hang back and let everyone else do the killing for me? Who should I count on for that? You already told me you couldn't do it."

Jowyn flinched like he'd been slapped, and Brysen knew he'd hit his mark. He was being cruel, but he wasn't sure why. He should apologize and tell Jowyn he was just upset, but he couldn't figure out exactly what he was upset about. Had he wanted Jowyn to encourage him to become an assassin, or had he just wanted Jowyn to believe he *could* so that he wouldn't have to actually do it? And why did looking at Jowyn always confuse him so much? The pale boy was as mysterious to him as the shapes in a flock of starlings.

"I . . . I didn't mean that . . . ," Brysen stammered. The pale boy took a deep breath, collected himself, and forced a small smile onto his face, making an effort to show Brysen forgiveness before he could even ask it. "It's just that, you know, I . . . I'm not used to anyone looking out for me." Jowyn raised an eyebrow. "I mean, other than my sister," Brysen said. "I'm not used to anyone but my twin sister looking out for me. And also . . . when you smile at me like that, it makes everything more complicated."

"Smile at you like what?" Jowyn smiled more.

"Like you're doing right now!"

"Am I?" He spread his smile wider, walking backward in front of Brysen and looking up and around like he was trying to find his reflection in the sky. He contorted his face into different versions of a smile. "I can't see it! How am I smiling? Like this? Like this?"

He was so intent on making Brysen laugh that he didn't see the seller's row of hand-carved perches lined up in the street behind him until he'd tripped over them. Brysen lunged forward and caught him by the waist, pulling him up. He felt Jowyn's hip bone press against him, saw the cracked pale lips and the gold flecks in his startled eyes. They froze there in the street like two albatrosses caught in a mating dance, and Brysen was keenly aware of all the eyes on the two of them—the gray-haired boy with all the scars and the phantom-pale boy with the dangerous mother.

Brysen's heart was a riot, and his hands felt hot where they held Jowyn. He cleared his throat and suggested they stop by the Broken Jess to get some ale.

"I'm not really in the mood for ale," Jowyn said.

"I don't really want to go home right now," Brysen replied. "My ma and the Altari will be there, chanting and praying and *thanking* me, and I can't deal with that. You go home if you want, but I'm going to the Broken Jess."

That was what he said, but all he could think was *Please, please, please come with me to the Broken Jess and talk me out of what I want to do.*

"That's my ma's place," Jowyn said. "I can't go back there."

"I need to get some advice from Nyck and the boys," Brysen told him. "They've all done work for Mama Tamir. Not killing work, but still . . ." He turned to go, hoping Jowyn would follow him in spite of himself. "We won't be there long."

Why was he dragging Jowyn around where he didn't want to go? It was like he was trying to push Jowyn away just to see if he would go. Was this what he'd done to his sister, too? Forced her to leave him before she could decide he wasn't worth staying around?

Before he and a reluctant Jowyn could reach the front of the Broken Jess, a high whistle sounded from the nearby barricades.

"Gliders!" one of the sentries shouted. "Twelve gliders coming in!"

The battle boys came scurrying along the barricades, some of them half-dressed, their colorful tunics flapping open, their hooded hawks on their fists. Overhead, a dozen shadows swiftly approached, wide-winged as ghost eagles, silhouetted black against the high sun. They soared over the barricades, weaving and turning. Before anyone could muster an order to attack, the warriors strapped into the fabric gliders began raining arrows to the street.

An arrow pierced the skull of an Uztari soldier who'd been standing watch not two spans from Brysen.

"Ahh!" Altari and Uztari villagers alike screamed and scattered for cover.

"Fly 'em down!" someone shouted. Nyck and his scrum in the front yard of the Jess unhooded their hawks and launched them up against the gliders, as falconers from all over the Six did the same.

These birds were trained from the battle pits to fight instead of hunt, and they flew, shrieking, toward the enemies in the air. The warriors steered with their shoulders and legs but drew blades with their free hands.

Nyck's colorful kestrel swooped at the first glider it encountered but turned before striking to avoid the slice of the sword. A sleek-winged peregrine flapped high above the gliders, then dove for a wing, dropping straight through the fabric and forcing the glider to dip sideways, plummeting for the river. A sentinel on the barricades loosed an arrow and took out the falling glider before it crashed, but in the moment after firing the killing shot, another glider dove low and impaled the figure on the barricades before they could nock another arrow. The sentinel screamed, hoisted on the end of a Kartami spear. As they were lifted off the barricades by the spear through their chest, Brysen recognized them as one of the Tamir attendants, a fearsome fighter he'd faced more than once in the battle pits at the Broken Jess and never once beaten.

The sentinel's peregrine circled above, rising higher and higher while its tamer's body was dumped onto the street. The bird didn't wait around, simply caught a higher breeze, rose on it, and skied out, gone. Brysen watched it, transfixed by its easy flight back to the wild. One less falcon for the defense of the Six Villages.

"Brysen!" Jowyn shouted, knocking him out of his reverie and out of the street just before an arrow thwacked into the earth in front of him. Their bodies slammed hard into the boarded front door of Dupuy's Equipery. The store had been shuttered when Dupuy's whole family left for the Sky Castle, after the first columns of Kartami smoke rose on the horizon.

In front of them on the street, bodies fell, either pierced by arrows or trampled in the panic. Overhead, four of the gliders turned, striking flints tied beside their dangling crossbows. They lit their arrows and took aim at the mews and falcon houses in the center of town.

With a *whoosh* they set fire to Groty's Breeding Hall, then targeted the Sygin Mews and Lannyer Mews and the Coop, which only bred bait pigeons.

"How do they know where to hit?" Nyck called out, whistling his kestrel back to his fist. He and the other battle boys eyed the scattering Altari refugees with suspicion. Somehow, the Kartami knew where the Villages kept most of their birds and bird feed. Somehow, they knew exactly where to aim their fire.

Spies.

And that was the true insidiousness of the attack, Brysen realized. They weren't just inflicting damage on the Six Villages defenses; they were sowing mistrust and fear of the Altari they'd forced into the Villages to begin with.

The other battle boys called their falcons back to defend the Broken Jess. Though no birds lived there, the amount of ale and liquor they'd stockpiled could ignite the whole town.

"How many gliders do you see?" Jowyn asked.

Brysen counted seven.

"With the one that crashed, that makes eight," Jowyn noted. "Where are the other four?"

They looked up from the doorway, scanning the sky, and Brysen saw the last four flying away from the heart of town, rising on the wind—cutting a straight path for Brysen's house.

Whatever spies they'd used had told them where Brysen lived, and his mother and the Altari were there right now, totally undefended. So was Shara, recovering in the mews, not ready to fly. He had other birds, too: a river eagle, green as the moss below a waterfall, and twin ice falcons, each bird not only worth more bronze than all the birds he'd caught in the past three seasons combined, but each a capable fighter and hunter, essential for the defense of the Villages. They were all trapped in cages, just waiting to be burned alive.

14

BY THE TIME BRYSEN AND JOWYN CROSSED THE NARROW FOOTBRIDGE
over the rushing meltwater stream that divided their house
from the rest of the Villages, the four gliders were already
circling their yard.

Brysen wanted to charge straight for the mews and get his
raptors in the air, but Jowyn stopped him, pulled him down
behind a boulder. He pointed up over the thorn-briar fence to
a quivering spear embedded in the mud beside the loose stone
path that ran to the outhouse. It took Brysen's mind a moment
to recognize that the spear wasn't stuck in the mud, but instead stood in the back of one of the old Altari he'd taken in.
The Altari was impaled, facedown.

The door to their house was shut, and he hoped his mother and the other two Altari with their baby were sheltered inside.

"I have to get to the mews," he told Jowyn. "We have to fly something against them."

Jowyn reached out his hand and touched it to Brysen's, then nodded. They held each other's gaze for a moment. Jowyn was a good talker, with quick jokes and a poet's soul, but when it came to fighting for survival, they both knew Brysen was the expert. He'd had to fight all his life in one way or another, and he had the scars to show for it.

Brysen squeezed Jowyn's fingers, then let go and ran for it, crouched low, zigzagging his way up the hill. Jowyn, with surprising speed, burst out in the other direction, yelling to draw the gliders' attention.

Brysen didn't look back; he just had to hope Jowyn would be okay as he slipped through a gap in the thorny fence and crept to the side of the hawk mews, sliding his back along it while he pulled the key from a chain around his neck.

In one quick move, he spun around the corner and put the key in the door, glancing over his shoulder at the one glider that swooped in low over him and fired a crossbow bolt at his feet. He had to dive away and roll before he'd turned the key, but he was alive. If they'd wanted to shoot him in the back, they could've, which meant they knew who he was and wanted him alive. His gray hair made him obvious, he figured.

If they had orders to keep him alive, though, he could use that to his advantage.

He got up while the glider flew away from the slope, making a wide turn to come around for him again. A glance down the hill showed Jowyn, picking his way among the boulders on the steepest incline, while two of the gliders weaved and dove, trying and failing to get an angle to fire on him.

Where was the fourth? As he scanned the sky for a sign of it, a bolt whizzed past his leg and thwacked into the dirt. He jumped at the door, turned the key, and threw himself inside, falling to the floor in the dim, mottled light.

"Prrpt," one of the ice falcons in its cage chirped at him.

"Eeee!" the river eagle screamed.

Shara sat wary and silent on her perch, staring at him and shifting back and forth on her feet. Her newly imped feathers wouldn't be strong enough to fly for another few days, so he'd have to leave her safe in her cage. But he got up, unlocked the ice falcons, pulled on his long dog-leather glove.

He whistled the best-trained one to his fist and closed the cage. He could only launch one bird at a time, but he hoped this one would be enough. He had no idea if she would even attack. She wasn't a fighting bird. He'd only just started training her to hunt gulls, not people.

The bird clenched her pale blue feet on his fist, ruffled her gray-and-blue feathers, and looked at him with her head turned to the side. He took a small hunk of meat from the game bag on the nearest peg. It was a few days old and probably halfway toward rancid, but she didn't mind. He only gave her a small peck at it while he tethered her to his glove, then tossed the meat away, leaving her mad-eyed and hungry. Keen for more. That was how he needed her.

Quick as he could, he ran to the door, then stepped into the light, thrust his fist up toward the nearest glider circling the house, and shouted, "Utch!"

The ice falcon shoved off his glove with a push of her feet and flew high over the house, even higher over the path and the gliders, up and up until she was a tiny speck against the sunlight.

He hoped there were no other prey in sight, because this falcon would dive for whatever made the easiest kill. She was used to hunting gulls around snowy mountain lakes, large prey with wide wings that flew in wobbly patterns while looking down for fish. That was why he chose her. From above, he figured the gliders might look a little bit like giant gulls.

"Watch out!" Jowyn shouted from below as a glider sliced across the mountain's steep upwind slope, heading straight for Brysen. It slowed as it approached, and the warrior leaned back, pivoting nearly vertical to come in for a landing. She wore a kind of sky-blue wrap and a scarf up over her face, with thick, polished-glass flying goggles. In each hand, she'd drawn small katar blades. The katar was a short-bladed knife with a crossbar for a handle, clutched in the fist and punched forward to stab. It was a close-combat weapon, and Brysen had only ever seen them used to take down wild boar.

So this was the plan, Brysen thought. *They're here to take me.* He glanced up toward the tiny speck of his falcon against the sun. *I've got other plans.*

Before the warrior could land, a teardrop of sky plummeted straight down through the glider's silk wing, crashing into one of her arms so hard, it broke without slowing the bird. The glider bent and spun out, smashing against the slope, while the ice falcon careened off in the other direction, stunned from the impact but making its instinctual turn to land on its prey, where it tore into the warrior's throat before the breath had even come back into her lungs.

The ice falcon would be feeding for a while now, and there were three more gliders left to deal with. He ran inside and called the next falcon to his fist, then stepped out with it.

"Utch!" He tried to toss it skyward, but the bird steadied itself and gripped his fist tighter, refusing to let go. Its wings spread, but even as he raised and lowered his arm, it wouldn't move. "Fly!" he grunted, but it only footed him harder. Just then, he saw an orange glow blossom at the tip of an arrow that had fallen onto his house. It flared against the tar roof but didn't catch. Two more flaming bolts rained down and dug in, and one of them caught. But the gliders stayed high. They were going to smoke his mother out.

He ran back inside the mews, the ice falcon still on his fist, and opened the river eagle's cage. The falcon cried— the eagle, too—and both frightened birds broke from their perches, the eagle chasing the falcon into the sunlight. Brysen ran out after them, shouting, "Utch! Utch! Utch!" and hoping one would heed the call to hunt. The falcon, in its panic, almost crashed into one of the gliders but dodged. The eagle, on the other hand, slammed right through it, tearing just enough of the fabric to force the glider off course, wavering and wobbling and whirling away.

It made a turn for the barricades, but crashed somewhere in the streets of the Six Villages, where the villagers mobbed it like crows.

The two remaining gliders fired more burning arrows into the roof of his house, but one broke off toward the site of the crash in the Villages, while the other circled high and vanished behind a rocky ridge.

In the moment of quiet, the door opened, his ma and the two Altari with the baby huddled in the doorway. His ma's dark hair was neatly braided, and she had on her nicest quilted robe, the one Brysen hadn't seen in as long as he could remember.

When he'd brought the Altari home, she'd rushed them in toward the hearth without being asked, tended their wounds, gave them water and milk, and started fixing a full meal. She'd even mashed up apricots for the baby. Brysen had been looking forward to those himself, but he couldn't begrudge the baby a meal. Still, he'd wondered why his ma's generosity had to extend to *his* snacks.

All the while, his ma had kept her eyes fixed at the ground, and the Altari, in gratitude for her gesture, had touched her feet with their fingers and pressed their palms against the dirt. It was an Altari thanks, one his mother probably hadn't seen since she was a little girl, when she'd fled the plains to the Six Villages herself. This had been her happiest day in countless seasons, a rainbow in a life of rain, so of course, like all things in Brysen's family, it would have to end in blood and death from above. If the sky blessed some people, it stood to reason that it would curse others.

Brysen tried to wave them back inside, but the Altari man holding the baby shook his head, pointed to the thick black smoke behind them. They couldn't stay inside, but if they ran, they'd certainly be killed.

The other Altari, dressed in a clean tunic and hunter's

pants that had been Brysen's father's, made a break for the outhouse at a full-speed sprint. She was surprisingly fast.

Not fast enough, though.

An arrow snapped into her back so hard, it sped her forward three steps before she fell, stumbling over the body that was already lying there. The glider had come around the other side of the ridge.

In the doorway, the baby wailed, and Brysen's mother looked across at Brysen, mouthing prayers. He had no choice. He went back into the mews and unlocked Shara's cage. Ready or not, he had to try to fly her.

"I'm sorry, Shara," he said, stretching out his gloved hand. "I know you just got home, but . . . I need you . . ."

The bird cocked her head at him and stepped delicately onto his fist. He heard a series of hard thuds on the roof of the mews, smelled smoke and burning grass, and knew they'd set fire to the building he was in, but it didn't matter. This was the last bird he had left to fly, and he stepped outside with her to try his best.

"Utch!" he called, raising his arm, and Shara bent her body, spread her wings, and thrust herself up and away.

She didn't make it far. Her wing wasn't fully healed, too tender still to fly. A few flaps halfway across the yard, and she settled again on to her feet, walking in a circle like she was surprised to find herself anywhere but in the air.

Brysen deflated. Across the grass, the baby wailed as thick black smoke enveloped the two people huddled in the doorway. Through the smoke, he couldn't even see the gliders.

And then his mother stepped out from safety, holding the baby in the crook of one arm, her other raised in the air, fingers spread, showing surrender.

"Ma!" Brysen called. "No!"

Like a vulture in a charnel ground, a glider cut through the smoke, wings flexed, dropping low and coming to land in the yard. It came in fast, the warrior running as he hit the ground, pulling lines to collapse the wings, which dragged in the dirt behind him. He released one rope and the harness fell away, allowing him to turn, dagger out toward Brysen.

With the sky clear, the Altari in the doorway staggered forward, coughing and wailing, and collapsed on his knees in front of the bodies of his two companions. Then he looked up at the warrior with an expression of pure hatred. "You seize the air where you've no rightful claim," he snarled. "Worse than any Uztari. Curse of the sky on you. On all your kind! I hope they grind you to dust and feed you to those you hate so much. I hope your bloody bones are—"

The warrior silenced him with a throw of his knife, driving it straight into his rib cage, piercing his heart. He gasped and clutched at the blade, mouth agape, but it was too late for him; his body just hadn't caught up. He didn't fall forward or backward off his knees, simply slumped, his head dropped forward, as the blood seeped through the rough cloth of his shirt.

Just then, Jowyn arrived from below, breathless from scrambling up the hill. The warrior's head snapped toward him, and he drew a knife to throw.

"No!" Brysen yelled, and threw himself between Jowyn's body and the warrior's blade.

The warrior didn't throw. He cocked his head sideways at Brysen, whose own reflection shone back in the lenses of the man's flight goggles.

A horn sounded, and cheers erupted from the Villages downslope. A lone glider retreated over the barricades, heading toward the distant columns of smoke and clouds of dust kicked up by the Kartami army. The first attack had been repelled. Only the glider warrior standing before Brysen remained behind, his mission not yet accomplished.

"I'm the one you want," Brysen said. "I'll go with you. Just . . . don't hurt him. *Them*. Don't hurt them."

Flames roared as they devoured his home and the empty bird mews that his father had built. The air was thick with the smell of blood and charred wood and smoking feathers. All his supplies and equipment, all his meager possessions, everything he'd ever known was going up in flames.

The warrior considered Brysen's offer, then moved forward to grab him.

But Brysen was not about to surrender.

The moment he was in the warrior's grasp, he fell limp, forcing the warrior to use both hands to hold him up, and that let Brysen sweep the warrior's legs out from under him. As he fell, he pulled his own knife from his belt, but he never got the chance to make a killing cut. Shara had leapt up from the ground to attack the warrior, clawing at his cheeks, pecking at his eyes.

"Ahh!" the man screamed while Brysen pulled away. He wanted to cut the warrior, to end the struggle, but he hesitated. There was blood on Shara's beak, on her talons as they dug into his throat. The choking screams were horrific, and they made Brysen's hair stand on end. He held his knife at his side; he couldn't bring himself to step forward and drive it home.

What's wrong with you? he scolded himself. *Just kill him. Do it now!*

Before he could will his feet to move or his blade to rise, Shara tore out the man's artery with a gruesome spray and pulled at it like a bloody worm from morning mud. With one final scream, the warrior grabbed her with both hands and ripped her away from him, hurling her hard, straight into the flames of the burning mews.

Any sound Shara made was drowned out by Brysen's scream as he buried his blade in the man's chest, but by that time, he was stabbing a heart that had already stopped beating. The warrior was dead, but across from him, Shara's body caught fire.

15

"NO, NO, NO, NO, NO!" BRYSEN STOOD, EYES LEVELED ON HIS BELOVED bird, who lay stunned as her feathers burned. The flames around her flocked, wind-beaten, blue-hot beaks and red-orange wings devouring the mews, sparking out, hatching new fires, spreading like condors on fresh carrion and pecking away at Shara's tender, feathered flesh.

He wanted to run to her but found that just as his feet had failed him before he could stab the warrior, they failed him now, holding him back. He couldn't move. The smell of smoke filled his nostrils, stung his eyes. The heat of the burning mews stretched out to him, kissed his cheeks like the rough grace of his father's beard. He could not look away.

We know you, the fire whispered. *We've missed you.*

He felt the scars that ran up his left side from waist to neck bursting opening, weeping, sizzling, like they had before, like they had the night his father punished him with the torch instead of the whip. His whole body shook. He could taste the burning flesh on the back of his tongue. He knew this taste. Was he on fire again? Had an ember caught him?

No, I never healed at all, he thought. *I was always burning. I lived with fire below my skin, and now it's breaking free!* He dropped to the ground, rolling and rubbing and trying to extinguish himself.

He felt Shara burning, like he had burned, like he was burning now. They were aflame together, the bird and the boy, and he didn't remember it hurting like this the last time, but it hurt so badly now.

He heard someone screaming far away and knew it was his own voice. "It burns, it burns, it burns!" he cried.

He didn't see it happen, but Jowyn had him in his arms, holding him tight, pale muscles smelling like smoke, and then his mother knelt over him, too, her dark hair glowing red in the firelight. He didn't even have hair, he thought. His was smoke. He should have known. It had always been smoke.

Jowyn held him tight, so tight he couldn't move. "It's okay, you're not burning," the boy whispered in his ear. The close breath fanned the flame in him. "You're not burning. You're safe. You're not burning."

Brysen screamed. He writhed from the fire inside. He could feel the flames cracking out of his skin. "Shara!" he screamed. "Shara!"

When he was a boy, when his father had torched him in the mews, he'd protected Shara, shielded her from the flames with his own body. He'd earned those scars saving her, only to have her die in flames anyway. Maybe he was still there. Maybe he'd never left. "She's burning!" he yelled. "She's burning!"

"Tell me you know that you're not burning!" Jowyn pleaded, still holding him tight enough to smother flame. "Breathe, Brysen. Breathe deep. One breath. In and out. In and out. Tell me you know you are not on fire."

Brysen took a breath. Gasped. Took another. He was not on fire. He took another. He wasn't burning. His clothes were cold. He was in Jowyn's arms. His mother's hands were on him. They were warm but not hot. He was cold. He shivered. "I'm not burning," he said. He tasted smoke.

"Breathe," Jowyn said, and Brysen shook in his arms. "Keep breathing."

"She's burning," Brysen's voice crackled like kindling. "Please. She's burning."

"Keep breathing," Jowyn repeated, and he let Brysen go, stood, and ran into the burning mews.

Brysen closed his eyes, tried to breathe deeply, tried not to smell flesh burning, feathers charring, and the choking smoke filling every hollow space inside him—his lungs, his tear ducts, the empty places in his heart. He felt the smoke pulsing in his veins instead of blood.

"Jo," he whispered, but Jowyn was already back, coughing and clutching a delicate bundle against his chest. He pressed Shara to Brysen like a baby. Brysen felt his bird against him, felt her body rigid and lighter than breathing. Breathless. Her feather shafts were raw and exposed, the feathers burned away. She smelled of smoke and cooked meat.

She was gone.

He'd raised her and fed her and protected her. He'd lost her and found her and replaced her broken feathers. But this . . . this could not be how she ended. There was life in her still. There had to be. He felt it, the way a mother must feel her child's tears the moment before they burst—an about-to-be, a just-before, an almost-now. That life was there, but it was fading, and he felt that, too.

He breathed in the scent of her charred feathers and still felt the smoke inside him, the burning beneath his flesh, but he knew he was not on fire. He *was* the fire. His father hadn't killed him with it; he'd *gifted* it to Brysen, a gift with the pain, with the flames . . . Brysen exhaled and felt the invisible smoke from his breath encircle the hawk, envelop her.

He whispered a word: "*Shyehnaah.*"

It was the Hollow Tongue, a word he'd heard his sister say to command wild birds of prey to kill for her, a word he'd said himself a hundred times to no effect, desperate or hopeful or pleading. He'd never once successfully commanded a bird to kill for him, but now he spoke it clear and pained and hopeful for the one and only thing he knew he truly wanted: for Shara to live.

"*Shyehnaah,*" he said again, not knowing what it meant but knowing what he meant by it: live.

"Prrpt," the hawk squealed, and stirred against him. Her tiny head lifted, nuzzled up against his chest to touch her bloodied beak delicately against his throat. She pressed against him, her heartbeat thrumming quick. She fluffed her feathers—all of them smooth and full and whole, and she stretched her wings, and they were even, level, and straight. The crooked wing healed. She hopped down from his arms and walked in circles, pecking at morsels in the dirt only her keen eyes could see.

"Brysen." His mother whispered his name, the first time he could recall her saying it in so, so long. "Brysen," she repeated, like it was a prayer in itself.

"Brysen," Jowyn said in the same near-reverent tone. "She was dead. I felt her in my hands; I *saw* her . . . She was dead."

"I called her back," Brysen said with a swelling inside him he'd never felt before, a fullness and lightness he'd never known. He looked at the smoke rising from the Villages, at the collapsing walls of his home. "I called her back with the Hollow Tongue," he said, and his mother dropped her head to the dirt, mouth moving in fervent, fearing prayer.

Kylee wasn't the only one with power, he realized while his mother prayed and Jowyn looked at him with gray-eyed awe. Shara hopped about, searching for grubs in the sizzling ruins of their lives, oblivious to her own impossibility.

"I can speak the Hollow Tongue," he said aloud to himself, to Jowyn, to the sky and clouds and wind and sun. "Me."

He knew he should have been confused or afraid, but never before had anything made as much sense as this did now. He'd always felt there was some reason he was alive, some reason he'd endured the torture of his childhood and never ran away nor succumbed, and this was it. The time had finally come when he was the one who had power, he was the one who could tell his own story and be the hero of it. His whole life had been a wing just waiting to open, and now, at last, it had.

He smiled as he watched Shara peck at the ground. He looked up and over her, past the smoking Villages and the falconers on the barricades to the rising cloud of the advancing Kartami horde. They burned bodies wherever they went, but Brysen knew he would not be burned. He felt unstoppable.

He pulled his knife from the dead warrior's chest and wiped the blade on the tattered glider fabric nearby. He'd hesitated to kill, and it had nearly cost Shara's life. He would hesitate no more.

"We don't have a lot of time," he told Jowyn. His mother still mouthed her prayers at the ground. "Will you help me train?"

"Train to . . . what?"

"To figure out what I can do," Brysen said. "And then to do it to these vultures before they can dip their beaks in any more Six Villages blood."

Jowyn swallowed hard but nodded. "I'll help you."

"We'll tell your mother that I'll take the job she's offered," he said. "As long as she keeps my ma safe."

"But who's gonna keep you safe?" Jowyn wondered.

Brysen, feeling the swell of pride he always felt before doing something gloriously stupid, winked at Jowyn. "That job's still open if you want it."

"I go where you go," Jowyn said, and they stood shoulder to shoulder, looking over at the distant columns of smoke beyond the barricades. "Even to the end of the sky."

Shara had found a juicy worm below the embers, and she flew with it to the charred branches of the sickly ash tree that now stood sentinel over the burned house. Her wings were strong, and so was her hunger.

Good, thought Brysen. *I'm going to need both.*

CORRESPONDENCE

*My most honored Kyrg Bardu, wishing you full skies
and fair days.*

*I do hope this letter finds you through the oncoming
siege. Not many birds are making it now, though I noticed
the boy you're interested in dispatched one this evening. I
have honored your request and made preparations for him
to infiltrate the Kartami siege when it arrives. His chances
of success are small, but I am sure you knew that already.
I will not question your motives, so long as you keep your
word.*

*As you know, once he is across our barricades, I have
no influence over his safety or survival, though I am*

certain my estranged son will keep an eye out for him, as much good as adding another reckless peacock to this endeavor might accomplish. He has no loyalty to me, but then again, I have none to you, yet our purposes remain in flight together. The boy will be with the Kartami. Now, when will you honor your side and elevate my eldest son from your dungeon to a seat on the Council? I will have a Kyrg Tamir before this war ends, as promised, or I do not know which of my promises I might keep . . . You are not the only one with spies and assassins in your employ.

That said, for now, the defense of the Six Villages will be strong enough to hold for some time, and I do hope the army you dispatch will offer our enemies nothing but the dirt's mercy when they arrive.

However, as we are sure to suffer heavy losses while we await your army, and have suffered some losses already, I will have to request, in addition to the elevation of my son, a sizable consignment of bronze. I have many mouths to feed, from the Altari who infest our streets to the battle boys who I keep at their heels. The cost of a busy populace is great. Another five hundred rounds would do, through the mountain pass, if possible. If not and I must wait for the siege to fall, then the fee should, of course, be doubled . . . for my hardship. One thousand rounds is a small price to pay for the gift I have given you. I imagine the boy's role in all this to be little more than bait for his sister, but if he should prove capable of the task you've set him through me, I would ask instruction on how to proceed? For now, I know, you must keep his sister happy, but when the time comes that they are no longer necessary, I would request your leave to avenge myself on both of them. We live in bloody times, as every generation does, and the lesson my family has long learned is that the predator who lets its prey escape finds starvation sooner.

I will not, good kyrg, starve, for food or bronze or blood or vengeance.

What is due I will receive, and no fanatical army on the plains nor pampered kyrg in her castle will prevent me.

Yours in service, as long as the sky blesses us,

Mem Cynari Tamir

KYLEE

OF TAMERS AND PREY

16

GRIEF AND FEAR SWAM TOGETHER LIKE MATING SWANS, TWIN MISERIES coiled at the neck, wide-winged and fiercely loyal. Grief had driven Kylee beneath her blanket, fear kept her there, and any urge to move or act was beaten back by the dark mourning of her cramped heart, crying out for her loss, for her loneliness, and for her guilt.

But, she had to pee.

With the same effort it took a hatchling to break through its shell, bursting blind and shivering into the light, she swung her feet out from under the blankets and set them on the cold stone floor. She paused there, head hung, staring at her lap, still wearing the same clothes she'd worn to Ryven's party, though not the same scent. Even in her miserable state, she knew she was ripe.

Two days since the party, and she'd spent the entire time lost somewhere in sadness for her friend and pity for herself.

Nyall hadn't come to see her, and no one had seen him since before the disastrous party. For all she knew, he'd been killed by the same assassins who murdered Vyvian. She feared there was someone after Brysen back in the Villages, and though she'd scrawled a quick note to warn him, she had no guarantee that it would ever arrive. Word was that the Kartami were closing in and shooting down any pigeons that drew near. No messages in, and no messages out. The first step of the siege of the Six Villages would be silence, which fed her fear and preened her grief.

"Look who's alive." Grazim's voice was a stick in a beehive, and Kylee's head shot up toward the girl, who sat on the edge of her own bed. Kylee found she lacked the energy to make her words sting. This was what her brother must have felt like in one of his dark moods, she realized, and let a new wave of self-recrimination mantle over her. She'd always told him to get some sunshine and exercise and he'd feel better, as if the world could be a balm for the very wounds it made.

"Word from Nyall?" she mumbled out.

Grazim shook her head. "He probably just came to his senses and ran off with one of those pub girls. *You* certainly weren't giving him what he was after." This was Grazim's way of offering comfort. No wonder she had fewer friends than even Kylee did. Or, at least, fewer than Kylee'd *had*. At this point, Grazim was probably the closest thing she had left to a friend.

"He wouldn't run off like that," she told the other girl.

"Because *everyone* just has to be all about protecting *you*, huh?" Grazim stood and pulled on her falconer's glove, stretched to a niche in the wall where her jackal hawk sat. Its spotted chest puffed and showed it keen to fly. Kylee hadn't even known it was there. "*Fiya*," Grazim whispered, and the bird stepped onto her glove. "So are you going to train today or keep wallowing? Üku's patience is running out, you know?"

Kylee grunted and stood, brushing right past the girl and her wild-eyed hawk to relieve herself in the water closet.

"In war, friends die as often as enemies," Grazim told her, speaking through the open archway. "But they don't have to die for nothing. Train for your friend, so that she didn't catch her last breeze for nothing."

Kylee hated that the girl spoke to her while she was peeing and hated more that she was right.

It was unfair that the only other student of the Hollow Tongue would have the personality of a hissing swan, while the people Kylee actually liked were far away, missing, or murdered. She swallowed that anger.

Grazim was right. The only way to avenge Vyvian and to help Brysen and the rest of the Six Villages was to white-knuckle through her grief and through training, and to master the Hollow Tongue, then win the war. Her own advice to Brysen about his moods was partially right, but it wasn't sunshine and exercise she needed. It was power, and it was revenge.

When she stood again, she was determined not to get back into bed. Instead, she crossed her arms in the doorway and met Grazim's eyes. The girl's short blond hair made her look severe, but her expression was softer than Kylee'd expected.

The girl nodded and turned to leave. "I'll tell Mem Üku you're on your way." She gave Kylee a withering glance over her shoulder. "After you wash off and change your clothes."

The sky was just reddening the high stone towers of the castle's central citadel when Kylee arrived at the mews beside the training courtyard. They always trained at dawn or dusk, when the birds of prey were most keen. After days away from her and from the hunt, every bird there was quite keen.

The ghost eagle had not returned, so she would train with one of the hawks and falcons Üku kept on standby. There was even a great horned owl that neither girl was allowed to touch.

"Owls are sacred to us," the Owl Mother explained. "And I will not risk this one on your sentimentality or her ambition."

Kylee noted how similar Üku sounded to Kyrg Ryven. Had they discussed her, or was it just that they both understood the workings of the Hollow Tongue?

Kylee had to choose which hawk to train with now, and she would be judged for her choice of bird as much as for her work with it. Different birds of prey had different skills and responded to different intentions. A goshawk was great for harrying attacks, but steep dives and precision assaults demanded something more like a peregrine falcon. A kestrel could do some damage but was easily distracted, while a jackal hawk had power but not nearly as much speed as smaller raptors. Redwings were good battle hawks but loud, like sharp-shinned hawks, and fickle in their loyalties. All their different dispositions could make as much difference in a battle as any command Kylee gave. She'd have to be able to deploy any of them to their own strengths on their own terms at any time. At least, she would have to if the ghost eagle could not be counted on.

She wondered what the ghost eagle had been up to during her time in bed. She wondered what Kyrg Ryven had been up to, and what they might have been up to together. She decided she would go see him after training.

For this morning, she chose a large goshawk that reminded her of Brysen's Shara. She thought the bird might be more sympathetic to her, being so close to her brother's beloved.

Stupid, she thought as she rested her gloved fist in front of its perch. *Birds aren't sentimental. This one doesn't have anything to do with Brysen or his hawk.*

This goshawk didn't step onto her glove. Skilled falconers didn't need to speak in the language of the birds to get one on the fist, but all the birds in these mews were recently wild and untrained. Trained raptors were for falconers who didn't command the Hollow Tongue.

"*Fiya*," she said, but the hawk didn't move. "*Fiya!*" she repeated, and this time the bird cocked its head. At least it didn't leap from the perch and try to fly away. It wasn't leashed, so if it flew, it was gone, and Üku would find ways to punish Kylee. Cleaning bird scuzz from the mews, or memorizing huge lists of words, like *zafla* and *crip*.

Zafla meant sleep; she knew from having once mouthed off to Üku. Her punishment had been to spend most of that night commanding every bird of prey in the mews to sleep, then waking them just to command them each to sleep again. *Crip* she learned while holding one of the birds. *Crip* was the Hollow Tongue word for bird scuzz. A huge white glob of it had oozed down her forearm.

"Just get on my scuzzing fist!" she cursed at the goshawk, which preened itself, ignoring her. A hawk didn't respond to scolding. It took gentleness to command one, and Kylee's boiling rage would only chase this one away. "Please," she cooed, and wiggled her fingers gingerly in front of the hawk's perch as she tried again, as sweetly as possible. *"Fiya."*

The hawk took a confident step from the perch onto her outstretched fingers. She moved her thumb on top of one of the bird's toes, a gesture that usually was enough to keep a hawk in place without a leash, and then she walked with it out to the courtyard.

"While the Hollow Tongue demands our patience with the raptors," Üku called to her, "my patience with you is not eternal, and you've long since run it out. You *must* perform the rudiments faster, or the enemy will have you and your birds cut down before you've flown a single one."

"Is there a Hollow Tongue word for *patience*, Mem Üku?" Kylee asked, staring cold iron at her instructor. "Perhaps you could teach it to me?"

Üku cleared her throat, ignoring Kylee's provocation, and gestured at the two girls. "Grazim," she said. "Command your birds to switch places."

"Sif-sif," Grazim chirped without any hesitation or consideration, and the goshawk on Kylee's fist leapt, flapping her way to Grazim, while Grazim's jackal hawk flew to Kylee.

"Kylee, the same," Üku said.

"Sif-sif," Kylee said, and nothing happened. Of course nothing happened. Why should the Hollow Tongue work for her when she wanted it to?

Grazim rolled her eyes, and Üku shook her head sadly. "Not every moment of your speaking must be life and death," she said. "Life is not lived in extremes. It need not be fatal to be important. Focus on the quieter needs. You *need* these birds to switch places, and in switching places, they will find their own needs met. Believe that, and they will, too."

Kylee focused on her wants in this moment. She *wanted* to find Nyall safe and sound. She *wanted* to avenge Vyvian's murder. She wanted to go home to make sure her brother was okay. The birds couldn't possibly care about any of that, no matter how much she did.

What did she want that they *could* care about? What want could they share?

For this to be over, she thought. "*Sif-sif*," she said, and this time, it worked. The birds changed places; the goshawk perched tall and proud on her fist, looking around the courtyard as if it had always wanted to be held by her, even though it had nearly refused altogether moments ago. She found herself proud to have done what took Grazim no effort at all. She couldn't help but smile at herself.

"Good," Üku said. "Now you will command these birds to attack."

She pointed across the courtyard to a grass-stuffed sack

shaped vaguely like a person. It held a spear and shield and somehow, it was moving. There was actually a person inside, protected beneath the padding.

"Grazim, you first."

"*Shyehnaah*," Grazim said. "*Kraas!*"

The bird on her fist flattened its wings against its body, lowered its head, shuddered.

"*Kraas!*" Grazim repeated to no avail.

"Kylee . . . you," Üku commanded, her voice sagging at her star pupil's failing. Her expectations for Kylee were clearly low, but Kylee had no intention of failing this time.

"*Shyehnaah*," Kylee said firmly, which readied the bird. She felt its muscles poised, its legs bend. "*Caleen!*"

She used the word she thought meant *chase* or *pursue* rather than the brutal *eat* that Grazim had chosen, and her bird took off, immediately going for the padded target. The man inside the suit tried to block the bird, tried to scare it away with his spear, but found that everywhere he stepped, the hawk harried him, forcing him back against the far wall of the courtyard. "*Shyehnaah-tar!*" Kylee said, and the hawk flew back to her fist.

Üku nodded. "And yet the bird did not attack?"

"I didn't want her to hurt this person," she said, rewarding the hawk with a small bit of meat from her game sack. "I couldn't send her to attack on a lie, so I told her the closest thing I could think of. To chase him."

"Interesting idea," Üku said. "But in battle, your commander will have orders for you that are part of a larger strategy. Your job is to execute those orders, translating the commander's desires into a command that the birds will obey. You will have to be precise. You and your birds are but one piece of a larger plan. There are other falconers doing simple tasks that do not demand the Hollow Tongue. There are foot soldiers and archers. In spite of what you think, this war will not be entirely won by you. There are some who do not want you to be a part of it at all."

Grazim had suppressed a grin. She was probably one of those people.

"So you must find a way to do precisely as ordered," Üku continued. "I assure you, deviation with a small hawk might not seem so dramatic, but deviation with the ghost eagle could be catastrophic . . . Grazim, your turn. Try again. Attack."

"*Shyehnaah! See-whet!*" Grazim used a word that Kylee didn't know, and the jackal hawk did take off, but instead of attacking the person in the padded suit, it flew up, flapping hard over the walls of the courtyard, catching a breeze and rising higher and higher. Was it going to dive at the padded man? Soon the hawk had flown so high, it wasn't even visible. The expression on Grazim's face was nonplussed. This wasn't what she'd wanted it to do. The star pupil had failed, and Kylee had triumphed. She was just as happy to see Grazim fail as she was to succeed herself. It wasn't a pretty feeling, but it was true nonetheless.

"What did you intend?" Üku asked Grazim.

"A dive," Grazim answered, keeping her eyes fixed up, searching the sky for the jackal hawk.

"But she isn't diving," Kylee noted as unhelpfully as possible. "I think she might've skied out."

"No," Grazim said. "Look!"

The jackal hawk was a streak in the sky, falling fast for the courtyard in a straight dive. Too straight. Too fast. It didn't even open its wings to slow, simply crashed with a splatter on the stones. On impact, it was more liquid than flesh.

A moment later, the ghost eagle appeared.

"*REEEEEE!*" it shrieked, settling on the parapet above them, now its favorite perch. The goshawk on Kylee's fist launched away, fleeing back inside to hide in the mews. The figure in the puffy padded suit scrambled back and fell, cowering in a corner of the courtyard. Even Grazim and Üku tensed.

Kylee stood firm and looked up at the great black bird, which spread its wide wings against the waning light of dusk over the mountains. She saw now, for the first time, in the amber light, how the gigantic bird wasn't all one solid black: The undersides of its primary flight feathers were striped in bluer blacks, while the secondaries were the reddish black of over-ripe berries. Its chest feathers, each larger than the hawk that had just splattered on the stones, were a shining, perfect black, while the skin of its feet was a black like the scales of a river snake, tinted with grayish green. Kylee thrilled at its shades and hues, the infinite variety of its gleaming darkness. She felt like the eagle *wanted* her to see it more clearly.

When it looked back at her with its glistening onyx eyes, eyes that shone with the depth of a night sky, did it see as much complexity to her darkness? Did it know the rage inside her? Was that what held its interest? Her skin prickled not with fright, but with the sense of feeling seen.

"*Khostoon*," she said, but in her mind she thought, *Where the scuzz have you been?* And also *Please don't kill me* and also *My friend was murdered* and also *Find Nyall*, and all the thoughts formed a quarrelsome flock until a new thought came, chasing the rest away.

Behind you, she thought, but Kylee knew it was not her thinking. *Behind you*, the bird told her, its voice in her mind, and just then she turned and saw the padded figure had stood from where he'd been cowering and revealed a small tube: a blow gun. He was aiming it not at her but at Grazim, who was too distracted by the ghost eagle to run for her life.

"*Kraas!*" Kylee called, and the ghost eagle shrieked and

dove from the parapet, scooping up the would-be assassin in its mighty talons. The giant bird lifted him, though he screamed and struggled, and carried him away into the sunset to feast, hidden from human eyes.

Grazim gaped at the space where the assassin had been, her mouth hanging open, shocked either at the assassination attempt or the fact that it was Kylee's command that had saved her life. Kylee was just as surprised. The ghost eagle had obeyed her, which meant she cared enough about the other girl to save her.

She hoped the feeling was mutual, because she needed Grazim's help for what she planned to do next.

17

ÜKU CANCELED THE REST OF THE EVENING'S TRAINING AND HAD THE girls confined to their room. She placed two guards outside the room's open archway, but they were not Uztari soldiers. Regal Owl Mothers, with chiseled features and shocks of silver hair like Üku's own, stood sentinel, vigilant owls on their fists.

"I just got *out* of this room. I don't want to be stuck back in here!" Kylee complained, but her protests splashed across the Owl Mothers' stony backs with as much as impact as a hummingbird's droppings on a cliffside. She looked with queasiness at her disheveled bed and decided to lean on the wall next to it instead. Grazim perched on the edge of her own, watching Kylee out of the corner of her eye, the way a snake watches a kestrel.

"This is ridiculous, right?" Kylee asked her, searching for common ground. She looked to the doorway to make sure the Owl Mothers couldn't hear them. "They're trying to kill us to stop us from using our skills against them. Cloistering us up in here is basically the same thing. Üku is handing them the victory they can't take by force."

"Üku has her reasons," Grazim said while she busied herself oiling the leather of her falconer's glove. "This is for our safety. We're too important for them to risk."

"We're not doing *anything* important here," Kylee complained. "I only agreed to come and train so that I could protect the Six Villages. If they're under siege, I should be going there to defend them, not sitting under guard a half moon's march away."

Grazim shook her head, muttered to herself, and spat on the floor.

"What was that?" Kylee pushed off the wall and loomed over the other girl. "You have something you want to say to my face?"

Grazim stood to meet her eye to eye. "The last thing the Six Villages need is you being reckless with your power. You could kill everyone because you have no control."

"I just saved your life, didn't I?"

"The ghost eagle saved my life," Grazim said. "And neither you nor I nor the Owl Mothers have any real idea *why*."

"*I* know why. It saved you because I wanted it to save you . . . and you haven't even thanked me."

Grazim exhaled through her nose. "You're angry at me. For what?"

"For . . . for . . ." In truth, Kylee didn't know. She was angry that Vyvian was dead and that Nyall was missing and that Brysen was far away. She was angry that the Owl Mothers had locked her away instead of letting her fight, and she was angry at Uztar for trying to use her to save itself but giving her no power at all. She wasn't really angry with Grazim.

"Anger is a fire," Grazim said. "Fire has its uses, but let one burn too long and all it will do is destroy."

"I still don't hear a thank-you," Kylee said back to her.

Grazim shook her head. "I heard your brother was the reckless one, but I can't imagine anyone is more reckless than a spoiled girl like you."

"*'Spoiled'?*" Kylee nearly choked on the word. "There were some ice-wind seasons when we nearly starved. It was up to me to keep my ma fed and my brother safe, and I always did. I had to do *everything*. Nothing ever came easy to us."

"Except the one thing that matters."

"What?" Kylee noticed her fists were balled again, proving Grazim's point. She relaxed them.

"Your gift," Grazim said. "The Hollow Tongue."

"It did *not* come easy," Kylee said. "You don't know what it costs me."

"I know better than you think." Grazim bit her lower lip. Training in the unshaded courtyards had made freckles erupt over the fair skin of her broad face and had bleached her short blond hair nearly bone-white. Her dark eyes were bloodshot, from emotion or exhaustion or late nights of study. Kylee had never looked this closely at the other girl and found that the longer she looked at her, the harder she wanted to punch her. Grazim was right; her anger was thrashing like a hawk in a trap, more likely to break its own wings than escape the hunter who'd caught it.

She sat down on her bed across from Grazim, softened her eyes. If they were stuck in this room, there was no sense in keeping their rage so keen. "I'm listening," she said.

"Both my parents were Crawling Priests," Grazim told her, easing back. Kylee relaxed her shoulders. "Like all pious Altari, I was raised to revere birds of prey and to curse falconry and all who practiced it. In the Parsh Desert, where my people lived in exile from these mountains—thanks to your people—we spent our days crawling from settlement to settlement, cursing the unholy blasphemy your people committed against the sky."

"My ma's Altari," Kylee offered. "Never touched a bird of prey in her life, though my da trapped and sold and battled them in the pits. She might've touched a hen once."

"We didn't have chickens in the desert," Grazim laughed, and Kylee felt relieved that they were having a conversation, sharing pieces of themselves. A story was a kind of tether, tying teller and listener together, and maybe this had been Üku's plan: to bind them. They were shut up in here not for the sake of their safety but for their partnership.

Clever old bird, Kylee thought. It was working.

"I had scabbed knees from the moment I could crawl until long after I could walk," Grazim said, smoothing the glove across her knees but staring past it, into her memory. "One day, in a mixed town in the Grassland Plains—one of the trading posts where Uztari come to buy grain and livestock from us—I saw a well-dressed man with a kestrel on his fist. A pretty bird, brightly plumed. It was hooded, and I thought I knew how that felt, seeing nothing. Most of what I saw was the ground just inches from my nose.

"My father went over to the man, clung to his foot, and

started preaching. 'Free the bird from its bondage or your soul will be tethered to the mud'—that kind of thing. The man didn't much like my pious dad, so he kicked him in the chin. I had never seen my father kicked before, and it filled my lungs with a holy heat, a fire I'd never felt before. I shouted—some word I don't remember and didn't understand. It was not my word to speak, but the kestrel knew it. It launched, still hooded, from that falconer's fist and attacked its own tamer's face. Pecking and scratching, bloodying him all over. My parents grabbed me, and we ran. Uztari justice never sided with our people.

"When we stopped at the next settlement, my father crawled to the filthiest latrine pit he could find and flung himself in to pray. The deeper the muck, the deeper the repentance. My mother, however, slapped me. She'd never done that before. She made me eat a mouthful of sand and told me never to speak like that again as long as I lived."

Kylee thought of her own father, exhorting her to use her talent and taking her reluctance out on Brysen, blaming him for her refusal to speak the Hollow Tongue, as if she didn't have a will of her own, as if everything she did was because of Brysen. Maybe it was. Maybe it had been.

"I did keep speaking, of course," Grazim said. "The words came up in me, no matter how hard I tried to stop them. You

221

know how it is, though? When you hold those words in and they burn and burn. You can't hold them forever. I had stomach pains, headaches. I tried to keep my talent a secret from everyone else, but having a secret like that at the core of me curdled my blood like bad milk. I hated it in myself. I bit my tongue until it bled, tried to cut the words out of my veins, but they never left me. I had this gift, and everything I knew of the world told me it was a curse."

Grazim laughed, a grunt of self-recognition. "Can you imagine? What any Uztari parent would celebrate as a blessing from the sky—what *your* community celebrates as a *gift*—my community hated in me."

"They didn't love it in me, either," Kylee said. "They just wanted to use it for their own purposes. They still do."

"I wish my community had wanted to use me," Grazim told her. "All they wanted was to bury me and my sin so far in the dirt that the sky would never see it. And all the while, I hated myself even worse than they hated me. I *wanted* to be buried in the dirt. I wanted to rot.

"But in my pain, I called out—in the cursed Hollow Tongue—and the sky answered me. A snow owl, too far from snow, flew over the pit of muck and scuzz where I was sleeping and hoping to die. It circled above me. It led me away, into the desert. It led me to water, and it hunted with me as I learned to command it. It led me to the mountains and to the

Owl Mothers. To Üku, who sheltered me. She taught me to use my gift. Made me *proud* of it. Proud of what I'd always thought was sin. And *that* made me powerful. I was powerful because I was proud. And then *you* came along, a girl who insulted the Owl Mothers and got so angry at the world that she ran away from her greatest gift."

"I'm not running away from it anymore," Kylee said softly, looking down at her hands, unclenched now. Her rage had vanished like mist in the wind. Grazim was just another broken-winged bird trying to fly to the safest branch in the storm. It was time to leap out and trust her.

"Listen: We're on the same side, and we want the same thing—to win this war. We've each got our reasons, but neither of us can do anything stuck in this room. I have to get out to see Kyrg Ryven."

"I thought you didn't get crushes like that. Because if this is some romantic thing, I really don't think—"

"It's not that." Kylee lowered her voice to a whisper. "He's helping me, okay? He's helping me with the ghost eagle."

"Ryven?" Grazim matched her whisper. "How?"

"The ghost eagle wants my anger," she explained. "Ryven's helping me understand how to harness it."

"I wouldn't trust that kyrg if I were you," Grazim said. "Anger has its uses, but held too close, too long . . ."

"I don't trust him," Kylee said. "But I can use him. *We* can

223

use him. You want to get into the war, too, right? Prove what you can do? Ryven can make that happen. He can put in a word with the commanders. He can overrule Üku if he chooses. But I'll need your help getting out of this room to see him."

Grazim narrowed her eyes at Kylee, considering. "You're going to get in trouble if you're caught outside our quarters."

"I know," Kylee said.

"And you won't be safe."

"I know that, too."

Grazim sighed. "Fine."

Kylee leaned across the space between them and startled Grazim by taking the girl's hand in hers. "Thank you, Grazim. Thank you."

Grazim shrugged, but a smirk played at the corner of her lips. "If you're dead or in the dungeons, maybe the ghost eagle will take an interest in me. I already know how to control my anger."

"Maybe." Kylee laughed. "Though I hope you're not *that* unlucky."

"Get ready to run," Grazim whispered, standing. She looked at the backs of the Owl Mothers in the doorway, then at their owls. Kylee's heart leapt in her chest. Once a decision was made,

Grazim wasn't one to hem and haw. Kylee envied that decisiveness. She grabbed her dagger and a cloak, and stood.

"*Thaa-loom,*" Grazim snapped, and no matter what she'd been thinking about her decision to help Kylee, she must have meant it, because both owls launched from the Owl Mothers' fists and dove away, making them leave the door to chase them.

The moment they'd stepped a few spans away, Kylee sprinted out behind their backs. She heard them shouting after her, but they seemed torn between chasing their beloved owls and chasing one disobedient girl.

She left them in the dust as she ran through the halls and winding stairwells to the street, where she weaved through dark alleys and doubled back, taking a longer route in case she was being followed. Soon she reached Ryven's gate in the Peacock District, sweating, out of breath, and exhilarated. She took the stairs two at a time, found the door open for her when she reached the top, and went straight through the entry hall to the great stone doors of his study. They swung open at her approach.

Ryven stood with his back to the open sky, his hands clasped in front of him. He was holding a rolled-up letter. Apparently he'd been expecting her, and so had the ghost eagle, standing at Ryven's side on a pile of fresh bones. The assassin from the courtyard. The ghost eagle had carried the body here, and had already picked the skeleton clean.

"We haven't got a lot of time," Ryven said without preamble. "The siege of the Six Villages has begun, and there is no telling how long they'll stand."

18

THE NIGHT WAS CLEAR, AND THE STARS CUT PINPRICKS IN THE DARK behind the eagle's back. As the giant bird paced, its talons scraped across the edge of the open room. Other than the *click click* of its steps, it hardly made a sound. It was more visible by the stars its shape blotted out as it moved than by the light in the room.

Click click. Its talons tapped as the darkness stalked her. *Click click. Click click.*

The great stone doors to the room were closed now, and as far as his servants knew, Kylee and Ryven were having a private moment for romance, her crying in his arms over her lost friends, him whispering sweet nothings into her dark hair.

Ryven gestured with the rolled parchment in his hand. "The Kartami have moved on the Villages and sealed off any hope of escape. Time is not on the Villages' side. So, are you ready for your lesson?"

"I need to go home," she told him, keeping her eyes fixed on the giant black eagle. "If the siege has begun, they need me. Üku's got us locked up for safekeeping, but I didn't come here to be safe. I need you to speak to Kyrg Birgund. I need to deploy with the army, to liberate the Six Villages. We need to march tonight. I don't need another lesson."

"You're angry at me?" His words echoed Grazim's, and Kylee burst out with a sarcastic laugh.

"Why shouldn't I be angry?"

"You should be," Ryven replied. "You are being attacked, lied to, manipulated, and controlled. You've got no power, and yet you feel responsible for everyone. Anyone in your position would be angry."

She clenched her fists. "I am," she snarled.

"Good," he replied, keeping his eyes both on the ghost eagle and on Kylee. "Why do you think it came to warn you today?" he asked.

"I don't know," she said. "Because we're partners?"

Click click. The bird shifted on its feet, talons tapping stone.

"But why do you think it chose you as its partner?"

"Because I speak the Hollow Tongue?"

"No!" Ryven clapped loudly, startling her and the eagle. It snapped its head around to him and shrieked, and she noticed Ryven shudder.

It can mess with his mind, too, she thought. *Good*.

"You misunderstand what the Hollow Tongue is," he told her. "Why do different people speak it differently? Why can some learn the words but not use it at all, while others, like you, could go most of their lives never knowing the proper words but speaking it just the same?"

"Because it's magic," Kylee suggested, annoyed at his pestering questions. Why did she have to analyze the language in order to use it? Why was he wasting her time with this questions-and-answers game? Was he trying to provoke her?

"It's not magic," he said. "At least, not more than any other language is magic. Language is just a way for two distinct minds to share their thoughts and desires. The Hollow Tongue is no different, except the minds it connects are not only human. It is *their* language"—he nodded at the ghost eagle, gestured with the rolled-up parchment in his hand—"and it is spoken for *their* purposes, purposes we can't fully know. We *do* know, however, that some people—people like you, like me, like Grazim and the Owl Mothers—have a connection to birds of prey that others don't. Maybe it's in our blood. Maybe it's in our history. Maybe it's chance. I can't tell you why, but I can tell you that the rules they obey are not human. Just as an eagle's sight differs from ours, so does its mind. It sees in colors we cannot, so why should it not think thoughts we cannot?"

"Let me see that letter," Kylee said, ignoring his lecture.

"Is it making you mad that I have information you want?"

"Yes," Kylee said.

"So take it from me."

"You don't really want me to," Kylee said. "You're just trying to make me angry."

"I'm trying to show you what your anger can do. Üku isn't pushing you. She thinks you're a caretaker. She thinks the eagle obeys you because of your deep love for your brother."

"That's what works," Kylee said. "And if that letter is about my brother, then I can make it work again right now."

"Show me."

"*Raakrah*," Kylee snapped the word for *take*, *gather*, or *find*. The ghost eagle lowered its head, looked at her sideways, but didn't move.

"It's not good enough," Ryven replied. "You don't want to be a caretaker. You're tired of taking care of other people. Tired of other people's demands and needs. Tired of serving. You know I wanted you to take the letter, which made you not really want to do it. You're defiant. You don't want to serve anyone."

"You don't know what I want," Kylee said, feeling the ghost eagle's black eyes boring into her with expectation, hunger, and promise.

"I *do* know," Ryven said. "I know because *it* told me. It sees."

The fine hairs on Kylee's arms stood on end. The air crackled with danger. She'd never felt so fragile before, never thought of how thin the layer of skin was that kept her blood inside her body, how fragile or how quickly the ghost eagle's beak could tear her open. But it didn't need to; its mind did all the work.

"Tell it what you really want. Why did you come all this way to fight for Uztar?"

"I want to keep my brother safe," Kylee repeated.

"No," Ryven snapped. "That's what other people expect of you. What do *you* want?"

"I want to go home."

"No!" Ryven yelled. "That's what you're *used to* wanting. What do you really want? For yourself?"

The eagle lowered its head until it was nearly flat with its back. Its shoulders arched up behind it, wings lightly flexed. One foot raised off the stones and its beak opened, like it was preparing to lunge. One talon clicked up and down on the floor.

Click click click.

She saw Ryven's reflection in its black eyes, and saw the reflection transform into her father's. His blond beard, his sky-blue eyes—the only feature she and her brother shared with him. How often those eyes had looked at her with disappointment, how often they had looked at her brother with pitiless hate. The vision was what the ghost eagle wanted her to see. Maybe what Ryven wanted her to see. But she didn't want to see her father's face ever again. The illusion turned back into Ryven . . . another man who thought he could control her.

"I want power," Kylee whispered, staring back at the bird, clear-eyed, but keeping her hands up to protect herself, as if her tiny hands could do anything against the giant eagle. She'd seen what its power could do to a mind, but worse, what its talons could do to a body.

"Why?" Ryven asked, unrelenting, as the eagle stepped forward, toward her, its stare fixed on hers. "Power for what? Power *to* what?"

"Power to . . ." The eagle took another step. "Power to . . ."

What do I want power to do? she pleaded with herself.

Click click. It came closer, talons tapping on the stones.

Why do I want to control this monster? No lying now. It will know you're lying. It will not forgive you.

Click click. Click click.

"I want revenge!" she realized, and the bird stopped, one foot still hovering in the air. Frozen.

"Against whom?" Ryven asked, and she could hear the smile in his voice.

"*Everyone*," Kylee answered, and she felt the rage she'd been carrying inside her for as long as she could remember spread wide its wings and soar. She'd been trying to harness that rage. Now she suddenly knew that she had to ride it like a breeze instead. "Everyone who's manipulated me, everyone who's threatened me, who's attacked me . . ." She snapped her head around to look at Ryven himself, the smug noble who'd presumed to teach her. "Everyone who's lied to me. I want to hurt them all."

Ryven smiled. "Good," he said. "Because that's what we want for you, too. That's exactly why we brought you here."

"'We'?" Kylee wondered, and the warmth inside her turned to heat, began to feel an awful lot like fear.

"Us," he said, and the stone door behind her opened again with a slash of light. Üku stood in the opening, arms folded across her chest.

"You've a defiant streak," she said, "so we had to give you someone to defy. In this case, we gave you me."

Kylee frowned. Another manipulation. Another set of lies.

"If you want power over others, you have to seize it," Üku said. "It will never be given willingly. We can help you take it, and in turn, you can help us take what we want."

"The kyrgs," Kylee said, understanding it all. Üku hadn't

come all the way to the Sky Castle just to train her. She'd come to cultivate Kylee, so she would overthrow the kyrgs and seize the Sky Castle. Ryven hadn't learned what he knew of the Hollow Tongue during his own study. He'd learned it the same way anyone who spoke it had: from the Owl Mothers.

Üku strode across the room to stand between Ryven and the towering ghost eagle. She stroked the black feathers on its side.

"*Khostoon*," Ryven said.

"*ṚEEEE!*" the eagle shrieked so loud, it shook Kylee's entire body. She felt a righteous rage boil in her, and she found that she loved it.

"We who are masters of the Hollow Tongue should rule all of Uztar," Ryven said. "Peak to valley, sky to mud. Imagine: to be at no one's mercy ever again. The apex predator."

"Along with you," she clarified.

"Along with *us*," Üku said.

The ghost eagle fluffed its feathers, and Kylee couldn't be certain if these words were Ryven's or the bird's, speaking through him. The bird's power bent reality around it, just like Ryven's honeyed tone, and she knew right away that, whether she said yes or no, she was perched on the edge of something, about to leap, to fly or to fall.

"Command the eagle," Üku told her.

"To do what?" Kylee asked.

"It doesn't matter," she said. "Show it you *believe* in what you want, and it will obey you."

"*Toktott*," Kylee said, the first word that came to her mind, the one Üku had taught her for *stop* or *block*. The ghost eagle swung its tail feathers around and knocked Ryven sideways, bumping him into his bird-flight model.

He laughed, but Üku glared at him. "Don't encourage her whimsy."

"Apologies." He saluted the Owl Mother across his chest and showed her his practiced smile, one that had surely worked on any number of lovestruck boys and girls in the past. It did nothing to cool Kylee's anger, which burned steady. This wasn't the wild flaring of fear that usually gave her the command of the ghost eagle; this was an indignation that told her she deserved more than she'd been given, that she'd been used and would be used no more. This was her will burning inside her and coming out at last.

"*Tatakh*," she said, and the ghost eagle took a jumping step, knocking Ryven to the ground and placing one foot on his neck, talons resting on either side of his soft throat but not yet squeezing.

"Okay, Kylee," Ryven said. "I get it. But that's not a word to use lightly."

Üku pursed her lips, looking pleased. Kylee considered

turning the bird on her next, but found she had no anger left for the Owl Mother.

"Where is Nyall?" Kylee demanded.

"I don't . . . I don't know," Ryven told her, and she found she liked the catch in his voice.

"You told me that your command of the Hollow Tongue comes from deception," she said. "Why should I trust you?"

"You shouldn't," he pleaded, staring up at the ghost eagle, who didn't look at him. It looked at Kylee. "But I swear I don't know where Nyall is."

"Who killed Vyvian?"

"You saw . . . ," Ryven said. "An assassin."

"Who *sent* that assassin?"

"How should I know?"

"You claim to know a lot."

"Listen, Kylee," he said. "Someone sent an assassin after me, too. Before I was seated on the Council. They tried to kill me before I could get any power. They're afraid of us, but we are stronger together. We can help each other."

Her heart was racing. She tried to think of the next word to use. *Release* or *crush*? She realized she didn't know either word. She looked to Üku, who offered her only the slightest shrug. The choice was hers; Üku would not make it for her. She wasn't, it turned out, a terrible teacher after all. She'd created the conditions for Kylee to learn, and now she had to put her learning to use.

We don't need Ryven, Kylee thought. *He has nothing left to offer us.*

She shuddered. Those thoughts were not hers. The ghost eagle wanted blood. It was an insatiable predator and would always choose blood over mercy, but Kylee was not a predator. Just because she wanted power didn't mean she knew how to wield it, didn't mean she *should*. She did not want to become what the eagle was asking.

"What's the word for *release*?" she asked.

"*Bost*," Üku said coolly.

"*Bost*," she said, but the bird did not obey. She didn't really want it to let go.

"*Bost*," Ryven choked out, and this, the eagle obeyed.

A wave of disappointment coursed through Kylee that she knew was not hers. Her great winged partner was still keen for blood.

Ryven rubbed his neck and pulled himself up by the edge of the stone table. The ghost eagle rose with him, up to its full height again, towering over the young kyrg and over Kylee. There was something in its stare other than menace. It was, she realized, curiosity. She'd learned something about herself, and it was learning with her.

Crows, she knew, were known to use tools—bits of

branches and small stones and leaves, whatever they could grasp—to test and investigate and explore. To catch a meal or a mate. They were the most intelligent of birds, except, of course, for the ghost eagle.

Are we tools for this bird? she wondered. *And if we are, what is it using us for?*

"Why ask me?" Kylee shivered, though the room was not cold. "Grazim has skill, and if the eagle speaks to Ryven, too, what do you need me for?"

"Because the eagle chose you," Üku said. "It *sees* you. You are a young woman whom this world has wronged too often, and there is nothing more powerful than your rage."

19

RYVEN AND ÜKU HAD PROPOSED TREASON, OPENLY AND WITHOUT apology. They wanted power because they felt they deserved it, and they wanted Kylee's help because they knew she wanted it, too. It was one thing to learn how to master the Hollow Tongue to aid the army and save her home, another thing altogether to use that knowledge to betray her rulers and conquer a kingdom.

And yet, she didn't refuse.

In fact, staring at the young noble in his fine clothes beside the massive eagle with its curious glare and the rough Owl Mother with her imperial stance, Kylee found that she *liked* the idea of joining them, though not to rule. She had no desire to administer territory and control taxes. She just wanted to tear down everyone who had stomped all over her, the kyrgs and their hangers-on, the Tamirs back in the Six, even her neighbors, who'd been all too happy to look the other way her whole life while her father heaped scorn on her and violence on her brother.

They should all suffer, she thought. *They should all kneel at your feet and beg forgiveness.*

The ghost eagle was still in her head.

She *did* want revenge on all those people, but she could not—*would not*—simply abandon her brother, no matter what these two thought she wanted.

If she seized power here, how could she help her brother in the Six Villages? The Kartami might this moment be sacking her home. She couldn't spend time plotting a coup when she had so much distance still to cross.

"You're still worried about Brysen, aren't you?" Ryven asked, sensing her hesitation. She nodded. "These kyrgs are using him, you know. They're using the Six Villages. Why do you think they've waited so long to dispatch the army? Kyrg Bardu wants the siege to distract and weaken the Kartami before the Uztari army engages. Birgund could've marched his army out days ago to intercept them, but he waited. He plans to let Six Villagers die to keep the kite warriors busy. These kyrgs don't care who suffers. They're using your home—your brother's home—as bait. And you've seen what happens to a bait pigeon when a hawk gets to it . . ."

"Even more reason for me to stay with the army," she said. "To end this war."

"*Their* war," Ryven sneered. "We have nothing to fear from the Kartami. They're a fanatical militia, nothing more, and their war with the sky will burn itself out soon. But with the Uztari army outside the walls, Bardu's small Home Guard won't resist us for long. They're terrified of you. You'd sacrifice all the power in the world to save one little foothill patch of mud?"

"It's still my home. My brother is still there."

"I thought we were past that." Ryven sighed.

"She still thinks she's his caretaker." Üku shook her head.

"He needs me."

"But what if he doesn't?" Ryven held up the letter and un-rolled it. Through the thin parchment, Kylee could make out Brysen's messy writing. "What if he has his own plans? What if he's daring great things while you hide behind your 'con-cern' for him?"

"That's from Brysen?" She felt the old rage boil up in her again. "You took my letter?"

"The Council has been intercepting all his letters before they reach you. They're worried about your loyalties," Ryven explained. "I decided to liberate this one before they got a look at it."

"But *you* looked at it?"

He held his palms up in apology. "Curiosity got the better of me. But I promise you, Brysen can take care of himself. He might even destroy the Kartami before Birgund's army has a chance to get there. And if he does, then we might miss our chance. If we don't seize control while they are marching across the plains, we lose our opportunity to seize the undefended castle."

"Give me the letter."

Ryven held it up but not out to her. She didn't dare snatch it from him, as close as he stood to the ghost eagle.

"If you spend your whole life protecting him, you'll never achieve your potential," Üku said.

Ryven extended the letter out to her. "You can be your own person. Take what's yours."

"I *am* my own person." She snatched the letter from him. "I am a person who cares about someone other than myself."

"He is holding you back."

She unrolled the letter, and her mind calmed at seeing Brysen's handwriting again. Ryven was right about one thing: All language is magic. Even the simplest writing, riddled with mistakes, could collapse time and distance as every word became a tether, binding the reader to the hand that wrote it. She could almost hear Brysen's voice as she read the first lines, as if he were in the room. It reminded her of who she was, where she came from, and why she'd come here.

> *Ky, I don't no if this will make it to you, but if it does, don't worry about me. Something amazing happened! I found Shara. She's safe and healthy and well . . . I can't tell you more yet, but its great and I am going to help you this time. I have a plan and am going to end this war, but it mite be danjerus tho I no I can do it. Trust me this one time ok? No matter wut you here, just trust me. I luv you sis.*
>
> *Brysen*
>
> *(Oh also Jowyn keeps looking at me like . . . you no . . . and I think maybe I do too. Is that stupid?)*

She found she had a tear in her eye when she looked up at Ryven and the watchful black bird. She shook her head. Her brother was reckless with his heart, but he could do worse than falling for Jowyn. The strange boy had saved his life before, after all, and clearly cared about him. If he was going to risk heartbreak again and again, better that it be with a friend.

But the rest of the letter worried her. He had some plan? Something dangerous? She did not like it when Brysen had dangerous plans. They usually ended with his life in peril.

What if I didn't save him this time? she wondered. He was, technically, the older one between them, though by only a few crows of the rooster. He had always wanted her to treat him like he was her big brother, and she never once had. Even mama birds give their babies more room to fall than she gave her twin. Why did she always need to control everything? *What if I trusted him and let him make his own decisions?*

Ryven had raised an eyebrow, watching her, seeing if she would, once again, go running off to save Brysen, to control him. Wasn't that the same as wanting power?

Before she could form a response, the large stone doors behind her burst open. Kyrg Bardu stormed in with a flock of soldiers at her heels, falcons on their fists. Behind them was Grazim with a new-caught tiercel jackal hawk, smaller than her old one and spotted gray. In the light of the hall beyond, she saw Ryven's servants, every one of them bleeding from the kinds of wounds that talons and beaks created. Two owls circled over them, until the two Owl Mothers called them to their fists.

"Ryven!" Bardu declared. "You are under arrest for murder and for treason. Surrender now or—" She hesitated when she saw Üku, the moon in her eyes widening. Kylee saw her confusion and her fear as clearly as the ghost eagle did. It took Bardu a moment more to see the ghost eagle itself, shrouded in darkness. When she did, she and the soldiers behind her froze.

"Or what?" Ryven grinned.

The ghost eagle lowered its head, raising its wings behind its back. Its sharp eyes snapped from side to side, studying the nervous birds on the fists of the frightened soldiers.

"It's time for you to step down, Kyrg Bardu." Üku squared her shoulders to face the woman. "The Kartami invasion is one among many of your failings. It is time for those blessed by the sky to rule and safeguard this kingdom."

The two Owl Mothers behind Bardu whispered, and their owls launched from their fists and hovered over them, waiting and ready to strike. Bardu's soldiers turned, knives out, nervous falcons on their raised fists. The owls blocked their escape back the way they'd come in; the ghost eagle and a sheer cliff blocked the other. It was a standoff, and Kylee saw no way for it to end without bloodshed.

"*Kylee,*" Bardu's voice warned. "Let the Council do its business. You do not have to be a part of this. Call off the eagle, and stand with us. Your brother's life depends on it."

"*Kylee,*" Ryven said. "The time is now. Do what you know you can do. Be free of these *politicians* and their lies."

"*Kylee,*" Grazim said. "I don't like you, but I know you're not a traitor. This isn't the war you came to fight. Don't do this."

"Quiet, you pet parrot," Üku snapped at her star pupil. "You'll never be more than a curiosity to these people, and you never should have sided with them over us." She turned to Kylee. "Trust your anger. You hate these people. You know what needs to be done."

"*Kylee*," Kyrg Bardu said. "Do not trust them. They sent assassins. It's Ryven's fault that Vyvian died. The poison was meant for her. It was his servant who gave it to you, he who made sure Vyvian, not you, was the one to drink it. He wants you to think everyone is trying to kill you, all while he takes out anyone you trust. He wants you afraid and alone. He is trying to isolate you, to make you dependent on him and only him."

They're all trying to control you, she thought as the ghost eagle opened its beak and screeched.

"*REEEEEEE!*"

The soldiers flinched, their trained birds cried out, and three bated from their tamers' fists to find themselves dangling, panicked, from the leashes on their ankles. Only the owls stayed calm. They were birds of the mountains and the night, and they knew this eagle's screams. They flicked their wings in hovering silence.

"Kylee," Üku tried again. "Listen to me. This is not about your brother. All of history hinges on what you now d—"

"Quiet! Quiet! Quiet!" Kylee shouted. She'd never hated the sound of her own name more than she did now, hearing these people scold and plead and cajole with it. They all wanted

246

her to choose a side when the only side she'd ever wanted was her family's. Now Brysen claimed he didn't need her.

To the mud with them all, she thought. *Let the ghost eagle devour them.*

She wanted to speak; she wanted to say the word that would unleash the great bird's wrath, and she knew the eagle wanted it, too.

But she hesitated.

Why was it waiting for her? Why did it need her command when it could kill whoever it chose? Why did its submission to her feel so much like she was surrendering to it?

The air was sharp; she could taste miner's iron and burning sulfur, the tang of sweat and the musk of gamey breath. Everyone was afraid, and everyone was expectant. None of them wanted to die, but the choice was not theirs and they all knew it. They were the prey, and Kylee controlled the predator. Kylee *was* the predator.

She had not come all this way to be prey.

"*Fliss*," she said with a wave of her hand. The ghost eagle hesitated, but she meant what she said. "*Fliss*," she repeated.

Her voice was a blade, and she would keep it sheathed.

For now.

The ghost eagle's eyes darted over her once, a judgmental glare from a bird that was capable of such emotion; then it turned, took three rapid steps to the ledge, and knocked away the failed assassin's bones as it spread its wings and leapt into the night. It first fell below the walls, then flapped up high enough to blot out the moon.

"*REEEEE.*" It screamed as it flew, a dark pupil in the white eye of the moon, growing smaller and smaller as it soared away. Kylee felt that scream on her skin, like a cold wind. She felt the eagle's disappointment, and its anger, and she knew those feelings were her own, too.

It wanted to kill for her, wanted its bloodlust to be hers. She couldn't tame it, and it didn't want to be tamed. It wanted her will to become its will, and only then would it submit to her command. She had defied its desires by showing mercy. As it shrank against the moon, she suddenly wasn't sure that it would come back to her.

And now she wasn't sure who she was without it.

20

"YOU FOOLISH CHILD," RYVEN SNARLED AS HE AND ÜKU TURNED TO the soldiers.

Bardu shouted, "Silence them before they can call out!" She produced a throwing knife from the sleeve of her tunic, and Kylee hardly saw the flick of her wrist before the needle-thin blade flew and sank into the throat of one of the Owl Mothers.

"*Thaa-loom!*" cried the other Mother as her owl swooped for Kyrg Bardu.

"*Toktott!*" Grazim cried, and her jackal hawk intercepted the owl, screeching and harrying it back. A soldier loosed her peregrine at Ryven, occupying him just long enough for the other guards to charge and shove a gag into his mouth. Though he fought, they tackled him and bound him, then jammed a heavy hood over his head and cinched it closed.

"*Tuslaash!*" Üku shouted. A wild snow owl flew to her aid from the night sky over the castle, but another flick of Bardu's wrist caught it in the air and dropped it from sight. Üku cried out in anguish, like her own body was falling, not the regal owl's. Kylee understood that *tuslaash* had meant *help* and that no more help would come.

Kylee's gaze snapped back to Bardu, whose wrist flicked again and again, and both Owl Mothers were on the floor now, gagging around the blood pooling in their throats, unable to speak, while their owls simply stood on the ground, summoned by tamers who could no longer tell them what to do next. They waited, blinking, and Bardu looked at Üku, daring her to speak again. Grazim's hawk circled the room and landed again on her fist.

Üku touched one finger to the cheekbone below her eye and glared at Grazim. "You chose the empire that hates you," she said. "Pathetic."

"I chose to keep my word," Grazim replied.

"Tie her mouth," Bardu ordered, and Üku was gagged, though not hooded. Kylee tensed, waiting for her own gag, but instead Bardu saluted her with the wings across her chest.

"Thank you," she said to Kylee. "You made the right choice."

"Is it true he had Vyvian killed?"

Bardu nodded.

"Is it true the siege of the Six Villages has begun?"

Bardu nodded again.

"Then I don't want to waste any more time," Kylee said. "We need to deploy with Birgund's army right away."

Bardu smiled. "Just what I planned to suggest," she said. "But first, if you wouldn't mind stepping inside." She motioned for Kylee to follow her deeper into Ryven's house, as Ryven and Üku were hauled away in chains. "I'd like to talk to you somewhere less"—she looked to the open wall and the dark mountains and the starry sky beyond it— "exposed."

Kylee had only seen the proctor of the Sky Castle from a distance before now. Now that she was seeing her up close, Kylee was impressed. The kyrg was younger than Kylee had imagined, but she radiated power. She had dark eyes hooded with long lashes, dark hair that she wore untied— obviously confident that no bird of prey would dare peck at it—and she wore rings on each of her fingers, rings so large that no falconer's glove could possibly go over them. Somehow, she ruled the falconer's world without the need to demonstrate her prowess with birds of prey. She didn't make a show of her power, and that confidence alone was enough to demonstrate it.

Kylee allowed herself to be led to Ryven's sitting room. Grazim started to follow them, but Kyrg Bardu shook her head. "I'd like to talk to young Kylee alone, if you please. Grazim, thank you for your service to the Council. Your loyalty will not be forgotten."

She saluted, and Grazim's chest puffed. She'd betrayed the teacher who had saved her from a life of abuse and misery, and in Üku's fall, Grazim rose. Her power came from her ambition. Üku should've seen the betrayal coming. Kylee couldn't fault the girl for doing what she'd done, even though it was far from admirable. Only the long dead get to be admirable. The living have to peck and dive at what they must to survive.

"You shouldn't hate her," Bardu told Kylee when they were alone.

"I don't hate her."

"Your whole body tensed like a talon about to strike," Bardu said. "Grazim might've saved your life, just as you saved hers. I wasn't lying to you about Kyrg Ryven. He did poison your friend and make it seem like it was an attack on you. He sent the assassin after Grazim in the courtyard. He holds no life valuable but those he can use, and he would've discarded you the moment he was done with you."

"How do you know that?" Kylee crossed her arms, skeptical. Maybe the Hollow Tongue couldn't lie, but the language of politicians lied all the time.

"Because Vyvian was working for me," Bardu said. "I sent her to keep an eye on you. To make sure you remain loyal to the Sky Castle. Ryven, however, wanted you loyal only to him and his ambitions. He had Vyvian killed to keep her from influencing you in my favor. He and Üku hoped to kill Grazim to further isolate you. They wanted you alone, unsettled, and vulnerable so they could exploit your gifts."

"Did they kill Nyall?" she asked as a fist clenched in the pit of her stomach. By not knowing, she'd been able to tell herself he was still alive. Once Bardu answered her, there would be no room for comforting lies anymore.

"No, they did not kill Nyall." Kyrg Bardu smiled gently at her, and Kylee felt that fist in her stomach loosen. "He might've," she added, "had I not protected the boy. He is, in fact, at this very moment, under my protection."

"Where?" Kylee stood, anxious to go see him. "Take me there."

"Ah, that, my young eagle tamer, is where we have a complication." Kyrg Bardu straightened the pleats on her long robe, looked at the shine of her rings in the glimmering light of Ryven's luxurious sitting room. "Ryven was not entirely wrong about us. We do have demands to make of you . . . and, of course, if you meet them, no harm will come to your friend."

The fist in the pit of her stomach became a claw. She felt it, sharp and stabbing. There was heat in her lungs—that burning anger returning.

But there were no birds in this room, no windows, either. Kyrg Bardu had picked this place to be completely safe from the wrath of the sky that Kylee could call down. Still, Bardu tensed at seeing the change in her.

Good, thought Kylee. *Let her be nervous. She doesn't know that the eagle might have left for good. She doesn't know I failed it.*

"You're keeping him hostage?" she asked.

"That's an ugly word for it," Bardu said. "But yes. Fine. *Hostage*. The ransom, however, is what you wanted anyway. I want all the speakers of the Hollow Tongue out of the Sky Castle, marching on the Kartami to defend our kingdom. You still want to protect your brother, correct?"

Kylee didn't answer. Of course she did, but she wasn't going to tell this woman any more than she had to.

"Well, I know a bit more about what your brother is planning than that letter Ryven gave you explained." Bardu laughed to herself. "Don't be so shocked. There isn't much that goes on in my empire that I don't know about."

"What is he planning?" Kylee couldn't help leaning forward, couldn't help showing her interest. Ryven was right: Her love for Brysen made her easy to manipulate.

"He's convinced he can infiltrate the Kartami and assassinate their leader." Bardu shook her head. "So many dead assassins these days. I wonder if this war really needs another one."

"He . . . he can't . . . Why would he think . . . ?" Kylee couldn't believe it, but she knew that this time, the kyrg wasn't lying. Her brother was a dreamer. Her brother was reckless. Her brother was always striving to matter, because he didn't think that just being alive and gentle and kind was enough. He'd been treated like prey his whole life, and he saw only one other way to be: as a predator.

I have a plan and am going to end this war, he'd written.

"Oh, Brysen," she said aloud. "No."

Bardu smiled. She had Kylee where she wanted her, and she knew it.

"As you requested, you will march out with Birgund's army," Kyrg Bardu said. "And Grazim will be your shadow. She is there to watch you. If she reports back poorly on you, it will not go well for Nyall. If you lose her or she comes to harm—even if it isn't even your fault—it will not go well for Nyall. She will protect you, even from yourself, and you, in turn, will unleash fury upon our enemies." Kyrg Bardu stood and patted Kylee on the shoulder, a gesture perfectly calculated to be insulting. "Smile, child. You'll get to save your brother and your friend and win our war, just like you promised. Nothing has changed. You flirted with treason but made a better choice. No harm done."

"You keep using the word *choice*," Kylee said. "But you're giving me no choice."

"True," Kyrg Bardu agreed. "But why fight it? You're getting everything you want without the responsibility of choosing. Why do you think birds of prey submit to their tamers? It's liberating to match your will with something bigger than yourself. A falcon's higher purpose comes from its submission to the falconer, just like a subject to a ruler. Their wills are one. Think of me as your tamer and you as my hawk. Hunt for me and return when I call and you will live in wealth and comfort. This"—she gestured at Kyrg Ryven's luxurious sitting room—"could be your mews."

"And all I have to do is make the ghost eagle keep terrifying your enemies?"

"Exactly," Bardu said. "Clever as a crow, you are."

As she turned to leave the room, Kylee's hands gripped the plush armrests of her chair as hard as a kestrel crushing a rabbit's skull. She called out, "Kyrg Bardu?"

The kyrg stopped but did not turn around. "Yes, Kylee?"

"Remember that even the tamest hawks can slip their leashes and turn on the fist that feeds them. No bird of prey is ever truly tame. Don't forget that."

"I won't, Kylee," Kyrg Bardu said, and she could hear the sigh in the woman's voice. "I definitely won't forget that."

BORROWED WINGS

IT MIGHT AS WELL HAVE BEEN AN INVASION.

Before the war began, there were intruders to the blood birch forest, of course. Lost souls fleeing inauspicious lives, hunting parties seeking shortcuts, the occasional trapper on the doomed path of the ghost eagle. They could be repelled, eliminated, or, when necessary, recruited into the community of the Owl Mothers and their covey of loyal boys.

But now they came every day and every night, sometimes alone, sometimes in small and ragged groups, harried and weary and in desperate need. They fled through the Six Villages, either from fear of the coming siege or because they believed the villagers themselves were worse than any danger the mountains might offer.

Except they had no right to cross this territory. Not without permission.

None of them had permission.

None of them made it through.

This latest group had taken to resting in a small copse of birches, where they'd discovered the remains of a campfire that a previous group had been foolish enough to light. These people were not that foolish, and they sat in the dark, eating dried fruits and napping, not speaking much, lest they draw unwanted attention from above or from below. Four of them, with the tops of their heads shaved like vultures', walked among the refugees, demanding food and water. They were feared, and therefore no resistance was offered.

The vultures were bandits, and they thought their petty violence gave them power here.

They thought wrong.

Nothing happened on the mountain without the Owl Mothers' knowledge, and no one had power here but them. Even now, a small number of watchful Mothers had their eyes on the group, debating the best course of action in low whispers. Their matriarch, Üku, was off in the Sky Castle with her advisors, and while she was gone, Malarmina, the next eldest, had taken over her role.

"We can send the boys down to frighten them off, chase them back to the Villages?" one of the younger women suggested. Sala. She was a sentimental type; she loathed the necessary violence that came with holding territory.

"Arrows or owls," Malarmina offered. "That's what we're choosing between. Their deaths are already decided."

"I don't recall deciding," said Sala.

"Outsiders are like crows," Malarmina explained. "They're cunning, flocking and determined. One or two are not a danger to us, but they never come in just ones or twos. We let these live and we'll soon be overrun."

"Mem Malarmina, with respect: If we chase them off, they can spread the story. Their fear will travel with them, and we might prevent further incursions."

Some of the other Mothers murmured their agreement, and Malarmina could feel her influence slipping to the younger woman. Leadership in the Owl Mothers was by mutual consent, and the moment that consent was revoked, she would find herself no more than one voice among many. Respected, perhaps, but easy enough to ignore. She did not want to be ignored.

"The Kartami are laying siege to the Six Villages," she said. "The longer it goes on, the more people will flee this way. First by the hundreds, then by the thousands . . . and they will be pursued. The war will come to us, here, where the power of life and death should be ours alone. If we show even the slightest mercy, we will lose what we've held since before memory."

"What if we let them stay?" another young woman interjected. Üstella. She spoke as if she was just curious, just asking questions, when she knew full well that what she proposed was an upending of everything. "What if we *did* show mercy to all who needed it? What if our strength came from opening our arms to outsiders, rather than closing our fists?"

Change was spreading. It had been ever since those two young eyasses came through the forest to capture the ghost eagle. The new generation thought they knew better than the old, thought that because they knew no history, they were not bound by it.

But Malarmina knew: She knew what the Owl Mothers protected, why Üku had gone to the Sky Castle to secure their power, and why outsiders could not be allowed to come to them so freely. The Kartami invasion was not the greatest threat; it would be nothing compared to what would follow if the young were allowed to do what they always longed to do: overthrow the world.

It had happened before. The last time, before history itself, had nearly destroyed everyone. Only the Owl Mothers remembered, and only the Owl Mothers could prevent it from happening again. The moment might demand mercy, but the generations to come demanded they show none.

So Malarmina was about to explain—when Sala spoke first.

"We might allow a few to stay," Sala said. "To add to the covey?"

Agreement fluttered among the group on silent wings; Sala had put another feather in her leadership nest.

"How many of you, like Sala and Üstella, want to welcome all these invaders?" Malarmina asked, hoping to assign an opinion to the young woman that she did not actually share.

"No one wants to welcome all the invaders," Sala said, clearly disagreeing. "It is a question of tactics. If all who go this way vanish, then others might think this way is safe. But if they return to tell about us, they'll know they cannot flee in our direction safely. We will not take any in; we will send them away to stop others from coming."

Scuzz, thought Malarmina. The girl was barely old enough to bleed and she'd made a better argument than Malarmina, and the rest of the Mothers knew it. Malarmina had lost, and that, she feared, would be just the start of her losing. She was not yet ready to resign herself to a symbolic role in her community. She needed to reassert her power.

"Is that the consensus?" she asked, and the others con-firmed that it was. "Very well. Sala—do what you will."

"*Mejeej*," Sala said, a Hollow Tongue command Malarmina respected. It was an elegant choice and left just enough room to spare a terrified life or two.

"*Mejeej*," the other Mothers whispered, and the leaves of the blood birches stirred.

The fleeing Altari and the bandits who led them looked up with just enough time to gasp as a parliament of owls de-scended on them. The small nest of Uztari bandits tried to fight back, pulling knives and slashing at the nocturnal rap-tors. Their resistance was quickly cut short by the owls' counter-attack. The bandits were eviscerated. One of them, who the others called Corrnyn, dropped his weapon when he tried to grab an owl by the foot that had torn into his gut, but while he was distracted and screaming, one of the Altari drove his own knife into his spine.

Sala's wide-winged boar owl lighted on the head of that one. His lover, kneeling in front of them, watched with help-less terror as the big owl squeezed and squeezed and finally caved in the Altari's skull.

Behind the pale, white trunks of the blood birch trees, the boys of the covey watched, soft and still as snow owls, waiting for the bloodshed to finish so that they might scavenge the belongings of the dead and drag their corpses to the open rocks to be carried by vultures to the sky.

When there were only four survivors left—the owls were tearing at the organs of the rest—Sala stepped from her concealment and announced to those who lived, "You will go back now. Return to the Six Villages, and tell them this way is forbidden."

The fear-struck Altari, gasping, stood and looked at one another, then ran back the way they'd come, down the slopes, nearly falling. One hesitated, however—the one whose lover had his skull crushed after killing the vulture-headed bandit.

"Why?" they asked.

"Why that one in particular?" Sala grunted toward the body at the Altari's feet. "Only we are allowed to take life on the mountain. Only we are allowed to give it, too. Yours is given. Now go!"

The Altari looked one last time at the body on the ground, then ran. They'd surely reach the Villages by late morning and, hopefully, would frighten anyone else from attempting this route.

"I understand your choice of three of the women to live." Malarmina sidled up to Sala after the quiet had returned to their mountain forest. "But that one whose lover's skull you crushed. They might not have been female. Why spare them?"

Sala shared a wry smile. "It's a new war and a new world,

Malarmina. The old ideas are falling like last season's molted feathers. You should question your assumptions about what makes a mother. Whatever happens with Mem Üku in the Sky Castle, or with the Kartami on the plains, no one's future in Uztar will look like their past. Change, or be crushed by the change."

You condescending scuzzard, Malarmina thought. *Who are you to lecture me, when I've been defending the Owl Mothers since before you were born?*

"It is time, I think," said Sala, "to consider new leadership."

"You intend to challenge me?" Malarmina asked.

"I already have," Sala replied.

The other women waited in silence. The only sounds on the mountain were the tearing and chewing of the owls at their new-caught feast. From the shadows of the trees, the covey of pale boys peeked, watching the unfolding drama with curious eyes. Sala was popular among them, too, and Malarmina understood that she would find no allies there.

She looked down at her brown-and-gray pine owl. The bird was pulling at a bandit's tendon, tugging until it made a wet *snap*. She betrayed nothing to the presumptuous young woman opposite her, even as she answered. "We will meet this challenge when Üku and the others have returned and we know where we stand. Now is not the time for division among us."

"*Tha-loom*," Sala said, and her broad boar owl looked up from its own meal.

All the owls looked up, blood on their beaks, eyes wide. Their heads swiveled toward Malarmina. There would be no delay, she realized, for this challenge.

Sala intended to force her to step down. She was young and confident and as foolish as an ambitious youth could be. She spoke the Hollow Tongue like so many before her—with ambition—where Malarmina spoke with a sense of history, a respect for community, and for all that their community protected through the generations. History, truth, language: a culture older than Uztar itself.

"A flock will always repel a lone hunter," Malarmina explained. "*Faash!*"

Sala hadn't expected her own owl to join every other as they launched themselves at her head.

A snow owl swooped and cut Sala's forehead with its talons before gliding into the trees, vanishing between their thin white trunks. Malarmina's pine owl snatched a chunk of Sala's hair, but she saved the killing strike for Sala's own broad-chested boar owl. It hovered over the frightened girl, who looked suddenly so much younger than she had a moment ago.

"I am borrowing your owl to make it clear to you that you should not have chosen this time of crisis to divide our community," Malarmina said. She looked at the hovering owl, which was beating its silent wings. "This lesson, however, will be of no use to you. Perhaps it will be informative for the others." She sighed, then spoke: "*Avakhoo*."

In the instant before Sala's own beloved owl took her life, Malarmina answered the question on her face. She would not let the young woman die wondering what that final word meant, the one that ambitious people never seemed to understand.

"*Avakhoo* means community," she said. Then, without making any sound at all, the boar owl dropped with such speed and force that Sala's neck broke before her skull collapsed.

Malarmina put her index finger to her cheekbone and waited for the other Mothers and the boys of the covey to return the gesture. They respected the challenge and saw the truth of its just result. She owed no explanations or apologies and would be asked for none. The community was bigger than any one person, and it would, as it always had, endure.

BRYSEN

SORE MUST BE THE STORM

21

THE FULL FORCE OF THE KARTAMI ARMY ARRIVED IN A CLOUD OF DUST beneath a clear and empty sky. Their kites dotted the horizon from end to end as they rolled to a stop in front of the barricades along the river, but they made no move to attack. They dug in for a long siege.

The warriors couldn't break through the barricades, and the ragtag defenders of the Six Villages couldn't come out and face their attackers on the open field. The stalemate was the strategy: The Kartami had supply lines behind them. The Villages were completely cut off.

Kartami warriors wore no uniforms and came in every shape and size and color imaginable. They were bonded by no nation or history but by one fanatical urge: to empty the sky and erase all falconers from the world. On the day of the army's arrival, a lone vulture fell from the sky into the charred ruins of a feed store. The killing arrow was wrapped with a scroll: the Kartami's terms of peace.

Unconditional surrender. There were no offers of mercy and no requests for dialogue, but they did demand one severed hand, still gloved, from every falconer in the Six, to be piled in the battle pits of the Broken Jess. They wanted all the Jess's ale, too.

"Sick scuzzards," Nyck groaned. "They can take our hands, but they'll never take our spirits!"

"How do they even know where and what the Broken Jess is?" Brysen had wondered. He'd been answered with stony silence. The thought that someone would willingly spy for the Kartami chilled them all, but it was the only explanation: The Kartami had an informant on this side of the barricades.

Tamir attendants and Uztari soldiers had begun gathering groups of Altari, taking them away for questioning. The Altari rarely came back.

When desperate groups tried to make their way out of the Villages by the mountain pass, the kite warriors used them for long-range crossbow target practice. Their corpses littered the slopes above Brysen's house, and no vultures came to devour them.

Even if the people could make it out that way, the Owl Mothers would never let them cross their territory.

"The Owl Mothers think any more than a handful of outsiders passing through is an invasion," Jowyn explained. Four ragged Altari who had tried to escape that way confirmed it. They were the only survivors from their group.

It had been some days since the first glider attack, and the siege had set in. Prices for everything were soaring, and Tamir attendants were getting bolder in extorting bronze from everybody. The Altari who weren't rounded up as suspected spies were pressed into service, digging latrines, fetching water, hauling refuse, and patching the barricades. As the days passed, the Six Villagers felt increasingly trapped and distrustful while they waited and hoped for the army of Uztar—for Kylee—to save them.

Brysen did not want to wait, and he did not trust himself to hope.

He stood in the blackened ruins that were once his hawk mews and held Shara perched on his fist, unhooded.

Two walls still stood, though they were so weak, he could have poked a finger through them, but they were enough for the privacy he and Jowyn needed to train away from his mother's prying eyes. Ever since he'd called Shara back to life, his mother had been impossible to be around. She cursed his beloved bird and spoke ominous warnings at

Brysen, like, "You've denied the sky a death it dealt, and now it will hunt for you" and "You speak with pride what should give you shame; the birds of prey are not yours to name."

The rhyming ones were the worst. He wondered if she lay awake at night thinking of new verses to inflict on him in the morning.

"I wonder what rhymes with *fire mole?*" Jowyn mused, holding the tiny mole he'd caught, cupped in his pale hands. Brysen noticed the nicks and cuts on the boy's fingers, the wear and tear everyone had but to which Jowyn had until lately been immune. The sap from the blood birch forest was truly wearing off, and his body was as vulnerable now as anyone else's. Maybe he'd always be unnaturally white, but the bruises and scabs that he quietly bore were the most beautiful things Brysen had ever seen. Every one of them told Brysen that Jowyn was here to stay.

"This is just to figure out what we can do," Brysen said. "We don't need to write odes about it."

"People would be happier if they wrote odes about the little things that make them smile," Jowyn said, then changed to a singsongy lilt.

"Caught mole in the ashes, wishing it were free,
If only the mole could see what I could see.

A bird on the fist, ready for the hunt,

Sometimes it's a curse, getting what you want."

With that, he set the mole down, and it scurried across the charred floor, racing for a burrow beneath the burned beams. Shara's eyes tracked the little mole, and Brysen, chasing away the smile Jowyn's song had given him, focused on the one word in the Hollow Tongue he knew, the one word he'd heard his sister say a few times to deadly effect.

"*Shyehnaah!*" he said. Shara, though she watched the mole run with a predator's eyes, sat on the fist like a tame parakeet, didn't even so much as spread her wings. He raised his fist to toss her the way he would without the use of the Hollow Tongue. "Utch!" he tried, but she gripped his fist harder and sat.

"Maybe she's not hungry," Jowyn suggested.

"That's not how it's supposed to work," Brysen said. "The command should overrule her own appetites, right? Otherwise, what good is a command?"

"I thought a falconer couldn't make a bird do anything it didn't want to," Jowyn said. "Just train it to do what it wants for your sake."

"But this is supposed to make me better than other falconers . . ." Brysen was at a loss. He'd brought Shara back from the dead with a word, and now he couldn't even make her hunt a mole.

The lucky fire mole vanished into the soot.

Shara's pupils, ringed in red like eclipsed suns, darted from Jowyn to the sky to Brysen to the ground, seeing everything faster and in more detail than he could imagine. Brysen wondered what it must be like, to see so much and so far. Hawks were nervous creatures, and goshawks more than most. Was it their powerful vision that made them that way? The more they saw, the more they realized there was to fear.

"It's okay," he cooed at Shara. "Let's try something simpler." He looked at Jowyn. "Hold your fist up."

Jowyn held up his fist, and Brysen raised Shara toward him. "*Shyehnaah!*" he said, hoping the bird would fly from his fist to Jowyn's. She didn't. She turned her head and started preening her neck feathers.

"She's even *less* well trained than before," Brysen groaned, staring at her. He loved this little bird so much that he never wanted any harm to befall her ever again. He also, at that moment, wanted to grab her tiny body and throttle it into pudding. "I don't get it."

"Maybe she no longer wants to kill," Jowyn suggested, resting his hand on the edge of the burned doorframe as if there were still a doorway there.

"A hawk that won't kill isn't a hawk," Brysen said.

Jowyn cleared his throat. "Maybe this isn't what she came back for."

"She didn't *come back*," Brysen noted. "I brought her back."

"But you don't know why or how."

"I don't need to," he snapped, wishing Jowyn weren't always questioning everything. Brysen liked the sound of the boy's voice, except sometimes it drove him mad, the way it turned up at the end, twisting like a hook to fish answers from Brysen's mouth. He wanted nothing more than to spend all afternoon chatting and training with Jowyn. He also, at that moment, wanted to grab Jowyn by the shoulders and throttle him into pudding, too.

His temper was acting up, like it did when he was tired or hungry or nervous. He was, right then, all three, but so was everyone else in the Six Villages. They were under siege, and being rested, fed, and calm were luxuries no one had.

"I *need* to figure out what she can do if she's going to help me kill their leader."

"If she won't kill a mole, I don't think she'll kill a warlord," Jowyn noted. "Maybe she's trying to tell you not to do it, either."

"A warrior who won't kill isn't a warrior."

"Maybe you aren't supposed to *be* a warrior," Jowyn answered. "Maybe your breeze blows in another direction. Think about it. You survived a father who wanted you dead most of your life. You survived capturing the ghost eagle, and fighting off Goryn Tamir, and two attempts to kidnap you, *and* the near death of your bird."

"Yeah," Brysen scoffed. "It's an impressive story of me not being dead. You can write odes about it."

"Surviving is no small thing," Jowyn said, then recited:

"The world's a beating, battered heart,
It bleeds through every land.
Rare the gentle healer's art,
Rare the soothing hand."

"You learn that in the blood birch forest?" Brysen asked.

"I wrote that last night when I couldn't sleep," he said. "I wrote it for you. I think you're meant to bring life to this world, Brysen, not death."

On his glove, Shara shifted from foot to foot, and Brysen rested his thumb over her toes to keep her still. He wondered why Jowyn stayed up at night thinking of these things to say to him. They were almost more annoying than his mother's curses. They didn't make him angry—they made him doubt, and he didn't really need help to do that.

"I can save a lot of lives if I end this war," he told Jowyn. "One killing to prevent thousands? I'm not great at math, but it's obvious to me: I have to do it." He didn't want to argue with Jowyn anymore. He wanted to stride the three steps between them, wrap his arms around the pale boy who had such misguided faith in him, and kiss until the war was over. He also wanted to shove Jowyn away and tell him to leave, tell him to stop looking up with that expression, like hope and disappointment all in one. He didn't want to care what Jowyn thought of him. He wanted nothing more than for Jowyn to think well of him.

But he had responsibility now. The Hollow Tongue had finally come to him, and he couldn't squander his chance. Lazy days full of kissing were for boys whose breezes blew fairer than his.

Instead of kissing or shoving or shouting, he planted his feet where they were and told Jowyn, "Your ma made arrangements with the battle boys to sneak me to the other side of the barricades through a smugglers' tunnel. I'm going tonight. You want to help me keep working, or you want to recite more poems about me?"

"Can't I do both?" Jowyn smiled, and Brysen found he couldn't remember anything that had annoyed him about Jowyn at all.

"Catch me another mole while you compose your next verse?" Brysen suggested, and Jowyn hopped off to do Brysen's bidding.

Four moles and most of the sun's downward slide later, Jowyn's pale face, hands, arms, and neck were smeared with soot and Brysen's throat was hoarse from trying the same word over and over in different tones. In that time, Jowyn had rhymed *carrion* with *barbarian* and *vows* with *house* and *arouse* in a verse that Brysen might've thought was flirty if it hadn't also been about dismembering fire moles.

In all that time, Shara hadn't flown at a single mole, though she had watched a butterfly in perfect stillness for so long that Brysen eventually had to set her down and leash her to a perch so he could go pee. She was still staring at the butterfly when he came back.

Now Jowyn had sat down on a fallen beam and was poking at the mews' ashes with a stick. He had a thick black smear of soot on his left cheek, and Brysen's mouth went dry as he wondered what soot and sweat tasted like. Shara, sitting on his glove, let out a small "prrrpt" and bobbed her head.

Now is not *the time*, he thought with a glance down the mountain, over the Villages and the barricades along the river, to the mass of the Kartami army, spread like a smothering quilt over the flame-red sunset plain. The day was circling down, and he'd made no progress with Shara.

"You ever stop to wonder why my ma's being so helpful?" Jowyn looked up at him. "She's got a lot of killers working for her. Why send someone who's never killed anyone before? Why send you?"

"She's seen me in the battle pits?" Brysen suggested. "She knows I'm a good fighter."

Jowyn raised an eyebrow.

"Fine," Brysen said. "Probably because she hates me and doesn't care if I die doing this. But if I succeed, she can take credit. And, I think, also because she knows you don't want me to do it. She's showing you that she's tamed me more than you have."

"I'm not trying to tame you," Jowyn said quietly. "That's not how I am."

Brysen looked down at him like a falcon who'd missed a dive at its prey. He had meant to explain Mama Tamir, not insult Jowyn. He should've known better than to talk about Jowyn's mother flippantly. Brysen's scars from his childhood were visible all over his body, but Jowyn's scars weren't so obvious. You wouldn't walk over a glacier without testing your steps for hidden pitfalls below the ice, and talking to someone you cared about was the same. You had to step carefully so you didn't break through the softest places. Brysen was used to being the one people talked gently around, avoiding certain topics to spare his feelings. He'd forgotten he wasn't the only one with a past.

"Jo, I didn't mean you're like her," he said.

Jowyn jabbed his stick at the ground. "I know," he said, and changed the subject, gesturing with his head toward the front lines of the siege. "So what happens after you cross the barricades?"

Brysen shrugged, performing a lack of concern where none existed. "I surrender."

"That's it?" The stick stuck in the dirt, and Jowyn wiped his hands on his pants, looked up, wide-eyed, at Brysen. "You just walk into the enemy camp and surrender?"

"Basically," Brysen said. "I tell them I know they've been looking for me and that I want to join them."

Jowyn blew out his cheeks. "Join them?"

Brysen nodded. "They tried to kidnap me, not kill me, which means they think I'm valuable, right? It's probably because of my sister that they want me for a hostage. So I'll tell them I'm even more valuable as an ally. How much would it mess with her head if I wasn't just their prisoner, but a soldier in their army?"

"Flaming sky, Bry, that's twisted."

"So's war," Brysen replied.

Jowyn nodded, considering the plan, which Brysen appreciated. He didn't start talking about how buzzard-brained the idea was even though, in reality, a buzzard probably made better plans than Brysen's. But it was the only one he could come up with. He had no idea if it would work or if they would just tie him up and hood him the moment he was caught, but he didn't see much other choice. If he stayed, Mama Tamir would probably punish him, his mother, and Jowyn before the siege killed them all anyway. A buzzard-brained plan of his own was better than waiting around to be the victim of someone else's.

After a pause long enough that a flock of gulls could've flown through it, Jowyn stood up and wiped his forehead with the back of his arm, smearing even more soot. "Did you notice how the Kartami fight in pairs?"

"Yeah," Brysen answered, and he felt Shara squeeze his fingers in his glove before he felt his own heartbeat squeezing in his chest. He thought he knew what Jowyn was about to say. He didn't dare hope at what Jowyn was about to say.

"You know I'm going with you wherever you go, right?" Jowyn announced.

"You don't have to," Brysen answered a little too quickly, trying to sound nonchalant even though his body felt like a spreading wing, his heart rising to endless sky. He was grateful right then that he had a rib cage to hold it in. He wanted Jowyn with him wherever he went; he felt, with Jowyn there, he could dare impossible things.

Or maybe he was just a fool for the way Jowyn's eyelashes curled or how two of his lower teeth were crooked or how he bit his lip while he thought about what to say. Brysen didn't dare look to see if he was biting his lip now.

"I'm going because I want to," Jowyn told him, "not

because I have to. You're my friend, and if I can't talk you out of it, then I'm getting into it."

"It'll be dangerous," Brysen said, which he knew was a dumb thing to say. Obviously it would be dangerous. Everything was dangerous right now, but saying the dumb obvious thing kept him from saying the dumb honest thing, which was *I want to tackle you right here in the ruins of my house and roll in the soot with you until our bodies are black as earth and night and the sky itself can't even see us anymore.*

"It'd be more dangerous here without you around," Jowyn said. "Who knows what kind of trouble I could get into?"

That smile again. How was it that Brysen could stand here, contemplating a deadly mission into the camp of a murderous army, and still be circling his own heart like a falcon with no fist to land on?

He was saved from his spiraling thoughts by the overloud shouts of Nyck and the battle boys. They were trudging up the slope to his burned plot of land with a pack Mama Tamir had filled for him.

"Delivery for the great hunter of men!" Nyck called. "Come and get it. I am *not* your pack animal."

"You sure you still want to come?" Brysen asked Jowyn one more time. "Anything Nyck thinks is a good idea is pretty suspect."

"I'm as sure as starlings," Jowyn answered, which didn't

mean much of anything to Brysen—no one had any idea why starlings flew the way they did. But Brysen didn't really care, because Jowyn smiled when he said it. And if Brysen was going to march into the Kartami's talons, he liked the idea of that smile by his side.

Nyck and the battle boys were looking around the yard, at the burned house and mews, at the tent his mother had set up for herself where her bedroom used to be, at the open-air pallets Brysen and Jowyn had been sleeping on since the fire. Nyck cocked his head, noticing that the pallets were pretty close together. Brysen just shook his head, a vague *no* that also could have been a *not yet*.

"You taking Shara with you?" Nyck asked. "Kartami aren't likely to trust you if you show up with a raptor."

"They aren't likely to trust me no matter what," Brysen said.

"And you're taking this strange bird with you, too?" Nyck waved a hand at Jowyn.

"Yes," Brysen said, keeping his voice flat. His other friends, he noticed, had *not* offered to join him. The battle boys were loyal but only to a point. Now that the siege had begun, they controlled all the ale in town, and the prices had risen higher than the mountain peaks. They were rich for the first time in all their lives, and not a one of them would give that up to march into hell.

"Whatever you say." Nyck shrugged, but his hand fidgeted with the hem of his tunic. "Whole thing makes as much sense to me as flightless birds . . ." His voice cracked and he looked anywhere but at Brysen. "But I know better than to get between you and a quest. You always were unstoppable."

"Thanks, Nyck," Brysen said.

"Hey, that wasn't a compliment." Nyck wiped a tear out of his eye before it rolled down his cheek. The battle boy rule was that it didn't count as crying if it didn't roll. "And you!" Nyck pointed at Jowyn. "You let this kid get hurt . . . or you hurt him in *any way*, I'll cut parts off of you I haven't even thought of yet."

"I'll do my best," Jowyn said.

"No," Nyck corrected him. "Do better."

Jowyn nodded. That kind of a threat was as close to saying "I love you" as a battle boy could get. Brysen hugged his friend, then looked for his mother, who did not come out from her tent to say good-bye. He wanted to be mad at her but found he had no anger in him. As frustrated as he got with his disobedient hawk, he couldn't imagine what his mother felt about her blasphemous, defiant, and reckless son. If he were her, he wasn't sure he'd say good-bye, either. Baby birds fly from the nest all the time without their mamas crying about it. He wouldn't expect more from her than he did from the sky.

"No time to lose," Fentyr said. "Gotta go."

Brysen took the pack from Nyck and heaved it on, then hooded Shara to follow Fentyr and the others back down into the Villages. As he and Jowyn followed them down the slope, Brysen looked back once more, but the tent and the ruined house were as quiet and still as if no one lived there.

In town, they slipped between the two round buildings that had been storage for Dupuy's Equipery. They entered a feed store that now gaped open, looted, empty, and half-charred to ash. Shara's head swiveled side to side, as if she could see from beneath her heavy hood or like she sensed the change in the air, the closeness of the looted shop.

"This was Krystoff's?" Brysen noted.

"Krystoff died in that first attack," Fentyr said with a shrug.

He led them to the back room, a small cubby with a hearth and a mat for the apprentice, Zyl. "Dead too," Fentyr noted. Under a moldy blanket in the corner, Fentyr revealed a small door. "This goes to a tunnel. When you get to the other end, you're on the other side of the barricades," he said. "It's a shorter distance than you think. Don't go until you hear our signal."

"Which is?" Jowyn asked.

This time Brysen and Fentyr grinned at each other, and Brysen answered for his old friends. "We'll know it."

"See you on the wind, brother." Fentyr gave him the winged salute across his chest and was gone. When Brysen and Jowyn were alone again, waiting, Brysen double-checked Shara's tether to his glove, then made sure her hood was secure. He felt a pang of doubt, wondered if maybe he was wrong to bring her, if maybe he should've left her with Nyck instead of bringing her into the camp of a thousand bird killers.

He and Jowyn crouched by the little door in silence as time melted away between them. The sky outside dimmed to red and gold and orange, then darkened to blue-black and purple.

"How will we know the signal?" Jowyn finally asked. "What are they going to do?"

"I think," Brysen said, "they're going to set the sky on fire."

22

THE SIX VILLAGES AT NIGHT WERE DARK BEHIND THE BARRICADES. NO
one wanted to give Kartami archers a target. Whenever a kite
or a glider got high enough to shoot over the wall, guards on
the barricades launched their falcons to chase them down.
Sometimes the falcons came back, sometimes not.

When a sortie of gliders rose up, people outdoors scurried
for cover. The Altari did their best to stay hidden beneath
tents or behind the burned-out walls of buildings. Nowhere
in the Villages was really safe, though, and the Kartami sometimes got off a flaming arrowhead, which sent Uztari bucket
brigades to douse the flames and draw arrow fire themselves.

No vultures came to eat the bodies. The siege denied the dead even their final flights.

Brysen wondered if anyone was keeping a tally of how many birds the Villages had lost, how many they still might have. He wondered if the Kartami spies were keeping that tally, too. Every bird the Six had was another chance at holding the line; every bird they lost was another heartbeat closer to their defenses failing. Never before had the fate of the Six Villages been so directly tied to the fate of their birds.

Brysen hoped to change that.

He and Jowyn waited in the close dark, leaning back against the little door, listening to these sudden bursts of activity, waiting for the signal, while Shara rested on a small folding perch on the ground beside them. They didn't speak much, but their forearms were touching, and sometimes Jowyn would move his knee to the side to bump Brysen's, who would then bump back. They played this knee-knocking game to pass the time until Jowyn threw a friendly elbow into the mix, jabbing Brysen in the ribs. Brysen tried to catch his arm but missed and found he'd put his hand on Jowyn's chest. Jowyn caught it and just held it there, let Brysen feel his heart thumping.

"Can you tell I'm nervous?" Jowyn asked.

"What's to be nervous about?" Brysen tried a joke but lacked Jowyn's skill at lighting a smile like a candle flame. His voice came out weak. The heartbeat below his palm was steady.

"You nervous?" Jowyn asked.

Brysen pulled his hand away. Yeah, he *was* nervous.

"What about what Nyck said, about bringing Shara with you?" Jowyn wondered. "Being responsible for her in their camp won't be easy."

"I can handle it." He cleared his throat. "I've always taken care of her before."

Jowyn nodded. "You don't have to end the war alone, you know?"

Brysen didn't want to hear Jowyn's arguments again, didn't want to be talked out of anything. "You said you wanted to come, but if you're just going to explain to me the whole time why I shouldn't—"

"No, Bry, I meant—" Jowyn sat up a little straighter, lifted his shirt, and Brysen tensed. This was *so* not the time for this kind of thing . . . but some people calmed their nerves in un-expected ways and . . . well . . . was this what Brysen wanted? His throat crackled like desert sand, but Jowyn just pointed at the tattoo that ran up his left side. He wasn't mak-ing an offer. He was telling a story.

"This shows the time an Uztari trapping party came to the blood birch forest to bag some owls. The Owl Mothers brought the covey of boys along to help defend the birds from 'defilement,' they called it. They warned the trappers to leave, but the trappers were being paid per owl they caught, and they had a quota to fill, to make sure they didn't lose bronze on the expedition. So they refused to go. The Owl Mothers killed them all, except one. He was a former attendant of my mother's, and I recognized him. I was still young then, and the sap hadn't fully transformed me, so he recognized me, too. And when they let him go to spread the word that any attempt to trap in their territory would be met with death, I followed him.

"I stalked him for two days, and when I finally jumped him, he used my name. He told me my ma would want to know I was still alive. They'd had a funeral. I told him he couldn't tell anyone. He promised he wouldn't . . . but I didn't trust him. I was no more than nine ice-winds old, but that was old enough to stab him in the neck. He bled out in front of me." Jowyn stared at the dark, his eyes seeing a scene that had happened a long time ago. The wounds you suffer when you're young stick with you forever, but so, too, do the wounds you make.

"The Owl Mothers found me with his dead body, told me that killing was forbidden on their mountain, that only those who carry life can take it. Not even all of *them* are allowed to kill. They forgave me, but they started this tattoo then. They wanted me to know that this boy's death was a part of my story now and always would be. That's why they give us the tattoos. Our stories are scars that we make beautiful. Just like when I saved your life. You are part of my story now and always will be." He touched one of his rougher and newer tattoos, one he'd gotten in the Villages. It showed two figures in silhouette in front of a giant moon. One held a hawk on the fist. The other held the first figure tight. It was the most literal of all Jowyn's tattoos, and Brysen's favorite.

Jowyn scratched his scalp, more of a nervous tic than an actual itch. "This is just to say I've killed before. It's not as easy as a falcon and a hare. We're not predators. When we kill, it echoes like thunder, in the world and in ourselves."

"I know that," Brysen said, although he didn't really. He'd never killed anyone.

"I don't *want* you to know that," Jowyn said. "I guess I'm just saying I've done it before and I can do it again if I have to."

"But I don't want you to kill for me," Brysen said. "Just be-cause we're fr"—he stumbled over the word—"*friends* doesn't mean you have to protect me like that. I can do this for my-self. I'm not looking for a hero to rescue me."

Jowyn finally looked at him. "I'm not trying to take away your—"

Just then, a bang like close thunder shook the building. Shara's feet clenched her perch and she opened her wings in fright. Shouts and cries rained from the barricades.

"That's it!" Brysen said, nudging the hawk onto his fist and kicking open the small door. "The signal!"

Jowyn went first, to make sure the way was clear, and Brysen followed awkwardly, stooped in the low space, carrying the bird. Dust fell from the commotion overhead, and as they scurried on a downward slope through the tunnel, the air grew thick and heavy and cold. The walls dripped. They were under the river and could hear it overhead. Brysen's stomach felt tight as he imagined a collapse, being buried alive and drowned, so far from the sky that his soul would never find its way up again. When he finally stepped out into the night air, he felt like throwing up and had to squat with his head between his knees.

They were on the open plain on the other side of the river, the wrong side of the barricades, with nothing but night air to shield them. Off to the right, the barricades rose along the riverbank——great heaps of petrified wood, boulders and wood scraps, broken carts and wagons, scrounged metal thrust out with sharpened points. And on top of it all, silhouetted by the light from a dozen torches, stood Nyck, laughing and cursing down at the lethal line of kites and barrows across the river from him. The ruins of a smoldering kite lay at the foot of the barricades, and a charred figure was still strapped inside.

"Beg the dirt for mercy!" Nyck yelled, and his voice

carried as clear as if he'd been an arm's length away. "You'll get none from us!"

He stood behind an upturned caravan wheel set atop a heap of timbers that made a parapet on the barricades. The battle boys scurried up beside him, towering over the siege plains like a nest of eagles in their eyrie, and at Nyck's high-pitched caw, they catapulted another of their precious kegs of hoarded liquor toward the heart of the Kartami lines, unstoppered, spraying the drink behind it. One keg, two kegs, then three and four— the whole, vast wealth of the battle boys, hurtling into the night.

At the same time, Nyck shouted "Utch!" and the boys loosed their hawks—the bright little kestrel, the heavy buzzards, the dart-fast falcons. Each bird carried a stick in its beak with a split cut into the end, and in those splits were burning strips of tree bark. As the birds flew with their burning sticks, each spark that fell caught the liquor spraying from the still-soaring casks, igniting in the air. Fire streaked up to the kegs, moving faster than the drink could drain, sliding like a thief through the kegs' stopper holes.

BOOM!

The casks exploded in midair. The birds above dodged the flames.

BOOM! BOOM! BOOM!

Fire poured on the Kartami army below.

"To air!" the Kartami shouted as arrows launched for the circling birds with their burning sticks, trying to knock them down before the next volley of barrels flew.

"To drink!" Nyck shouted with a roar, and launched three more barrels.

"Run!" Brysen urged Jowyn. Every Kartami eye was on the flame-streaked night, but it would only take one of them to look Brysen's way and cut off their approach before they had a chance to surrender.

They ran farther, to the flank of the Kartami army, and Brysen dared a glance back, then stopped at what he saw. Kartami kites had risen already, warriors strapped in and flinging spears at the barricades. The barrow tenders below held the kites steady and sent more spears up the lines that bound the warriors to the earth below.

A spear cut through Fentyr's hawk and nicked the wing of Nyck's dashing kestrel before it could get back to him. His raised fist hung in the air, clenched, like he'd held his own heart up above his head only to find his hand empty.

How many birds of prey did the Six Villages have now? How much longer could they fight off a siege from the air when their birds were cut down one by one, and how many was this assault sacrificing, all so Brysen could enact his reckless plan?

He looked at Shara, so newly returned to him, and he

looked at Nyck, whose head swiveled now, fist still up, searching for where his injured bird could have fallen. His whistle for her even carried across the din, so desperate and true. But the bird had fallen somewhere in the dark on the wrong side of the barricades and would not be coming back to him. His fist dropped to his side and his shoulders slumped. He stood like a mourner's crow on the plinth of a monument, frozen in grief even in the heat of battle.

Brysen knew what Nyck was going through and knew, too, that he could help. He was scared to part with Shara, but she had no place coming to the Kartami camp. They'd surely kill her, and her presence on his fist wouldn't look good for Brysen. It had been selfish to think he should bring her. It would be a kindness now to let her go.

He didn't want to. She'd only just come back to him. He slipped her hood from her head.

Her wide eyes darted to the sky. The streaks of fire against the starlight shone in miniature across her wide pupils.

"I know it's scary," he said to her, more for himself than for any understanding the bird could have. "But this isn't somewhere you can go with me . . . and they need you."

He held up his fist. "Sorry, friend," he whispered, and tossed her up, calling "Utch!"

She flew from him as if for a hunt, and he dropped his hand and pulled off the falconer's glove, stuffing it into his belt. She circled back in the dark, afraid of all the noise and light in the sky, looking for the fist she knew so well, the place that meant safety and food and comfort, for the fist that was her home.

She screeched and tried to land on Brysen, but he waved her off. She circled once more and tried again, and again he waved her off, toward the barricades. "Go!" he yelled.

She flapped her wings and rose, and Nyck in the dark distance looked out in her direction. Birds of prey remember faces, and Shara knew Nyck as well as she knew anyone who wasn't Brysen. He hoped Nyck could see what was happening now. Brysen waited with bated breath until Nyck raised up his fist again. Shara saw it but circled back over Brysen one more time. As she swooped in to where his fist should have been once more, Brysen found his voice, in fear and love for her, and spoke:

"*Li-li!*"

She turned with all the speed of a hunter after prey and flapped straight and fast over the siege, dodging flame and arrow alike, to settle perfectly on Nyck's fist. He startled at her sudden landing, her obedient perch.

"What did you just say?" Jowyn asked, just as startled as Nyck was at the sudden change in Shara's flight.

"I don't know," Brysen said, too stunned himself to even wipe the tears from his cheeks. Like the first time he ever remembered being hit as a child, he understood the pain but couldn't understand its cause. Why did she only obey him now, in the moment he was losing her? What kind of stupid power did he have?

"Keep her safe," he whispered into the dark, and knew that she would be taken care of until they met again. If Nyck needed an ally in his defense of home, he'd find no better bird than Shara.

"So what now?" Jowyn asked. They'd ducked behind a berm that the invaders had piled high in defense of an attack from the Six Villagers' side, whispering to each other in case sentries waited on the other side of the great heaping mound of dirt.

"We find the nearest sentry and surrender," Brysen replied. "If your ma was telling the truth and they've been trying to abduct me, they'll know who I am and be pretty glad to see us, right?"

Jowyn nodded. "The truth is a big 'if' when it comes to my ma. She might've just been trying to get you to walk to your death."

"No risk, no reward." Brysen grinned, playing as nonchalant as he could, trying to pretend he hadn't just sent a piece of his heart flying on feathery wings to someone else's fist.

"And how will you explain me?" Jowyn wondered.

"Easy," Brysen said. "You're my valet."

"You think they'll buy that?" Jowyn gestured at himself. Even with the long tunic on, it was obvious he was too pale, and the tattoos poked out above the collar and at the cuff on his left wrist.

"I'll charm them. People do find me irresistible."

Jowyn shook his head. "Since when?"

"I figure, starting now. I plan to be irresistible starting now."

Jowyn's smile could have set the sky on fire a second time. "Great, we're all set then." He rested his hand against the small of Brysen's back. Brysen felt wings sprout up his spine where those fingers touched him, felt every bone in his body soar, though in truth, not one part of him moved. Not one part of him dared.

Brysen couldn't help but think they were both stalling. Planning a thing and doing it were very different birds, and he found he liked perching with this wild plan a little longer before seeing it fly.

"Ready then?" Jowyn asked.

"Not just yet." Brysen took a deep breath.

He exhaled.

"Ready," he answered, and made his way on his belly up the steep dirt berm and into the vast Kartami lines. He was, obviously, far from ready. He was scared, and he was grieving, and he was falling in love at the worst possible time, but he was determined to do this one thing right. He was determined to kill a warlord.

23

THE WARRIORS WHO FOUND THEM FIRST WERE NOT WHAT HE HAD expected. They were not the bloodthirsty monsters from the stories the Altari told when they arrived in the Six Villages, and they were not the ferocious predators prowling the sky on gliders who had set his home ablaze.

They were two girls, about Brysen and Jowyn's age, and they were caught by surprise when the two boys walked up.

"Stop!" one of them yelled, popping to her feet. She'd been giving the other girl a foot massage. That one frantically tried to pull her boot back on one-handed while drawing her thin rapier blade. The movement nearly caused her to topple over and fall out of the back of the war barrow in which they'd been lounging. "Uztari?" she demanded.

Brysen held his palms open and facing the sky to show his fists were empty. He'd moved his black-talon blade around to the back of his belt. He didn't want to be caught hiding it, but he also didn't want it to be the first thing his captors saw. "We're of no people," he said, and hoped his wild gray hair and Jowyn's near colorlessness would make them look the part. "But you have been looking for us."

"Who—uh—who are you?" one of the girls asked. She had short dark hair and was slight—probably the one who went up the lines and strapped herself into the kite for battle. The other girl was taller, more powerfully built, with skin the color of Brysen's and a blade curved like his. She might've been Uztari once, but now she drove a Kartami war barrow, which meant she'd renounced falconry and proved her worth to the murderous horde. He hoped that augured well for his own chances.

"My name is Brysen, and I was born in the Six Villages to a worthless falcon trapper, as cruel as he was stupid, deserving of the death the sky gave him." Brysen found that the truth was the best plumage for a lie, so, just as he'd imped flight feathers onto Shara's broken wing, he now imped as much truth as he could onto the wings of his lie. "I am brother to a Hollow Tongued sister, who left me here alone while she tames the ghost eagle for the Sky Castle, chasing glory and power though I struggle to survive. I've lost my hawk and had my heart broken, been attacked and beaten and betrayed, and I come here now, with my . . ." He glanced at Jowyn. *Valet* was a stupid lie, and after seeing the pair of warriors side by side in front of him, both nervous and keen, he decided this truth, too, would serve him better. ". . . dearest friend to renounce my former ways and pledge myself to the Kartami, the shards of the faithful, who will empty the sky that has only brought me pain. We want to help."

At that, he dropped to his knees and looked at the dirt, in the best imitation he could do of his mother's gestures. The Kartami leaders had all been Altari once, even though they had renounced that faith, and he thought maybe the gesture would still be appreciated. Jowyn followed his lead and knelt beside him.

Brysen stole a glance, as the girls looked at each other. He recognized that glance. Anyone who'd ever been in love for long enough developed invisible talk that bound their minds to each other without the need for words, and Brysen understood that these two—frightened as they were of their first war and maybe of their first real duties guarding this one spot—*wanted* to believe Brysen.

He took Jowyn's hand in his. The other boy tensed and nearly pulled away but let Brysen interlace their fingers and raise their linked hands to the girls. "Please," he said. "Accept us in your ranks."

The larger girl's face twitched a tiny bit, and the smaller girl nodded. "It's not up to us, Brysen from the Six Villages. You need to see Anon."

Jowyn squeezed Brysen's hand before he let go, and they stood. "Thank you," he said. "We will see him with our hearts as open as a windless plain."

Brysen was sure he saw the bigger girl smile a little as she turned to lead them into the heart of the Kartami camp. She didn't even bother to check him for weapons. Maybe she was overeager and glad to have caught a valuable prisoner or was happy to see another Uztari pledging himself, or perhaps she liked the strange pair he and Jowyn made. Or maybe she was just happy she didn't have to fight anyone that night.

As she guided them through the camp, Brysen felt a lightness in his step. It was more than he could have imagined he'd feel walking through an army of thousands, an army that had cut a swath of bloody murder from ground to sky across the plateau and would happily spill the blood of everyone he'd ever loved. These weren't monsters or nightmares made into flesh. They were people, and they could be beaten, and they could be afraid, and they could also be killed.

So far, anyway, Brysen's half-considered plan was going perfectly. He even felt a little proud of himself.

Until they were brought into the Kartami leader's tent. He stood from behind a campaign table, where he'd been studying what looked like detailed maps of the Six Villages and surrounding mountains. He'd had good spies. Even with the brief glance Brysen got, he recognized the climbing paths and herders' passes that would make the most likely escape routes for Six Villagers if the barricades fell.

The man introduced himself as Anon, dismissed the girls, and ordered an older woman named Launa to disarm Brysen, tie him and Jowyn up, and put a sword against the throbbing artery in Jowyn's neck.

Cold metal had a way of breaking perfect plans.

"After all we did to try to catch you . . ." The Kartami leader gazed down at him. "I must wonder whether it's a blessing or a curse that made you come to me of your own free will. And to bring your lover as a hostage?"

"We're not—" Brysen started, then stopped himself. He didn't need to give Anon more information than necessary. Let him think whatever he wanted. He and Jowyn certainly weren't "lovers." Even the word made Brysen uncomfortable, like their whole complicated relationship could be reduced to one word.

Anon smiled and leaned back on the table. He was an

imposing person, as big as—if not bigger than—the stories described him. His arms were thicker than Brysen's thighs, his neck was as thick as his arms, and his long hair hung down to a chest that was almost as wide across as Brysen and Jowyn side by side. He wore no shirt, and the taut skin over his muscles was nicked with the scars and scabs and scratches of a constant warrior. He was not some back-of-the-line commander like the kyrgs in the sky castle. His fingers were rough and calloused and stained with the blood of his enemies.

And yet the eyes looking down at Jowyn and Brysen were kind. He didn't stare at them like a hawk, filled with hunger, but like a sun rising red over the mountains—distant, indifferent, but promising warmth.

"So you're saying you're not lovers?" The skin around Anon's eyes wrinkled with his grin. "Or you're not hostages?"

"Both," Brysen said. "Er . . . neither, I mean." His confidence was faltering under the oddly benign gaze of a warlord.

"Why have you surrendered to me tonight, Brysen and Jowyn?" he asked them, signaling that he knew quite well who they were. "An exile from the Owl Mothers and the brother of the great commander of the dreaded ghost eagle. To *what* do I owe the honor of holding you at my mercy?"

"We want to join you," Brysen said. Anon raised an eyebrow. "You know who we are, so you know our story, I guess," he said. "Life in Uztar has brought us nothing but pain." He steeled himself to tell all his most painful memories in order to buy the trust of this mass murderer. He'd show his scars and talk about his father lighting him on fire. He'd talk about his mother's indifference, her curses on him. His last boyfriend betraying him and his sister leaving him behind. Losing his hawk and losing his home.

He was ready to weep, and none of it would be a lie, but before he could begin, Anon crossed to where Brysen knelt with his hands tied behind his back. He lifted Brysen's chin with two fingers and looked down at him. Anon's hand was rough and meaty and could've snapped Brysen's neck before his next heartbeat, but instead the warlord nodded at his lieutenant to remove the knife from Jowyn's throat and step back. Still holding Brysen's chin, Anon narrowed his eyes at him. "So your family, your bird, and your village itself betrayed you, and your solution is to run to me."

Brysen blinked, because he couldn't nod while Anon held his chin.

"And I am supposed to invite you two mourning doves into my army just like that?"

"You like to spread fear," Brysen said. "Imagine how scary it will be to the Uztari to learn that I've joined you."

"You don't actually believe he wants—" Launa scoffed, her hand still on the hilt of her knife, but Anon silenced her.

"You're not quite the foolish boy the stories about you suggest," he said, which Brysen tried not to take as an insult.

How come stories about his sister were all terror and power and glory, but his made him sound like a fool? *Let them think I'm a fool after I've cut this man's neck from ear to ear,* he thought.

"I'll do you the courtesy of telling the truth: You make a valuable hostage," Anon continued. "But I also see your point. As a warrior with us, you make a potent symbol of Uztar's decay. And I admit, I have wanted to capture you. But I could break your sister's heart just as well by slicing your stomach out and hanging you like a flag from a pole."

Brysen shuddered.

"Her rage makes her powerful," he replied. "But imagine what it will do"—he struggled to get the words out, certain again, that they were true—"when my sister hears I've joined you to fight against her. We know your warriors fight in pairs. So you know that it's harder to fight with a broken heart."

Anon pursed his lips, studied Brysen with eyes as still as stars, then let go of Brysen's chin and loomed above Jowyn. "What about you? The long-lost Tamir. You know, I had an alliance with your older brother, Goryn. He failed me and now rots in a Sky Castle dungeon. Why should I trust you to be any better? Aren't all Tamirs treacherous vultures?"

"They are," Jowyn said, "which is why I left my family long ago."

"The Owl Mothers who fed you their sap are no better," Anon said. "Trusting an owl's stillness is the last mistake a rodent ever makes."

"I would never call you a rodent." Jowyn gave Anon the same smile he so often gave Brysen, and it felt at once like a betrayal and a brilliant lie.

Brysen held his breath, every part of him tensed with what this warlord might do in the face of a joke, but Anon simply waited it out, expecting more from Jowyn than a little wit.

Jowyn had to sell this plan he didn't like to a man who didn't want to buy it, and Brysen was afraid the entire enemy camp could hear his stomach rumble with nerves.

"You know enough, Ser Anon," Jowyn said, lowering his voice, "to know that my family is full of monsters, the Owl Mothers disowned me, and the one person beneath this blasted sky who I've felt truly knows me is tied up right here at my side. I don't care about fighting for or against you or your cause. I'm not a falconer or a fanatic." He turned his head sideways to look at Brysen. "But I'd slice the sun from the sky if it would keep him safe."

Both Anon and Jowyn had their eyes on him now, and Brysen shivered. He was empty air in the shape of a boy, and if he turned his head to look at Jowyn, he might just blow away.

"I've always liked the frankness of the young," Anon said at last. "And I appreciate that you both appear to believe what you've said to me." He returned to his campaign table, studied the curved black blade of Brysen's knife, and tested its point for sharpness. He frowned. Brysen had never taken as good care of the black-talon blade as he should've. "But your beliefs don't actually matter, nor do your pretty words. The one thing I ask of all my warriors is *deeds*. Your deeds will reveal you more than any words can do. Deeds do not lie. So . . ." He looked at each of them again, then nodded. "You will train as a pair with Launa and her son, and if they are satisfied with your abilities, you will join our next attack on these Villages that you say betrayed you. We'll allow word of your participation to escape the siege lines so that your sister might hear of it, and if it is as you say and we gain the advantage, you will have my thanks. If not, your bodies will rise as smoke to the sky, like everyone else's. That's the offer. Are you ready to kill your old friends, Brysen? Are you ready to put a blade through a falcon's beating heart?"

"Yes," Brysen told him without even the slightest quiver in his voice. It was easy enough to lie once you'd convinced yourself it was true.

"Good," said Anon, nodding at Launa to take them from his tent. "You'll have your chance to prove it. But if you fail"—he

paused, and any slight hint of warmth drained from him—
"you'll watch each other die screaming, and not a soul on either side of the barricades will mourn you."

Brysen was used to being threatened and didn't much fear
pain, but one thing scared him more than he'd expected: His
plan was working, and that was, for him, something entirely
new.

24

"IT WORKS WITH WIND AND WEIGHT," LAUNA EXPLAINED AS THE bleary-eyed boys rubbed the sleep from their faces. Brysen and Jowyn stood in front of her and her grown son, beside a rough wooden war barrow. Its wheels were as tall as they were, and a large carved-bone-and-stretched-silk kite was lashed to its side in a harness. All kinds of oiled ropes—which Launa called *lines*—were tied around metal hooks—which she called *cleats*—that cluttered the upper rim of the barrow. This, she called its *strake*.

There were as many strange terms for the parts and principles of the war barrow as there were for falconry, and

Brysen found memorizing them just as dull. He was having trouble focusing in the bright red morning dawn.

Red at night, a hunter's delight. Red at morning, all hunters take warning.

"Brysen!" Launa's son, Visek, snapped at him and slapped him across the back of the head. "Focus!"

He glared at the younger warrior, a few seasons older than he was, and wondered what it must be like to fight alongside your mother, rather than against her. These two, as much as he wanted to stuff a pigeon down their throats, were the key to gaining Anon's trust. He had to play nice with them. They looked so much alike, with skin dark as healthy soil and features sharp as mountain peaks. Their only differences were in their scars. They both had scars but in different places—a reminder that the winds of the world did not buffet all families equally.

"Apologies," he told Visek. "I'm just tired."

"The blasted sky doesn't care if you're tired," Launa said. "The barrow will break you if you do not respect it."

He stifled a yawn as she continued her lecture about how the driver's job was to launch the kite to the sky using the tension in the sling line, and then control its path through the wind with tension on the guidelines. Meanwhile, the smaller warrior—in their case, Brysen—would climb the rigging line and strap into the airborne kite. She droned on and on about "points of wind," "luffing and leading," "kite dynamics," "speed and weight" . . . and Brysen lost focus again.

Last night, he and Jowyn had been taken to separate tents and left tied up to sleep fitfully under guard. All night Brysen heard the sounds of shouts and taunts from the barricades to the Six Villagers and from the Six Villagers to the barricades, each side playing a game of provocation but neither escalating to a full-out assault. The Kartami were waiting for the Villages to surrender or starve; the Villages knew they would be wiped out if they left their fortified barricades.

Brysen wondered if he'd be able to get close to Anon before he had to prove his loyalty by leading an assault on his home. Would Shara see him in the heat of battle? Could he call to her like he had before? Would she hear him and finally kill for him when he asked her to?

"*Shyehnaah,*" he'd whispered to himself in the dark of his tent. "*Shyehnaah, li-li, shyehnaah.*" He said the words but felt nothing. He'd tossed and turned and sweated all night and hadn't slept for even an instant.

"So, driver!" Launa quizzed Jowyn. "Where do you stand?"

"Just forward of the wheels," Jowyn answered, a diligent student. He stepped into the barrow, his palms resting on the smooth, oiled strake. To his left sat a rack of gleaming spears, their tips made of polished metal alloys—whatever the

Kartami could seize and melt down in their rolling forges—and their shafts a mix of woods—again, sourced from scavenging. To his right was a system of ropes and pulleys. Some connected to the wheels, others to the large kite. They were the mechanism that let the Kartami catch the wind and roll so fast across the plains.

"The kite warrior stands behind him," Launa continued, "and when it is time to mount—" She gestured to her son, who stepped into the barrow behind Jowyn, their bodies pressed so close together that Brysen could've driven a knife through Visek and pierced Jowyn with it. He didn't like it. "When it is time to mount, the flier unhooks the kite and launches it much like you would launch a hawk." She said that part with disdain as Visek demonstrated, grunting with the effort to slingshot the kite into the sky. "It's easier to throw if you're already moving, by running behind the barrow and pushing, as the wheels and the momentum do more of the work. But with practice you can throw from a standstill."

Above, the kite's folding flaps opened like clunky wings. The wind caught and filled its silk, pulling it higher. Ropes unspooled behind it and the war barrow lurched forward, though the wheel locks kept it from rolling away. "When the kite has enough height and wind, the flier grabs the climbing line"—Visek held a thin rope that was dangling down from the kite—"and goes up."

Visek grabbed the line and scurried into the sky. With stunning agility, he slid his arms through the straps under the kite, while his feet settled into looped holsters at the kite's tail. Now, with the strength of his arms and by twisting his body, he could steer the kite on the end of the line, moving up and down and side to side.

He demonstrated weaving and turning, dipping and diving.

"On the open plains, there is always a steady wind to catch," Launa said, "but this close to the mountains, the breezes bend and blow wilder. A barrow pair must observe the patterns and adjust. No daydreaming up there. No admiring the view."

Brysen nodded, looking up at Visek's sleek movements. He was gliding like a sand-swimming albatross high above a long-hauler's desert caravan. Asking him not to daydream was like asking the sun not to burn. Ask all you want, but the sun can't change its nature. Brysen was already dreaming of flight.

"I have the wheel locks on," Launa explained to Jowyn. "In battle, I would not, and you—the driver—would help him steer and be steered by him. If he does not have a crossbow mount, then you also must send up spears as he throws them." She showed how the other end of the climbing line had a hooked pulley-and-counterweight system. The driver could attach a spear and send it up to the warrior.

"There is a bond that must exist between driver and

warrior, wordless and sightless and soundless. They must be able to anticipate each other. This is Anon's wisdom and his genius. I fight alongside my son, as I have since the beginning. Others fight alongside their siblings or their lovers or their friends. The bond must be unshakable and complete. Your lives are for each other and bound to each other. If one dies, so does the other. Are you two prepared for such a bond?"

What could Brysen say? There was a tether between him and Jowyn that wasn't like that of a tamer to a hawk, a hunger that leashed. Theirs was more like starlings flocking, a bond of song and wind that their blood knew and their wings obeyed, making shapes that no one else could understand, that even they themselves did not understand. They flew together on the faith that flying would tell them why.

"Yes."

Launa looked at Jowyn, waiting.

Jowyn nodded.

"Let's see you fly, then." Launa whistled, and her son unstrapped himself and slid down the line. The kite bobbed and waved as Launa held the line steady.

She motioned for Brysen to step up into the creaking war barrow.

"Climb," Visek ordered, and Brysen, with the muscle memory from countless climbs above his house in the mountains, found himself creeping up like a vine worm. As he climbed, the wind pulled and pushed him, buffeting him, and the rope felt suddenly too thin and somehow too heavy to possibly stay aloft, to possibly hold his weight with nothing but wind against fabric. What if he slipped? What if the wind changed? What if the fabric tore?

His palms were sweating, but he gritted his teeth and climbed the last length to reach out for the harness.

The rope slackened as the breeze changed and he fell forward, missing the strap and nearly losing his grip. The ground below heaved at him and he felt dizzy, like an ale-addled battle boy at the end of a night at the Broken Jess. He clutched the rope, terrified to reach out again. The kite swirled and shook as Jowyn tried to steady it from below using the ropes.

And then Brysen caught the harness. He squirmed and kicked and climbed into it with all the grace of an eel in a bucket, but he was, all of a sudden, soaring.

Oh, how he was soaring!

With a bend of his arms, he changed the curve of the kite's wings and rose with an exhilarating *whoosh*. Another bend and he sank. If he bent farther, he dove. He leaned and pivoted, pressing his feet back in the straps, which straightened or turned him as he needed. He'd spent a lifetime staring at birds, watching the waft and whirling of their airy bodies, and now he felt like one of them, part boy, part breeze. *This*, he thought, *is where I am meant to be.*

He looked down and saw Launa removing the blocks from the wheels, and now the barrow was rolling!

Jowyn tugged the guideline, and Brysen answered with a slight turn. The motion shuddered down the rope and the barrow veered. Jowyn looked up, struggling with the line that held the kite and the lines that steered the barrow, but he was getting it. Each turn and each tug sent tension up to the kite, which Brysen felt in his arms and legs, his torso. Every part of his body was in tune with the kite, and by imagining the kite stretching down to the barrow, he could imagine Jowyn, seeking out his desire on the wind. He felt even the slightest shudder of the lines and turned with them.

The wind above pulled at him, but the rope held him to the ground. He was in balance between earth and sky. He bent an arm and pulled against the lines, which Jowyn eased up, and he rose higher. He bent the other way and changed the flex of the tail with his legs, and Jowyn reeled him slightly in.

They were two bodies flying with one mind. He was the falcon and Jowyn the falconer. He found he could fly wherever he wanted as long as Jowyn wanted him to, and he could *make* Jowyn want him to just by simply wanting it. It was absolute freedom. It was absolute submission.

This must be how a tamed falcon feels, bound and free, soaring on a tether tied in the mind. Two wills united.

He tested a dive, speeding low ahead of the barrow to feel the weight of it pulled behind him. He tasted the salty wind on his lips. He was sweating and thirsty and found himself overwhelmed with *want.* He wanted to fly. He wanted to fight. He wanted to hunt.

"WOOOOOO!" he couldn't help but yell as he curved up from the dive with skin-peeling speed, grinning.

As he rose and slowed, the kite wobbled and wavered, then started to drop. He'd tilted too far back, lost the wind. He was falling and wanted to flap his arms. He yanked one sideways, trying to bend back into the wind, but the kite fell faster. On the ground, Jowyn shouted something he couldn't hear, but he stopped moving to listen and Jowyn pulled a line, eased it around the wind, and the kite caught and steadied and Brysen had control again.

He couldn't stay aloft without Jowyn. Jowyn couldn't move without him. This was the way the war barrows fought, the same way that falconers hunted. The line that tied them was the visible tether, but there were deeper bonds, stronger bonds.

He tried to signal for a spear, but unhooking one arm caused the kite to pivot wildly to the side, then drop. His foot slipped from its stirrup. He dangled and clung and the kite plummeted once more.

The line snapped taut, righting the kite as it fell. It caught the wind but too late, slowed its fall but not enough.

Brysen crashed into the ground with a thud and rolled in the dirt as the barrow skittered up to him. Jowyn was on his feet before it had even stopped moving, running to Brysen, grabbing him up.

"Are you okay?" Jowyn shouted.

"Hahahahahaha," Brysen cackled through bloody lips. "That was . . . fun!"

"We will have to work on your fighting balance." Visek jogged up to them. "But that was a good start. You can stand?"

Brysen nodded, heaving himself to his feet with a painful groan. Nothing was broken, although it felt like he'd chipped a tooth.

He smiled at Jowyn for confirmation, but Jowyn rolled his eyes. "'Fun'?"

"I'm at your mercy up there," Brysen said. "I thought you'd like that."

"I like it better when you're on the ground."

"I'm not sure I ever want to be on the ground again," he said, and Jowyn cocked his head sideways, a tiny frown flashing on his face. He wasn't sure if this was a performance for

Visek and Launa's sake or if Brysen really meant it. Brysen wasn't sure, either. In spite of the fall, he loved the flying.

"The kite is unharmed," Visek announced, studying the dirty silk and carved-bone frame. "Go again."

Brysen got back into the barrow, catching his breath, and pressed against Jowyn's back.

"Ready?" Jowyn said over his shoulder.

"Ready," Brysen said as Jowyn pulled the kite back against the tension in the ropes and launched it into the sky. Once it caught, Brysen climbed up after it.

They practiced all morning and Brysen fell over and over. Jowyn couldn't stop him falling every time, but he learned to brake the ropes to slow the crash into something almost like a landing, learned how to keep the barrow rolling long enough on its momentum to quickly launch the kite again.

They stopped for water and for dried fruit and groundnuts that, Brysen noticed, didn't grow anywhere near the Six Villages, and then they started up again. While they worked, learning to follow instructions from flags and signals on the ground, Brysen stole glances at the vast Kartami army below—first looking for Anon, then to memorize the route to his tent, then searching out the sentries on the ground and in their own stationary kites—and then he looked across the river to the barricades guarding the Six Villages.

He knew he was too far away for anyone there to know it

was him in this kite, but he did wonder: Could they tell by how he flew or by his shock of gray hair against the bright blue sky? Could Shara, with her keen hawk eyes, see him from afar, and could she understand that he was still, even now, trying to protect her?

Was it wrong that he was also having fun?

25

WHEN THEIR DAY OF TRAINING ENDED, THEY WERE ESCORTED AWAY
under guard, stinking and sore and tired. They were tied to
posts in separate tents, where meals were brought to them
by people who wouldn't make eye contact. Brysen wanted to
lie awake and plot his next move but must have fallen asleep
instantly, because the next thing he knew, daylight glowed
against the tent flaps and Visek was nudging him awake with
the tip of his boot.

He was sore when he opened his eyes and sorer still when
Visek untied his ropes and shoved him outside.

"We run," he said, and Brysen found himself jogging the

perimeter of the entire Kartami camp. Visek passed him a skin of water but never let him stop moving. Even when he doubled over to vomit, Visek pushed him. The sun had peaked when he was finally allowed to rest. After Brysen shoveled a few handfuls of mashed beans into his mouth, Visek made him run to an open clearing, shoved a spear in his hand, and ordered him to throw it at a grass-stuffed pelt target.

"First on the ground, then in the air," Visek said.

He lifted the heavy shaft, cranked his arm back, and let it fly.

He missed.

He had to chase after the spear, bring it back, and try again.

He missed again and had to run after it again.

"From now until you are allowed to join us, when you go *anywhere*," Visek snapped at him, "you go running."

It was sundown when he was finally allowed to stop the target practice, and he hadn't gotten much better at it. He hadn't seen Jowyn all day, and he hadn't seen Anon, either. His legs and back and shoulders felt like the charred embers of a plague pyre, but this time, after Visek left and the Uztari girl who'd first captured him went to tie him up for the night, he found the strength to resist slightly. He caught her by the wrist.

"Is he okay?" he asked. "Jowyn?"

She looked away, but he squeezed her tighter. "*Please*, tell me."

"He's fine," she whispered. "You'll train together again tomorrow."

"Thank you," he said, slumping back against the post. He noticed her smile slightly before she left him. "By the way, my name is Brysen," he added.

She shook her head slightly. She was a cold-blooded fanatical killer with the Kartami horde, but Brysen swore he saw her mouth *Duh*.

"And you are?" He smiled.

"Morgyn," she whispered as she was leaving.

"Morgyn," he repeated after the flaps closed behind her. *Good*, he thought. *An ally.*

The next day, he was woken by the same rough boot and dragged outside again to run, but Jowyn was there waiting.

"You'll run three laps of the camp," Launa told them, "and then, to the barrows."

Brysen was excited to be near Jowyn, dirty and stinking as they both were. He hoped to tell him about his plans, but they had no chance to talk. Visek ran right behind them and could hear anything they said. Brysen couldn't explain how he hoped to identify Anon's tent from the air so he could target it later, that he was working on Morgyn to get her to help them escape when the deed was done, or that, in spite of it all, he was actually enjoying his time in the Kartami camp. He loved flying. He felt like it was what he was meant to do. He wanted to see if Jowyn felt the same way about driving the barrow, that if it weren't for the brutality of this army, maybe this actually *was* where they were both meant to be.

And with Visek there, Jowyn couldn't tell him he was being foolish. No Kartami guard was his ally just because she'd told him her name, and so far, all Brysen had done was train, and not all that well. He was a middling warrior at best, and he was no closer to killing Anon than he'd been when they'd arrived, even if he managed to spot the leader's private tent. They still hadn't even given him his knife back.

Brysen had the whole conversation in his head. By the time the sun had reached its peak and their run was finished, he wasn't sure who had won the argument.

They spent the rest of the day training on the war barrow.

By sunset, Brysen could mount the kite in ten breaths, grab a spear without falling, and throw it absolutely nowhere near a target. But he didn't crash. Not even once. And as he

soared above the camp he saw Anon, walking with two warriors. The man gave some sort of instructions and then looked
up in his direction to watch Brysen train.

Brysen turned the kite against the wind and dove, showing
off. When he pulled out of the dive and steadied himself again,
Anon had gone.

They only stopped training because evening storm clouds
boiled on the horizon, rolling their way. The moment their
practice ended, every muscle in Brysen's body burned or
ached or both. He was covered in dirt and blood and sweat,
but he happily could have kept going right through the storm.
He wondered what it would be like to fly through lightning.
Not even hawks liked to the fly in the rain, though.

Once he'd come down for a final on-purpose landing,
Visek supervised them as Jowyn inspected the kite for tears
in the fabric and then folded and stowed it for an easy launch
the next day. Visek watched Brysen oil the lines and sharpen
the spears, then cover the barrow against the oncoming rain.

"So . . . how am I doing?" Brysen asked Visek when their
work was done. He tried out an insouciant grin. "Like what
you see?"

Visek was immune to his charms.

"Tomorrow you learn to strike where you aim, or else
you're not worth wasting another day on," he said.

"I suppose I could use some more target practice."

"You will have it," Launa interjected. "When you were above, did you see the dust cloud on the horizon?"

Brysen told her that he had.

"That is the army of Uztar approaching. They will be here by sunup," she said. "When they are in eyesight tomorrow, Anon wants you leading an assault on the barricades. We'll let your friends see whose side you're on. Kill one of them—*and be seen doing it*—and then we can decide how it is we think you are progressing."

Brysen blanched. Even Visek looked doubtful at his mother's orders. "Isn't it . . . too soon to fight? I'm not ready."

"This is a war, boy!" Launa slapped him so hard across the face, his head turned. Jowyn's fists clenched. "You are ready when you are needed or you are a deadweight. Dead-weights get carried in the guts of a vulture. Your sister will see you fight, or she will see you bleed out on my spear. Either way, tomorrow is the day one or the other will occur. Understood?"

He looked at the ground as he nodded, cheek stinging, but the woman's voice suddenly softened. "But you've done better than either of us expected you to," she said. "And I believe you will like tonight's training regimen, although some your age find it the most terrifying part of all."

"What is it?" he asked, still not looking at her.

"Sealing the warrior's bonds to each other," she answered him. "Or breaking them for good."

This time, Visek and Launa led Brysen and Jowyn away together.

26

THEY REACHED A SMALL TENT ON THE EDGE OF THE CAMP, WHERE
Morgyn and who Brysen now figured was her girlfriend stood
guard.

"For new warriors," Launa said, opening the flaps. Inside
was a plush rug with cushions all around it and a small wash-
basin on a stand with clean water and soft brushes. Skins of
water, milk, and wine hung from pegs on the tent poles, and
a tray of food on a low table sat beside a burning brazier under
a pot, which steamed and warmed the night air.

"This is not forever, so don't get comfortable," Visek
grunted. "Only new pairs on the first night." He looked to the
risen moon and snorted.

"Your bond is vital to your fighting power," Launa explained as her son left. "Whatever vows you make tonight must be unbreakable. They may be your own—we do not have dogma on what ties one soul to another—but you must be tied, completely. You are responsible for each other, as Anon is responsible for all of us. To fail each other is to fail him, and to fail him is to fail us, and failing us will invite retribution."

They both nodded. Just because they'd survived a few days with the Kartami didn't promise them the next ones.

"Good," she said. "Tomorrow, you will wake with the sun, and then the sky will test you as it never has before. Rest well, or don't. The choice is yours. Until then." She bowed her head to the dirt, the Altari way. Brysen returned with the winged salute, which startled her. He noticed Morgyn, who was still holding open the tent flap, suppressing a smirk.

"Careful," Launa warned. "Not all Kartami have as warm a sense of humor as we do."

She left them, and they both exhaled. Brysen chugged a skin of fermented milk while Jowyn collapsed against a support pole, staring at him. When Brysen had finished drinking, he looked around. "Nice place we've got here." Sarcasm was his only defense against the words he didn't know how to say.

Jowyn, however, had no such reluctance. "What under a blazing sky of fire do you think we're doing?" he whispered. It somehow also sounded like a shout. "If I didn't know better, I'd say you were having fun."

"I am," Brysen told him.

"They want us to attack the Villages tomorrow!"

"They're just trying to get a rise out of my sister," Brysen said. "If she's with the army that's coming, they'll want her to see me, get mad, and attack. It'll kick off a battle for real, and that's when we can make our move."

"'Our move'?"

"I'll kill Anon during the battle," Brysen whispered. "I'll be up above. I'll have the drop on him."

"You'd miss the ground if you were aiming at it, Bry." Jowyn sighed. "You've got a lot of talents, but aim isn't one of them."

There was no cruelty in the comment; it was simply true. "But what if I don't have to aim? What if I don't use a spear?"

Jowyn was listening.

"There will be hawks sent up to fight us off," Brysen explained. "I can use the Hollow Tongue to command one to attack."

"Brysen . . ." Jowyn shook his head. "You don't know if you can do that. You never even got Shara to hunt a mole. You don't know anything about how the Hollow Tongue works, and if you screw up, they'll kill you for trying. You'll be strapped in that kite and they'll drop you before I can do anything to help."

"That's only if I fail," Brysen said. "I don't know why you assume I'm going to fail."

"I don't assume that," Jowyn said, "but even if you succeed, he's just one warrior among literally thousands."

Brysen shrugged. "You see how they worship him. It will break them if he dies. They won't know what to do, and while they're confused, we'll make a run for safety behind the barricades."

"They don't look like the sort who get confused."

"Why won't you trust me on this?" Brysen hated the whining pitch that his voice took. "Why won't you *believe* in me?"

"Because I *do* believe in you," Jowyn answered, his own voice bending like a knee to dirt. "I just don't want to see you killed and I don't want to see you throw away the gift you've been given just to spread more death in this world. We have enough death. You can do something else. I've seen you do it."

"You saw me command a bird to do what I wanted it to, even though it was impossible," he said. "That's what I can do. That's what I *will* do."

"No." Jowyn crossed the tent to stand directly in front of Brysen, making eye contact so hard, it pressed Brysen back against the tent's canvas. "I saw someone kind and beautiful and brave start to find the kindness and beauty and bravery in himself and to harness it for something other than the bloodshed our stupid world has taught him. That's the impossible thing I saw. Not the Hollow Tongue. You. I saw you."

Brysen felt the blood rush to his face. He looked at his feet; he looked at the floor. His lower lip quivered. The anger he felt toward Jowyn tipped its wings and dove, faster than any living thing could fly, and became pain. He didn't trust that sort of kindness, couldn't believe that kind of faith in him. He had power now, and a great and bloody purpose, but he still couldn't believe he was beautiful or brave or kind. He hadn't proven it yet. He had to kill Anon. Maybe then he could believe it. Regardless, so far Jowyn's praise felt like lies, and they hurt worse because Jowyn believed them to be true. He was embarrassed to think these same stupid thoughts that always clipped his wings, and being embarrassed hurt, and being hurt embarrassed him more, and so his tired old thoughts dove and dove and dove and found no ground beneath them.

If I could just do this one great thing, he thought, *then I'd break this tired turning of my mind. If I could just do this one great thing, it wouldn't just change the world. It would change me.*

I'd slice the sun from the sky, Jowyn had said, and Brysen wanted to be worth that statement.

He longed for proof that Jowyn meant what he said. He felt ridiculous and stupid, but all he could think of were reasons not to trust Jowyn, even if he was making those reasons up on the spot. Jowyn had seen his scars; Jowyn had seen his moods; Jowyn had seen his ridiculous faith that he could be more than people thought he was, that he could change the world. Brysen couldn't hunt a weasel, let alone a whole world.

Some assassin I'll make, he thought, and he was crying now. He felt like such a weakling, such a wimp.

"Hey, it's okay." Jowyn put his hands on Brysen's shoulders and bent his neck so their eyes would meet even as Brysen turned away. "Please, hear me, Brysen. I meant everything I've said—I go wherever you go . . . but I truly think you have another path. You're a healer, Brysen. Wars are lousy with killers, but those who can heal? They're rare birds. Irreplaceable. *You* are irreplaceable, and I fear what happens to this world without you in it."

Brysen let Jowyn's thumb touch his cheekbone below his eye, let him wipe the tears off.

"If you say something about my 'gentle soul,'" Brysen sniffled, "I'll punch you in the mouth."

Jowyn smiled. "But there are so many better things my mouth can do than get punched."

Brysen laughed and wiped his nose. "You have a terrible sense of humor."

"I have a terrible desire to kiss you," Jowyn replied.

Brysen's eyes were wet, but his lips were suddenly dry. His heart pecked at his throat. He felt dizzy. Wasn't this what he wanted? He had thought his heart was a circling hawk, carving the same path in the sky over and over, but maybe it was a hawk on the fist, bound and tamed and terrified to fly. Maybe he had to let it go, risk it to the world and trust its safe return, though the wind was wild and predators stalked its shadow.

"I have a terrible desire to let you kiss me," he said, allowing his hawkish heart to fly at last, and Jowyn took his face in his hands, looked into his eyes, unblinking, and the tiniest twitch in his lips sent a smile through Brysen's entire body. The air between them became that smile.

Brysen breathed in, and in that breath he reached his own hands up, pulled Jowyn's face to his. And he kissed him. He felt Jowyn's rough smile against his lips, and their mouths bent together into a laugh.

"What? Did I—What?" Brysen pulled his face away, ears burning like a bonfire. Had he kissed wrong? Had Jowyn not wanted that? Had he ruined everything?

"The hairs on your chin," Jowyn laughed. "They tickled. I was never ticklish before."

"Things change," Brysen whispered, relieved.

"I'm glad they do," Jowyn replied, his hands on the back of Brysen's neck. With the tiniest pressure, he nudged their faces back together again.

Like a drowning body gasps for breath in desperate heaves when it breaks the surface, Brysen gulped the air from

Jowyn's lungs. He might've lived his whole life drowning had he never shared his breath like this, would never have known what it was to breathe through lips like these.

When Jowyn pulled back, a small trail of saliva bridged between them, stretching to break on Jowyn's chin. They laughed at the absurdity of it, how strange it was to have bodies when both their hearts were only wind and light.

His hands dropped to Jowyn's side, felt the heat of him, the pressure as he pulled them together, and now they were nothing but bodies, and they crushed their lips together so tight that no wind could blow between them, no heat escape. Like when a log falls on a blazing fire, sparks burst to the sky as Jowyn's hands slid down Brysen's back, to his hips, to the hem of his tunic.

He let Jowyn lead.

"Is it okay?" Jowyn whispered, and Brysen said, "Yes," and let the hands touch the skin of his side, where the old burn scars made a map of the moments when he'd wanted to leave his body behind. He sank into his skin under Jowyn's touch, let his shirt rise up over his head and off. He never wanted to leave this body again, he'd never loved it so much as now, broken as it had been, whole in all the broken places.

Their limbs entangled. Brysen turned. He felt Jowyn's breath on the back of his neck, one arm wrapped around his shoulder to his chest, hand pressed, open-palmed, holding him like a falcon holds the fist. The other hand rested feather-soft on his jutting hip. He tripped a little and they nearly fell forward, which reminded them they were still standing.

They laughed.

Jowyn whispered into his ear again, "Is this okay?" and Brysen nodded yes, because his only language was his body, pressing back, and Jowyn moved to the rhythm of Brysen's breathing, just like in the war barrow. There was pressure, Jowyn's grip tightened, and Brysen let out a sound he hadn't meant to, a high yelp with a warble, like someone had stepped on a songbird.

"Sorry," he said, and Jowyn's gentle laugh had no unkind-ness in it.

Jowyn asked him again, "Is *this* okay?"

And Brysen found the word for *yes*, and he said it and weighted it with every other word he could remember—*yes* for sunrise, and *yes* for laughter, and *yes* for crying and for wanting and for cursing. *Yes* for needing and for hunting, and *yes* for flying and for heartache and for grieving, and *yes* for then, and *yes* for now, and *yes* for later. *Yes* for the yesses he never got to say before, and Jowyn repeated "yes" and meant the same and meant the opposite. And it was every word they'd ever said together and every word they feared they'd only ever say alone, and they said *yes* like breathing, *yes* like wind, like sky, like storms. *Yes* like lightning. Like lightning. Like lightning.

It rained all night and was still raining in the predawn dark when Brysen slid out from under Jowyn's heavy arm and dressed himself. He ducked under the tent's side flap, crawling through the mud and the dark past the two sleeping sentries in their trenches. He had a smile on his face as he crawled, the happiest he'd ever been and, he figured, the happiest he'd ever be again.

He had decided that he couldn't risk Jowyn's life in battle. He wouldn't. As precious as Jowyn had told Brysen he was, that was how precious the strange pale boy was to Brysen. And though he was used to being invulnerable, Brysen had seen the changes in his skin, the easy bruising, the blisters and scabs. Jowyn's body would break like anyone else's in a war, and the thought of that strange skin tearing was too much for Brysen to bear. He would not allow it.

He'd used a bit of berry wine from the tent to scrawl a quick note on a tiny, torn piece of tent cloth and gently reached up and slipped it into the folds of Morgyn's robe, safe from the rain, where she'd find it if she went for her knife. He hoped she'd read it and understand. He wanted it to be clear Jowyn had no part in this; maybe she'd see fit to let him escape when the deed was done. He hoped she'd heed the message, a kindness from one person who'd been in love to another.

Before the sun came up, one way or another, Brysen would fulfill his destiny. He hoped that if he didn't come back, Jowyn would eventually forgive him, or at least remember the best of him.

SOME LITTLE BATTLES LOST

FENTYR LOVED HIS FRIENDS, BUT NOT MORE THAN HE LOVED HIMSELF, right?

His family was old-fashioned; his parents had pushed him out of the house the moment he could talk in full sentences, and he'd been looking out for himself ever since, first by begging for what he needed, then by taking it. Fentyr couldn't even remember what his parents looked like, and he wondered if they'd recognize him now if they saw him, a bright-clad battle boy with a condor's hard-eyed glare. For all he knew, he'd rolled his own father for a half bronze in some brawl or another.

Not that he wanted pity for his childhood. There were a lot

like him in Uztar. Keeping your kids in the nest until they decided to leave on their own or, like Brysen's ma, letting your kids take care of you—*that* was a new trend in parenting. You didn't see baby birds feeding worms to their mamas in old age. Unnatural. Fentyr liked Brysen, of course. *Everyone* liked Brysen, poor kid. He was always up for a good time, which was a miracle given the rough winds he'd flown against his whole life. They'd gone swimming once, and Fentyr had seen the burn scars and whip marks all over his back. After that he hated letting Brysen pay for an ale at the Broken Jess. The other battle boys agreed with Fentyr: Brysen had paid enough for his old man's ale. He should never have to buy his own again.

But Brysen was weak. He was a romantic and a sentimentalist, and it was no surprise that Mama Tamir preyed on him the moment his sister was gone. Brysen was just one of those boys who the world abused no matter what they did. Do you blame the world for that, or do you blame the boy? It wasn't Fentyr's fault the Kartami had targeted Brysen's house. He did what he had to do to survive, same as anyone would.

"That's a load of scuzz, right, Fenny?"

Fentyr startled. He'd been lost in his thoughts, convincing himself of his own righteousness. "Huh?"

"Nyck says the Kartami are gonna attack at dawn, but I say they're waiting to starve us out," Wyldr said. She was one of Nyck's latest girlfriends and would, no doubt, not be around that long. Nyck never could settle for one person, and usually Fentyr didn't invest too much in getting to know whoever Nyck had perched on his arm. But Wyldr was a good one and, as far as the battle boys knew, the only one right now. It'd be a shame to see her go.

"Doesn't matter," Fentyr said. "If they want to fight, we'll fight, and if it comes to starving . . . well, battle boys don't starve. We do what we need to survive."

"You're a vicious one, aren't you, Fen?" Wyldr smirked. Fentyr wondered if she was flirting with him. She knew Nyck's reputation. Maybe she was angling for her next love interest already. Or maybe she liked to date more than one person at a time, too. The thought was not at all unpleasant.

He gave Nyck a look, like would he be okay if Fentyr flirted back at her, but Nyck wasn't in a noticing mood. He was distracted—probably worried about Brysen. But Fentyr knew Brysen wasn't in real danger. The Kartami wanted him alive. They'd even told Fentyr so themselves when he pointed out the house. That was why he'd agreed to spy for them. They said they wouldn't kill Bry once they caught him. So Fentyr told them where Brysen lived. Helped draw a map. They made him fill it in with other details, too—the Broken Jess, some hawk mews, food stores. It wasn't his fault how they used that information. He just answered some questions. Nothing that happened later was his fault.

"Nah," Fentyr said, covering his wandering thoughts with a shrug. "I'm not vicious, just ready. We'll fight till the last bird falls out of the sky. Six Villagers to the end, right, Nyck?"

"Right," Nyck said, looking up and down the road, eyes rising to the clouds. Thunder clapped and everyone flinched, even Brysen's hawk, Shara, who was hooded on Nyck's fist. Fentyr got a little sad looking at the bird. He knew how Brysen doted on it, hated to think of the poor kid off being held hostage in enemy territory without his beloved bird. Then again, the Kartami would've sliced the head off that hawk faster than flies on dung. On the barricades over their heads, birds screeched as soldiers waited for the storm clouds to burst.

They'd said the army of Uztar was approaching from behind the Kartami lines, and everyone was on edge. If not tonight, an attack would come soon. The Kartami would have no choice if they got squeezed between the Villages in the foothills and the army of Uztar on the plains. Not every person would survive the fight, but if the army had come, the Villages as a whole might endure. Fentyr, of course, meant to endure with them.

Lightning flashed. Then came the next clap of thunder. Nyck was so distracted, he didn't react to the sound. In the stormy light, Fentyr saw that Nyck's jaw was clenched, his eyes set straight ahead—straight at him.

"What's ruffling your feathers?" Fentyr asked, not liking how distant his friend was being.

"Something I heard," Nyck said. "Something I heard about you, actually."

Fentyr tensed, tried not to look like he'd tensed. "I am not going to date you, bro," he said, grinning.

Nyck didn't laugh, which was a bad sign. Nyck *always* laughed at the idea of dating Fentyr. Fentyr was not, as everyone liked to remind him, the prettiest peacock in the Villages.

"Heard you got caught on your last smuggling run across the river," Nyck said. "Day before that first glider attack."

"Caught? Me? What?" Fentyr looked around. They were alone on the street. Everyone stayed inside at night now, terrified of gliders in the dark, spears hurled from the stars. The falconers on the barricades above had their backs to them. "If I got caught, I'd be dead."

"Yeah," said Nyck. "You would. And yet . . ."

"Nyck, I don't know what you're—"

"Did you get caught?" Nyck stepped into his space. The boy was so much smaller than Fentyr. People who didn't know Nyck thought he'd be easy to take out in a fight, but Fentyr had fought at Nyck's side often enough to know he was like a blue jay: fiercer than his bright feathers or tiny size suggested. He didn't want to fight Nyck, and not just because they were friends. He didn't want to get beaten to a pulp.

"If you're accusing me of something, at least tell me what it is."

Nyck just shook his head. Suddenly a knife pricked Fentyr's back and an arm wrapped around him. Wyldr had snuck up behind him. It was now clear that she hadn't been flirting at all. She'd been distracting him.

"You want to keep your spine in one piece? Tell me what you did," Nyck threatened.

"Flaming sky, Nyck, what are you—ow!" The knife broke the skin, but it didn't drive through him.

Yet.

"Right. Okay. Look," Fentyr began. "I slipped out with two of the Altari, like always, to forage hunter's leaf by the riverbank. Kartami scouts snuck up on us. Cut the Altari down straightaway, but they let me live. Dragged me to one of their, like, officers or something. He knew who I was . . . at least, knew who the battle boys were. And he asked me questions about Brysen, asked me where he lived . . . said he wouldn't hurt him, but that Brysen had a bigger role to play in this war. I told him. I had no choice."

Nyck frowned.

"Brysen's tough, and that pale kid is, too." Fentyr tried to minimize what he'd done. "I figured they could handle themselves."

"But that's not all you told them?" Wyldr whispered in his ear. Her breath was warm.

"They asked me where stuff was in the Villages. The mews,

the feed stores, the battle pits. I had to tell them! I didn't have a choice."

"You keep saying that," Nyck said. "But it's not true. There is *always* a choice."

"Their full army wasn't here yet and the barricades were strong. I figured, what harm could it do? Everyone was safe behind the barricades, and the Uztari forces would probably be here before long. I didn't think Brysen would just, like . . . surrender to them! And I didn't think they'd burn down the places I told them about. Didn't think they could! I . . . I didn't know what they'd do! Mud take me, I swear I didn't know."

His voice hitched. He regretted the oath the moment he said it. Oaths like that were hawks you couldn't call back. Once loosed, they had to hunt. *Mud below and mud between, the dead can't rise to a sky unseen.*

"There were a hundred other things you could've done to help, and you did none of them." Nyck spat on the ground at Fentyr's feet. "Mud below," he said.

"No, come on, Nyck . . ." Fentyr groaned. "I'm sorry about helping them make a map, but it's not like that's the worst sin in the world. We've both done worse for less. I had to save my own life. You can't blame me for that. We're battle boys. You can't just—"

In a flash, Nyck's hand was on Fentyr's windpipe, choking

off his words. "We were all supposed to be brothers, you gnat. You wingless cockroach. You betrayed all of us. Brysen. Me. The whole scuzzing town. Even the blasted Altari you left dead on the wrong side of the barricades so their people can't mourn them. You don't have a flock anymore, not with us, not with them. You're a vulture, and you should die like one."

Fentyr saw the hate in his friend's eyes—the disappointment, too—and he knew what he'd done in spite of all his rationalizing to himself. He'd been happy to oblige the Kartami spies. They'd given Fentyr a sack of bronze and spared his life, and it wasn't like he cared so much what happened to Brysen anyway. The kid wasn't even a battle boy, not really, and that pale boy was just weird, and who wouldn't have done the same in Fentyr's place?

The answer was staring him in the eyes.

Nyck.

Nyck wouldn't have done the same.

Nyck would die for his friends. He'd have even died for Fentyr.

So that was that. Fentyr was who he was and he had to live with that . . . but he didn't have to live with it long.

He saw Nyck and his girlfriend walk away just as another flash of lightning lit the barricades and the clouds opened up with rain.

Funny, he thought. His back felt soaked before the first

drops hit him. Then he saw the red puddle pooling around his feet. He hadn't even felt the girl's knife go in. That, at least, was a mercy. Nyck had found a winner. Wyldr was good.

As Fentyr fell to his knees, he watched the lightning and the rain. He was bleeding out in the street. In spite of it all, he didn't regret a thing. He had lived his life as a solitary hunter, free as a falcon filling his gullet. It hadn't worked out, but so what? You can't win every battle, and no one lives forever.

He did kind of wish he'd lived a bit longer, though.

KYLEE

THE WIND AND THE RAIN

27

WHAT NO ONE TOLD KYLEE ABOUT WAR WAS ITS MONOTONY. ENDLESS days of marching followed by evenings pitching camp, digging ditches, cooking and eating, cleaning, studying maps, then sleeping, then marching again. The melt-wind season threatened rain and the air on the march grew more humid every day, and so much of the talk around her was about when the storm would finally break. A few more days, most thought. Just in time for them to reach the siege lines.

Among the soldiers and officers, valets scurried about with cadges and cages and perches and boxes full of birds. The falconers rode a mixture of mountain horses and crossing camels, while their best valets rode in carts with the birds and infantry soldiers marched on foot.

Kylee, however, who didn't know how to ride so much as a rock mule and had no valet nor any birds of her own to care for, was forced, in spite of Grazim's objections, to ride behind the other girl as a passenger.

"An oversight in your training," Kyrg Birgund grumbled. "I should've known the treasonous Owl Mothers wouldn't have thought through the realities of military requirement. I only hope you prove your worth when the time comes." He glanced nervously at the sky, as every one of the soldiers did when Kylee was around.

None of them knew she hadn't seen or heard the ghost eagle since the night she'd spared the kyrgs from the eagle's wrath. She was afraid the dreaded bird wouldn't return and she'd find herself on the battlefield struggling to command haggard hawks and tulip falcons. Only Grazim suspected something was wrong, but she said nothing about it. She also said nothing about Kylee's almost-betrayal of the Council and the attempted coup. Only Grazim, Kyrg Bardu, and Kyrg Bardu's guards knew what she had done—or nearly done— and they had pledged their silence. Ryven and Üku, ensconced deep in the Sky Castle's dungeons, were not about to tell any-body. And so Kylee rode behind Grazim in silence. She was glad the other girl didn't feel like talking, either.

The mad scramble to leave the castle had been all excitement and anticipation as supplies were wrangled and bags were packed. The forecourt where the army mustered was a riot of squawking birds and braying camels, clattering weapons and soldiers shouting and cursing, laughing and chanting. Lovers embraced as they parted, fathers and mothers said good-bye to children, and children wondered if their parents had come to see them off. The youngest soldiers were about her age—all of them foot soldiers, none of them in the falconer brigades—while the oldest soldiers were gray and grizzled falconers, veterans who'd fought with trained hawks and eagles before anyone dreamed that the Hollow Tongue would become a tool in their arsenal. In the awe that surrounded Kylee and Grazim, there was also, she sensed, a portion of resentment. The rising young always frightened those accustomed to soaring over them.

Each brigade of falconers was commanded by an officer who answered to an aide of Kyrg Birgund's. Birgund commanded the entire army with his overfed golden eagle on his fist. Kylee wondered if the bird could fly, spoiled as it was. Maybe it didn't have to fly. Maybe Birgund had brought it for show. Maybe none of them expected to fight, as long as Kylee came through with the ghost eagle.

The *talorum*. *Bound to death*. It had been days since she'd heard its terrible cries or seen its wings darken the sky. What happened when death slipped its tether? Would that spell death for her? For anyone she cared about?

She feared, for Nyall's sake and for her brother's, that she would fail. If the ghost eagle didn't return, she was as useful a falconer as she was a horseback rider. Mercifully, no one knew she had no idea how to call it back.

On the third day of riding across the plains as Grazim's passenger, the other girl finally broke the uneasy silence that had held between them since that night in Ryven's study. "You still think I betrayed you," Grazim announced.

Kylee grunted. "I know you betrayed Üku."

"We both know you had no love for her," Grazim said, "so don't go crying saltless tears. She made her choice and so did you."

"When you told Bardu I went to Kyrg Ryven's house, did you know they wouldn't throw me in the dungeons, too, or is it a disappointment that I'm not hooded in the dungeons along with them?"

Grazim paused, then answered Kylee with startling honesty. "When I saw Üku had gone to his house, too, I thought you all might end up arrested, making me the only Hollow Tongue speaker the army could deploy. In your fall, I would rise." She slowed the horse to get some distance from the others. "But I took no joy in it. I don't hate you, no matter what you think."

"But if you knew about the plot, why not try to join it?"

Kylee asked. "Why side with the same kyrgs who take every opportunity to keep the Altari people down?"

"Because with you and Üku at Ryven's side, the plan might've worked," Grazim said. "And who would I have been in your rise to power? I know you've got no love for me. Anyway, I don't want the Council overthrown. I want to be *on* it. Bardu promised me that, in thanks for my service, she will try to elevate me to kyrg after this campaign against the Kartami."

"No Altari has *ever* been on the Council," Kylee reminded her. "Not even the proctor could make the other Council kyrgs go along with that."

"No Altari has ever been a speaker of the Hollow Tongue, either," said Grazim. "I'm not sure I care about what no Altari have done before me. I care about what they will do after me. *Because* of me. I'll be the first but not the last."

Kylee let out a soft laugh. Grazim sounded so much like Brysen, thinking she could do something to win the approval of people who had long ago decided to hate her. At least Brysen had only tried in vain to prove his worth to one person: their dead father. Grazim was trying to justify herself to an entire culture that hated her. Two cultures, really. But neither Uztari nor Altari would ever want to claim her, and surely Grazim was smart enough to know that.

"You think by serving Uztar well, you'll show them you're

not a servant?" Kylee scoffed. "You think by defying Altari faith better than anyone ever has, you'll convince the Altari you're not damned? That's naïve."

"Maybe," Grazim grunted. "But it's no more naïve than you thinking Bardu will give your friend Nyall his freedom after this war is won. You're too powerful and you love those dumb boys you're surrounded by too much. Nyall and your brother make you easy to manipulate. Your need to protect them is your leash, just like ambition is mine. Everyone has a leash, so don't go judging me for mine."

"Caring about other people makes me stronger," Kylee replied, but she wasn't sure that was true, either. Caring about Nyall and Brysen *had* made her easy to manipulate. Even caring whether the ghost eagle killed Bardu and Üku and Grazim had made her easy to manipulate. Was that why the ghost eagle flew off? It had chosen her as tamer but found her already tamed.

Grazim didn't press the conversation further, which was a relief. They'd circled too close to each of their hardest truths for either girl's comfort. Grazim was smart and ambitious and could think whatever she wanted about what gave Kylee power. Kylee didn't need Grazim's explanations or her friendship.

They rode on. Kylee's hips and butt were sore from riding the horse, but she'd never let her discomfort show. Grazim would love it if Kylee got off and walked, so Kylee stayed just where she was, staring at the back of Grazim's blond head, smelling her sweat, glancing every so often at the overcast sky, and waiting for something to break the monotony of the long and miserable march to war.

Toward sunset, it happened.

Three pigeons flew up from the scouts ahead of the column, each with whistles tied to their tail feathers. They rolled and tumbled, creating a chorus in the sky. Kylee knew the dirge-like tune of the whistles worn by mourners' crows, but she had never heard the shrill whistles of signal pigeons before. All eyes looked to the sound just before they dove again, returning to their handlers.

Shouts went up, and Birgund's gilded eagle launched heavily from his fist with his cry of "Utch!" It made one lazy circle over the heads of both wings of the brigade and then returned to the commander. The march stopped.

"Kartami squadron," the nearest officer said. "Two dozen strong, chasing an Altari caravan." Only the officers knew how to read the pigeon code, which changed every day to prevent spies from cracking it. The number of pigeons released and the pitch of their whistles somehow carried the information. Kylee found herself jealous of the officers who could decode it. She hated when someone had more information than her, and lately, it seemed *everyone* had more information than her.

"Which direction are they headed?" Grazim asked, reaching down to the falcon box on the side of the horse to coax the tiercel jackal hawk to her fist.

The officer looked at her with a frown, uncertain how much information to share with the girls who spoke to birds of prey in their own language.

"The caravans are headed to the Sky Castle," she said. "Probably seeking shelter."

"Two dozen kite warriors?" Grazim frowned. "We have to attack."

The officer glanced up at the gray sky and sucked her teeth. The peregrine on her fist stayed hooded. "Orders are to let them pass and keep marching for the Six Villages."

"But they'll all be killed," Grazim objected.

"Probably," the officer said.

Grazim shook her head, then spurred the horse forward to the front of the column, seeking out Kyrg Birgund. She moved so suddenly, Kylee had to grab her around the waist to keep from falling off. Grazim's jackal hawk stared over her shoulder at Kylee, its meat-hook beak too close to Kylee's face for comfort.

"Kyrg!" Grazim called. "We have to intervene!"

Kyrg Birgund looked aghast to be spoken to by the young girl. Kylee hoped Grazim was about to get a dressing-down in front of the officers, but instead Birgund composed himself and told them to return to formation.

"Respectfully, my kyrg," Grazim said with a defiance Kylee couldn't help but admire, "I think we *must* attack. Not only to save the civilians from a massacre but to sharpen our skills. We've never gone into battle before, and this is a smaller force than we will face when we reach the siege lines. What better way to practice than when the enemy is so greatly outnumbered?"

"You've not studied war," the kyrg grumbled at her. "You perhaps don't understand that this is likely an attempt to draw us away from the Six Villages. An intervention now might delay us long enough that the Villages' defenses will fall. I imagine your"—he glanced behind Grazim to Kylee—"*partner* would not like to see that outcome. Is that your preference, Kylee? To aid these people and risk your home? Your brother?" The kyrg knew exactly where Kylee was vulnerable, and that was where he pecked. "We keep marching," he ordered Grazim.

His valet released a small berry-picker falcon that flew a quick circle around the army, signaling resumption of the march. Grazim let the horse fall back as they trudged on.

It didn't take long before the first column of smoke rose from the caravans in the far distance. Kites flew ahead of it like pinpricks in the sky, swooping and diving. The army was close enough to hear the screams of the people on the ground, even if they couldn't see them through the dust that the war barrows kicked up. With every diving kite, more screams pierced the air. The Altari had no birds to defend themselves with, of course, and were no match for Kartami soldiers on the ground.

It was a massacre, and it was happening within earshot of the largest military force the Uztari plateau had ever seen. Kylee could feel every muscle in Grazim's body tighten.

"Call your eagle," Grazim told Kylee, snapping her words like an order.

"You heard the kyrg," Kylee responded. "We're not to in-tervene."

"Since when do you care about a kyrg's commands?" Grazim groaned. "The army won't need to do anything—the ghost eagle can fight the Kartami off alone."

"I wouldn't want you to report my disobedience back to Kyrg Bardu," she said. She hated herself for it but added a barb nonetheless: "Besides, you didn't say 'please.'"

A lump like a ball of dry bread formed in Kylee's throat. She wasn't heartless, and she wished she *could* call the ghost eagle to stop the massacre, but she couldn't admit that the eagle was gone. If anyone knew, she'd have no use in the war and would likely be thrown in the dungeon alongside Ryven and Üku. She'd be no help to Nyall or Brysen or anyone else. The secret was the only thing keeping her free. She hid behind Kyrg Birgund's orders. Because she was afraid of the truth coming out, these innocent Altari people would die.

"Fine, I'll do it myself," Grazim snarled. She whispered to the jackal hawk on her fist, "*Praal uz.*"

The hawk launched from Grazim and flapped madly over the heads of the army, straight for the distant kites. A shout went up.

"Loose hawk!" someone called.

"Hawk loose!" someone else echoed.

"*Praal uz,*" Grazim repeated, and the peregrine on the young officer's fist leapt away from her so hard, it snapped its tether. It flew after the jackal hawk.

"Hawk loose!" the officer shouted.

"Loose hawk!" someone else called.

"*Praal uz!*" Grazim yelled, and this time a half-dozen hawks snapped from the square frame of a nearby cadge, all flying toward the Kartami attack. The falconer brigade was in disarray, shouting after their birds, whistling and raising their fists, but the command Grazim had given them was stronger than any tamer's training.

"What did you say?" Kylee asked as Kyrg Birgund double-checked the leash on his own eagle and then raced back through the army toward them.

"*Praal uz?*" Grazim shrugged, then turned to look at Kylee over her shoulder. Kylee could hear the smile in the girl's voice before she saw it. "It means *seize the sky*."

28

"WHAT DID YOU DO?" KYRG BIRGUND BELLOWED AS SEVERAL OF HIS officers maneuvered their horses to surround the girls.

Grazim bowed her head and spoke quietly, her defiance wilting in the face of the kyrg's rage. "I helped them," she said, barely above a whisper.

"You've put nearly a dozen of our hawks at risk—birds that were not yours to command! And for what? Some fleeing glass grinders?"

Grazim's shoulders tensed, and Kylee felt the urge to defend the girl against the slur but, still stewing in her own worry, said nothing.

She hadn't expected Grazim to risk all her ambitions to save some strangers, strangers who probably would have cursed and spat on her before they'd have recognized her as one of their own. Just because Grazim was proud to be Altari didn't mean the Altari were proud to claim her. Still, it was interesting what she was willing to risk for them. Maybe she hated what she saw as Kylee's weakness—caring—because it was identical to her own.

"The birds will be safe," Grazim assured him as he and his officers raised their hunter's glasses in the direction of the attack. Grazim did the same, and Kylee had to search through the various pockets and pouches of her riding robe before remembering where she'd put her own pair. She lifted them to her eyes, focused the lenses, and saw an awe-inspiring display of aerial combat.

The hawks had taken Grazim's command to heart, circling over the kites and diving through their silks like hail. As the kites crashed, the hawks whirled on the barrows below, harrying the drivers off the open backs and then mantling over their faces, tearing loose the flesh. The moment the fallen warriors stood from the wrecks of their own kites—if indeed they could stand—they were set upon by the bloody-beaked hawks, faces slashed, guts pulled out like worms from the dirt.

The Altari survivors had dropped to the ground, shielding

their eyes from the horror, and a few of them, in a traditional show of supplication, stuffed their mouths with dirt while praying. They'd been saved, but only by what they believed was blasphemy.

Kylee noticed Grazim flinch. If Grazim's own pious parents had been among the survivors, Kylee felt certain they'd have cursed the salvation their daughter delivered them. Kylee suspected her own mother would, too. She felt something in that moment like kinship with the other girl. Neither of them could make their parents proud.

Before the birds could finish seizing the sky above the Altari, a spear flew from the ground and impaled a peregrine in its dive. Its falconer cried out, as did Grazim. Heartened by the victory, the surviving warriors on the ground regrouped and took aim at the birds. Grazim's jackal hawk had a near miss with the swipe of a large hooked sword, and a sunset hawk had its head lopped clean off when it tried to harry a barrow driver off the back of their cart.

"It's turning against them," Birgund growled. "Kylee, intervene. Now."

"I . . . um . . . ," Kylee stammered. She looked up, desperate, toward the smoke and the gathering clouds above. "*Talorum*," she whispered, hoping no one else could hear her plea. "*Praal uz*," she tried.

No eagle shrieked from above; no dark thoughts twisted

anybody's mind but Kylee's, and those thoughts were entirely her own. This was how it ended for her: failing a minor skirmish before they even reached the war. She had to do *something*.

"I won't risk the ghost eagle," she announced, pretending she had a choice. "But if you unleash your eagle, I can help."

Birgund looked at her skeptically, and she felt Grazim draw in a breath and hold it . . . until the commander untied his bird's jesses from the leash on his glove. He nodded to her.

Kylee searched herself for her truest want. She wanted to avoid failure. She wanted to keep her secret safe. She wanted to get away with her lies.

"*Tuslaash!*" she called out, and in answer to her plea, Birgund's gilded eagle launched from his fist and flapped high over the fight, nearly out of sight. It then dropped hard onto a spear-wielding warrior with such force, the warrior's head caved in like rotten fruit. Then the eagle leapt from him, wide-winged, and latched onto the face of another warrior, shrieking and clawing. With the sudden favor of the fight turned back toward them, the birds Grazim had called resumed tearing down the Kartami and their kites, and the gilded eagle turned back in a wide circle for its master.

Except it didn't stop when it reached Birgund's fist. It raised its feet and crashed hard into his chest, knocking the commander from his horse.

"Ahh!" he screamed as his own bird jabbed her sharp beak for his eyes, for his mouth, for his neck. He rolled and swatted, trying to escape the heavy bird, which had a chunk of his chest in its talons and was not letting go. "AHH!" His cries grew shriller.

"Call it off!" someone shouted, and Kylee couldn't think of how.

"*Fliss!*" she tried. "*Fliss!*" But the eagle ignored her. She'd asked for help keeping her secret safe from the kyrg, and the eagle was following her desire. Dead, he would never learn she'd lost the ghost eagle. "*Fliss! Fliss! Fliss!*" she pleaded.

"*Fliss!*" Grazim snapped once and meant it, and the eagle ceased its attack, hopped off its bloodied master, and stood on the ground, staring up at the people on horseback like a baby who'd just passed gas and expected to be praised for it.

Birgund's valet helped him to his feet and pressed a clean cloth to his wounds. He looked at Grazim and Kylee with a stare that could've burned desert sand to glass. If he gave the order now, both girls might find themselves executed for treason on the spot. His officers had their hands on the hilts of their weapons even before their hawks and falcons made their way back from the battle they'd just won.

"Perhaps my command was too strong for your eagle," Kylee confessed. "Lesser birds are easily overwhelmed, and for that, I apologize."

She punched the word *lesser* to remind everyone, especially the injured and embarrassed commander, that she directed the bird that haunted their nightmares and could turn it on them just as easily as she could command it to protect them. The threat of the ghost eagle, she prayed, was enough to back them down.

Kyrg Birgund took the cloth from his valet and shoved it in his belt, then heaved himself back onto his horse. He glared down at his eagle, then ordered a valet to take it away, have it checked for injury, fed, and returned to him. Only then did he speak to Kylee and Grazim, trying to regain his dignity. "Quick thinking for an effective attack," he said. "I am glad we worked out the errors in your thinking, and I expect we will never see such errors again."

Kylee saluted him, and he signaled the march to resume but stayed a moment after his officers and valet had returned to their positions to whisper toward Kylee and Grazim.

"If you ever defy my orders in front of my soldiers again or do *anything* to cause me harm," he hissed, "I will have you chained to a post and whipped to the living bone, and then I will do the same to everyone you have ever cared about. Brysen's cries will echo past the mountains and the entire Altari people will choke on their own innards as they curse the name *Grazim*. I will not be made to look a fool by two fledgling falconers who think they're mightier than the sky, understand me?"

Kylee nodded. Grazim nodded, and the commander left them, no eagle on his fist.

"I assume you lost control," Grazim said. "But I won't pretend it wasn't fun to hear him scream."

"Thanks for stopping that," Kylee told her.

"Didn't look like you were able to," Grazim replied. "Anyway, why did you help me out?"

"Because you proved me right," Kylee answered. "Caring about others *does* make you stronger. And you care about your people as much as I do about mine."

After a long pause in which they bounced along to the slow trot of the horse, its hooves clomping on the packed earth below them, Grazim finally mustered a quiet "I guess so."

"You're welcome," Kylee told her loudly. She'd been the bigger person, and it felt good.

Her pleasantly smug satisfaction did not last long, though, as Grazim had her own barbed gratitude to show. "I suppose I can keep your secret, too, then."

"What secret?"

"That you've lost the ghost eagle," she said. "And you're all alone out here."

Kylee felt her stomach drop like a broken kite. "It's not true."

"You're a terrible liar, Kylee," Grazim said. "We both know you've been looking for it since we left the castle. I've seen

371

you glancing up every night, trying out words under your breath, trying to summon it back. You even tried to call it down on those Kartami and it didn't come. But don't worry," she added. "I won't tell."

"Just like you wouldn't tell that I'd gone to Kyrg Ryven?"

"No," Grazim said. "This time I think we're on the same side. Just try not to lose control when we're in a real fight."

To lose control meant you had to have control to begin with, and Kylee feared she had none at all.

No, she thought. *I never lost control. I wanted to hurt Birgund, and I did. That is who I am, and now they know it.*

She looked up and hoped that, wherever it was, the ghost eagle knew it, too.

29

SOME DAYS LATER—KYLEE HAD LOST COUNT IN THE MONOTONY—AS storms clouds churned on the horizon, the army made camp in sight of the Six Villages and the Kartami's forces.

It was as if a great city had come to rest, panting smoky breath at the sky. Tents popped up and trenches were dug. Soldiers built pens, stables, canvas hawk mews, and fire pits. Behind the army, traveling merchants hauled everything an army could want: food and water, clothing and birdcages, tanneries and bakeries, metalworks and glassworks and breweries. They had herds of goats and flocks of pigeons. Anything you could think of, anything for a price.

Kyrg Birgund spent most of his time in camp in the guarded

tent where the army's bronze was stored, and the valet who kept the official ledgers was never far behind him. That valet, Kylee noticed, wore the signet of Kyrg Bardu, the taloned dove, and not Kyrg Birgund's eagle emblem. He commanded the soldiers, but she controlled their purse. It amazed Kylee how much of war turned on accounting.

Kylee and Grazim had barely spoken since becoming guardians of each other's secrets.

"I like this new, quiet you," Grazim told her as they sat crosslegged in the dirt to eat bowls of stew and flatbreads fresh from the battalion ovens. A retired falconry officer tended the wheeled bakery, his blind fisher's eagle perched beside the warm hearth, staring at the flames with unseeing eyes. Kylee wondered which had retired first, the man or the bird.

"No need to hood old Heela here, and no need to tether her, either," he chuckled. "She's got nowhere to go . . . except for that one final breeze. The one we all fly on without the need of wings."

"I could do without the morbid bread-man," Grazim grunted, not looking at the baker. He frowned and returned to his work, leaving the two girls staring at each other. Grazim filled the silent space with her ideas about the kyrg's strategy against the Kartami. He meant to push the Kartami forces forward against the barricades, while the Six Villagers pushed them back into the Uztari forces, squeezing them from both sides like a hawk crushes the skull of a rabbit. Kartami couldn't flee to the mountains, where the wind shears and rough terrain would hinder their fighting kites and barrows, and if they tried to retreat to the plains, the larger army of Uztar would chase them down and crush them. "And obviously, he still thinks you'll call the ghost eagle to pick them apart . . ."

"Maybe I still will," Kylee said.

"If the sky wills it." Grazim bowed her head to the dirt, a show of piety she certainly didn't feel. Their relationship was a tense standoff, but now at least they understood each other. "So your brother is in that camp?" She glanced across the plain to the silhouettes of kites rising on long lines around the Kartami perimeter.

"Bardu said he was going to be."

"You believe her?"

Kylee shrugged. "I don't have anything else to go on."

"Word is he plans to kill their leader," said Grazim.

"You heard that?"

"Gossip flies faster than falcons."

"But misses its mark more often."

"So he isn't planning an assassination?"

"My brother makes lots of plans," Kylee said. "He doesn't always think them through."

"So you're the smart one and he's just the pretty face?" Grazim chuckled. They were twins, and she knew it. "I do like his bright blue eyes," she added, amusing herself even more. They had the same ice-melt eyes—their father's eyes—and they both hated them, which Grazim also knew.

"Brysen's just impulsive." Kylee defended her brother without taking Grazim's bait. "He thinks in big gestures. He doesn't really sweat the details."

"Like keeping himself alive?"

"Well, yeah, for one."

"Seems like a smart person would figure that detail out ahead of time," Grazim told her. "Unless he's not actually smart or maybe doesn't actually want to live."

"Are you trying to make me angry?" Kylee pulled apart a piece of flatbread like she was ripping the wing off a baby bird. She glared at Grazim while she did it.

Grazim grinned and popped a chunk of flatbread into her mouth, then spoke while chewing. "Yep. I am."

"Why?" Kylee demanded, throwing her bread down into the bowl of stew. "Why are you *always* trying to make me angry?"

"Because I've seen what you do when you're afraid, and it's dangerous." Grazim sucked her fingers clean. "I don't want to become collateral damage at your side. I've also seen what you can do when you're angry, and if you can harness *that*, we'll win this war . . ."

Kylee stopped with the bread halfway to her mouth. *Was that . . . a kind word from Grazim?*

Grazim leaned forward and dropped her voice to a whisper. "Even without the ghost eagle."

"I'm not so sure," Kylee said.

Grazim chewed her bread, thinking. "You don't deserve what they're doing to your family," she said. "Bardu's preying on your fear because she thinks it gives her power. Let go of that fear and she's powerless."

"I thought you worked for her now," Kylee said.

"I am as loyal to her as I was to Üku," Grazim said. "The difference is Kyrg Bardu knows it, so we get along fine."

"What about me?"

"Do you think we get along fine?"

"I meant are you as loyal to me as you were to Üku?" Kylee asked.

Grazim smiled. "That's easy. I'm not loyal to you at all."

Kylee nodded and went back to eating, glad they felt the same way about each other.

"I don't hate you, though," the other girl added. "Even if you hate me."

"I don't hate you," Kylee said. Grazim raised an eyebrow, doubtful. Kylee elaborated. "I don't trust you and I'm not sure I even *like* you . . . but I don't hate you. Every one of these kyrgs has lied and manipulated to get what they want from me, but you don't want anything from me. I guess I . . . appreciate that."

A brief laugh lit Grazim's face. "Well then, I am happy to continue to want nothing from you. Scuzz it, if I never have to see you again after this war, we could be best friends."

Kylee laughed, too, and they went back to eating. She thought about that word: *hate*. There were people she thought she hated—her late father, the kyrgs, the Tamirs, the Kartami, the assassin who killed Vyvian—but picturing them didn't burn the air in her lungs the way she needed to summon the Hollow Tongue. Hate and anger, she realized, were different things, and only one of them was useful. She'd have no need for hate if she could find her rage.

To the rear of the army, storm clouds rolled across the plateau, racing low and heavy, while in front of them, the deadly Kartami horde waited. From the barricades beyond the Kartami, torches blazed.

Kylee felt a pang of longing. She was so close to Brysen and to their home and the world she knew. Yet what stood between her and them was a vast field of killers keen for blood and an army that expected her to fight with a weapon she no longer had. There would be no homecoming for her before vultures ate their fill of flesh.

Except there were no vultures in the sky—not over the Kartami and not over the Six Villages. An empty sky was more unsettling than the armies massed against each other. It wasn't natural, and it sent ripples of worry through all the falconers of Uztar.

"We don't have to worry about an attack tonight," Grazim said, throwing the last of her dinner into the fire and bowing her head to the dirt. Whether this was an Altari custom or just a Grazim one, Kylee didn't know.

"Why do you think that?"

"Falconers' hawks won't fly in a storm," she noted. "And Kartami kites won't, either."

There was a mischievous twinkle in Grazim's eye, one that made Kylee sit up straight.

"We can command the birds to fly in the rain, though," Kylee noted. "We could surprise them."

"We'd have to *want* it," Grazim said, leaning in, conspiratorial. "We'd have to want it more than the birds' own will to stay safe and dry. That's no small thing to ask."

Kylee looked around the camp. Everyone was tying stakes and settling in for the storm. If Grazim was right, then the skies would be quiet and the sentries on the ground would be lulled into complacency. If Kylee had any chance of rescuing her brother from his foolish assassination attempt in the heart of the Kartami camp, she'd never have a better night than this, under cover of the storm, before the real fighting started. If Brysen was still in the enemy's clutches when the battle began, she'd never be able to focus. Fear would overtake her, just like Grazim predicted.

Bardu held Nyall on one side, the Kartami held Brysen on the other, and she was stuck in between, fighting with her heart split in two.

But if Brysen was safe behind her, maybe she could get back the anger she needed, free herself to unleash the sky's full fury on her enemies even without the ghost eagle. There were other birds to command, and with Grazim as her ally, what couldn't they accomplish?

Yes—once the people she loved were safe, there was no limit to what she could do. She could tear down the kyrgs herself if she chose, rip the foundations out from under the Sky Castle, and proclaim herself ruler of all that scuttled under the sky.

The hunger for power latched onto her thoughts like a tick. Power to do what, she still didn't know, but maybe that was the point of power. Those who had it didn't need to know what it was for. A bird doesn't question the breeze that carries it. Why should the powerful question the power they wield?

The first step was to rescue Brysen.

Grazim watched her as she studied the Kartami camp in the distance. She must have seen the problem work across Kylee's face. "You're thinking something reckless," she said.

"You presume to know my thoughts."

"I'm responsible for you, remember?" Grazim reminded her. "My instructions are to know your thoughts."

"And to report them back to Bardu," Kylee added. "But I notice you haven't dispatched any letters. You haven't reported that I lost the ghost eagle."

Grazim pursed her lips.

"I want to save my brother tonight," Kylee said. "And if you want to win this war with my help, you're going to want to come with me to save him."

"It seems to me that you're afraid of who you are when you aren't saving him."

"I'm not afraid of who I am when I'm not protecting him," she said. "I'm afraid of what I'll do when I've got no one left to protect."

Grazim's eyes narrowed. "You really want me to be your partner in this?"

Kylee nodded.

"Prove it," the other girl said.

Both her and Grazim's people revered birds of prey—birds that did not flock, that flew alone, that hunted alone, and, more often than not, that met their violent deaths alone—but Kylee knew that a mob of crows was more powerful than a lone hawk and that a pair of kestrels could catch more than twice the prey.

They were stronger together.

"*Khostoon*," Kylee said, and at the word for "partner," Grazim looked at the red-dusk sky that warned old hunters of storms. No bird swooped down on her. Then Grazim looked over at her own jackal hawk, which sat on its perch in the ground beside her. The hawk was now looking straight at Kylee, poised, untethered, ready to fly at her command. "Your hawk believes me," she said.

Grazim's thin lips turned up into a tight smile and she repeated the word. "*Khostoon*." The hawk turned its head, swiveling its eyes between the two of them, ready to raid the enemy's nest, ready to fly into the storm between them.

30

WHEN THE STORM BROKE HARD OVER THEIR CAMP IN THE EARLY morning dark, it turned the earth to heavy mud, the black sky to slashing needles of rain. The rain blotted out the torchlight from tent to barricade. Visibility was terrible, and it was hard to hear anything over the deluge. It was the perfect time to sneak away.

Grazim had tucked the jackal hawk under her dark robe, and the girls slipped out so close to the sentries at the edge of camp, they could have tickled their noses with a dove's feather.

They crouched as they ran across the vast open field

between the armies, but Kylee didn't think they needed to be so careful. The storm that kept the birds and kites grounded covered their approach completely. The only time they paused was during flashes of lightning, when the eyes of the soldiers perched like soggy falcons on their barrows might've been drawn to movement.

As they neared the enemy camp, sopping from their zig-zagging dash through the rough mud and trenches dug between the armies, they could hear the screech of metal on metal, the crunch and grind of bones bent and shaped. The sounds told of weapons being forged or fixed and of kites and gliders being patched. They were close enough now to see torches flickering and spluttering at odd intervals among the Kartami tents and barrows. The torches were arranged to deceive the Six Villagers on the barricades about where the warriors were assembled. Firecakes steamed and smoldered, burning low and wet in the rain.

Kylee had promised Grazim she had a plan and just didn't want to share it lest one of them was captured. The less Grazim knew, the better. In reality, Kylee didn't know how she was going to find her brother. It had been nearly half a turn since she'd seen his letter and left the Sky Castle, more days than that since he'd sent it, and for all she knew, he was dead or maybe he'd never left the Villages at all.

Except she felt certain, for reasons she couldn't explain, that she would be able to find him. They were bound to each other, tethered from heart to heart, and there was no distance so far nor storm so great that she couldn't find him in it.

She was acting like Brysen, rushing into danger without a plan. She wondered if, the longer they were apart, the more like him she was becoming. Was he on the same journey in reverse, becoming more deliberate and reserved while she grew reckless and enraged?

"So your plan is to interrogate someone?" Grazim suggested, offering a good idea in the form of a question. "Take one of their sentries and interrogate them on where they keep prisoners?"

"Yeah," Kylee agreed, grateful for the other girl's tactical mind. She wondered if she and Grazim might end up friends after all of this, if they both lived.

Lightning flashed, and the girls froze again. Kylee was awed by the size of the siege up close. It stretched far past the edges of the Six Villages, bending to the riverbank, and blocked the road that led one way toward the Sky Castle and the other toward the Talon Fortress in the distant south. The Six Villages were truly cut off, and on the barricades its own protectors perched like a mob of roosting crows soaked in anticipation as much as in rainwater.

The Villages' birds wouldn't fly in this weather, either, but it seemed every able fighter had assembled to hold the line, preparing for a sneak attack that the Kartami might yet launch. The storm was no guarantee against sudden violence. The Kartami were known to mobilize faster than breath.

"First we have to actually find someone to question," Kylee noted, and Grazim nodded. Between them and the rows of tents were high dirt berms running with mud, there were trenches to traverse, and there were certainly defenses they couldn't see.

Grazim brought her hawk out from under her cloak. The bird tensed. Its eyes smoldered at Grazim as it shook out its suddenly sopping feathers. The bird looked like it might turn on its tamer for the insult of the storm, but she whispered something to it and it calmed, docile.

After a few steps closer to the Kartami camp, Grazim released her hawk with a command to fly. The moment it flapped away, a lump of prairie grass outside an isolated tent stirred, turned, and tracked the hawk's low flight. A whistle signaled a second hidden guard, this one rising from a trench just high enough to nock and raise an arrow, tracing the hawk's flight path.

They'd flushed their quarry from the brush, and now they had to bag it.

Without a word, each of the girls charged at one of the sentries, while the noise of the rain covered the sound of Grazim's shouted word, which turned her hawk and sent the first arrow flying wide.

A second arrow was not loosed.

Kylee tackled the archer into the trench, slamming the warrior's head against the mud and shoving the hooded face into the ground with all her weight. She leaned over and whispered into the back of the hood, "If I let you breathe, you stay silent. One shout or whistle or sudden move and your companion will be gutted by that hawk before any help arrives. Understand?"

She hoped Grazim actually had subdued the other warrior. Kartami loyalty to their companions was the only leverage they had.

The sentry facedown in the mud did their best to nod, and Kylee pulled their head up hard, just far enough to breathe but angled back so they would have a hard time doing more. At the first sign of trouble she could push the warrior's head into the mud again. She wondered if she'd have the nerve. She'd used birds to kill before but never her own hands.

"An Uztari boy was taken prisoner," she snapped. "Where is he?"

"Many Uztari boys are taken prisoner," the warrior answered

with a Sky Castle lilt to her voice. This was an Uztari girl fighting for the Kartami. *How many others*, Kylee wondered, *have chosen this side?*

"There's just one I'm looking for," she said. "Gray-haired but too young for it. He might've been with a pale-skinned boy."

"All the dead are pale."

The girl felt like being defiant. Kylee had to break her of that mood. "What's your name?" she demanded, pulling the girl's head back harder.

"Morgyn," the girl grunted.

"Well, Morgyn, pray to whatever earth or sky you love that these boys are not dead," she snarled, feeling the familiar heat of rage in her. She whistled to Grazim. Through the rain and stormy winds, a high cry carried.

Whatever Grazim had commanded her hawk to do to the other sentry, it hurt.

"I know you heard that. You all fight with companions, right? Imagine how yours is suffering this instant. Now imagine me in fury, seeking my twin brother." The girl tensed beneath her. "Imagine what I might do, and *fear it*. You *will* tell me where he is, or the sky itself will carry you to my vengeance."

The words she'd spoken were as precise as any she had said before, and every one of them was true. She shoved the warrior's head in the mud and counted to twenty, then lifted her up to breathe again.

"He's alive," the girl gasped, spitting mud. "Brysen. I know him. He's . . . kind to me. He and the other boy . . ." The girl hesitated.

"What?" Kylee gripped her hair, yanked her neck back harder. "Speak!"

"They're in the bonding tent," she shuddered. She was . . . *laughing.* "For new warriors."

"For . . . wait . . . what?"

"He's one of us now," Morgyn said. "He talked about you. How you left him behind. How you always let him suffer, made him live in your shadow. How he wanted to step into his own light. He looked happy up in the kite, you know? He'll make a good warrior."

"No," Kylee said, imagining Brysen saying those things about her, fearing the truth of them. "You're lying."

She could not abide a lie.

The heat in her was a full flame now, like when she spoke to the ghost eagle, but there was no ghost eagle here, just her and this treacherous girl, and the wind was howling around her and it howled inside her, too, and she shoved the warrior's head forward, pressing it into the mud, leaning all her weight onto the neck and base of her skull. The body shook and then it squirmed and then it shuddered and flailed and then its movement ceased, and still Kylee pressed on it and pressed on it and pressed on it.

You lie, she thought. *You lie, you lie, you lie.*

"Your brother and that owl boy are in the bonding tent," Grazim said, sliding down into the sentry pit beside her, covered in mud from nose to toes. She glanced at the lifeless body under Kylee's knees and the rain washing the tears from Kylee's face.

"She said the same," Kylee confirmed. Her voice came out hoarse. "Did yours tell you where it is? I . . . didn't get a chance to ask."

"She said it's right there, though who knows if that's true? She'd have said anything to save this one." Grazim poked at the corpse Kylee'd created. "I guess not everyone gets to be saved."

Kylee looked up at her, cold filling the spaces where rage had ignited her. "Everyone on my side does."

She meant it, but she didn't know if it was true.

"This way." Grazim pointed, then raised her fist for her jackal hawk to return. It flew heavy, with blood on its beak and the sated looked of a predator after a meal.

They left the bodies where they lay in the rain and the mud. They'd be found, but Kylee meant to be gone before they were. When she looked back at them, Grazim gave her hand a reassuring squeeze. "Relax," she said. "It's war and they're the enemy. That's two fewer warriors we'll have to fight later."

Kylee couldn't relax. They crept low near the tent and listened for any sound. It was quiet, and she reached for the flaps and ducked inside.

31

THE ONLY LIGHT WITHIN THE TENT CAME FROM THE EMBERS BURNING
in an open brazier next to a fur-covered pallet. In the dim
glow, she saw Jowyn's pale skin gleaming. The strange tattoos
looked almost like elaborate cutouts up his side.

He seemed so peaceful, lying on the pallet in the flickering
light, his chest rising and falling slowly, that it took her a moment to realize he was alone. Brysen wasn't there.

"Where's Brysen?" she whispered as she rushed to him. The
boy gasped, bolting upright, and turned to her wide-eyed, sleep
and confusion flapping across his features.

"Uh . . . I . . . what . . . who?" His confusion looked

suddenly like fear, and she realized she was soaking wet, covered in mud, and probably looked more like a monster than a person.

"It's me," she said, making sure he heard her voice. "Kylee. Where is Brysen?"

Jowyn frowned at her and then looked at the pallet beside him, like he expected to see Brysen sleeping there in the empty space. "He's . . . he was. He was here."

The boy jumped up, all sleep gone from him, and did a quick survey of the tent. He was stark naked in front of her, but either he wasn't shy or hadn't yet remembered.

It turned out to be the latter, because the moment he realized he was completely exposed, he yelped, covered himself where he felt most vulnerable, and scurried around the tent picking up his clothes and yanking them on haphazardly. He tore his tunic's collar in the process.

"He was here," he repeated. "When we went to sleep he was right next to me."

"Where could he have gone? Is there a latrine?"

"They wouldn't let us go without a guard," Jowyn said.

"There were two guards nearby," Kylee noted.

"'Were'?"

"They aren't guarding anything anymore."

"If they were both there, that means he didn't go to the

latrines," Jowyn said. He was too worried about Brysen to question what had happened to the guards. Or he simply didn't care.

"So where?"

Jowyn looked up at the top of the tent, but Kylee suspected he was looking well beyond it, to some imagined sky. He was shaking his head. "Oh, Brysen, no."

"What is it? Where do you think he went?"

"I think he went to look for Anon," he said. Seeing Kylee's confusion about who or what an Anon was, he added, "The Kartami leader."

"To try to kill him," she confirmed. Jowyn nodded.

"They were going to make us attack the barricades tomorrow. He thinks he can stop it."

"We have to stop him," Kylee said. "They'll kill him."

"I've been trying to talk him out of it," Jowyn told her. "Since before we left."

"And you've done a great job," she snapped. It was unfair, but her anger needed a place to perch and Jowyn was convenient. No matter what she did or how far she went, it seemed she was the only one who could keep her brother safe. She tossed the worried boy a halfhearted "sorry" and then asked if he knew where Anon's tent was.

Jowyn shook his head. "Brysen had views of the whole

camp while we were training in the war barrows, but he didn't tell me that he saw anything."

Kylee gritted her teeth but popped her head outside the tent flaps to speak to Grazim. "We need to find someone else to question," she said. "We need to know where the Kartami leader's tent is."

Grazim nodded and crept away. A few pecks and one painfully placed talon later, they had their answer. There might've been a time when the thought of making someone suffer to get what she wanted would have bothered Kylee, but when she searched herself for any remorse for whatever Grazim had done, she found none.

A hawk feels nothing for a hare, so why should I feel anything for these people? she thought, even though she knew these warriors were not hares and she was not a hawk. Easier, though, to think of them that way. There'd be more pain to inflict before the night was done; she couldn't leave it all to Grazim and her hawk.

The three of them made their way out into the rainy morning dark, moving fast between the tents, staying as low as they could to avoid being seen. The sun was on its way up the back of the mountains but hadn't shown itself yet. If they could beat the full dawn, find Brysen, and flee before light, they might get away without rousing the entire camp. Grazim kept looking to the far horizon, anxious to get back to their army's camp before their absence was discovered.

"You can go," Kylee told her. "We'll catch up."

"As long as you're here, I'm here," Grazim assured her. "And if it comes to it, there's no reason we can't do what Brysen was planning to do for ourselves."

"Is *that* why you came?" Kylee realized. "You assassinate the Kartami leader, *you* get to be the hero?"

"The idea crossed my mind," she confirmed, shrugging. "I won't apologize for being ambitious."

The idea to do the job themselves hadn't even occurred to Kylee. She wanted to get Brysen and get out of there, but Grazim was already plotting how to turn this rescue mission to her advantage. She'd probably make a great kyrg, Kylee realized, if she lived that long.

They reached what they'd been told was Anon's tent and saw it was well-guarded. A pair of warriors walked the perimeter, each dark-skinned and muscled.

"That's Visek and Launa," Jowyn whispered. "They've been training us to fight. There's no way Brysen could sneak past them."

"So if he's not inside, where is he?"

Jowyn looked around. They'd ducked behind a tall war barrow. Several more were sitting around the tent, all pointed with their noses out, ready to roll at a moment's notice.

And one of them, Kylee saw, sat heavier in the mud than the others.

"He's in there." She pointed. They watched the barrow for any signs of movement, and sure enough, she saw a flash of gray as Brysen shifted inside it. He was only two spans from where Visek and Launa patrolled and a straight run from the front of the tent. What his plan was from there, Kylee couldn't imagine. Maybe he couldn't, either. They watched and waited, and he made no more movements.

"We need to distract those two guards," Kylee said.

Grazim stroked her hawk's spotted chest feathers and whispered to it. "She's getting tired, I think, but we've got a little more left in us." She raised her fist and tossed the bird into the wet morning air. The hawk flapped across the distance, swooping right in front of Visek and Launa, who turned after it, and while they were looking away, Kylee sprinted, leaving the others behind and rushing to the war barrow. She leapt into the open back and ducked down, practically tackling Brysen as she clamped her hand over his mouth so he couldn't scream.

"I'm here to rescue you," she whispered to his wide, wet eyes. He'd been crying. She took her hand away, ran it over his arms and chest, looking for bleeding. "Are you okay? Are you hurt?"

"I didn't do it," he whispered. His blue eyes gleamed in the brief flashes of lightning, so much softer than their father's eyes, but still so unsettling to find staring back at her in the dark. "Anon came right outside to stretch in the rain, right here . . . his back was to me . . . I could've done it, and I didn't move."

"You were scared," she reassured him. "It's okay to be scared. That's your mind telling you something's wrong."

"I'm not *scared*," Brysen said, sounding so much younger than his seasons. "I *chose* not to do it. After everything I put Jowyn and the battle boys through, all the big promises I made myself about ending this war . . . and I decided not to do it." He shook his head, like he couldn't believe what he was saying. He had the faraway look of a dazed augur, a mystic who'd stared too long at the sky.

"That was smart," she said. "This isn't some singer's tale where the big bad gets killed and all the monsters turn back into clouds. You'd never have gotten out of here alive if you'd done it."

Brysen's expression shifted, like he was just realizing this conversation wasn't happening in his head, that Kylee was really there, in front of him. He looked at her and frowned. "Wait. What . . . what are you doing here?"

"I *told* you," she repeated, "I'm here to rescue you."

"Kylee." Brysen squeezed her hand. "Kylee," he said again. "I have so much to tell you."

She smiled at him, squeezed his hand back, and felt the anger that had been boiling inside her melt away. There was something different about him. He'd always seemed like a storm held together by scar tissue, but sitting in the dark of the war barrow in the midst of an actual storm, he seemed calm, like the mist that comes when a storm has passed.

"It's good to see you, too," she said. "Now can we flutter out of here while we still have heads attached to our bodies?"

Brysen nodded, and they rose to peek the tops of their heads out from the war barrow together.

The rain had slowed, and fog shrouded the camp in a hazy light. The rising sun in the distance made a rainbow that ran like a bridge behind the Six Villages, over both war camps, all the way to the far end of the Uztari plateau, over the landscapes the two of them used to dream about as kids.

Maybe we'll explore them one day soon, far past the reach of any armies or kyrgs or nightmare birds, Kylee thought.

"*Shyehnaah!*" Grazim's voice cut through the morning, and Kylee's head snapped up to see the hawk, turning hard, falling fast with a spear through its chest, and then Jowyn running after her as she charged at Visek, who'd already raised another spear in her direction. Jowyn tackled her out of the way and the spear grazed over his back, slicing a thin red line between his shoulder blades.

"No!" Brysen yelled, bolting up from the barrow, leaping

over his sister, and running to Jowyn, grabbing the boy in his arms and looking up at Visek with red-eyed rage.

"*Shyehnaah*," he snarled, and Kylee felt dizzy. She'd never heard him speak the Hollow Tongue before and didn't know to what bird he could possibly be speaking.

On the ground, the hawk with the spear through its chest looked like a chicken on a spit over a flame . . . but it stirred. It flapped its wings and tried to stand, charging madly at Visek with the wood shaft dragging in the mud behind it. The warrior cocked his head, then raised a boot and stomped the bird straight into the ground, crushing its skull as he heaved the spear out of its back with a wet crunch.

Brysen collapsed where he sat, like a tether had been snapped between him and the bird. He held Jowyn's bleeding back against his chest, his jaw hanging open in a silent scream. The tent flaps opened and a large shirtless man stepped out, his long hair hanging past his shoulders and a huge hooked sword clenched in one hand. The sword probably weighed more than Kylee.

"Gag them before they speak again!" he ordered, and warriors descended on Kylee, Grazim, Brysen, and Jowyn from all sides.

She was hauled from the back of the barrow as a rag was stuffed into her mouth, and though she wanted to fight, wanted to scream out and call down the wrath of a furious sky on her captors, she found she could only stare at her gray-haired, teary-eyed brother, who had chosen not to end a man's life and had, somehow, called a bird back from the dead.

A SKY OF STONE

THE CEILING WAS PAINTED LIKE SKY, THOUGH IT WAS CRACKED.
Soot-stained clouds gave way to exposed stone, and what passed
for a sun was smeared with blacks and browns, the origins of
which Nyall didn't want to question.

There was no real sky. No window. No light. No fresh air.
This was the Sky Castle's dungeon, and Nyall had no idea how
long he'd been down there. Days? Weeks? They say time
slows for prisoners, and some foolish part of him hoped it had
only been a long night, that the hangover he had when he'd
first woken up here had created an illusion of endlessness. He
knew better, though. The world was moving on without him,
and somewhere in it, Kylee was in danger. He'd been her

protector, or at least, he'd convinced himself he had been. Some good he'd do protecting her from this cell.

He took comfort in the fact that she could look after herself. She always had. She'd taken care of Brysen and her mother, too. They'd never starved, even when there was no bronze because her da gambled or drank it all away or her ma gave it all to Crawling Priests. They didn't starve when Brysen spent his days mooning over his trainer instead of taming new birds for sale. And they didn't starve when Kylee left, because she had Nyall sending back letters of credit, even though Brysen promised he didn't need her help in every reply.

Would Brysen starve without those letters now? Had Nyall failed *everyone*?

Self-pity flocked around him, beating relentless wings. No one had even told him *why* he was in this cell. Those two goons from Kyrg Bardu brought him food at odd intervals but wouldn't tell him anything. He cringed when he heard the metal crossbar sliding back, because whenever he got too close while his cell door was open, the bigger one, Chit, punched him in the gut.

"I could aim lower if I wanted," she told him the first time.

The second time, she demonstrated.

After that, she didn't even look for reasons to beat him.

At least the bruises helped him tell time. They'd turned

more yellow than black, which meant at least three or four days had passed.

This is my life now. I measure my days in bruises.

When the door creaked open again, he braced himself, but Chit entered all smiles. She didn't have her falcon with her this time, which Nyall found curious. After so much time alone, any change in routine felt monumental.

"Your fist is empty," he said, mostly to test that his voice still worked. How long had it been since he'd spoken?

Chit clenched it. "I could fill it with a chunk of your hair, if you'd like," she snarled. Nyall found the new threat entertaining. He'd grown bored with being punched and kicked.

Behind Chit, her equally hulking companion blocked most of the light from the hall. He, too, carried no bird. They'd never come down to the dungeons birdless before. Nyall wondered why but knew better than to ask directly. Instead, he asked the same question he'd asked every time they came to him.

"Where's Kylee?"

"She's gone," Chit said. "Off to war. You should hope she fights well, because your life is tethered tight to hers."

Nyall chuckled. "Same as it ever was."

Chit pulled a rolled-up flatbread from her robe. It was wrapped in cloth, and when she unrolled it, steam rose. He smelled the cheese and roasted nuts and dried fruit that stuffed it. His mouth watered.

"Hungry?" Chit asked.

Nyall shrugged. He didn't want to look desperate.

"We made this just for you," Chit told him. "And we would love to give it to you while it's still warm."

"Well, I won't stop you." Nyall smiled and put out his hand. "Go for it."

She raised the bread to her nose, took a deep sniff, and sighed. Then she spat in it and held it out to him.

Nyall seethed, and in that moment, he realized four things.

The first was that she hadn't asked him any questions or made any threats. She had something he wanted, but she wanted nothing in return. She didn't want information or a confession or any of the things he assumed jailers usually tried to extract from prisoners. He was simply a hostage, and the only thing he had of value to her was staying alive.

The second was that they were never going to release him. He was their leverage over Kylee, and if she had gone off to war without him, that was because they hadn't given her a choice.

Kylee deserved choices. Nyall never wanted to be someone who limited her choices. That was the third thing he realized. To free his friend, he had to free himself.

The fourth thing was that he was going to enjoy shoving that flatbread down Chit's throat.

"I'm so hungry," he whined, and stepped forward as meekly as he could, head bowed and hand out to accept the soiled food. Chit dropped it on the filthy floor, forcing him to bend down at her feet to pick up.

Perfect, he thought as he bent. With his head down and his long, coiled locks hanging over his face, she couldn't see him smile.

"Say thank you, bird scuzz," she commanded him.

"Thank you, bird scuzz," he repeated with just enough snark so that her leg bent back to kick him. That was when he made his move, springing straight up to smash his skull into her chin and then shoving her backward into her partner. As she fell, he threw the hot bread at the man's face, forcing him to reflexively shield his eyes.

If this were a brawl in the yard of the Broken Jess, he would've swept their legs out from under them right then with a kick, but he had to play this fight a few moves ahead. He wasn't trying to beat them into submission; he was trying to escape. In spite of every instinct he had, he backed off, stood his ground by the waste bucket in the corner, where he'd been forced to relieve himself for days, and let them both recover their footing to charge him in the cell.

One hard kick was all it would take to get the waste bucket

in the air, sloshing its foul contents over both of them. He twirled around, not going for a strike but faking like he was, so the last thing they both saw before getting a face full of his crap was his body off-balance for a high kick.

Shut-eyed and gagging, they both lunged for where he'd been standing, thinking to tackle him as he struck, but he danced around, avoiding hitting either of them. He was now standing in the doorway to his cell, while they stood inside it.

"Thanks for the hospitality," he told them, and saluted with a flourishing flap of his fingers across his chest before realizing they couldn't see past his own crap in their eyes. As they rushed for the sound of his voice, he slammed the cell door shut and slid the metal bar across, much preferring the sound of it ramming home from this side of the door than the other.

The frame shuddered as they slammed their massive bodies into it, but he couldn't even hear the oaths and curses they were no doubt screaming. There was a viewing slot in the upper part of the door, which he slid open.

Chit's filthy eyes blazed out at him, much brighter than the painted sun. "You will never get out of this city alive," she growled, and he realized he didn't have anything else he wanted from her. He slammed the slot closed again.

Down the hall there was another door, closed. He figured there would be guards on the other side. He'd need some sort of plan to get past them. He also noticed that the row of cell doors along the hall were all closed, but not barred, except for the three next to his cell. He cocked his head, wondering who else he might find locked up at Kyrg Bardu's pleasure. What if Chit had been lying and Kylee was a prisoner, too? It was worth checking.

Opening the first viewing slot gave him a start.

There, sitting cross-legged on the floor with her hands resting calmly on her knees, was Üku, the Owl Mother, in a kind of meditative state. She didn't react to the slot being opened, and he slid it quietly closed. This explained why Chit and her partner didn't have their falcons with them. You wouldn't want to bring birds anywhere near Üku.

When he slid open the slot in the next cell door, he saw a slightly bruised and battered Kyrg Ryven. The young lord was muttering to himself and shaking his head, repeating words that Nyall recognized as the Hollow Tongue but didn't know the meaning of. He frowned. The kyrg spoke the Hollow Tongue, or at least thought he did. *That* was interesting.

When Ryven saw the slash of light from the open slot, he bolted to his feet and rushed for it. "*Shyehnaah!*" he yelled, but there was no bird for his word to work on.

"Sorry, kyrg," Nyall said. "It's just me. But if you care to tell me what's going on, maybe I can be of some assistance."

"Let me out of here and I'll explain everything." The kyrg spoke fast, frantic. "Kylee is in danger and only I can help you protect her."

Nyall snorted. "Why don't you explain from in there? I feel safer with this door between us."

"I know hidden ways out of this castle. Help me help you."

"*That* was not an explanation," Nyall said. "Maybe take a heartbeat to think about your position. I'll be right back."

He slid the slot shut over the kyrg's objections. It was petty, but Nyall needed to humble the noble prisoner a little, remind him who had the power at this moment, especially since he probably would need the young kyrg to show him those hidden ways out.

He slid the last slot open and saw a skinny figure in tattered clothes, looking like the skeleton of the man he used to be.

"Goryn Tamir," Nyall whispered. "Never thought I'd see you again."

The fallen heir to the Tamir family raised his head toward the slot in the door, squinting at the dim light, shielding his eyes as if he were staring into a cloudless midday sky. His mouth moved to speak and his tongue lolled inside it, but no sound came out at all.

Nyall slid the slot shut and leaned against the opposite wall, glancing at the locked door to the tier of cells.

An Owl Mother, a kyrg, and a gangster all at my mercy, and all of us locked underground together, he thought. *Looks like I just got some bargaining power.*

Now he just had to decide what it was he wanted and how each of them was going to help him get it.

BRYSEN

OPENING WOUNDS

32

BRYSEN WAS ON HIS KNEES, TIED TO A POST BEHIND HIS BACK. THEY
had been dragged inside Anon's large tent. It was still dim in
the early morning light and a few dung-lamps blazed, casting
distorted shadows on the cloth. The light made Anon's shadow
change in size, looming huge before them, then turning tiny
as he paced about the space.

Jowyn, Kylee, and that girl whose name he couldn't remember were tied up in a line beside him, though with the
way they'd bound his neck, he couldn't turn his head to see
without choking himself. They'd also tied a rag in his mouth,
and from his peripheral vision it looked like they'd done the

same to the others. Even Jowyn, whose voice could make Brysen's heart flutter but not much else. He wasn't even a falconer by normal means, let alone one who spoke the Hollow Tongue like Brysen and Kylee.

Like me and *Kylee.*

There was irony in the fact that Brysen had longed his whole life to have this gift, to truly fly out from under his sister's shadow. Now that he'd finally done it, a barrel of bird's scuzz it was worth to him.

The moment he'd had Anon within a blade's reach, he found himself without a weapon to wield or a bird to call. He'd left his bird behind to keep her safe and Anon still had his black-talon blade, which wasn't even really Brysen's. It had been his father's knife. He'd picked it up when his father was killed and had been trying to wield it ever since.

The knife that had cut him so many times as a child had been with him through countless brawls in the battle pits and fights on the mountain. The only time it had felt like his own was when he used it to imp Shara new feathers, and then any knife would've done.

All his life, he'd prayed for the gifts his sister had—the power to command a bird of prey to hunt and kill with perfect ease—but had never found his voice. Squatting in the war barrow, staring at Anon's exposed back, he'd realized he was a bird flying against the wind. He'd been flapping like mad to chase his father and his sister with the idea that the only greatness in this world was a predator's power and if he could master it, he too would be great.

But Brysen was not a hawk. He didn't have to choose between predator and prey. He could, if he wanted, be something else entirely. He could call a bird to heal itself, summon it back to life; his sister had never done that. He'd never even heard stories of *anyone* doing that. He really was unique in all the world, and all he had to do was embrace this gift, turn and glide on the wind he'd been flying against his whole life. Be a healer.

He'd slumped back in the barrow then, his choice made. Jowyn was right—of course the boy knew the best parts of Brysen better than he knew them himself. Jowyn had looked for them in a way Brysen never had. At that moment Brysen had decided he needed to get them out of the camp and back to safety, so he could figure out how, exactly, to use this gift he had finally accepted.

That was when his sister appeared, like a falcon returning to the fist, and the two of them were reunited. Through his tears he'd even smiled. For the first time in a long time, things just felt right.

So of course it didn't last.

He was a prisoner now, and the jackal hawk he'd healed had been crushed beneath a boot just moments after he'd brought it back to life.

Nice job, as usual, he sneered at himself. *Another brilliant victory in a long and glorious life.*

"The First Falconers believed they could divine the future from the entrails of a hawk," Anon said, standing in front of Brysen and dropping the mangled corpse of the jackal hawk in front of him. "Of course, their civilization was wiped out, leaving nothing but ruins and rock paintings." He laughed to himself and then squatted so his face was in front of Brysen's. He'd put down his sword and now held Brysen's curved black-talon blade. He raised it so the tip touched Brysen's nose. "Do you see your own future in the ruins of this bird, Brysen? Do you see theirs?"

Anon looked down the line of prisoners, then stood, turning his back on all of them. Visek and Launa watched from the shadows as outside, the clattering of the Kartami army grew louder. They were on edge, preparing for an attack either from the barricades or the Uztari army, or both. They were pinned between the two, and it made Brysen wonder about Anon's military genius, if he'd let his army get stuck like this. Unless he'd done it on purpose. Unless there was a trap to spring that no one yet saw.

"So you think you're here to end this war?" Anon said, and Brysen tensed. Had he known Brysen's plans the whole time? Was he toying with him? "The young always think they can change the course of the wind. It's nothing new. I thought so, too, when I began. I thought I could topple Uztar and rebuild the world, free from this sky cult that corrupts everything it touches." He shook his head and toyed with Brysen's knife between his hands.

"I was wrong, of course. There is no tearing down Uztar. It's far too strong and the lies that built it are far too insidious. However many believers I recruit, there will be a hundred more on your side, prepared to die to protect the world they find familiar. An empty sky is more terrible to them than a corrupt one."

He set the knife down and kicked the dead hawk's entrails, splattering them on Brysen's face. "Still not seeing your future?" Brysen worked the cloth in his mouth with his tongue. If he could get a word out, then maybe . . . maybe what?

He had no idea what to do.

"There *is* no future there." Anon stepped on half the corpse, further desecrating it. The part of Brysen that still remembered his mother's lectures and prayers about the sacredness of every bird of prey winced. The part of Brysen that devoted all his time and energy and care to taming birds of prey felt nauseated. "This is your future! You are here—all of you ambitious children—as *bait*. I am picking a fight, but not with the armies massed around us. I couldn't care less about conquering territory, and I have no way to hold it long if I did. I am trying to pick a fight with the sky and, I hope, empty it at last, even if it kills me and every one of my warriors."

The ghost eagle, Brysen thought. Anon wanted Brysen in order to lure his sister—he'd been honest about that from the start—and he wanted his sister because the ghost eagle followed her. But why would he want to pick a fight with the ghost eagle?

"Your people think the Hollow Tongue is a gift," Anon said. "You think just because it is useful to you that it belongs to you. Using a thing and controlling it are not the same. The weapons we choose wield us. A blade wants to cut, and an eagle wants to hunt. Have you ever wondered why beings of blood and air allow themselves to be tamed by heavy lumps of bone and flesh who walk and crawl and rot on the ground? You worship these birds like gods and then you presume to tame them. How do you tame a god? Why do you assume it is you who is doing the taming? You think the Hollow Tongue has been taming birds of prey for you, but it has, in truth, been taming *you* all along. Putting you in position, teaching you how to serve it, keeping you hungry for more. The ghost eagle is an intelligence like you cannot conceive, and there is no controlling it."

Anon laced his fingers together, leaned back against the campaign table, and softened his tone, like a bard for children beginning a storytime.

"In my youth, wandering in the Parsh Desert, I encountered an ancient shrine, a monument of the First Falconers, built to honor these great and terrible birds, and when I meditated upon it, I had a vision. I *saw* what the eagle saw and *knew* what it wanted for all humanity. It is the only word I've ever known in the Hollow Tongue: *vayara*."

Brysen knew the word without understanding how or why. He'd felt it in the moment when Shara nearly died in the fire and again when the spear tore through the jackal hawk. Now he felt it echo through him, the feeling that all was lost.

"It means," Anon explained to his prisoners, leaning forward, his hands on his knees, "apocalypse. An end of all things. And with your screams and blood, I will stop it. I am needed to lure you here, Kylee, in all your distress, to bring forth an angry ghost eagle. And in its rage, I aim to kill it. I am going to save humanity and set us free from this eagle, no matter who I have to kill to do it. Nestlings die, but the flock survives."

Finished with his speech, he strode toward Kylee with Brysen's black-talon blade drawn, and Brysen was helpless to stop him. They, it appeared, were the nestlings who had to die.

33

HE SQUIRMED, TRIED TO TWIST AND BREAK AWAY FROM THE POST, BUT the movement just squeezed his windpipe tighter.

"Agh!" he groaned, and Anon shot him a glance.

"Relax, Brysen. You'll get your turn," he said, then called back to Visek and Launa. "The impatience of these young ones is exhausting. I'm sorry I made you spend so much time training them."

"We do with happiness all that service demands," Launa answered with a bow at the waist. Anon smiled at that and then turned the black blade to Kylee. He cut the cloth that gagged her.

She spat. "You know nothing, and you'll suffer for it!"

Anon ignored her and came back to Brysen, who tensed as the warrior squatted in front of him again. "Well, that's the screaming. Now for the blood."

He lifted the knife and touched the tip lightly to Brysen's cheek. With his other hand, he grabbed Brysen's chin to hold his face steady. The metal was warm.

"Call the eagle," he told Kylee.

"Rot in mud!" she snarled back at him, which made Brysen smile against the thumping of his heart. He was so close to Anon that the scent of sweat and rope oil filled his nose, covering the stench of the mangled hawk's corpse. Sweat raced down his own back, and his breath came ragged through the cloth in his mouth. He clung to his defiance, remembered the pain he'd endured all his life. Pain was nothing to him. He could manage pain. He cast his mind like a hawk in the air, flew his thoughts back through the rainy night to the moments when he and Jowyn held each other, the awkward laughter, the unfamiliar joy. He could mantle those memories over whatever pain was about to come. He'd shelter himself in those memories of joy.

But there was no sheltering himself from *this* pain. The knifepoint did not slice down across his cheek like he'd expected. It twisted upward and dug its metal into his left eye, drove in. The scream he let out chased off any memories he could find. There was nothing else but clean, white agony. He could hear the knife scraping the bone in his eye socket, could feel the hot stream of blood and pus that flowed down his cheek.

Through his gag, Jowyn screamed and thrashed against the ropes.

When Anon pulled away, Brysen was dizzied by the throbbing pressure of pain, unable to control his breathing and struggling to make sense of his new vision—one-eyed, depthless, fuzzy, and dark.

"*Brysen!*" Kylee shouted, and then she said a word in the Hollow Tongue he didn't know, a word he could barely hear through the roar of his own pulse, a word he hoped meant something like death and vengeance. He wanted to hurt these people, he wanted to rip them all to shreds. He wanted the black wings of the ghost eagle to beat on them so hard it would blow their camp to sand, blow their flesh to ash, and blow time backward to last night, to those last moments before he'd screwed up by coming here, by dreaming too big for himself, before turning everything to pain.

But time only went one way, and he couldn't undo what had been done to him. He screamed again, but screaming didn't dull the hurt.

"Don't let him die," Anon snapped, and Visek rushed to

Brysen, shoving some kind of salve into the socket of his eye, which stopped the bleeding and cleaned the wound, even numbed the pain a bit. Boiled sunroot maybe, or a compound of sage root and some other herbs, similar to what he used for imping hawk feathers. He felt pressure and an ache as Visek worked on him the way he'd work on an injured hawk. He even saw phantom spots where the man's fingers pressed the wound, but lost the sight of him on that side of his body. There wasn't black in his vision but a void, a lack of light and darkness, a *nothing* that Visek bandaged over. His other eye had trouble focusing now and that was only partly because of the tears that blurred it. His eye was a swan grieving for its mate. The thought made him laugh. *My widower eye.*

"His suffering can stop," Anon told Kylee, "when you do as I ask, Kylee."

"I can't!" Kylee cried out. "The ghost eagle left me. I disappointed it, and it left."

"No," Anon said. "It can't be finished with you. Perhaps you need more motivation." He moved back to Brysen with his knife but was stopped by a commotion outside the tent.

"Kites up!" someone yelled outside. Visek and Launa glanced at each other.

"To air!" someone else yelled, and Anon paused.

Another barrow pair came into the tent, breathless. "The rain has stopped and the Uztari are advancing on our position across the field," they updated him. "The villagers on the barricades are preparing their hawks to fly. We're pinned between them."

"Only so much as an ice-snake is pinned by a hawk it is about to bite," Anon told them. "Set up defensive kites against the Six Villages, but don't push through yet," he ordered. "Roll out four battalions against the Uztari. One left, one center, two right. I want to push them toward the mountains, cut off their supply lines."

The messengers bowed their heads toward the ground, then left to execute his orders.

"The war is begun," Anon spoke only to Kylee. "For now, my forces are set on bloodying this ground on which we stand . . ." He sucked his teeth. "Give them something to fight in the sky, and who knows how many lives might be saved."

"Why do you think I can *make* it fight you?" Kylee asked.

"Because, Kylee," Anon told her, "*that* is what *it* wants to do. The ghost eagle is not what you think it is. It is not controlled by the Hollow Tongue; it *is* the Hollow Tongue. It is the word made flesh and feather, held together by a power older than history, and it wants to tear every one of us apart: Uztari, Altari, Kartami . . . it sees no distinction. I alone among those who walk this world am fighting against it. I, my foolish child, am trying to save all humanity. I can only do that, however, if the eagle will fight me, and it will *only* fight me, it seems, if you command it to. I took Brysen and I let him train, all to summon you here. It was a great effort, as you can see, so perhaps you'll make some effort yourself?"

"It won't come to me!" Kylee pleaded. "It's changed. It doesn't care who I'm protecting anymore."

"Then find a better way to call it!" Anon demanded. "If it won't come to your fear, find what it *will* come to! What does it want from you? What has it always wanted?"

Brysen's breathing was ragged. He felt dizzy, and he strained to hear what Kylee said next over the humming in his head. She spoke so quietly, even Anon had to lean over to hear her.

She repeated herself: "It wants my rage."

"And you won't give it?" Anon held the bloody knife up so she could see it before it went back to Brysen's eye. "Are you not angry at me, Kylee? Do you not hate me? I've done everything I can think of to earn your hate, and still you won't unleash your anger?"

"If I do," she said, "I may never be able to stop it."

Anon broke out in a smile. He rested his heavy hand on Brysen's shoulder, patting it softly. "That's fine, Kylee," he said. "I will stop it for you. But first . . . to work."

He held the knife in front of Brysen's other eye.

Jowyn managed to spit out the gag and scream. "I'll bury your bones so deep worms will look down on them!" He thrashed and bucked against the ropes that bound him. The threat was as empty as it was creative.

Brysen, in spite of all his determination to be strong, to be defiant, simply squirmed. His body tensed as he tried to pull his head away, straining against the ropes. The blade loomed up in his remaining eye's vision, blotting out anything else. It was hard to tell how close it was. He couldn't triangulate, struggled to focus on it. That blurry black blade would be the last thing he saw, the blade that had been his and his father's before he took it. This was the blade his father would've killed him with had he lived, and now it was coming for him again. He was that little boy in the mews, his back flayed by his father's whip, his arm slashed by his father's black-talon blade, his skin burned by his father's flame.

He wet himself. It was humiliating, but pain has no pride, and as the knifepoint pressed forward, he whimpered. This was what complete loss felt like—not even his body was in his control anymore. He was at Anon's mercy, and Kylee's, and the ghost eagle's. He'd always been at everyone else's mercy. Jowyn had his heart now, and Anon his body, and Kylee his fate. What good was a healing power if he couldn't even heal himself?

He cried and it stung and was maybe the last time his eye would ever well with tears, and he tried to calm himself, to soften himself against the pain that was to come, to remind himself he'd never liked his eyes anyway, that blue that was so like his father's. *Good riddance*, he thought, but the thought was a lie. He didn't want to lose any more. He didn't want any more pain. Just before the tip of the knife broke his cornea, he cried out, in desperate terror, like a broken-winged bird shuddering before a fox, and his sister twinned his scream with her own and their cries were answered with a high shriek.

The tent's fabric roof tore open in half a dozen places as a rain of falcons dove into the dark. One slammed straight into Anon's forearm, knocking down the blade. Another hit his back with talons up, tearing his skin and pulling him backward, off his feet. Two more went after Visek and Launa, while one hit hard on the post to which Brysen was tied. The post wobbled in the dirt, came loose, and, with a shove, fell. Brysen slid free of it, then worked his hands out of the rope. He grabbed his blade to cut the others free.

"*Caleen!*" Kylee yelled, and the stunned bird who'd hit the post suddenly snapped back into focus and launched itself at Anon's face when he tried to stand up again.

"*Kraas!*" Grazim yelled, and the bird tried to tear Anon's windpipe out, but the warrior dodged and landed a punch that knocked the bird out of the air. Grazim lunged for him herself, but backed off when he turned to meet her. She'd never survive hand-to-hand against him. From Brysen's view, it looked like she was directly in front of him, but it was a trick of his sight. Anon was at the far back of the tent, and two more birds attacked him, keeping him from coming for Grazim.

"Hey, Bry, any time now," Jowyn said, showing his wrists still bound behind his back.

Brysen struggled to line up the blade's edge with Jowyn's ropes. He wasn't used to the depth perception with one eye and found there was a blind spot he couldn't understand. When he reached for the rope, he felt himself holding Jowyn's wrist. He tried again and missed completely.

"I don't want to cut you," he said.

"I trust you," Jowyn replied, which was nice but didn't actually help him aim the blade. On the third try, he got the rope and carefully pressed the knife to it, sawing more than slicing so he didn't risk missing. His hands shook, but he soon felt the ropes snap.

"He said they trained you?" Kylee asked urgently as Brysen untied Jowyn and the Kartami fought against the birds Grazim commanded against the warriors. "You know how to drive one of their barrows?"

Jowyn nodded but looked questioningly at Brysen. "Can you—?"

"I think I can fly," Brysen said. "As long as you're steering below. I can't aim so well. But I won't need to. I'm not trying to kill anything."

Jowyn gave him the softest of nods, and Kylee called to Grazim to fall back.

"But——!" Grazim objected. She was still trying to kill the warlord, though her birds were not faring well. The man knew how to fend off their attacks. His hands and forearms were bloody, but he was undaunted. Grazim relented and the four of them ran together from the tent straight into a battle raging outside.

On the ground and in the air, birds and soldiers clashed. The scene would've been dizzying even if Brysen hadn't just lost an eye.

He'd seen violence and death in his days, but he had never seen anything like this.

34

THE SKY WAS SO THICK WITH KITES AND BIRDS AND ARROWS THAT HE could barely feel the freshly risen sun on his face. The Six Villages had thrown everything they had against the Kartami siege, and the Kartami kite warriors were fighting just as hard.

Overhead, a reddish-brown sunset hawk zipped across Brysen's peripheral vision and then vanished. Brysen realized he'd have to turn his head to track it now, that half the light of the sky had been stolen from him. But that didn't mean it was gone. He just had to learn how to find it. He could use the background to guess at the bird's speed and distance. It would be hard on a clear blue day, but the chaos in the air actually gave him a lot of focal points to use. Adjusting his sight was going to take practice, and practice would take time he didn't have right now.

He tracked the hawk as it sliced straight through the silk of a kite, which whirled and curved and fought to stay aloft. The hawk turned around and landed on the warrior's back, tore at the frame and then at the warrior strapped inside it. An arrow shot by the barrow driver below ripped right through the bird. Brysen searched himself for the words to heal it as it fell, but even though he wasn't yet sure how his use of the Hollow Tongue worked, he knew now that it demanded he feel *some-thing*. He didn't know this bird, was too focused on his own struggles, and he couldn't find the desperate hope he needed to save it. He watched it fall.

Nestlings die, but the flock survives.

He had to keep his focus on the bigger picture. Saving his friends and family. The shock of the morning was setting in, and he felt a welcome numbness. Pain, fear, and hope were all dulled, and in their dullness, action became possible.

Anon's war barrow was sitting right in front of them, wheels locked but otherwise rigged to fly. Both barrow and kite were larger than most of the others, as Anon was larger than most of the other warriors, but Brysen guessed that meant it could haul the weight of three of them in the barrow, while he would mount the sky to pull them.

"Are you sure you're okay to fly this thing?" Jowyn asked

again, gently, but this wasn't like last night, when it was just the two of them in their tent during a storm. This wasn't a time when his readiness would matter. When he could say no. He had to be ready now. Wounded and aching and frightened though he was, he was a survivor. He would fly.

He unlashed the kite and almost dropped it from the cleat where it hung. It was heavier than the kite he'd trained on, and it took Jowyn, Kylee, and Grazim pushing the barrow forward to get the wheels moving, while he stood inside and struggled to position the kite for throwing. As they rolled, tension built on the slingshot line to help him launch it, but even with that help, he nearly threw his back out and fell off the barrow with the effort.

With a *whoosh* the kite went up, and Jowyn jumped into the barrow and slid in front of him to steer as the wings of the kite opened and caught the wind. Brysen leaned on his shoulder a moment, relieved to feel the steadiness of Jowyn's muscles as he wrangled the lines into control. Brysen needed to know that when he went up, Jowyn was below to keep him from falling.

The barrow gained speed, surprising warriors, who dove out of its path. One quick-thinking sentry nocked and raised an arrow toward them, but Kylee snapped a short word that made Brysen think of crossbow bolts. At the command, a peregrine flew from the tent and slammed into the sentry's head, knocking their neck back at a terrible angle and sending the arrow wide and wild.

Kylee then jumped into the cart, followed by Grazim. Brysen pressed himself to the side so they could get in front of him. He'd hang off the back so he could climb the line without kicking them in the head—and so they wouldn't see how clumsily he climbed now that he couldn't be so sure of his hands gripping the rope when he reached for it.

It took him two tries to get his hands around the guideline, but he found by moving his head to the side as he reached out, he could estimate the distance a little better than looking at the rope straight on. As his hands wrapped around it, he felt a swell of pride. He was adapting. He was winning. He would not be stopped.

He pulled himself hand over hand, feet pressed together to grip the rope, hauling himself higher and higher. He felt like a caterpillar on a branch that knows there are magpies with hungry eyes watching him climb. His new blind spot frustrated him as he climbed; where the hectic sky beside him should have been, he saw only a vague whiteness. He had to turn his head completely to look around and get a true sense of where he was in relation to the barricades and mountains. The shadows on the ground looked like part of the objects that cast them, and the effect was dizzying. People, barrows, tents, and mountains . . . they were suddenly bonded to the darkness they cast. They were one with their own darkness. *This was always true*, he thought, *but now I can see it.*

As he climbed, it became very clear to him that this was *not* a training kite. He knew he was higher than he'd thought he'd be just by the size of the figures on the ground. Another facet of his new sight: If he'd been able to tell how high this kite was flying, he might never have found the nerve to climb it.

From this height, he could see the lakes of rainwater in the low hills that held pieces of the sky on their wind-rippled surfaces. They looked close enough to touch. The wet air stung his face like tiny flecks of gravel; the speed ruffled his hair. He struggled to strap himself into the harness—grabbing things was so much harder than he wanted it to be—then adjusted it to fit his smaller size rather than the size of whatever warrior normally flew above Anon.

As he settled into his skyward perch, a volley of blazing arrows shot across his sightline, lethal fireflies heading from the barricades to the kites. Brysen's heart leapt to his throat as he flexed his arm to turn and dodge, though the arrows were actually nowhere near him.

He had to get better at judging. He was lucky that volley hadn't been meant for him, but the defenders of the Villages didn't know it was him up there. They would shoot down any kite they saw.

The arrows fell into the camp below, where the flames

burned out against the wet fabric of the tents or the wet ground. Kartami archers returned a volley of arrows, sending the Six Villagers on the barricades scrambling for cover.

But the moment the arrows ceased, the villagers launched their birds—a screaming scrum of mismatched buzzards, dusky hawks, and delicate collectors' falcons. The birds of prey rose higher than the kites. Brysen couldn't see clearly enough to know if Shara was among them, screeching and calling and jostling for position. Some were obviously better trained than others, but all were keen for fighting.

The first to mount the sky were the true falcons, peregrines and gyrfalcons and kestrels. Once at a killing height, they folded their wings and dropped like deadly hail, beaks pointed for the silk-strung kites below them—including Brysen's.

A colorful flycatcher falcon dove for Brysen but had to dodge an arrow fired from the Kartami, which forced a near miss. Its wing clipped the edge of his kite, making him turn but not tumble. Then another wave came at him, this one composed of short-winged hawks—buzzards and goshawks, red-tails and sunsets. All the beautiful birds Brysen had devoted his life to trapping and training were now sky-bent and talons-up, screeching for his blood. He weaved and turned, dodging the onslaught as best he could with his new vision. A talon slashed his thigh but didn't grab on, kept flying. His head ached from the effort of decoding everything he saw.

Below, his weaving and turning had slowed the war barrow, which was struggling in the mud. Grazim and Kylee were busy, using their voices to commandeer the birds that the Villages had just launched against the Kartami. Foot soldiers chased their barrow through the camp.

"*Toktott!*" Grazim shouted so loud, Brysen could hear from above, and the falcon that had just missed him changed its flight and knocked away a spear that one of the other barrow drivers had thrown at Jowyn.

A spear flew past Brysen, and he turned to see Visek strapped into a kite, giving chase while his mother steered after them on the ground. An unexpected benefit to Brysen's one-eyed, unpracticed flying was that he was uneven, wobbly. If he'd been flying straight and true, Visek's spear would've hit him in the chest. Visek took aim and loosed the next spear. This one wasn't going to miss.

"*Toktott!*" his sister yelled, and a grand golden eagle, probably one of Mama Tamir's prized birds, dove from chasing a Kartami kite above to spread its lustrous wings wide between him and Visek. For a moment, the eagle's back was all Brysen saw, and then the spear point tore through the bird. The eagle screeched and fell, but the spear fell with it.

His sister had saved him, though not with the ghost eagle. She could command birds of prey to their deaths for him but could not summon the one bird that might save them all. He could heal birds of prey on the verge of death with just a word but couldn't make them fight for him.

What if Anon is right? What if the birds aren't the ones whose wills are being bent?

On the ground, Jowyn struggled to steer. The over-weighted war barrow moved too slowly, half-mired in mud, and the Kartami were flanking it, though they tried to weave through the tents and trenches, searching for a way out of the camp, a way to escape, any path to safety at all. With the Six Villages to one side and the advancing army of Uztar to the other, a measure of safety was impossibly close, but they were hemmed in on all sides and Brysen couldn't see a way out in any direction. The Kartami horde was too vast.

Brysen could feel the kite straining to pull and knew they weren't covering much ground. He could see from above what they couldn't from the barrow—they were outflanked and surrounded, and warriors were closing in around them like a hawk slowly squeezing the life from a hare. The Uztari army was still too far away to help, having just collided with huge Kartami battalions. The only thing keeping Visek's kite from overtaking Brysen were the birds that harried him back. Grazim barked commands to fight off the warriors below, while Kylee's eyes were fixed on Brysen, trying to defend him. But it wouldn't be enough. They'd never make it before the Six Villages exhausted themselves and the four of them were cut down dead.

Anon stood in front of his tent, bloodied but calm, as officers ran to him to receive orders and then ran off again to implement them. As Brysen watched, a new war barrow arrived for the leader, and he mounted the back without waiting for someone to pair with him. He heaved the kite from the side one-handed and hurled it into the wind, then began his roll in their direction. A warrior held out two big katar blades sheathed on a belt, which he grabbed as he passed. His eyes were locked on Brysen's kite, and he steered through the camp with the easy grace of an eagle gliding.

Brysen had to do something to help, other than steer poorly for an escape they couldn't reach. He had to fight back. If the Hollow Tongue demanded his pain, then he had to open himself up to that pain. He had to let himself see everything in himself that he hated—everything he'd ever lost or feared to lose, everything he wanted that he knew he couldn't have— and he had to accept it.

A body that did not repulse him with its scars.

A chance to laugh and dance and play at peace with Jowyn.

His sister free of all the burdens she bore for him.

A future that he got to decide for himself.

He'd never have any of those things if they all died here today; he'd never even learn how to try.

As the birds swirled in violent clouds around the gliders and bloody, mangled bodies fell, he sent out one more hopeless wish: that he might see Shara one more time before he died.

He whispered her name, but it didn't come out as "Shara." He stumbled on the word, his sadness catching his voice, and said, "*Sharaya.*"

He knew even as he said it that it was a Hollow Tongue word and that it meant friend.

And she came.

Screaming from the barricades, weaving through the arrows as if guided by the sky's desire, she flew to him and slowed to match his speed. They were side by side in the air. One of her blazing eyes looked into the last of his and he felt, for the first time, that he'd called her by her proper name.

How did I know that word? he asked himself. *When could I have learned it?*

Four things happened then in the space of four heartbeats.

First Visek loosed a spear that clipped Shara's wing.

Next the goshawk cried and twisted, falling, and Brysen cried out with her, turned fast and dove, out of control, to follow her down, so fast that Jowyn on the ground could barely break his fall.

Third, the war barrow, now without the kite's pull, finally slowed as the Kartami closed around it. With one swipe of her blade, Launa severed the rope that tethered Brysen to the barrow, and the line, now slack, fell into the mud. Unleashed, Brysen and his kite spun off, falling fast.

And last, a shadow cut across the sky, arrows bouncing off its deep-black feathers like raindrops off a boulder. The ghost eagle screeched.

KEEN AND SEARCHING

THERE WAS BLOOD ON THE WIND. IN ALL DIRECTIONS, A HUNGER, KEEN *and searching.*

Armies rise, and intrigue swirls through them. They play their games in the dirt, seek power, seek glory, seek and seek and seek.

They have such little lives, these flightless ones. So short are their memories, tied deep inside their bodies. All they know in every life, death takes from them. They invent ways of cheating: form words, learn stories, make writing. They carve faiths from stone and pass secrets down to children, but it wins them little. Generation to generation, they forget what once they knew, circle wider and wider from their truth. In time, they don't even know what they once forgot.

But the eagles know. The night-black eagles whose memories stretch through bodies, past time, over space and consciousness. They never forget; they live, they die, but they lose nothing. The eagle roosts and waits and hunts and waits, spreads tales and fears and dreams through generations of these scuttling creatures, and when they find the vessels they need, they strike.

These people call them "ghost eagles," though this is not their name. Such short-lived things cannot possibly know their name. They do not try to learn, not so long as they think they can control them.

Oh, these falcon tamers who do not know they are nothing more than prey.

Their armies were in place now; all the little seeds planted in a blood-soaked world were bearing fruit. The eagle flew above the castles and towns and the armies in their fury, and it screeched, and in its call, the blood below rose up. The falconers had been prepared and did not know whose will they served.

They call her death. They call her hunger, and they call her ghost. Her name is all those things and more. She has too many names for their little minds to hold. Her name is fear and forgetting. Her name is truth and vengeance. Her name is as changing and as constant as the winds. Her name is the end of all things.

Her name today was war.

KYLEE

SEIZE THE SKY

35

"REEEEEEEE!"

The ghost eagle screamed as it swooped over the battle-field, arrows blunting against its stone-hard feathers. On the barricades, the defenders of the Six Villages dropped to their knees, covering their ears. Whatever dark thoughts the ghost eagle put into their minds, Kylee couldn't know, but in her mind, she thought clear as a bronze bell, *Now I'll make them pay.*

She didn't care if the thought was hers or the ghost eagle's. It didn't matter. It belonged to both of them and it was true for both of them, and she couldn't wait to tear them all to shreds. Her true partner had returned and so had her rage.

Except the Kartami were not cowering from it. Not on the ground and not in the air.

"*REEEEE!*" it shrieked again, but none of them appeared to hear. Though every other bird in the sky turned and fled and every Six Villager winced and wept at the great bird's screaming, Kylee saw, looking at the Kartami warriors surrounding her, that they'd stuffed their ears with wax. They couldn't hear the ghost eagle's cries, so it couldn't put its thoughts into their minds.

Even the ghost eagle had a limit to its powers. The Kartami were prepared. They'd been expecting this.

She saw Brysen's kite plummet, untethered, toward the mud. About a hundred paces diagonally ahead of them, Visek pursued him, hefting another spear up the line to hurl on her brother's prone body. The young warrior's mother drove the barrow after him, racing to where Brysen lay. Even if Brysen was able to get up and dodge the spear from above, Launa had her sword. She would cut him down without even slowing. Jowyn tried to turn the barrow sharply toward where Brysen had crashed, but caught a wheel on the edge of a trench. The barrow tilted, then lurched to a stop, tottering and about to topple. Jowyn cursed, then dropped the lines and jumped over the front, splashing in the mud to race to Brysen's side . . . except he was unarmed and there were over fifty warriors between him and Kylee's brother.

"What's the word for *them*?" Kylee asked Grazim, who had no birds left to call to defend them on the ground. Kylee took a spear from the rack beside her, which was far too heavy for her to wield, but she managed to heave it sideways to Jowyn, who caught it and swung it around like a club, trying to clear a path for himself. His arms shook under its weight. He wouldn't be able to hold it long. These were not their weapons, and they would be nearly useless against the experienced warriors around them. The one weapon they had left circled them in the sky.

"*Dees*," said Grazim.

"*Dees*," Kylee said, and the ghost eagle knew. It tucked its wings and dove, smashing through Visek's kite without even slowing. It came through the wreckage clutching the warrior's body in its talons and dove, using Visek like a club to knock the warrior's own mother backward off her war barrow. She landed with such force that her neck snapped.

The ghost eagle dropped Visek's body as it rose again with a few mighty flaps.

The soldiers surrounding them in the war barrow tried to press in. Jowyn held off one flank, but they'd made a circle, and it was tightening. Kylee would never make it through to Brysen, not until this army was wiped out.

More, Kylee thought. *They wanted us to suffer. Make them suffer.*

"How do you say *suffer*?" Kylee asked.

"Careful," Grazim cautioned. "If you lose control . . ."

"HOW DO YOU SAY *SUFFER*?" Kylee demanded.

Grazim cocked her head at the fury in Kylee's voice and told her, in a whisper, "*Yeef.*"

"*Yeef,*" Kylee said, and the ghost eagle screeched. Kylee felt a rush from her fingers to her toes, a heat that wasn't like the helpless rage she'd felt while tied up in Anon's tent. It was like drinking hot broth during the worst days of the ice-wind. It was like lying on a high boulder on a clear day, when all the world is sun and light and sky. Now she understood. It was pure, animal pleasure.

The ghost eagle crashed through two more kites, knocking their warriors loose so they fell, but it didn't dive after them. They were not its target. It flew fast and straight for the barricades and over them into the Six Villages, then dove out of sight. Jowyn still batted and swung his spear, though the point drooped toward the mud a little farther with every thrust, and the warriors closed in.

"Where did it go?" Grazim asked.

Kylee didn't know. She was afraid that maybe she'd told it the wrong thing, that it had left again . . . but she didn't feel the heat inside her cooling. She still felt warm and flushed and full. She'd not made a mistake.

She'd made a discovery.

The ghost eagle had seen more than she ever could. It knew

who had plotted and who had planned and who had made her friends and family suffer. And it knew who had to suffer in return.

When it rose again above the barricades, it held a woman in its talons, a stout woman in tailored leathers with a finely wrought falconer's glove, who was flailing and punching at the black foot that held her.

Mama Tamir, screaming over the river.

Mama Tamir, screaming, tossed into the sky.

Mama Tamir, no longer screaming as her head was severed with one quick snap of a great black beak. Her body dropped into the mud in separate parts.

"REEEEE!" the ghost eagle cried, and Kylee wanted it to do more, so much more.

"This one I know," she told Grazim.

"Kylee, help Brysen!" Jowyn cried as a warrior knocked the heavy spear from his hands, and he simply tried charging through, though they blocked him at every turn. He was too quick for them to kill, but he was getting no closer to Brysen.

Kylee looked again to where her brother had crashed. She couldn't see him through the warriors that surrounded him. Above, kites circled like birds of prey and the ropes that held them to their barrows creaked. The kite warriors hefted spears. They aimed.

If she ran to him now, they'd cut her down at the same

time that they cut him. She had no plan, nor any strategy. What she still had, though, was power, and she wasn't done using it.

If only they'd surrender, she thought. *Don't they know they can't win?* But out loud, she shouted: "Praal uz!"

With a soundless beating of its wings, the ghost eagle turned for the kites above Brysen. It cried out its gleeful screech, and Kylee thought, *Leave no survivors.*

The black bird dove, severing kite ropes with its snapping beak, hardly slowing. The kites spun off, struggled for control, and fell away from their barrows. A few brave archers from the barricades poked their heads up and loosed arrows at the falling warriors. Blood rained down red on the eagle's black wings as it dropped below them, going after their drivers.

From the ground, Kartami soldiers aimed up at it with spears and arrows. The great bird made a large target, and as much as it weaved, the Kartami were practiced archers. Its feathers were hard enough to repel the arrows, but a spear finally penetrated a weak point at a leg joint, which made it scream. An arrow found the tongue in its open mouth. A second hit its left eye.

Blood blood blood, Kylee thought in the eagle's voice. For a moment, her own vision blurred. Her legs wobbled, then steadied. The ghost eagle's flight wobbled, too.

Across the battlefield she saw Anon. He towered over his

warriors as he jumped from a rolling war barrow and ran to where Brysen lay tangled in the wreckage of his kite. With one hand, Anon lifted Brysen's half-limp body by the arm. With the other he tore away the mangled kite frame.

Kylee felt her heart rise into her throat. Her brother struggled in Anon's grip. His bandage had come off, revealing one gory eye socket and one panicked eye, blazing bloodshot blue. He was clutching something under his arm, trying to shield it with his body. A hawk. A goshawk . . .

Shara!

Brysen tried to turn away from Anon, to protect the little bird with his own body, but the great warrior punched him to the ground with one fist and took the wounded, panicked hawk away with the other. Brysen tried to rise and draw his black-talon blade at the same time, but Anon kicked down again, knocking away the blade, then holding up the flapping bird in front of him. Brysen reached up, his one eye pleading.

Whatever he said, Kylee couldn't hear and Anon didn't heed, because he snapped Shara's neck and then pulled her head from her body.

Brysen screamed, though he couldn't get a whole word out because Anon's hand shot forward and gripped his throat, squeezing his windpipe and lifting him from the ground. His warriors parted, so Kylee could see clearly as Brysen's face began to purple. The entire scene felt rehearsed, like Anon and his warriors had planned for all of this, had trained for it. The entire battlefield was a show designed for Kylee's benefit.

She knew what Anon wanted her to do.

She wanted to do it, too.

"*Kraas!*" she yelled, and the wounded ghost eagle flapped toward them, taking a barrage of arrows on its feathers as it slowed and spread its wings to land in front of Brysen and Anon. It hobbled where it stood but lunged forward with a ferocious snap of its beak.

Anon dodged and dropped Brysen. As Brysen fell, limp and gasping, into the mud, Anon drew two long, thick katar blades, one in each fist. The eagle snapped at him and he dodged low, swiping at its leg and cutting a thumb-thick notch in the ghost eagle's onyx ankle.

"REEEEE!" the eagle screamed, and Kylee pictured a rain of blood falling from the sky, soaking the earth; she pictured the corpses of birds falling like a nightmare blizzard; she pictured the ground covered in human skulls. She shut her eyes against the images, but they only grew clearer.

When she opened her eyes again, Anon was behind the ghost eagle, delivering one-two stabs at sharp angles to get underneath its feathers, a knife in each fist. He struck with the speed of a battle pit boxer, and the eagle opened its wings and spun around to try to knock him away. Anon jumped back and crouched in front of it. Though the eagle kept screaming,

Anon's ears were plugged and his focus would not be broken. He lunged quickly to try to slice the bird's face. It dodged, tried to flap up to grab him in its talons, but its wounded wings failed it and it stumbled into the mud.

Anon rushed forward and drove both his blades into its thick neck. Black blood spurted up his massive arms. He pressed the full weight of his body on the ghost eagle, breaking its feathers, driving the blades deep into its throat. The eagle's eyes stared across the field at Kylee, locked with hers. Though its mouth opened and its tongue hung out, it made no sound.

She felt a wave of nausea pass through her, like she'd been tossed high as the clouds and then yanked swiftly down. She doubled over and vomited in the mud, but when she looked up, she saw Brysen, standing, his hooked knife raised as he stepped around behind Anon, who hadn't seen him yet.

"Look!" someone warned from the Kartami forces, but Anon couldn't hear the warning through his wax-plugged ears.

Brysen shifted his stance, preparing to kill the great warrior—when a spear flew at him.

"No!" Jowyn and Kylee yelled in unison. Brysen turned his head just in time to spin away from the throw, sliding in the mud and falling on the other side of the ghost eagle's body, in front of Anon. As the spear passed over him, Anon looked up, saw Brysen with his blade. He ripped one of the katars from the ghost eagle's neck. Black blood coated it, but he adjusted the slick knife in his fist and then lunged for Brysen's skull.

From Kylee's vantage in the barrow, still a hundred paces from her brother, all she saw was Anon's arm thrust forward with astounding speed. There was a stiff jerk and then she saw Brysen's arms flail out to his side as he fell backward and away, behind the ghost eagle.

For a terrible moment, all Kylee heard was her own screaming. Time itself moved slow as mud. Jowyn wrestled away from the two Kartami warriors who'd tackled him, and tossed them off like they were down-feather dolls, and sprinted across the battlefield toward Brysen. Before he could reach Anon, he was tackled by another warrior who pressed a knee into the wound on his back. His scream broke through Kylee's own. For a few heartbeats, the world itself was nothing more than mud and blood and screaming. It was not a word in any language, but it was, Kylee understood, the ghost eagle's truest name.

But in the chaos, Brysen stood. His head was cut from the crash, his neck bruised from Anon's grip, and his shirt torn to expose his scarred and bloodied chest, but he still held his knife. He looked at Anon with his one bright blue eye. The great warrior's blade had stopped short. He did not move.

Anon had a giant black talon shoved through his heart.

The warlord and the ghost eagle had died together.

36

"TO AIR!" NYCK'S VOICE CARRIED OVER THE STUNNED AND SILENT battlefield as, from the barricades, hiding defenders emerged. Their birds, unafraid of the massive black-feathered corpse lying in the mud, launched again.

The Kartami army took longer to regroup. They stood stunned at the death of their leader, the sudden loss of direction, of plan. They looked at one another like survivors of a fire, tallying what was lost and what was saved.

But they were warriors, and they had officers, and those officers saw the incoming attack from above and responded with orders.

"Parry!"

"Squads up!"

"Advance!"

The bloody battle resumed. Whatever dramas played out for Kylee and Brysen and the birds they'd lost were not enough to stop this war. *They probably never will be*, Kylee thought. *What could two fatherless fledglings from the foothill Villages ever have done to halt a world sky-bent for war?*

Tamers whistled their hawks to air as Kartami soldiers turned their spears and arrows up after them, mounting more barrows and flying more kites. Without Anon's orders to hold them back from conquest, one pair of warriors on gliders raced straight for the barricades.

Nyck stood tall in front of them, holding a sword that was too big for him and wearing a falconer's glove with no falcon to fly. Beside him, Kylee recognized Wyldr, his sometimes girlfriend. She tossed a rat-catcher falcon, and it flew to harass one of the glider's pilots, who slashed at it and missed but forced it off and away. It circled high but didn't come down. The other glider tried to shoot a crossbow bolt through the bird but missed. The distraction the small bird caused made enough time for Wyldr, though. She flung throwing knives from her belt one after the other until both gliders fell, bloodstained, into the river.

The battle boys cheered her, and then one of them, a red-haired boy with colorful feathers tattooed around his neck, began climbing down from the barricades to meet the Kartami on the field in front of the barricades. Two brothers followed, and Nyck looked at Wyldr, shrugged, and started the climb down, too. Some of the Tamir attendants, themselves now leaderless, let the battle boys charge forward and rushed to join the fray.

"Here they come," Kylee said as, in the distance, a dust cloud raced for the camp. The army of Uztar making their move at last, when the worst of the fighting was already over.

On the ground the Six Villagers were outnumbered and exposed and largely untrained in hand-to-hand combat. The Uztari war machine was coming in like an avalanche, but Kyrg Birgund didn't care what became of the Six Villagers, and protecting them would not be his priority. He had no need of Kylee anymore, nor of her brother or her home. They might be ground to dust along with the Kartami for no reason other than the kyrg's spite.

Before this day was done, Kylee feared, the rambunctious battle boys and their friends and allies and every last bird they'd tamed would be shredded to bits. Already, Kartami archers had resumed shooting hawks from the air without much concern for the threat Nyck and the rest posed on the ground.

The battle boys, though, weren't merely fighting to take back the banks of the river and defend their home. Nyck was leading them with wild slashes of his sword and the most terrible battle cries his cracking voice could muster, heading straight for where Brysen stood over the body of the ghost eagle.

He was, through it all, trying to reach his friend.

In the midst of the chaos, Brysen stood still, looking down, but not at the body of the ghost eagle. He held Shara's headless corpse in his bruised and bloodied hands, cradling it, whispering and weeping, but to no avail. Whatever of the Hollow Tongue had worked for him before was not working for him now.

"I could use your help!" Grazim grunted, which snapped Kylee's attention back to where they stood in the idle war barrow, completely surrounded by Kartami foot soldiers. Every time one of them stepped forward, Grazim called a buzzard or a hawk or a falcon to push them back. Every arrow they fired, she had a bird block with its body. The ground around them was a gruesome flock of slaughtered birds and broken feathers, and the sky above was emptying fast. They wouldn't last until the Uztari army arrived. They wouldn't even last long enough for Kylee to comfort her brother one last time.

Four Kartami warriors rushed for him, and she couldn't even find her voice to speak the simplest commands to aid him. Jowyn couldn't get out from under the warrior who had him down, who was choking him with the shaft of a spear. His eyes bulged, his lips were turning purple. He, too, would lose.

Kylee saw it all so clearly. This fight was hopeless. The bodies would pile up, new tyrants would emerge, and new grievances, too, and new fights would break out. History was just like Ryven's model of migrating birds; it followed the same paths over and over and over again, flocking and falling, circling and diving, different wings flying the same patterns for generation after generation.

She had thought the ghost eagle might break that pattern. They had *all* thought the ghost eagle might make something new with blood and terror. But the ghost eagle was dead, and with it Kylee's hopes of changing anything.

She felt hollowed out, empty as a fanatic's sky. She'd tied her dreams of power and of triumph to this one bird, but in the end, powerful as it was, it was just a bird. Her anger had been satisfying to unleash but had ultimately gotten the bird killed. Anger unleashed had its limits, just like pain did, just like love. None of them, on their own, were enough.

Brysen was surrounded now, and her vision narrowed to a tunnel. She felt something brush her cheek; a near miss from an arrow. Blood trickled warm down to her chin, but she didn't care. She'd lost Vyvian and Nyall, the ghost eagle, and the war. She was about to lose her brother. What was the point of resisting? What was the point of fighting when the fight couldn't be won?

Through the scrum of warriors, she could just make out Brysen dropping to his knees, and for the first time in a long time, she thought they were feeling the same thing at the same time, like when they were little kids. Twinned completely once more, at last.

Except he wasn't kneeling to surrender. He wasn't giving up, though he wasn't fighting, either. He was kneeling over the body of the ghost eagle and had rested both his hands across its massive, morbid wing. He spread his fingers in the way he'd hold the broken wing of a bird to imp new feathers in. The way he'd often work to heal his little hawks' hurts.

His lips began to move, like he was singing. Or praying.

The Kartami around him hesitated, then raised their weapons to impale him, but he didn't flinch, didn't even appear to see them. Nyck wouldn't make it there to save him. He was caught up in hand-to-hand combat against a kite warrior who'd crashed. Jowyn was up, limping now, but alive—unlike the warrior who'd tried to kill him—but he was running too slowly. Kylee's voice was still stuck in her throat.

She looked toward the barricades and hoped their mother wasn't watching, wouldn't have to see both her children die on this sunny morning. The clouds had burned away and golden light shone across the mountains. It was amazing to Kylee how hope could fail and life could end on such a perfect day.

Except . . . the sky wasn't so perfect all of a sudden. A black rose bloomed and blossomed against the blue over the mountains behind the Six Villages. It pinched and whirled into a tornado, then spread like smoke, shrouding the horizon, shifting and shaping itself, looming ever larger, like a murmuration of starlings returning from the icy wastes on the other side of the mountain—except the flock was too big for starlings. The birds themselves were too big.

The first fighters to notice this black cloud froze, and then others looked and saw. Once again the fighting ceased. Even Jowyn stopped his run and stumbled, looked up at the flock spiraling in.

The entire bloody plateau held its breath—Six Villagers, Kartami, and the whole pursuing army of Uztar. All watched in awe and terror as the blackness dropped.

The blazing sun cast the hills and mountains and mud and river and plains and corpses of the countless dead in its rich gold light, but as the black spread, the sky took on the red of warning, the red of storms, the red of a fresh kill. The light reflected off a thousand black wings diving down. Each wing gleamed.

Ghost eagles. Hundreds of ghost eagles, flocking.

The black-red wings and black-red bodies and black-red fury swooped over the battlefield, smothering the sun, and then they turned as one, like a hurricane, rising in a black-red vortex. In the middle, in the eye of the black-red storm, the golden sun shone down, straight onto Brysen and the black and bloodied ghost eagle's body, where his tears and his whispered prayers were falling.

37

THE GHOST EAGLES TURNED AND TURNED LIKE A GRINDING STONE, pulverizing the Kartami kites still in the air. Bits of fabric and bone rained down like chaff falling to a bakery floor.

The great flock shrieked as one, so loud that no amount of wax could stop the sound. Every warrior dropped to their knees, covering their ears. Kylee also dropped, and she saw things she had never seen before.

Brysen fighting off bandits to save a few haggard Altari in the mountains; Kyrg Ryven instructing an assassin on the poison; his view as he took the cup from her hands and passed it to Vyvian; her own mother kneeling in quiet prayer as their father raged and whipped her brother, while he bent over

Shara, protecting her. She saw Kyrg Bardu drafting letters, and Nyall taking Üku and Ryven from the Sky Castle's dungeons. She saw the Owl Mothers slaughtering strangers in the blood birch forest, and she saw Brysen again, smiling as he drifted off to sleep in Jowyn's arms in the rainy Kartami camp.

She saw everything the ghost eagle had seen, and she knew, the way lightning knows thunder, that the story she thought had been hers all along—her longing to protect, her blood-thirsty rage, her hope and shock and disappointment—had never been hers at all. She was part of a bigger story, the ghost eagle's story, and she had done exactly as it had trained her to do.

She'd been tamed and used to hunt, like every other unfortunate soul on this field of battle. They were the falcons and the ghost eagles were the falconers, watching from unseen heights for longer than time could record.

Now they struck.

One by one, giant birds broke from their great, turning flock and dove, landing among the soldiers and their minuscule birds of prey, their paltry weapons, their fragile flesh. Battle-hardened soldiers covered their heads, curled like they were hiding in the womb, and wept as large black feet with long black talons were planted in the mud beside them. Uztari, Altari, and Kartami cowered together, all labels lost of their meanings in the mud and blood and terror.

Grazim found Kylee's hand and held it wordlessly, met her eyes with a look of both shock and apology. Whatever visions Grazim had seen had softened her and frightened her. They had made her reach out to the one person she might call a friend, and Kylee, to her own surprise, was glad.

"Is this you?" Grazim whispered, and Kylee shook her head. This was not her doing. She could not find words for this. There *were* no words for this.

The throng of black-feathered bodies converged with hopping steps on the spot where Brysen knelt over the ghost eagle that Kylee had thought was somehow hers. They ignored the warriors cowering around it as they lowered their great black heads, forming a circle of beaks ringing Brysen, a circle of deep black eyes watching him, so still that even the wind dared not ruffle a single feather.

Brysen's gray hair in the center of their circle looked like a single puff of smoke in a heap of coal. As his lips moved, Kylee thought she saw smoke come out of him, thick gray plumes pouring from his nose, his mouth, his eyes. It surrounded him and wrapped around the ghost eagle's body. The other eagles were still, their beaks bent into that eternal scowl, while overhead hundreds more still glided in a perfect circle, turning and turning but making no sound, beating the air so the smoke pouring from Brysen also turned, curling like a ribbon for the golden hole in the heart of the black-feathered sky.

"What is that smoke?" Kylee whispered.

"What smoke?" Grazim asked. "There's no smoke."

She couldn't see it even as it grew thicker and thicker. This was another of the ghost eagle's tricks, an illusion. She tried to make herself see through the hallucination, but the smoke darkened. She wanted to rush forward, to grab her brother and pull him out of the smoke that wasn't there, that was somehow more dangerous *because* it wasn't there, but her feet wouldn't move. She couldn't make them move.

"*REEEEE!*" came a shriek from within the smoke.

"*REEEEE!*" every ghost eagle on the plain answered, which made all the warriors and battle boys and villagers and soldiers scream again. Jowyn, never one to despair, was sobbing on the ground. Grazim squeezed Kylee's hand tighter. The creatures were filling every head with their darkest thoughts, but Kylee now thought of nothing. She heard nothing but her own heartbeat.

When the smoke that only she could see had cleared, her ghost eagle—her *partner*, the fearsome *talorum*—stood again, alive and gleaming black, looking down at Brysen, who now lay on his face in the mud. The eagle rested one massive foot across his back, its talons slick with battlefield blood.

Kylee felt that burning inside her lungs return. She knew the word to speak. *Bost*, which meant release.

"*Bost*," she commanded, bending every thought she had to

that of the eagle letting her brother go. *"Bost!"* she said again, and she meant it. She knew she meant it. She knew it was what she wanted more than anything and that it should work.

But the eagle did not obey.

"Bost, bost, bost!" Kylee shouted.

"They don't hear me," Kylee cried. Had she lost her voice? Had she lost the Hollow Tongue? Had they *taken* it from her just as they had taken her brother? "They don't hear me!"

As one, the ghost eagles on the ground turned their great black heads to her, staring with dark, impassive eyes.

We hear you, she thought, and knew it was them.

We hear you, she thought, and then the ghost eagle mantled over Brysen, enveloping him with its wings. The eagle looked up, meeting her gaze. Its eyes were blue crystals, like a winter sky, like a frozen lake.

Like hers.

Like Brysen's.

Like their father's.

The eagle opened its wings and there Brysen stood against its breast.

I hear you, Brysen said, though his lips didn't move. It was *his voice.* She heard *his* voice in her head.

His one eye snapped open, and it was black from eyelash to eyelash, a gleaming onyx orb. He looked right at her.

We hear you, and we defy you, and we will tame you all.

With that, the ghost eagle dropped Brysen into the mud and launched itself to the sky. As one great flock of a thousand wings, the others followed. While every person on the battlefield and in the foothills of the Six stood still and followed the dreaded birds skyward with their eyes, Kylee and Jowyn sprinted across the bloody ground to Brysen's side.

She slid into the mud beside her brother, cradled him in her arms. He looked up at her, his one eye blue again. "They're going to come back," he said.

"I know." She held him tight.

"Is Jo—?"

"I'm here." Jowyn bent down and held his hand.

"Shara's dead." Brysen cried and curled in on Kylee like he used to as a little boy, though he didn't let go of Jowyn's fingers. "I saw what they saw," he gasped.

"Anon was right," said Jowyn. "They'll kill us. Every one of us."

"No," Kylee said back to him. "Not us. Not our people. I won't let them. Ever."

As she said it, she had never believed any words more than these, and in the black sky above, the ghost eagles shrieked. She saw the field of human bones and trembled, but she looked up at them and told them, "No."

"REEEEEE," they answered. They'd heard her, and she would teach them to believe.

ACKNOWLEDGMENTS

IT'S HARD TO WRITE THE SECOND BOOK IN A TRILOGY, BUT IT WOULD have been a lot harder without the guidance, support, and brilliant work of the people who make this series possible.

Grace Kendall edited this book with care; it's not hyperbole to say working with her not only improved the book, it improved me. Along with Elizabeth Lee, Kayla Overbey, and Mandy Veloso, they made sure the book flew straight and true and on time, in spite of the headwinds of the world. Publicist Morgan Rath and marketer Ashley Woodfolk have been indefatigable in spreading the word on this series, and Elizabeth H. Clark's gorgeous design continues to astound me. There isn't space to name the entire team at FSG/Macmillan Children's

Books, but the publishers, production staff, school and library marketing, digital marketing, conference planning teams, and the sales reps and warehouse crew—all work long hours with little fanfare to help readers connect with the right book at the right time, and I'm grateful for their efforts on behalf of mine. Every single one of them deserves a full page of thanks and more and I'm so grateful to publish with these amazing professionals.

I never would have been able to maintain this career without the advice and support of my agent for over a decade of publishing now, Robert Guinsler. He's held together far more than my book deals.

Thanks also for reasons they already know to Adib Khorram, Isaac Fitzgerald, Brendan Reichs, Marie Lu, Holly Black, Cassandra Clare, Veronica Roth, Adam Silvera, Kendare Blake, Dhalia Adler, Mackenzi Lee, Eric Smith, Laura Silverman, Sarah Enni, Sam J Miller, Fran Wilde, Dhonielle Clayton, Margaret Stohl, Adam Sass, Phil Stamper, Corey Whaley, Ally Condie, Claire Legrand, Roshani Chokshi, Libba Bray, Kami Garcia, Holly Goldberg Sloan, Kiersten White, John Green, Caleb Roehrig, April G Tucholke, Ngozi Ukazu, Marissa Meyer, Tomi Adeyemi, Neal Shusterman, Phil Bildner, Rose Brock, and Katherine Locke. If this reads like a who's who of YA, it says a lot more about the kindness of the YA community than it does about me. Also their books are wonderful.

I'm grateful to the teachers, librarians, and booksellers who've supported me more than I deserve and more than I can thank them for. They are too numerous to list here, a fact that remains a delight and an honor. Rachel Strolle does, however, deserve a special shout-out for the years and years of support and, well, the gifs! And bookseller Emily Hall brought raptors to the launch event, which was definitely a first for me.

Last, thanks to my husband and our new daughter, the two loves of my life. He makes all things possible, while she didn't help much in the writing of this, but still managed to make everything under this wild sky better simply by existing. I'm gonna try to be worthy of her for the rest of my life.

GOFISH

QUESTIONS FOR THE AUTHOR

ALEX LONDON

As a writer famous for having written books in both the science fiction and fantasy section, do you believe there is any particular distinction to writing in these genres versus what many people would call "mainstream" fiction or contemporary realistic fiction?

A good story is a good story, but I do believe fantasy and sci-fi can play a unique role in shaking off the dust of our assumptions that our world is the only possible world, and that systems of power in it are the way it has to be. Sci-fi and fantasy, when done well, can spark the imagination to look at our world in a new way, can ignite the imagination for other possibilities. To invent a landscape is to question our understanding of geography; to invent a religion is to look with new eyes at faith; to invent different gender constructs or ways society treats sexuality is to look at heteronormative assumptions anew . . . and to do it all in a ripping yarn with all kinds of cool inventions makes tearing the veil off reality a damn fun prospect too! There's a reason so many of our devices look like something out of *Star Trek*: The engineers who invented them were once dreamers inspired by the possibilities imagined by fabulists. No one who read Douglas Adams's *So Long, and Thanks for All the*

Fish in middle school looks at dolphins or human folly the same way again. I hope my series can do that for birds of prey . . . and also human folly . . .

The Skybound Saga is set in what seems to be a Eurasian epic fantasy focusing on falconry and magic, a dramatic shift from your last series, featuring an American sci-fi dystopian world. Why the dramatic shift, and where did your inspiration come from?

For me, the story dictates the world (and vice versa), so it's hard to say exactly where the inspiration comes from. Writing a novel is like throwing logs on a bonfire. There are a lot of individual sparks that make the flame and I can't say which spark or sparks are the ones that caught, but I was deeply drawn to falconry, as both a literal really cool human thing that every culture on earth where there are birds of prey has invented at some point and also as a metaphor for longing, for the dichotomy of gentleness and cruelness, and for the struggle to understand minds different from our own. Once falconry was the central piece of the world building the rest flowed from there—a culture that would be bent toward the sky would live at high altitude, the characters would organize their lives around birds of prey and around hunting, even the religion would be bent skyward. While I didn't draw only on one cultural tradition in creating the Skybound Saga, the landscape is very much inspired by the Himalayan region, our planet's closest habitable land to the clouds.

In addition to including gay representation, you also include a female character who could be coded as asexual and/or aromantic. How will you be

exploring this character's queer identity in the rest of the series?

I don't want to give away too many spoilers, but you did read that correctly. I didn't import any of our labels around sexuality into the fantasy novel on purpose, as it is not set in a world where cis-gendered heterosexuality is assumed or even the norm, so trans characters are not labeled, gay characters are not labeled, and ace characters are not labeled, even as they all exist and live these experiences in their own context. Not being asexual myself, I did have to tread very carefully when writing Kylee, because I don't want to get her representation wrong. While she would not call herself any one thing or another, she definitely does not have romantic or sexual feeling, and I wanted to write the experience as honestly as I could in a world that did not judge her for it or see her as somehow incomplete for it. She's a teen and surrounded by some very horny other teens, so there are challenges for her, but it's a world that affirms a variety of identities so this aspect of herself is not a great struggle on her life or among her peers (while of course, for the writer to get it right had to be a great struggle . . . getting it right matters!). Even the boy who is in love with her understands and accepts their relationship.

In various interviews you mention how you write books featuring the queer representation you needed as a young adult growing up. If you could deliver a message to your younger self, what would you say to them?

I'd say: Your story hasn't been written yet, not by your parents, your community, or even your favorite author. Your possibilities are as infinite as your imagination.

What advice would you give to aspiring authors today?

Ignore trends and write the book you want to read. The more authentically it comes from you the more likely it is to find readers who need it. The more specific to your dreams it is, no matter how silly or serious, light or dark, realistic or fantastical, the more likely it is to succeed. That and read a lot, because whatever you want to write, someone else is writing in that vein well and has something to teach you. Learn what's out there to know the writing you aspire to and ignore what's out there to create something wholly your own. Basically, it goes to that old Yiddish paradox: "You must invent your own religion else it shall mean nothing to you. You must follow the religion of your fathers else you shall lose it." Or to put it in a Sondheim quote, "Anything you do/Let it come from you/Then it will be new . . ."

Who and what are some of your favorite LGBTQ+ authors and novels, and what titles are you looking forward to reading?

We're in an exciting time for LGBTQ+ novels for young adults. The doors that people like Malinda Lo and David Levithan and Bill Konigsberg opened for queer YA (which they are all still writing too) have led to a wonderful array of voices being widely available, from a thriller like *White Rabbit* by Caleb Roehrig to the genre- and gender-bending magic-mafioso of Amy Rose Capetta's *The Brilliant Death* to the poetic meditation on grief in Will Walton's *I Felt a Funeral, in My Brain*. Mackenzi Lee and Katherine Locke both write great alternative history queer YA that are joys to read, and I'll read anything Nina LaCour writes. I love Mark Oshiro's writing and Adib Khorram's debut, *Darius the Great Is Not Okay*, and Lev Rosen's recent *Jack of Hearts (and Other*

Parts) is the sex-positive gay YA contemporary I never could have dreamed would exist when I was a teen. Julian Winters's *How to Be Remy Cameron* is not to be missed. Oh, and my baby daughter and I are loving Kyle Lukoff's picture book *A Storytelling of Ravens.* While it's not a "queer" book, the author is an out transman and his *When Aidan Became a Brother* won a Stonewall Award!

As a relatively new father, do you believe your writing for younger audiences will be affected or influenced by your parenting experiences in the future?

So far the main impact has been that I'm not getting much writing done at all! So many diapers! So many feedings! But I do think being a parent will impact the kind of stories I write—how could it not? Everything in life influences a writer, and my daughter is the biggest thing in my life. I want to imagine a world where her possibilities are limitless and tell stories that contribute to a culture that values the safety, dignity, autonomy, and opportunities for women and girls, and I want to lift up and center the voices of women writing those stories now. Time will tell how she leaves her mark on my work, but I'm excited to find out. She's definitely leaving her mark on my sleep schedule!

Read an excerpt of *Gold Wings Rising*,
the final installment in the Skybound Saga!

GOLD
WINGS
RISING

ALEX LONDON

AN OLD SONG

THEY'D LOCKED THEMSELVES INSIDE CAGES BUILT FROM THE wreckage of the world.

The occupants of the Six Villages had strung up heavy netting to cut off any open sky, from roof to roof and fencepost to chimney, layers of nets and bars and beams sagging over streets and courtyards, casting patchwork shadows. They tied lines to the half-crumbled barricades—structures left over from a half-won battle they'd only half given up fighting—and looped the opposite ends on boulders. Every rope that once held a kite to a war barrow had been repurposed to create a shield between earth and sky.

As if the sky could be kept out by nets of rope and wire.

As if the sky hadn't wanted this cage built in the first place.

As if a net could keep the sky from falling.

The ghost eagles did not know their own thoughts were anything other than the sky's. They believed themselves the sky's talons, the sky's will, the only beings truly beloved by wind and air. They believed humanity was exactly where it was meant to be: cowering inside a cage. The ghost eagles believed they were winning.

The ghost eagles were right.

When the ghost eagles flocked down from the high mountain peaks, the Sky Castle had sealed itself underneath nets and behind walls, cut off from its own army. No messages came in or out. Any stragglers on the plains or in the mountains or crossing the desert had been chased into shelters or torn to shreds. The Sky Castle took in no more frightened masses, closed its gates completely. Inside, the occupants were beginning to starve and, in desperation, beginning to riot.

The blood birch forest was quiet. None who entered left. The Owl Mothers had retreated, as they always did.

The ghost eagles attacked the Talon Fortress straightaway, leaving it abandoned and crumbling. They perched on the tops of its huge curved walls, which were shaped like talons breaking through the mountainside. They feasted on those who did not flee fast enough, and they built their eyrie from ruined stone and broken bones. This place had been theirs long ago, before the people, and now it was theirs once again. They perched by the hundreds and, from there, saw everything.

The flock of humanity scattered, and each settlement was its own cage, and each cage was all alone.

The ghost eagles ignored most of them but could never ignore the Six Villages. Through rage and hunger, the Six called them back, night after night after night, for reasons not even they could quite understand. The girl and her brother haunted their dreams. The ghost eagles saw memories, fragments of thought that were not their own, feelings so utterly human that they were incomprehensible to the convocation of ancient birds. They screeched back with their own voices, trying to chase out these thoughts that drew them, over and over, to the sky above the Six.

The once-broad main street of the Six Villages was clogged with tents and shacks, divided and subdivided into narrow twisting alleys and paths barely wider than a gull's wings. Awnings protruded at odd angles, crossbeams cutting this way and that. The bent shells of war barrows capped alley entrances, forming arches over which the inhabitants strung their nets and ropes—anything they thought might impede an attack from above. Everything was built with a bird's-eye view in mind.

What a person might consider laughter fluttered through the ghost eagles' thoughts.

People had no idea what a bird's-eye view entailed, nor what the eyes of these birds could see. One mind with a thousand eyes—they saw everything. They *thought* they saw everything.

In the Six, people fought over territory. Some lived in mountain caves just above the towns, stretched to the very limit of the nets' reach. The nets were strongest wherever they met stone.

Fights broke out, houses changed hands, and violence in the narrow lanes was as common as cardinals scuffling with blue jays. Survivors of Kartami violence attacked ex-Kartami warriors—or people they believed to be ex-Kartami warriors. Kartami warriors not ready to give up their cause slaughtered Uztari soldiers in their sleep or slit the throats of the precious hawks and falcons they still viewed as blasephemous.

Then there was the violence born not of ideology or grievance but of survival: new gangs extorting people over food and water, gangs competing with each other after the collapse of the Tamir family's control, freelance criminals, starved to the point of petty violence.

And, as in any society, there were people who loved

violence simply for its own sake, who ran fighting rings with both bird and human bouts, who jumped anyone they didn't like for any reason they could think up. There was too much ale and hunter's leaf in town, and also too little. Supplies were starting to run low. Prices were soaring. Some people always found ways to profit from pain.

Kyrg Birgund, the nominal defense counselor of the Sky Castle, tried to maintain order, but there'd been little respect for the authority of kyrgs before the current calamity, and the situation hadn't made anyone *more* respectful. Soon the soldiers would be hungry. Soon they would take what they needed from the people, who would, of course, fight back.

These were the thoughts that occupied the brother and sister, the thoughts the ghost eagles heard. The boy fretted. The girl plotted. The ghost eagles listened.

These human dramas played out in the crowded town during the day. Volunteers raced to patch tears in the nets, which the ghost eagles would then shred at night. It was endless maintenance. The people tired as they hungered.

The ghost eagles did not tire, though they did hunger as well. They could eat and eat, of course, but they would never be full. Want of meat was not what starved them. Still, at night, they ate.

Every morning the huddled multitudes of the Six Villages

tried to mend their barriers against wrath from the predators above, and every night, from the moment the sixth star appeared in the sky until the first red light of dawn, those same predators came screeching down upon them.

People waited out the long nights with wax stuffed in their ears. At first the wax was for keeping out the ghost eagles' cries, but it served a second purpose for the hard-hearted: not all the night's shrieking came from ghost eagles.

Each morning, more people were found missing. The ghost eagles snared lifelong falconers of Uztar. They grabbed Altari Crawling Priests who'd never so much as looked at a bird of prey, let alone captured or trained one. They seized ex-Kartami warriors stranded in the Six Villages after their army was crushed. They massacred Uztari foot soldiers and Uztari officers and Uztari traders and merchants and trappers and cooks. They took old and young, lovers and loners, sick and healthy—all forms of mind and body that the sky had ever seen. There was no discrimination. Death came for anyone unlucky enough to be caught.

Crowds gathered in the dawn sunshine each morning to breathe fresh air and share news about who had been taken in the night, how they had screamed, and what pieces of them might be found tangled in the web of ropes overhead. People placed bets on hands and limbs. The odds of a head were so low, a gambler would make a fortune if one were ever found.

The children sang new songs:

> *Fix the nets and tie your line*
> *Or a ghost eagle will break your spine.*
> *Every night they shriek and cry.*
> *Who will live and who will die?*
> *Me or you? You or I?*
> *The eagle takes every-bod-die!*

The last rhyme stretched thinner than the protective nets, but so it went with humanity. When happy, they sang; when sad, they sang; and when afraid, they sang. They were beings of song who knew well that song would not save them.

Sing on, rodents, sing on!

The ghost eagles had a song, too—an old, old song—and they'd sung it before and would sing it again. They sang this song every few generations, and it was always the same. They *thought* it would always be the same.

They wondered what might happen if it changed. They dared not wonder what might happen.

The song could never change.

The ghost eagles shrieked.